BABY TIGER

K.J. Graham

ISBN: 1537534289
ISBN 13: 9781537534282

ACKNOWLEDGMENTS

George Kean
Callum McMeekin
Anna Lesniara
Fiona Graham

TABLE OF CONTENTS

CHAPTER 1

A FOOL'S ERRAND

Flight Lieutenant Andy Paxton parked his Ford Fiesta in the visitors' parking space outside the Sunny Brae care home. He paused, removed a letter from his attaché case, and reread it. Andy was the newest member of the Royal Air Force legal team based at RAF Northolt. Andy had the feeling because he was the newbie in the team, he had been sent on this wild-goose chase to his native Scotland.

Andy had been summoned to his commanding officer's office, where he had been given the task—allegedly because he was a Scotsman and would be travelling back to his beloved Scotland. Andy had other ideas about this. He thought the truth was more to do with this being a thankless task no one else could be bothered with.

The letter Andy studied was the latest of more than twenty letters sent over the past year requesting a meeting between the sender, Jan Powlak, and the serving air marshal.

The letter stated that Mr. Powlak had fresh information about an RAF pilot who had not been recognised for his actions during the Battle of Britain. Mr. Powlak had apparently been contacted by mail but refused to give details of his claim until he spoke face to face with the head of the Royal Air Force.

Andy was shown into the head nurse's office where he introduced himself to Lisa, who was in charge of the day-to-day running of the home. "Good morning, Lisa. We talked on the phone earlier this week. I am sorry to put you to all this trouble, but my boss wanted to put this matter to bed once and for all and asked me to come up here to speak to Mr. Powlak."

Lisa smiled as she studied Andy closely. "Flight Lieutenant Paxton, believe me when I tell you we are glad to see you. Jan has been driving us mad with this obsession of his. He has always been fond of telling us over and over about his time in the RAF, but about a year ago, he started driving us round the bend. He has had my staff running backwards and forwards to the post office with his letters, mostly to yourselves."

Andy needed to know if he was wasting his time here and attacked the problem head on. "Lisa, sorry to be blunt, but can you give me your opinion as a professional on the mental state of Mr. Powlak? In other words, Lisa, do you think I am wasting your time and mine coming up here?"

Lisa did not like the way the question had been put to her, and her head-nurse mentality kicked in, coming to the defence of her patient. "Mr. Paxton, Jan has been with us for the last five years. He has a wicked sense of humour. He sleeps a lot, and his mind can wander, but mentally, he is as sharp as a tack. For a man approaching his hundred-and-first birthday, he is remarkable."

Andy could tell from Lisa's tone that she was not best pleased with his direct approach. The last thing he wanted was to fall out with her after only being here for ten minutes. "Lisa, I am sorry for the way I put that, but I am a lawyer, and it's better to be clear about these thing than find out later Jan is not fit to be questioned."

Lisa frowned at Andy while studying his uniform. "A lawyer? I thought you lot were pilots. And anyway, do you not think I would have told you when you phoned that Jan was away with the fairies if that was the case? On a good day, Jan could run rings round us both."

It was Andy's turn to frown. "And on a bad day?"

Lisa got up from behind her desk. "On a bad day, he sleeps. One day, Mr. Lawyer Man, Jan will not wake up, so let's go. You can find out for yourself why he needs to speak to you while you still have the chance."

Lisa led Andy through a maze of corridors. They ended up in a large conservatory overlooking a pond and fountain. Andy watched as Lisa walked over to a window seat where a frail old gentleman sat watching the world go by.

Andy studied the old man while Lisa fussed over him, brushing away some crumbs that had landed on his lap from a previous snack. Despite his age, Jan had a full head of pure white hair neatly set in a side parting. He was dressed in a shirt and tie and wore a silk waistcoat, complete with pocket watch and chain. His trousers, although neat, gave away the frail state of his worn-out body. They probably had fitted him at one time, but Jan's body had shrunk since the trousers had been bought for him. His shoes screamed military. They stood out from the rest of his attire, gleaming black in the sunlight from the big window.

Andy knew instinctively that the first thing Jan did every day was bull up his shoes. It was a military thing that had been drummed into them all. Clearly, in Jan's case, it refused to die, even after all these years out of the service.

Jan Powlak regarded Lisa's guest with searching eyes. He had already checked out the young man's uniform for rank and insignia. Before he even uttered a word, Jan knew this young man had been sent here as a courtesy, with no real intent to fulfil Jan's request.

At first, Jan was having none of it. How dare they send the office junior to brush him off with a pat on the back. It was Lisa who eventually persuaded Jan to listen to what the RAF officer had come to say. "Come on, Jan. Let me introduce you to Flight Lieutenant Paxton. He seems a nice chap, and he has come a long way to hear what you have to say."

Jan tilted his head to the side so he could get another look at the young officer. "*Pajac.*"

Lisa stared at the old man, waiting for him to explain the word he had just uttered, but Jan was not qualifying his outburst. "Jan, I take it that was Polish. I have told you before, it is rude to speak like that unless you explain what you are saying. Come on. Don't be so grumpy. We have all helped you to get the attention of the RAF. Don't spoil it now. Please, Jan, behave."

"*Puppet.* Pajac means puppet. This man is only a puppet. I need the one who works his strings, the puppet master. Very well. Let me speak to the pajac!"

Lisa introduced the men to one another. For a second after Lisa left, they sat staring at one another, each one trying to decide the first move, like two chess grand masters.

Andy decided to take the plunge first. "So, Mr. Powlak, I take it from your letters you were involved in the Battle of Britain. It would be good if you could let me know a bit about yourself and why you have requested this meeting."

Jan scowled at Andy before forming a reply. "Firstly, young man, I did not request a meeting with a messenger boy, and secondly, you had better get pen and paper out so you can write down my details to tell your superior officer."

Andy decided to play it cool and retrieved a pen and notepad from his case. Without waiting any longer, Jan launched into his relevant history.

"I was born in Dukla, Poland, in 1914. I became a mechanic at fourteen, and at sixteen, I moved to Italy. In 1937, I moved to England and joined the Royal Air Force, eventually joining 303 Squadron and being reunited with my Polish comrades fighting against the Bosche."

Andy stopped writing. "And is it 303 Squadron that this meeting concerns?"

Jan looked away to the garden, not wanting to make eye contact with the young officer. "That is a matter I will discuss with your superior, young man."

Andy was stuck between a rock and a hard place. He badly wanted to go back to Northolt with a result for two reasons. One, he wanted to prove to his commanding officer he could be trusted with his own project, and two, he wanted to rub their noses in it for sending him on what they thought was a wild-goose chase.

Andy was not impressed by the manners of the old man, and this was a factor in what Andy did next. "Mr. Powlak, as I see it, you have two options here. You either tell me your story, and I will decide if it goes any further, or you can hold out in the hope someone of higher rank will listen to your story. In my opinion, this will not happen after I go back to RAF Northolt and submit my report saying you were uncooperative. You decide, Jan. Talk to me, or take it to the grave with you."

Jan Powlak was now the person with the dilemma. He looked into the eyes of the young officer, trying to decide if he was bluffing, but he was met with a steely glare. Jan was worried that if he told his story to the young man that he would not believe him. Jan needed time to think and, if required, some evidence to back up his story.

"I am too tired to continue at the moment. You will come back tomorrow, and I will decide then what to do."

Andy had planned to take a quick deposition from the old man, then head for his parents' home in the little village of Muckhart, which was a fifty-minute drive from his present location in Dundee. He would get fed and watered there, then head off first thing in the morning for RAF Northolt. The old man had just shot his plan out of the sky.

"OK, Mr. Powlak, I will call back tomorrow morning, but I will need a decision from you then, or I will recommend that this matter be closed once and for all. Good day, Mr. Powlak."

On his way out, Andy introduced himself to the new nurse who had replaced Lisa at the desk and explained that he would be back tomorrow.

Andy had just climbed back into the Ford Fiesta hire car when his pocket started to vibrate. A quick look at his phone showed a new text from his mother.

His parents had decided to go out for the evening, leaving Andy to make his own meal plans. Another part of Andy Paxton's plan had just bit the dust.

Now in no great hurry, Andy decided to call the RAF records section before they split for the evening. He wanted to find out a bit more about the uncooperative old man now that he had a few more details of his previous career to go by.

The officer in charge of records promised to look up Powlak's record then e-mail the findings to Andy's RAF mailbox that evening.

At the end of the street, Andy was about to turn left down the hill towards Dundee Airport and the quickest way out of the busy city when he spotted a pizza restaurant opposite. It reminded Andy that his evening meal had been cancelled. With any luck, the fast-food joint would have Wi-Fi, and Andy could study Jan Powlak's history while tucking into a big pizza.

Ten minutes later, Andy had ordered a meat-feast stuffed-crust pizza and was busy logging onto the shop's Wi-Fi with his laptop.

Bill the records officer had been true to his word, and waiting in Andy's inbox was an e-mail and attachments detailing the RAF records for Leading Aircraftman (LAC) Jan Powlak, 1937–1948.

The first document told no more than Jan had already stated, other than specifying Jan's rank and serial number.

The second document was more interesting. It contained a number of reports from Jan's sergeant to the commanding officer of the day. It described how Jan had been assigned to Pilot Officer Artur Krol. Jan had been commended for his tireless efforts in keeping Krol's Hurricane airworthy.

Yet another document noted that Jan Powlak had been reprimanded for removing serviceable parts from other

Hurricanes to keep Krol's plane airworthy. A footnote stated that due to Krol's success in the air, the incident had been overlooked.

The final document was a recommendation that Jan Powlak be recognised for his part in keeping Artur Krol in the air, allowing him to become one of the highest scoring Polish fighter aces of the Battle of Britain.

Andy studied the final page with huge interest. It was an image of a handwritten note from Jan Powlak's previous employer, commending him to his new employer in Great Britain, whoever it might be. The note had been written on headed notepaper emblazoned with the logo of Alfa Romeo.

This handwritten note stated that young Jan Powlak had worked with the car company for a while without taking any vacation or sick leave and was a good timekeeper. Due to his excellent engineering skills, the letter said, he had been promoted to the Scuderia racing team of Alfa Romeo and would make an excellent addition to any mechanical or engineering business. The letter was signed "Enzo Ferrari."

Andy was in shock. The old man in the nursing home had been one of Enzo Ferrari's race mechanics and the leading aircraftman to a Battle of Britain fighter ace, one of the "few" whom Winston Churchill had commended in his famous radio address to the nation.

Andy was staring open mouthed at the laptop screen, still struggling to take in what he had stumbled across when a voice broke his concentration. "Well, well. If it isn't Lieutenant Paxton. Don't you have a home or a base to go to?"

Andy Paxton looked up to find Lisa staring down at him. "Hello again. I was going to say good-bye at the nursing home, but you had been relieved by another nurse. I take it you are having pizza for tea as well."

Lisa glanced at the laptop before replying. "I just popped in for a takeaway. How did you get on with Jan after I left you?"

Andy shook his head. "What's the hurry? Sit in and keep me company, and I will bring you up to speed about Jan."

Lisa was clearly wavering on the offer, so Andy attempted to persuade her further. "Come on, Lisa. I don't bite. Just get what you want to eat, and add it to my table bill. I'm sure the RAF can stand you dinner—that is, unless you need to get home?"

Lisa gave in, removing her scarf and coat and sitting down just as a waitress appeared. She ordered then returned her attention to Andy. "I suppose I can keep you company. After all, it will just be my goldfish that misses me. It's not as if he needs to be walked or anything."

Lisa sat opposite Andy, studying him while the waitress served them soft drinks. "So, Andy, did you get Jan to tell you anything today? I was run off my feet and never managed to get back to you or Jan this afternoon."

Andy took a sip of his cola and shook his head. "No, he was not for talking. I had to give him a bit of a wake-up call. I will be back tomorrow, but I warned him if he doesn't want to talk to me, that will be his one and only chance of talking face to face with any RAF staff. I could see he was close to saying something, but he said he was tired so I backed off. Hopefully, it will give him time to weigh up his situation. Tell me, Lisa, do you have any idea what this is all about? Has he ever during his war stories alluded to any wrongdoing or anything he seemed passionate about?"

Lisa sat quietly, thinking through what Andy had just said to her. "Honestly, no, he has never said a thing. Before he started sending you letters, he seemed resigned to the inevitability of death, just counting down his last days. But then the letters seemed to give him purpose once more. We were shocked at the level of determination he had found. For a gentleman of his age, it is quite remarkable."

There was a pause in the conversation as the waitress delivered their pizzas. After a few seconds, Andy broke the silence. "You know, I feel I have only scratched the surface regarding Jan Powlak, but already I agree with you. I think we are dealing with quite a remarkable man. It makes me very curious as to the nature of his request."Andy took a big bite. "Did he ever tell you he worked for Enzo Ferrari during his time in Italy? He also was part of the most famous Polish fighter squadron of the Second World War, not to mention that he was the mechanic for one of their aces."

Lisa finished a mouthful of pizza before replying. "He said nothing about Italy, but he did speak about the war. He hated the Nazis with a passion. He lost both his parents and a little sister in the war, poor guy."

Andy was just about to ask Lisa a question when her mobile phone started to vibrate on the table in front of her. Lisa checked the number before apologizing that she had to answer as it was the home calling. Andy took the time Lisa spent on the phone to study the nurse he had only met that morning. Lisa was not big, especially considering the work she was expected to do. Andy estimated her height at around five foot six. She had an athletic build, probably due to all the running about she did at work. Lisa's natural-looking blond hair was short, but she had obviously had it cut by a professional stylist. As for her makeup, he noted it was sparse but expertly applied. Even her clothing spoke volumes about her attention to detail. Her jacket was folded neatly with her folded scarf neatly on top of it. Andy studied Lisa's pale-blue eyes as she focused on the tablecloth while she spoke to her colleague. Andy got the impression that Lisa would be no different at work. Heaven help anyone who didn't make her patients' beds properly. One crease in the wrong place, and Lisa would come down on the sloppy bed-maker like a ton of bricks.

Then the phone call came to an end, and Lisa returned her attention to Andy. "Sorry about that. One of my favourite old ladies isn't doing too well tonight. I believe you were about to ask me something?"

"Oh, it was nothing really. Just killing two birds with one stone—a terrible chat-up line and trying to satisfy my curiosity at the same time. I was wondering why a lovely looking girl like you has only a goldfish to go home to at night?"

Lisa was single and used to her fair share of chat-up lines, but for some reason, this one, although corny, got to her more than most. It took Lisa a major effort to appear calm. "Well, before you jump to the usual idiotic male conclusion that because I am single, I must be gay, you would be wrong. There are three reasons I am single. Work, work, and more work. I am too busy for a relationship, and I am not a good person to be around when I lose a patient, and in my line of work, unfortunately, that happens quite a lot. So you see, that is why only my goldfish will put up with me." As Lisa spoke, she stood up and started to put her jacket on. "The pizza was nice, thanks, but I need to go."

Andy finished his cola and started to get up from the chair. "Oh, right, listen. It's raining. Can I give you a lift home? No more chat-up lines, I promise."

Lisa smiled and tucked her scarf into the top of her jacket. "No, thanks, Flight Lieutenant Paxton. I'm not going home. I need to go and see if there is anything I can do for my old lady friend at the home. I will see you tomorrow, and I promise, we will both work on Jan so you can find out what his secret is. Thanks for the chat. It was nice—even the corny chat-up line. Bye."

Andy watched as Lisa made her way across the busy road, heading back towards the home.

CHAPTER 2

AN OLD MAN'S SECRET

It was almost ten o'clock the next morning when Andy pulled up outside the Dundee nursing home once more. The traffic had not been kind that morning. Andy locked the car, checked his attaché case, and headed for the reception area where he stated who he was over the intercom and then waited patiently for the duty nurse to buzz him in.

As Andy approached, he was glad to see one of the nurses behind the desk was Lisa. The nurses whispered and giggled to each other before Lisa broke away and headed in Andy's direction. Andy reckoned he had been the topic of conversation but was glad to see that Lisa looked to be in a good mood. Her patient must have made a good recovery.

"Hello, Andy. I thought we were going to have to send out the search parties for you this morning. You will be glad to hear in your absence, I have been working on Jan this morning. I got the chef to make his favourite breakfast, and I have left him reading one of his flying magazines. Oh, and I have my fingers crossed as well."

Andy smiled as Lisa gave him a run-down of her efforts to get Jan into a good mood and fell in behind her as she led him through the corridors of the big care home.

"You must have got in bright and early to get all that done already. I take it your patient is on the mend, the one you went to check on last night?"

Lisa stopped outside the door to one of the bedrooms before replying. "Yes, she is sleeping at the moment. We are just waiting for the doctor to pop in and give her the once-over although I am sure now she will be fine. As for being in early, I haven't been home yet. It's amazing what a shower and a big mug of steaming coffee can do for you."

Lisa opened the door to the room they had stopped outside before Andy had a chance to respond to her statement. Lisa marched into Jan Powlak's bedroom, startling the old man who was poring over a magazine in front of him. He wore a pair of glasses that looked like someone had stolen the bottoms of milk bottles to make them. Lisa took the bull by the horns, taking advantage of Jan's surprise.

"Jan, shame on you. You have made this nice gentleman come back again today. Now you have had a good breakfast and a good night's sleep, so let's have no more nonsense. Andy here has bent over backwards for you. I am a good judge of character. If he can help you, I am sure he will. I will leave you for the moment. Be good, boys, and no fighting." Lisa caught Andy's eye as she left the room and winked to him.

Andy couldn't resist getting his oar in the water. "Thank you, Matron!"

Lisa shook her head as she closed the door, enveloping the room in a deadly silence. Andy looked down at the old man's magazine. It was an American specialist publication on air racing, a subject Andy had no knowledge of. Andy pointed to the front cover—a photograph of two planes in flight.

"Would I be correct in saying that the two planes on the cover are P-51D Mustangs? I am a bit rusty on the old ones, Tornados or Typhoons, no problem." There was an uneasy silence for a few seconds. Jan seemed to be making his mind up whether to speak to him or not.

When the reply came, Andy was not expecting the answer. "The machine on the left was one of mine, and yes, they are Mustangs, both of them."

Jan was sitting at a table by the window of his room. Andy dragged a second chair across and sat down next to the old man without invitation. "I didn't know the Polish squadrons were equipped with Mustangs?"

The old man nodded. "Towards the end of the war, some of our unit were equipped with them, but I never worked on them until I moved to America."

Jan removed his specs, folded them, and placed them on the table next to the magazine. "After the war, I was offered a job in America with a flying circus maintaining their planes. They had two Mustangs and no one who knew a thing about Merlin engines, so I jumped at the chance. One thing led to another, and I eventually ended up owning my own aviation company—Powlak Air. My company specialised in Rolls Royce aero engines, specifically the Rolls-Royce Merlin and the later Rolls-Royce Griffon. During the sixties, air racing in America had taken off in a big way, and Powlak Air went from strength to strength, tuning Merlin and Griffon engines for the racing Mustangs." Jan pointed to the magazine on the table. "I like to keep an eye on my old girls. They will still be flying long after this old body of mine has turned to dust." Jan started to laugh but this brought on a fit of coughing. Andy handed Jan a box of tissues from the table as he tried to bring the coughing back under control.

"Jan, you have had one hell of a life. You should write a book about it. Between Ferrari, the war, and America, you would have plenty of material for it."

Jan had brought the coughing under control, but he regarded Andy through bloodshot, watering eyes that were wary of the young air force lawyer. "So, young man, I see you have been checking up on me. Did your investigations bring up the name of the pilot I worked with in the war? Artur Krol?"

Andy sat back, watching the old man's expression. He was sure the old man was about to start spilling the beans. "Yes, Jan, his name did come up. I believe he was the second highest scoring fighter pilot from 303 Squadron, and you were his mechanic, I mean aircraftsman."

Jan sat looking out the French doors of his room onto the central garden of the home. It was clear to Andy that he had come to the make-or-break moment of the meeting. "Fight Lieutenant Paxton, look me in the eye and tell me that if I inform you of a military miscarriage of justice, you will do everything in your power to put the record straight." Jan produced a tattered old Bible, signalling Andy to place his hand on it and swear on the Bible to do his duty.

Andy obliged the old man and did as he asked. Jan placed the Bible by his side and started rummaging in an old wooden box for something. Eventually he found what he was looking for and placed a picture in front of Andy.

The faded photo was of a young man in his twenties sitting on a grassy bank and a younger, much smaller girl with short, light-coloured hair sitting by his side, knees tucked up to her chest, smiling at the photographer. Jan pointed a shaking finger towards the two figures in the photo. "The picture is of myself and my friend Miss Jean Bruce."

Andy waited for some explanation for the picture, but it never came. Jan was once more busy digging through his wooden box. Finally he came up with a second picture, this time of a group of men gathered together and dressed in air force uniform. "This group of men formed part of 303 Squadron. Not a lot of people, certainly not the historians or British senior staff, knew that 303 Squadron was effectively two units operating under the guise of 303 Squadron. This group of pilots were scattered and reformed in Romania before eventually being drafted into 303 Squadron while most of the rest of our men escaped via Dunkirk.

"These men in the picture had suffered the worst Hitler could throw at them, and the group had lost many fine men. They learned the hard way how to fight the Germans, and they were not for taking orders from either the British officers or the rest of 303 Squadron. You must understand, their only purpose left in life was to kill Nazis."

Jan was on a roll, so Andy let him continue without interruption, waiting patiently for Jan to get to the reason he had called in the RAF.

"If you look at the bottom left of the picture, the man kneeling on the ground is Artur Krol. My recollection of him is that he was a nervous young man who spoke little. Artur was the only member of the team who had not flown a combat mission, having just finished his training." Jan paused, gathering his thoughts before continuing. "What I am about to tell you is the truth. I swear on the holy Bible to prove it to you, young man." Jan picked up the Bible, waving it in the air before placing it on the table next to the picture. Jan pointed to the picture of the airmen, making eye contact with Andy as he spoke.

"This picture was taken only weeks before the Battle of Britain began in earnest, and two days before Artur Krol deserted the RAF. Artur was never seen again, and to my knowledge, he vanished forever."

It took a second for Andy to register what he had just been told. "Wait a minute, Jan. That can't be right. Artur Krol is documented as one of Poland's great fighter aces of the Second World War and one of the *few*—a Battle of Britain hero. That can't be right, Jan!"

Jan had obviously been expecting this reaction, so while Andy was speaking, Jan started pulling more pictures from the wooden box. "These are all that remain of the pictures of the Romanian unit, as they were named by the other Polish members of 303 Squadron. I was tasked with recording the efforts of our unit. Take the pictures. Study them at your leisure. Then come back, young man, and tell me why this so-called fighter ace is not present in any other picture bar the one I have just shown you. He was not present, and for years, his name was used in the same sentence as *hero,* though less of a hero one could not get!"

Andy studied the faded old photos while Jan sat quietly, getting his breath back. Andy noted that Jan had held onto one picture that he seemed to be guarding jealously.

Jan was correct. Artur was not present in any of the pictures, although this in itself was not conclusive proof of what Jan had told him. Jan could simply have destroyed any other pictures of Artur to make his claim seem real. "Jan, if what you say is true, then who shot down the German planes? Surely the other pilots would have claimed the kills. Why would they give credit to a deserter?"

Jan seemed troubled. Still staring out into the garden, he slid the last photo back and forth through his fingers. Then, without a word, he leaned over and handed Andy the photo. He then continued watching the wildlife in the garden without saying a word.

Andy studied the picture. Again it was a group of pilots gathered together. There seemed to be a bit of celebrating going on, and it appeared from the dress code that the unit had just returned to base. Some men still sported flying helmets and goggles and life preservers. Their grinning faces, covered with grime from air operations, stared into the camera lens to be recorded for posterity. Andy studied each face, looking for Jan's reason for holding onto this picture until now.

From the middle of the group, a face jumped out at Andy. For a second, Andy screwed up his eyes, trying to get the faded image as clear as possible, but no matter how Andy looked at it, in the middle of the group, a smiling girl complete with helmet and goggles stared out of the picture at him, willing him to ask Jan the fateful question. "Jan, this can't be an operational picture. One of the pilots is a girl. Was she one of the Air Transport Auxiliary pilots?"

Jan sighed, mumbling to himself, "And so it begins!" Jan turned his attention back to Andy, pausing to recollect the facts before speaking.

"The Air Transport Auxiliary was not formed until June 1941, my friend. That picture was taken by me in August

1940. The girl in the picture is Jean Bruce, and the picture was taken after Jean scored the first kill for the Romanian unit of 303 Squadron in the so-called Battle of Britain."

Andy was in shock. What the old man had claimed was outrageous. Andy wanted to ask more questions, but he didn't know where to start. His head was spinning with the revelation.

Andy was about to launch into a verbal assault when the door opened and Lisa appeared carrying a tray with coffee, tea, and biscuits. She entered with a beaming smile, but she took one look at Jan, and the smile vanished. Lisa handed Andy the tray and went over to Jan, reaching for his hand.

"Jan, honey, do you feel OK? Your colour is not good." Lisa busied herself checking Jan's temperature before calling for a second nurse. "Andy, can you go and wait in my office by reception? I will be along shortly."

Lisa had a haunted expression that told Andy to leave any questions he had until later.

Andy was not sure how long he spent in Lisa's office. It felt like hours. Andy needed to get back into the old man's room. He had so many questions to ask Jan.

Lisa arrived just before lunchtime. It was clear to see that her overnight stint combined with Jan's problems had taken its toll on her. She looked fit to drop. "Andy, I don't know what you spoke about in there, but Jan is shattered. He is sleeping for the moment, and unfortunately, I think it is best he be left for the rest of the day to give him a chance to recuperate."

Andy could have screamed. He could not stand being left hanging like that, but he had little choice. He did not need to ask Lisa. He knew she would not let her patient be put at risk. He would have to wait for Jan to recover before he could ask the hundreds of questions that were flying about in his head. He watched as Lisa wrapped her scarf round her neck before reaching for her coat. "Sorry, Andy. Come on. Let's go and grab some lunch. It's my turn to pay today, no arguments."

Andy could think of no good reason to object to this. After all, it wasn't every day a pretty nurse offered to buy him lunch, and he was at a loose end. Andy picked up his attaché case and followed Lisa past reception and out into the car park.

Lisa's idea of lunch proved to be somewhat different to Andy's. A quick visit to a mini supermarket filled a basket with the ingredients for lunch. Andy said nothing but followed Lisa around the store like her pet dog. In truth, he was still turning Jan's revelations over in his head. A few minutes' walk towards the city centre, and the pair arrived at a three-story building split into flats. Lisa punched in her code entry and held the door open while Andy, carrying the shopping bags, entered the premises. Lisa led him up the spiral staircase to the second floor, arriving at flat 5. She held the door once more so Andy could deposit the shopping in the galley kitchen on the right just off the tiny hall. Lisa showed Andy to the living room. "Well, Andy, I'm afraid this is it. Not much, I know, but it's all mine, and it's easy to clean, so it suits me fine. Has the cat got your tongue? You have been very quiet?"

Andy unbuttoned his heavy jacket, looking around the room before replying to Lisa. "I'm sorry, Lisa. My manners are terrible. Thanks for inviting me to lunch, and forgive me, but Jan has taken the wind out of my sails. Lots to think about, you see."

Lisa fluffed up the cushions on the sofa. "I will sort lunch. Grab a seat, and feel free to use my Wifi. The password is on the back of the router. Just shout if you need anything. I will be in the kitchen.

Andy needed no second invitation, and five minutes later, his laptop was online. Andy searched for Artur Krol who, due to his glittering career, was not hard to find. Strangely, not much was said about Artur on the Polish historical websites. Andy had more luck with the British historical websites. Artur Krol's first confirmed kill was dated August 31, 1940, when he shot down a Messerschmitt Bf 109. Krol's career continued with him scoring various kills until he'd achieved a total of sixteen confirmed kills, three unconfirmed, and five damaged, making him not only one of the top Polish pilots of the Second World War but one of the top all-time Allied fighter pilots, but what became of him? Andy read on until he found his answer. Artur Krol took off from RAF Northolt on May 12, 1942, on a routine channel sortie. His Spitfire was never seen again. His last radio transmission stated he was about to engage two enemy Focke-Wulf 190 fighters. Neither Artur Krol nor his Spitfire was ever found, despite exhaustive searches by the navy and the pilots from 303 Squadron.

Andy found a footnote relating to this page. The Luftwaffe claimed that they had engaged and shot down a Spitfire Mk V over the English Channel on that date, but that claim was unconfirmed.

Andy sat back relaxing on the sofa. His head was exploding. Jan must have been mistaken. How would it be possible for a woman to fight in the Battle of Britain and no one to find out until 2014?

For a second, Andy let himself believe it was true. What was he going to do next? He was a lawyer first and foremost, and lawyers needed proof. The pilot, male or female, was dead, and all Andy had were a few old photos that were circumstantial at best and the testimony of a 101-year-old man in failing health. Even if this yarn were true, bringing it to his superior's attention would get him laughed out of the Royal Air Force.

Andy's mind snapped back to the present as Lisa placed a tray in front of him. "I hope you like smoked ham and cheese, Andy. Just say if not, and I will dig you up something else."

Andy smiled and picked up the baguette Lisa had prepared for him. "Perfect. Thank you. You must have read my mind." Andy tucked into the crusty bread, washing it down with coffee that had arrived on the same tray. There was a short silence as they both tucked into their meals. Andy was first to finish, and then he sat back watching Lisa.

"Sorry to talk shop, Lisa, but what do you think is wrong with Jan? Do you think I will be able to speak to him later today?"

Lisa smiled, shaking her head playfully in mock disgust. "There is nothing wrong with Jan. He is old, very old. Even drinking a cup of water at his age is a challenge. He just gets tired. Maybe one day you will find out for yourself. To answer your second question, unless it's a life or death situation, I would leave your questions until tomorrow and give the old boy a chance to recover after the grilling you gave him today."

Andy was mildly annoyed by the accusation that he had been the cause of Jan's tiredness. "Excuse me, Matron, but

I mostly listened. Jan did all the talking. I take your point though. When I talk to him again, I would like you to sit in on the conversation. That way, if you think he has had enough, you can intervene."

Lisa sat back in her chair studying Andy. "So you think the head nurse has nothing to do other than become your personal assistant?" Lisa sat forwards suddenly, remembering Andy's previous comments. "Oh, by the way, Squadron Leader, when did I become a matron? I'm not too sold on the image of a chubby, bossy, middle-aged spinster. Is that how you see me, Mr. Paxton?"

Lisa paused, waiting for Andy Paxton to either redeem himself or crash and burn. "You're wrong, Lisa. That is not what 'matron' says to me. It means someone a little old fashioned, always professional, running things like a Swiss watch, and a little tiny bit bossy. That describes you perfectly."

Lisa knew he had got himself out of deep water, but she wasn't for letting him off the hook that easily. "So you think I am bossy, do you? I must introduce you to my second-in-command, Susan. She would have given you a slap on the head if you called her 'matron,' so think yourself lucky I took your call about Jan."

The mention of Jan's name reminded Andy why he was here. He decided to try and find out more about Jan Powlak from Lisa.

"Lisa, do you know if Jan has any relatives or friends who visit him? Maybe they can shine a bit more light on Jan's story, or has anyone else visited Jan since he started writing to the RAF?"

Lisa started to tidy away the lunch dishes. She remained deep in thought for a second before replying. "I really don't know how much I should be telling you, not that there is much to tell. I suppose I can tell you this much. As far as I know, Jan has no family. I think all his family were wiped out in the Second World War. Jan signed himself in and pays his own way in the home. He has no friends who visit him, only his lawyer who visits once a month. So sad to see such a lovely old man so lonely."

Andy had been surprised when Lisa mentioned the lawyer's visit every month. "Lisa, do you have any idea why his lawyer visits every month? Did Jan ever say why?"

Lisa shook her head. "No idea, we were just glad somebody came to see him."

Andy followed Lisa into the kitchen, watching while Lisa started washing up the dishes. Andy grabbed the tea towel and started to dry the dishes that Lisa had just placed in the drying rack. "Lisa, do you know the name of the lawyers that visit Andy?"

Lisa stopped washing and thought for a second before replying. "It was an Edinburgh company. The card had three big Bs as the heading, but I can't recall at the moment. Stupid of me. They say who they are each time they call to make an appointment. Sorry, Andy."

Lisa finished up in the kitchen then handed Andy the TV controller, proclaiming she was heading for a shower. Andy dismissed the TV, instead logging back onto the Internet, looking for an Edinburgh lawyer with a three-B logo.

Andy had been busy on the Internet for five minutes when Lisa's phone started to vibrate on the table. At first, Andy was happy to ignore it, but the caller rang off only to call again. Andy looked at the screen. The only words on the screen were "Sunny Brae." Andy lifted the phone and walked into the hall. The shower was still going. Andy had a dilemma. The call could be urgent.

Andy pressed the green call button, and before he could say anything, a clearly panicked woman started talking. "Lisa, thank god you answered. I called Susan. She is on her way, but you are closer. It's old Morag. Can you come?"

"Listen. This is Lisa's phone, but she is in the shower. I will get her to call you back. She will call right back, OK?"

Andy hung up and then followed the hall along to the bathroom door. It took more than a few knocks before the shower was turned off and a flustered Lisa appeared at the door, a small towel only just covering her dripping body. "Can a girl not have a shower in peace? Please tell me this isn't to ask another lawyer question."

Andy handed the phone in through the slightly open door. "The home has been trying to get you. It sounds urgent, something about Susan being too far away, something to do with old Morag?"

The words had barely left Andy's lips when the bathroom door was flung open, and Lisa barged past him, heading for the bedroom. Andy returned to the living room to await the charging nurse. Andy didn't have to wait long before Lisa reappeared, pulling a jacket on. Andy stood up as she entered the room. "Sorry about interrupting," he said, "but I thought it was best."

Lisa grabbed her phone and headed for the door. "Need to go. See you in a bit."

Lisa was gone before Andy could say another thing. Andy noted that in her rush to leave, she had left her house keys on the living-room table. It looked like Andy had the option to either stay put or lock the place up and drop the keys in at the home on his way past. After all, his car was still parked outside the home. Andy turned the options over in his head and decided it would be rude to leave without saying good-bye.

Andy returned his attention to the Internet. His efforts were rewarded twenty minutes later when he came across a lawyers based on the outskirts of Edinburgh. The Murrayfield lawyer had an advert sporting the three Bs that Lisa had described. Andy checked his watch. There was still a chance there might be someone in the office. Andy was in luck and was put through to the office of one of the senior partner in the business after explaining he was a lawyer working for the Royal Air Force.

"Hello, Mr. Brentford. Thank you for speaking to me on such short notice. I am in need of some information regarding one of your clients, a Mr. Jan Powlak."

Brentford butted in before Andy could go any further. "I assume Jan has passed away. I have been expecting this call for some time now. I must say I am at a loss as to why the RAF legal department needs to get involved. There is no need for your assistance. Jan has left quite specific instructions in the event of his death. No grey areas, and there is only one benefactor. So why do you need to be involved exactly?"

Andy had not expected that the conversation would head this way, and it took him a second to regroup. "No, Mr. Brentford. We have our wires crossed. Jan is still alive. The RAF are looking into certain claims made by Jan. I just needed to know a bit more about him and why he needs your company to visit him once a month. So Jan has no family who gets his estate, his cat?"

Andy had chanced his arm. He knew he was out of order, but it was worth a try. Brentford was not happy. He had already told Andy too much, and he was not planning on giving anything more away. "Sir, if you are a lawyer, you will know I cannot answer that question. I suggest that you talk to Mr. Powlak if you require any further information. Good evening."

The phone went dead. Andy sat thinking things through before contacting his commanding officer. "Hi, Bill. It's your long-lost Scotsman here. Just checking in. Listen, this might be a wild-goose chase here, but I need to tidy up some loose ends before I head back. I take it that's OK with you?" Andy could hear laughter in the background as his request was passed around the office by Squadron Leader Bill Hardy.

"No problem, Andrew. Would your 'loose ends' be tall and blond with big tits? I have no problem as long as you fill out the report when you get back. Speak to you later."

Andy helped himself to a cup of coffee while strolling round the flat. It was clear that Lisa only used this as an overnight stop. It had almost nothing more personal than you would find in any modern hotel room—only the goldfish and a neat row of framed nursing certificates proudly displayed, along with a framed letter from the head of nursing at Ninewells Hospital wishing Lisa Preston good luck with her new venture in the private sector.

Lisa was a bit of a mystery. Andy made a mental note to find out more about the pretty blond nurse who had made such an impression on him.

It was after nine, and Lisa arrived at the door of her flat to find she had no keys. Another search of her handbag proved fruitless. It was the final straw. Lisa tried to check again, but the tears blocked her vision. She had been on her feet for more than forty-eight hours, and her patient and friend, old Morag, had just passed away in her arms. Lisa had managed to hold it together until the doctor had confirmed time of death. Then she had contacted Morag's only relative in Australia and made arrangements with the undertaker. She just wanted to sleep away the pain in her heart, and the missing keys were the final straw.

Andy was not prepared for what he found when he opened the door. Lisa was a mess, pale as a ghost and sobbing openly. In the turmoil of recent events, Lisa had forgotten all about Andy. When she saw who had opened the door, Lisa launched herself at him, flinging her arms around his neck, clinging to him as if her life depended upon it.

Andy wasn't quite sure what to do next. In fact, he wasn't at all sure what the problem was. All he knew was that at that moment, Lisa needed him. Whatever the problem was, it was bad. The poor girl was breaking her heart.

Not wanting to cause a scene for the neighbours, Andy gently scooped Lisa up in his arms and carried her inside the flat, using his foot to close the front door. Inside the hall, Andy attempted to find out what the problem was, but he was having problems making any sense of the words Lisa was trying to get out in between a string of huge sobs.

Andy gently removed her arms from around his neck and led her through to the living room by the hand, sitting her down, then sitting down by her side, still holding her shaking hand.

"Come on, Lisa. Take a couple of big breaths and try to calm down. You're home, and I'm here for you." Andy squeezed Lisa's cold, shaking hand in a friendly gesture.

It took a few minutes of them both sitting quietly before Lisa started showing signs of recovery.

"It's Morag, Andy. She died in my arms, and I could do nothing about it." It was all too much for Lisa, and she was off again, sobbing loudly. Andy's natural instinct was to try and comfort her, and he gently put his arm around her and cuddled the poor girl.

For a second, her body was rigid, but Andy felt her relax as she let her cold body rest against his warm chest and shoulders. Gradually the sobbing subsided.

Andy said nothing, not wanting to risk setting her off again. For Andy, it wasn't an unpleasant experience. Since his first year of study, he had thrown himself into his work, shunning a social life and accepting the inevitable lack of female company. Even for all the wrong reasons, Andy was happy to let Lisa cling to him. Her heartbeat felt strong through her thin jacket. It was with some regret Andy let her go as she sat up, pulling a box of paper hankies from the table and using them to wipe her eyes.

"I'm sorry, Andy. Give me a second to pull myself together. I wasn't expecting to find you still here. Thanks for putting up with my stupid antics. In a normal hospital situation, you tend not to get too close to the patients, but that's the thing about this bloody job. I have never got used to it, and probably never will. The old ones become part of your life, working every day with them. It's so hard to let go when they pass away."

To Andy's surprise, Lisa leaned back, cuddling back into Andy's side again. "I hope you don't mind, Andy, but this is the first time I have had anyone to speak to. You have no idea how much better I feel with someone to talk to. Help me take my mind off poor Morag. Can you tell me what Jan wanted? I decide I am going to be in the room tomorrow."

Lisa was right. There was no point not warning Lisa, as she would find out tomorrow anyway.

"Well, Lisa, where do I start? Your old pal Jan has well and truly thrown the history of the RAF into disarray." Andy explained the conversation that he had had with Jan.

Lisa although intrigued did not yet grasp the enormity of Jan's statement. "So what's the big deal, Andy? The RAF had women pilots. I am sure I watched a programme on them at some point." Andy shook his head, turning round on the sofa to face Lisa. "Not during the Battle of Britain they didn't. When they were eventually deployed, they were never allowed to engage the enemy. We will hear more from Jan tomorrow, but it looks like he is claiming this girl fought in the Battle of Britain, which, if true, will send the historians into meltdown."

Lisa and Andy sat for some time, Lisa visibly calming down. Andy decided his job here was done and stood up, ready for his journey home. "OK, young lady, I will see you tomorrow morning bright and early."

Lisa glanced at the wall clock. "Too right you will, Mr. Paxton. Look at the time! It's not worth going home. You would just have to turn around and head back here. You can sleep here. Relax—I'm not inviting you into my bed. I have a spare quilt and the couch is a sofa bed. Breakfast is on me, no arguments!"

Andy winked at Lisa, who was watching him closely for his reaction to her offer of a bed for the night. "It's OK, Lisa. I can handle it if you want to keep your spare quit unused. I'm sure I could find a corner of your bed that would do me fine."

Lisa smiled at Andy while shaking her head. "Nice try, mister, but no deal. The tongues at the home are already wagging after you answered my phone and announced to the world that I was in the shower. Thanks for that, by the way."

Andy was not too worried by the brush-off. He was sure the twinkle in Lisa's eye meant that his suggestion was not dead in the water just yet.

The next morning, Andy was woken by a gentle shake on the shoulder. He found Lisa standing over the sofa bed, holding a tray with his breakfast on it. Lisa was already dressed, ready to leave for work.

"Good morning, Andy. I take it the sofa bed was comfy enough?"

Andy screwed up his eyes to stop the sun streaming in through the window distorting his view of Lisa. "Are you going already? Don't you have breakfast in the morning?"

Lisa was already making for the door. "No time for food. I will grab something when I get there. You have breakfast, feel free to use the shower, and I will see you when you get in. Give me a call at the home before you leave just in case Jan isn't up to a talk today. My key is on the table. Bring it with you when you come. Bye."

Andy made up the couch, then tucked into the croissant and coffee that Lisa had left for him. A thought suddenly crossed Andy's mind, and seconds later, he was on the phone to his old university mate Cammy.

Andy had two reasons for this. Cammy now worked for a company that researched ancestry, mainly searching for relatives who had been willed the estates of people who had died but also for people researching their family histories. The second reason was that he had nothing to do with the RAF.

Andy had only to wait a few seconds before his old friend Cammy picked up the phone. "Cammy, it's Andy Paxton here. How are things with you? What is happening in your world these days?"

There was a slight pause while Cammy computed who was on the other end of the phone line. "My god, if it isn't my mate that the RAF stole from me. Long time, no hear buddy. How are you doing yourself?"

Andy would have loved to catch up with Cammy, but the imminent meeting with Jan was weighing heavily on his mind, "Sorry to be a bore, Cammy, but I am in need of your genius at finding people, and I don't have much time. If I gave you a name, do you think you could try and come up with something for me?"

"Andy Paxton, why do I get the feeling that this is going to be a freebie? Don't the air force have their own people for this kind of thing? OK, give me the details, and I will see what I can do for you."

Andy breathed a sigh of relief, but he knew he wasn't home and dry yet. "Thanks, Cammy. You're a good man. The girl's name is Jean Bruce. She was a pilot in her late teens to midtwenties in England around 1940. I am afraid that is all I can give you at the moment, pal."

Andy heard the loud sigh from Callum before he replied. "Seriously, that's all you have? It's not a genius you need. It's a miracle. OK, I will have a poke about and see what comes up."

Andy thanked Cammy and rang off just before his phone battery died completely. Andy plugged in his phone to charge while he grabbed a quick shower. He had heard nothing from Lisa, so he presumed his meeting with Jan Powlak was still on the cards.

The walk to the home took less than fifteen minutes. On the way, Andy thought over what to ask Jan. If his superiors were going to believe a word of Jan's story, he was going to have to come up with conclusive evidence of events. This was why he had enlisted the help of his friend Callum.

Andy knew what Callum was like when he got his teeth into a project. He knew his friend would leave no stone unturned. If there were something to find, Callum would find it.

CHAPTER 3
JAN'S STORY

On arriving at the home, Andy was asked by the girl at reception to take a seat in the waiting area while she contacted Lisa. Andy noted the girl was trying hard to suppress a smirk when she mentioned Lisa's name. She had obviously heard about Andy's visit to Lisa's flat. Andy wondered if this were the girl he'd told that Lisa was in the shower.

Andy didn't have long to wait. Lisa soon appeared at the far end of the corridor, walking towards him. Andy had seen her that morning, but he was still taken by her sheer presence. As she walked towards him, she almost glided, her short blond hair glowing in the morning sunlight. Andy discovered that without realizing it, he had fallen for her charms. Here he was, possibly just about to rewrite RAF history, but at the moment, he could think of nothing but the pretty blond nurse.

Andy was still studying Lisa as she walked past reception. The girl who had asked him to take a seat said something to Lisa as she passed. By the time Lisa arrived at the waiting area, her face was positively glowing.

"Hi, Andy, I hope breakfast was OK. I am not used to company, so I'm a bit rusty when it comes to hospitality."

Andy stood up smiling, "You are a busy lady, no time to practice hospitality, but if you find the time, I would be happy to let you practice on me."

Lisa broke eye contact and turned, trying not to show that her rosy complexion had just got rosier. Lisa led the way back to Jan's door, pausing outside and still not quite looking Andy. "I have arranged with my number two to look after things for the next couple of hours. She will only disturb us in the case of an emergency."

Lisa was still avoiding eye contact when Andy reached down, taking her hand and giving it a gentle squeeze. "You're an angel. Thank you."

Jan Powlak was seated in the same position as yesterday. His colour had improved, and someone had been hard at work cutting his hair. Lisa sat next to him, taking the old man's hand, while Andy sat opposite him so he could study Jan's features.

"OK, Jan, shall we start where we finished off yesterday?"

Jan's expression was blank. "Forgive me, officer, but I do not remember what we said yesterday. Can you bring me up to date?"

That was the last thing Andy wanted to hear. In the future, if Jan were questioned about Andy's involvement, he would make Andy look stupid if he said he had never met him. Andy caught Lisa's eye before continuing. Lisa jumped in before Andy could say anything to upset the situation. "Don't worry, Jan honey. It will come back to you. You'll see. Andy will help jog your memory for you, won't you, Andy?"

Andy placed his attaché case on the floor, switching on a Dictaphone in the process and placing it on the table between the chairs. "No problem, Jan. Yesterday, you were telling me how Artur Krol had deserted before the start of the Battle of Britain and that Jean Bruce had flown with 303 Squadron. Does that help, Jan?"

Jan was nodding in agreement. "That's correct. You must be wondering how it came to be that a young girl ended up flying with 303 Squadron. You must understand that some of what I tell you was told to me. Initially, I was not aware of Jean's presence and did not know her.

"Jean had an uncle in Canada, and she learned to fly on his farm, but I believe after a family row, she ran away to America where she joined up with a travelling flying circus. I believe she would have stayed in America. They say she was a highly regarded stunt pilot with no fear whatsoever. Fate, however, decreed she would return to Britain, caused by a situation out of her control. Her parents had gone missing during a holiday trip to the continent.

"Jean arrived and met up with another one of her uncles in England. She tried to get the necessary permits to fly to France to begin her search for her mother and father. As you will understand, it was not a time for civilians to be wandering about Europe, and she was turned down. I think it was only days later that someone got word back to the government that Jean's parents had been executed on the Swiss border, shot for allegedly being British spies. The Red Cross version was somewhat different. While skiing, they had wandered into Nazi-held territory and paid a terrible price.

"Jean's uncle in England worked for the Hawker aircraft company and was trying to get Jean into the company when war broke out. Although refused a pilot's job, Jean worked with her uncle delivering spares to the RAF airfields.

"Tomasz Zajac, a squadron leader with the Romanian section of 303 Squadron, was the first to meet Jean Bruce. While her uncle unloaded and checked off the spares, Tomasz chatted to the young girl. He was somewhat surprised to find out Jean was a fellow pilot, and he let Jean poke around his newly delivered Hurricane. He even let Jean sit in the plane, going through the flight controls with her. Looking back at it now, he must have taken a shine to her—no one, not even Tomasz's flight crew, was ever allowed to sit in his machine. Jean was the only one.

"On the twelfth of August in 1940, the Romanian section of 303 had been on a flying exercise over the west coast. Fate again arrived to knock on Jean Bruce's door. I remember the day well since it was the first day I first set eyes on the girl. Her uncle had arrived and was in the back of his truck, searching for parts. Tomasz Zajac and two other pilots had just arrived, first back from exercise. Tomasz was in a foul mood, which he had been in all day. He did not want to admit to his British commanding officer that one of his Polish pilots had deserted even before a shot had been fired. We were proud people. It was not good for us to admit weakness.

"I was walking out to my pilot's machine to give it a visual check when the first bomb landed—no air raid sirens, no warnings, just a huge explosion. At first I thought one of our Hurricanes had exploded. It was only when the second bomb fell, and I heard the scream before it detonated that I realised we were under attack. Jean Bruce was only feet from Tomasz's plane. She was frozen to the spot, a rabbit caught in the headlights. Tomasz was battle hardened and reacted instinctively, looking for his men. He was just in time to see his men halfway across the strip being strafed by a Me 109. One pilot was cut to pieces by the bullets from the Germans' guns while the other dived for cover, narrowly avoiding being hit.

"Tomasz turned, screaming at his frozen ground crew to get the Hurricanes started. You see, in the early days of the war, these fighter planes were like gold dust. I watched as without hesitation, he turned to Jean and screamed at her to get into the Hurricane that was parked closest to his own machine. I think she wavered, but I am not sure. Tomasz was screaming at me to help her get the machine started.

"Tomasz got his machine away first with the girl trailing behind him. Zajac's Hurricane was up and away while the girl's machine was still trundling down the runway, bombs going off on either side of her. The last Hurricane was up and banking hard left away from the falling bombs. I watched as at the last minute, the girls Hurricane lifted its nose just retracting its undercarriage as it cleared the boundary hedge at the end of the airfield. I was still watching, mesmerised by the situation, as Jean's plane banked hard left, too hard. It looked as if there were no way she could keep the machine in the air. Her air speed was too slow to allow it to stay airborne. It was then that I saw why she had made this crazy manoeuvre. Just to her right, the yellow nose of a Messerschmitt Bf 109 appeared, banking hard the other way. They had both been on a collision course. The Nazi pilot, intent on destroying the planes on the ground, had not counted on one taking off in his path. The German pilot was not as lucky as Jean, and the tip of his wing made contact with the boundary hedge, cartwheeling his Messerschmitt to destruction and killing him in the process.

"Jean was lucky. I watched as she recovered and looped round out of sight of the airfield. For sure, she would have crashed if her Merlin engine had been cold. It would have stalled for sure, but luckily for her, it had just returned from operations, and it was still at operating temperature."

Lisa was as engrossed in Jan's tale as Andy Paxton, but she was watching Jan closely. His complexion was similar to a beetroot as the memories came flooding back to the old man—some good, some bad, and some terrible.

Lisa pressed the call button next to Jan's bed, and a few minutes later, a flustered nurse appeared. Lisa asked her to fetch some refreshments for them in an attempt to allow Jan to calm down for a bit and save his ebbing energy levels.

Lisa's ploy failed miserably as a fired-up Jan charged on with his incredible tale, a story that had remained bottled up in Jan's brain for decades. Now that the cork had popped, there was no stopping the flow of knowledge from Jan Powlak.

"I was still in shock that Zajac had let a girl fly one of his precious Hurricanes. Tomasz Zajac was the first to bring his Hurricane back to the ravaged air base. The girl trailed him home like a lost puppy dog. I held my breath as she landed the fighter. To my surprise, as well as remembering to drop the landing gear, she managed to put the Hurricane on the ground with only one slight hop as she adjusted her landing speed to compensate.

"By the time, the girl had taxied the plane next to Zajac's. A small group had gathered around the planes.

The girl was elated, not a nerve in her body, cool as a cucumber. I think that was the first time that I realised that this young ginger-haired girl was something very special. At that moment, I could not understand Tomasz Zajac's mood. His face was one of thunder while everyone rejoiced that we had survived the German attack.

"It did not take long for the reason for Zajac's mood to become apparent. The young girl was being patted on the back by everyone present, but he walked up to her and took her hand, and with a stony face, he led her to the edge of the group. He pointed to the smouldering crater in front of the workshops where only minutes ago Jean's uncle's lorry had been parked. Only one axle, a wheel, and a mudguard remained to show what once had stood there. Next to the axle stood a man's boot. Jean collapsed into Zajac's arms at the sight of the bomb crater, her brain registering for the first time her uncle was gone.

"Later that afternoon, after placing Jean in his room, Zajac held a meeting in the bunkhouse, and all from the Romanian section attended. Zajac started by saying a prayer for Pilot Officer Peter Kalinowski, who was the first member of the team to have lost his life in this latest conflict. All the pilots present swore an oath to hunt down the Nazi pilot who had gunned him down while he was running for cover.

"Squadron Leader Tomasz Zajac then changed the subject. Tomasz was not a man you would argue with, but what he said next shocked me to the core. Tomasz brought up the subject of the deserter Artur Krol. He was worried that reporting his desertion to his British RAF superiors would have a knock-on effect for 303 Squadron, who had not yet been given operational status. Tomasz painted a bleak picture for us—already bombed and now two pilots down, with men running away. He was not sure the RAF would trust us to do the job. Zajac declared he had a solution, but that we all had to agree then and there to do as he said to keep our unit effective. It was then he explained his clever but crazy plan. Jean Bruce had proved her flying skill in dramatic fashion, and as far as the authorities knew, she had been in the truck with her uncle when it took a direct hit from a German bomb. Her uncle's body was utterly destroyed, so there would logically not be a girl's body either. Jean would fly in place of the deserter Artur Krol, using his identity. Only the people present would know. Not even the rest of 303 Squadron would be told, only the Romanian section of the squadron, men he could trust to keep a secret.

"At first, there was a lot of grumbling. No one wanted to stick his neck out for Zajac to chop off. I think Zajac sensed the disquiet and continued with the hard sell. He asked the group what the problem was. Had they come here to kill Germans, or were they afraid a little girl would show them how to fly? Zajac kept chipping away until he had the majority of his men behind him.

"As the meeting broke up, I headed for the workshop to start clearing up the mess our German friends had left us. I only got as far as the hut door when Zajac intercepted me. I was to be the girl's lead ground crew. Zajac did not want the girl in the bunkhouse for two reasons. He did not want the rest of his men in close proximity to her, and she could not be present if an outsider visited the barracks. I was ordered to clear a space for a bed in the tool store in the hangar for her.

"I was in the process of doing this when something blocked the light from the doorway. I looked up and saw

Jean watching me work. There was no sadness left in those young eyes, only a hatred for an unknown enemy that once again had struck at her family. I could tell that Tomasz had not had to do much persuading to get Jean to sign onto his crazy scheme. That evening, I introduced myself to Jean but said little to her. I had no idea what to say. It seems foolish now, but the only thing I commented on was her manoeuvre at the end of the airfield. I told her if she tried that move again, she would not walk away to tell the tale. She smiled at me, but her eyes gave away her true feelings. She did not like to be told what to do when it came to flying."

Lisa had been watching Jan closely and had decided enough was enough. Jan and Andy both protested, but Lisa was having none of it, Jan was struggling to string sentences together, so Lisa called a halt to proceedings, declaring it was time for Jan's afternoon nap. Reluctantly, Andy agreed. Lisa stayed, helping Jan to drink a little water as his throat had dried up from all the talking and then getting him into bed. "Well done, Jan. I bet that felt better, getting that off your chest after all these years. You get the eyes shut for a while, and Andy and I will be back later to finish our chat."

Jan stared into Lisa's eyes. He nodded to her, mouthing the words *thank you*, but he was so exhausted his wrinkled lips only moved. No sound escaped.

Within two minutes of lying down, Jan was asleep, dead to the world. Lisa watched his chest rise and fall rhythmically before drawing the curtain silently over the window. Then she cleared away the cups before shutting Jan's door.

Lisa was worried. Jan had made it his mission to speak to the RAF. Now that he had done it, what motivation did he have to go on? Lisa had seen it before in her patients.

They set a goal, and then, when that was reached, they had nothing left to fight for and faded like wilting flowers. Lisa went looking for Andy. She needed to know what more he needed from Jan.

Andy sat outside in the car park, soaking up the sun-rays while sitting on the boundary wall of the care home car park. Lisa was not the only one who was worried. Jan Powlak had convinced him that he was telling the truth. There was only one problem—the rest of the world would require more than just the testimony of an old man before they would be willing to agree that history must be changed. Andy Paxton had no idea how he was going to be able to prove to the world Jean Bruce was Britain's first and only Second World War woman fighter ace.

Andy had been sitting thinking for some time before Lisa appeared and sat down by his side. Although each of them was aware of the other's presence, they sat quietly, absorbed in their own thoughts. Lisa broke the deadlock.

"Andy, I don't know how much more we can ask of Jan. I know you need to find out the details as quickly as possible, and I suppose we could get him up again, but would you do me a huge favour and let him rest until tomorrow?"

Andy listened to Lisa's plea but said nothing. For a second, there was silence again. "Lisa, I swore on the old man's Bible in there I would follow this through. Honestly, Lisa, I don't know where to start." Andy jumped to his feet, reaching down and pulling Lisa up by the hands until she stood looking into his eyes. Then he nodded.

"We will worry about that tomorrow. You have your wish, Matron. I will leave Jan to sleep on one condition and one condition only. You have to join me for dinner, my treat. I am going home to get changed. So what time shall I pick you up?"

Lisa smiled, trying not to blush. "You do know, Flight Lieutenant Paxton, that if you keep this up, people will start to talk about us."

Andy shrugged his shoulders. "I will take that as a yes then. What time can I pick you up, Lisa?"

Andy pulled up outside Lisa's flat at exactly 7:30 p.m. He had flatly refused to tell Lisa where they were headed, only that it was a bit better than a pizza shop, so she could dress up, but only if she wanted too.

Lisa emerged from the flat wearing an off-the-shoulder dress, black and covered in black sequins, with shoes and clutch bag to match. The black clothing made her blond hair stand out and almost glow. It made Andy's white shirt and grey chinos look rather underdressed, although at that moment in time, Andy was far too preoccupied by Lisa to even realise he was hopelessly outgunned in the fashion department.

CHAPTER 4

A DATE WITH MATRON

Lisa stepped carefully into the Fiesta and was greeted by a low wolf whistle from the driver.

"I take it from the whistle that I will pass inspection, Squadron Leader?"

Andy smiled at Lisa's attempt to wind him up. "Right back at you, girl. You know, for a matron, you do scrub up pretty well."

Lisa giggled and hit Andy a playful slap over the head. "Andy, I am warning you. If this is your idea of a joke, and we end up in a pub for a bar supper, you will need a real matron to look after you in hospital when I am finished with you, understood?"

Andy smiled, checked his watch, then pulled away from the kerb. "We better get a move on, or we will be late. Buckle up. We have a bit of driving to do."

After a few minutes driving, they reached the motorway, and Andy pushed the little Fiesta along quickly, heading in the direction of Perth.

"So are you going to tell me why I have got all dressed up, or will I have to beat it out of you, Mr. Paxton?"

Andy's eyes never left the road ahead, but he was smiling and enjoying keeping Lisa guessing. "No, part of the fun is the surprise. Don't worry. You will knock them dead dressed like that. Trust me. The only rule of the night is this. It's a get-to-know-each-other evening. No talking about work for either of us. Jan Powlak is off the menu tonight, and if either one breaks the rules, we'll owe the other a forfeit."

Lisa was watching Andy closely as he drove. Were it not for the military haircut, his short brown hair would almost certainly be curly. There was not a wrinkle or blemish on his face, giving him a boyish look. Lisa guessed he looked younger than his actual age. Lisa did not imagine that with his looks he would have much trouble finding girls to date. She felt slightly flattered that he seemed to be focusing his attention on her.

"OK, Mr. Paxton. I will take the bait. I have decided on my forfeit. If you talk about work first, you have to get me a flight in an RAF aeroplane of some description. That's mine, so what is yours?"

Andy was shaking his head. "You don't believe in selling yourself short, do you young lady? OK, that was my fault, so I will stand by my mistake. I just hope I win. OK, my turn. If you slip up, my forfeit is a kiss from the best-looking girl in Dundee."

Lisa had suspected that they were heading for one of the posh restaurants in Perth, so she was somewhat surprised when Andy sailed past Perth and continued south towards Stirling.

Andy parked the Fiesta in the overspill car park of the Gleneagles hotel at 8:20 p.m., ten minutes before his table booking. He squeezed the little Fiesta in between a Range Rover on one side and a Maserati on the other. He had deliberately picked the overspill car park in the hope his transport would not be shown up. He was wrong. It wouldn't have mattered. Everywhere they looked, the next car was bigger and better than the last one.

"Well, Lisa, it looks as if we have well and truly been beaten in the flash car department."

Lisa looked around her, gobsmacked. On their right, swans glided by in the hotel pond. Behind her, the famous golf course stretched out into the distance, and beyond the car park rose the impressive Gleneagles Hotel.

"Andy, I can't go in there. I mean, I have never been in a place like this. I'm just a nurse, for god's sake. This place is for mega rich people, not me!"

Andy walked round to the passenger side of the car where Lisa sat frozen to the spot. He was surprised to find that the confident, in-control nurse he had come to know was shaking like a leaf. Andy took her arm, holding her warm hand, and winked at her.

"Lisa, loosen up, woman. You look a million dollars. Who knows and who cares what we do. No one is going to ask to see your CV. It's just food, and I bet you half the punters in this car park are ticked up to the eyeballs. Or as my father would put it, two pianos and no knickers. Come on. We are here to relax and enjoy each other's company. Why not in nice surroundings?"

As they were being led to their table, Andy was glad to see that it was in a quiet corner of the room. It appeared that this was the place to dine tonight as there was not an empty table in the house. Once they were seated, Lisa seemed calmer and was studying the menu with interest. Andy studied her as she examined the menu. Tonight, Lisa had intensified her makeup slightly, using it to emphasize her misty blue eyes. A quick look around the room confirmed what Andy had proclaimed earlier. There was no other woman seated in the room who could match Lisa in looks. More than a few of the men in the room had checked out the pretty nurse as she had entered with Andy.

They ordered drinks and food, and for the first time since entering the room, Lisa turned her attention back to Andy. "Andy, this is lovely, but I think I would have been more at home eating pizza again. I feel like a fish out of water."

Andy decided to change the topic. "So I think it is time to find out about each other. I will start, and if you need to know something specific, feel free to ask. I am twenty-six years old. I have another five years of service to do with the RAF. I come from the little village of Muckhart. I am single, and when not on base at RAF Northolt, I live with my parents for the moment. I studied law at Edinburgh University and qualified as a lawyer before joining the air force. Pretty boring really. It's your turn, Lisa."

Lisa sipped on the wine she had ordered, thinking before she replied. "Not so fast flyboy. What the hell do lawyers actually do in the RAF? How many girlfriends have you had? And why does a twenty-six-year-old lawyer still stay with his mum and dad?"

Andy was smiling while removing the condensation from his glass of mineral water with his finger. "Straight for the jugular! There is no messing around with you, lady, that's for sure. OK, RAF lawyers can do a variety of things from giving council to RAF personnel to advising on flying laws to studying law in different countries to assisting with overseas operations. Girlfriends, total three, two from school and one from university. The only reason I stay with my mum and dad is because I have been rather busy studying law and haven't quite got round to that chapter of my life yet. Your turn, madam."

Lisa shook her head. "No, I'm not finished yet. You're still under the spotlight, Andy Paxton. Why did you split up with your last girl, and what hobbies do you have other than being a law bookworm?"

Andy waited until the waiter had delivered the first course before replying. "Lynn was her name. She is a lawyer now. We split up because I needed to study, and we drifted apart, no real reason. I suppose if it was meant to be we would have got together again, but it never happened. My hobbies are Formula One, boxing, and chasing pretty nurses!"

Lisa was tucking into her smoked-salmon starter but stopped when Andy mentioned the pretty nurse part.

"OK, I guess it is my turn to introduce myself. I am twenty-five years old. I trained at Ninewells Hospital in Dundee as a nurse and then moved to private care. I was brought up in the village of Errol before moving to Dundee to be closer to my work. My work is my hobby and my life at the moment, and I can't really think of anything else to say, so over to you. Is there anything you want to ask about me?"

Andy rubbed his chin. "How many boyfriends have you had? And when was the last time you accepted a dinner date from an admirer?"

Lisa finished her starter and avoided eye contact with Andy. "Just the one long-term boyfriend, who left me for my best friend after I started in the hospital, and I had a pizza not that long ago with a gentleman who I suspect is an admirer, but I may be wrong."

Just as Andy was about to reply, the main courses arrived. They both sat in silence as the waiter served the main course. Andy made eye contact with Lisa who started to blush before turning her attention to straightening the cutlery.

Lisa had a premonition that Andy was about to embarrass her and jumped in before Andy could say any more. "Andy, tomorrow you will be as quick as possible with Jan, won't you? Sorry to be a bore, but I am worried about my old pal. He is very frail, you know. We need to be careful. I will stay with you again if you don't mind, Andy."

Andy leaned across the table, taking Lisa's hand. "I promise I will keep it to a minimum, Matron. Oh, and by the way, you just lost your flight in an aeroplane, but it looks like I should be all right for a good-night kiss."

Lisa rolled her eyes and shook her head in mock disgust but said nothing. Andy was left to carry on the conversation.

"So what made you move to the private sector of health care? To me, it looks like you have gone as far as you can in the nursing-home business."

Lisa once again found her tongue. "Well first and foremost, it was obviously the money. Sunny Brae is owned by Sir Anthony Moorehouse, the billionaire property tycoon. He wanted to set up someplace where he and his family could live when the time came to be looked after in old age. His staff, like the equipment and the premises, are second to none. I was headhunted by his personnel manager to be in charge of the day-to-day running of the business and to help recruit the other staff. It was a dream come true to be given the ability to mould a team around you. The only part of the team missing at the moment is a resident doctor. Our last doctor was a retired consultant who decided after two years, it was time to brush up on his fishing. His replacement starts with us in three weeks' time, and it can't come quick enough. Depending on local doctors is a pain in the backside."

Andy was pleased that Lisa had found her tongue again, but something crossed his mind, and he butted into the conversation while it was still fresh on his mind. "So if it's all the best staff and no expense spared on equipment, Sunny Brae must be a rather expensive place to stay?"

Lisa nodded, taking a sip of her wine. "Yes, I have seen the bills, and they are eye watering. You have got to have money to stay at Sunny Brae."

Andy thought for a second before his next statement. "Old Jan must be worth a few pounds then, to stay with no family to support him. His time in America must have been lucrative."

The time passed quickly for the pair, and before they knew it, they were one of only two couples left in the dinning room. Andy paid the bill and escorted Lisa back to the little Fiesta for their journey back to Dundee.

The Fiesta pulled up outside Lisa's flat, and the chat, which had continued all the way from Gleneagles, dried up as both parties realised this was the end of their evening.

Andy broke the silence before the situation became awkward. "Well, Nurse Preston, I believe you lost the challenge tonight, and I do believe the prize was a kiss from the best-looking girl in Dundee."

Lisa smiled to herself as she reached for the door handle of the Fiesta. "You're right, Mr. Paxton. I had better go and look for this girl for you."

Andy gently grabbed her arm as she was about to get out and pulled her back in. Lisa turned to speak, but Andy kissed her before she could. He felt Lisa relax and fall back onto the seat, but she did not pull away from his kiss, and both parties stayed entwined for some minutes before Lisa eventually broke off the embrace.

"I think I have fulfilled my part of the deal, and I don't want the neighbours taking about me, so that will have to do for the moment, Andy."

Andy was smiling at Lisa. He had not broken eye contact with her and was still holding her hand. "I like 'for the moment.' That kind of implies there may be more to come?"

Lisa blushed but did not draw away from Andy's hand. "You do know it's past midnight. Are you going to drive to Muckhart tonight?" Lisa stared into Andy's eyes waiting for his response.

"Why? Are you offering me the couch again?"

Lisa let go of Andy's hand and stepped out onto the pavement, looking back into the car where Andy still sat. "I might be able to find a corner of my bed for you as long as you make me a coffee when we get in."

Lisa walked away towards her front door without looking back. Andy locked his car and followed. Coffee was the last thing on his mind, and he was pretty sure it wasn't high on Lisa's list of priorities either.

Andy stepped through Lisa's open front door to find her waiting for him in the hall. She draped her arms around his neck, giving him a gentle kiss on the lips before pulling back.

"You put the kettle on, and I will tidy the bedroom. Agreed?"

Lisa didn't wait for Andy's reply and headed down the hall to her bedroom. Andy filled the kettle, switched it on, and hunted about until he found two mugs in the cupboard above the sink. Andy made his way to the bedroom to ask what Lisa took in her coffee to find her trying to remove her necklace. Andy came to her rescue, removing the necklace just as Lisa spun round into his arms, pushing him back on to the bed. They were both busy undressing one another when the kettle finished boiling in the kitchen. Coffee was off the menu as they both now had other things on their minds. Lisa was better at the undressing bit and was some way to removing Andy's shirt when she gave a little gasp as the last button came undone. She paused for a second before pulling Andy's shirt off his shoulders, then standing back, leaving Andy with no option but to stop his side of the undressing. Lisa was staring at Andy's torso as if she had seen a ghost. Andy slid his arms out of the sleeves, removing the shirt completely.

"Wow, I mean, wow. Are you sure you just do law? I mean that is impressive. You're not a male stripper part time? Please stand up so I can get a better look at you." It was Andy's turn to feel slightly embarrassed as Lisa ran her hands over his chest, stomach, and shoulders. "Since when did lawyers have a six pack and a chest and shoulders that make Superman look like a wimp?"

Andy pulled Lisa gently against his chest as he recommenced removing Lisa's clothing. "I find it helps when you are the Royal Air Force light heavyweight boxing champion, as well as their lawyer."

Andy removed Lisa's dress and was about to embark on a voyage of discovery with her black lace bra when her matching clutch bag began vibrating on the bed behind them. Lisa looked at the vibrating bag then back into Andy's eyes.

She picked the bag up and tossed it farther up the bed before lying back on the bed and looking up at Andy. Andy gently ran the back of his hand from Lisa's belly button upwards over her taut milky-white belly to the edge of her lacy bra. Andy hesitated as he struggled to control his emotions. He reached past Lisa and retrieved the still-vibrating clutch.

"I know and you know, if you don't answer the bloody thing, it will play on your mind, and I really would like your full attention. Call me selfish, but I kind of think it helps in these situations."

Andy kissed Lisa on the cheek, handed her the bag, and removed his torso to the kitchen to reset the kettle.

Although somewhat frustrated, Andy was not too worried by the latest setback to his love life. He now knew Lisa was attracted to him, and for the moment, that was the important thing. Sex would have been nice tonight, but it wasn't a deal breaker in his book. Andy had just finished making the coffee when Lisa appeared in the kitchen doorway dressed in jeans and a knitted sweater. Andy was somewhat taken aback to find his date fully clothed. Lisa was chalk white and looking every place other than at Andy.

"Sorry, Andy, but I am needed urgently at the home. Please don't go. I will be back as soon as I can."

Before Andy could even offer her a lift, she was gone, Andy listened to her footsteps as she took the stairs two at a time. Lisa was in a big hurry. Andy found it hard to believe ten minutes ago he was on the verge of making love to Lisa, and in the blink of an eye, she was gone. He was not sure what to make of the situation. He watched from the window as Lisa sprinted down the street in the direction of the nursing home.

CHAPTER 5
DISASTER

Andy was fast asleep in Lisa's bed when he heard the front door close in the hall. Sunlight was streaming through the chinks in the curtains as Andy sat up, getting his bearings.

Lisa came into the room silently and sat down at the end of the bed without saying anything. She began to remove her shoes, her back to Andy.

Andy Paxton sensed all was not well but decided it would be better if he let Lisa explain in her own time. A deathly silence fell on the room.

Lisa was still looking at the floor when she at last broke the silence. "Jan died in his sleep last night, Andy."

Andy wanted to scream but contained himself for Lisa's sake. He had witnessed firsthand how volatile Lisa was when one of her patients passed away. He had also seen how close Jan Powlak and Lisa were.

"That's terrible news, Lisa. Are you OK? I know how close you were to him."

Lisa shrugged her shoulders. "As well as can be expected in the circumstances. The only consolation is that Jan passed peacefully in his sleep, poor old boy. I'm sorry, Andy. I should have let you finish your interview. I have well and truly screwed up your case."

Lisa started to get up, but Andy reached for her hand, pulling her back onto the bed and into his arms. Although Lisa was holding it together, tears streamed down her face, making their way onto Andy's bare chest.

"I'm sorry, Andy. Can you just hold me for a bit?"

Lisa eventually fell asleep in Andy's arms. Andy did not want to disturb her, so he sat cradling her while he tried to think what he was going to do now. Really, there was not much to think about. His case had as good as died with Jan. No hard evidence, no witnesses. It was nothing more than a myth. Andy knew if he tried to take it any further, he would be the laughingstock of the RAF. The only problem was the old man had convinced him. Andy knew in his mind that Jan was telling the truth. Two things were stopping Andy Paxton from dropping this adventure like a hot potato. One, if this story were true, it was his duty as an RAF officer to investigate it. Second, he had given Jan his word that he would investigate the situation.

Andy needed proof. He needed to look through Jan's personal belongings. Maybe, just maybe, Jan had not shown him all the evidence. Andy knew someone not a million miles away who could let him into Jan's room. Andy looked down on the pale girl curled up in his arms. She was indeed lovely, even more so when she slept. Her mouth formed a kind of natural smile. She was so angelic—did

Andy just dream that last night she was trying to tear his clothes off?

A few hours later, Lisa woke up when she heard the front door to her flat close. A quick search of the bed proved fruitless. Andy was gone. Lisa could scarcely believe the time—the alarm clock next to the bed said 5:00 p.m. Lisa's head was thumping as she made her way to the hall to investigate the closing door. She found Andy in the living room removing his jacket.

"Hello, sleepyhead. Feeling better?"

Lisa's eyes travelled to the coffee table, which had two large pizza boxes on it. Andy followed her gaze.

"I hope you don't mind, Lisa, but I thought you had better eat something. I wasn't sure what to get, so I went for the safe option and ordered the same pizza as you had the other night."

Lisa sat down on the couch still half asleep. Andy joined her, handing her a pizza.

Lisa had somehow read Andy Paxton's mind. "Listen, Andy. I was thinking on the way back from the home, if you want a look through Jan's belongings, we better do it today before we start clearing out his room. After that, his stuff will be put into storage until it is decided what happens to his things."

Thirty minutes later, after picking her way through the pizza, Lisa declared it was time to go, and twenty minutes later, Lisa let Andy into Jan's room, telling him she was heading for reception to let them know Andy was here to pick some RAF documents.

After a hasty search of the room, Andy found what he was looking for in Jan's bedside cabinet. Two old biscuit tins and one folder were the sum total of Jan's life. It shocked Andy that a man who had done so much and seen so much could be reduced to two tins and a folder to house the contents of his life on earth.

Andy started with the folder, which mostly contained receipts for bits and pieces Jan had bought while in the home. Other than this, there were only three things that caught Andy's eye. First and probably high on Jan's list of things to keep was his birthday card from the queen. Next was a letter from the managing director of Powlak Air, inviting Jan across for a visit. But it was the third letter that stopped Andy in his tracks. It was not a long-winded letter, but its contents made Andy read it three times before he allowed himself to believe what he was reading. Andy read the letter aloud to himself one more time.

> Dear Jan,
>
> I suspect this will come as a great shock to you. Please forgive me for not seeking you out before now, but recently, during the course of business, an associate of mine had dealings with an American company called Powlak Air.
>
> For many years, I have not came across that name, and I think destiny had a lot to do with it. I had the company looked into and found that it was you who had founded the company after the war. In turn, that allowed me to trace you to Scotland and the home you now stay in. I hope and pray you have found peace and beauty in my home country. Myself, I have lived a full life, far removed from the terrible days of the war. I just wanted you to know

that *Tygrysek* thinks of you every day. I surely would have lost my life in those dark days were it not for your engineering skills.

Rest easy, my old friend, for one day soon, we will meet again. It may not be in this world, but we will meet again.

Yours always, your friend,
Jean x

Coming out of his shock, Andy realised he had already spent far too long in the old man's room. He needed to move fast. He could hear approaching voices and footsteps. Andy grabbed the two biscuit tins and emptied the contents into his briefcase before returning them to their original resting places just as the door opened and Lisa appeared, followed by two elderly gentlemen in suits. As the men entered, Andy made a show of picking up Jean's letter from the file and popping it into his attaché case before snapping it shut.

"Hello there. No need to send for help, nurse. I have just found the letter that I dropped in for Jan. It's so sad he won't need it anymore. Well, I won't bother you anymore. Thanks for all the help, folks."

Both men had faces of thunder. One reached down, grabbing the folder while the other frowned at Andy's presence.

"Nurse Preston, this is highly irregular. You know Mr. Powlak's room was ordered to be sealed until we arrived, but yet we find a stranger sifting through his belongings!"

Lisa Preston hustled Andy towards the door, speaking to the men as she went. "Flight Lieutenant Paxton was only picking up RAF paper work that I myself witnessed him dropping off with Jan. I can see no harm in letting him pick up his own documents. I will be back to help in a moment, once I have seen the officer out. I take it that's OK with you, gentlemen."

Lisa did not wait for a reply, almost frog-marching Andy out of the room.

Back at reception, Andy could tell all was not well in Lisa's world. "Listen, Andy, leave your mobile number with reception. I have no idea how long I will be. There is trouble brewing here, and I need to stay put for the moment. I will give you a call later." Lisa forced a smile onto her pale face, gave Andy's hand a squeeze, and hurried back towards Jan's room.

Andy passed his number to reception, then headed back out to his Fiesta. In the car, he sat for a second, his head still spinning from his latest revelation. Then he noticed his phone blinking away silently. Andy picked it up and examined the call log. He had missed two calls that morning, one from Peter, one of his colleagues at Northolt, and a second from his mate Cammy.

Andy waited patiently while the call centre put his call through to Peter in the office. When Peter answered, he sounded relieved that Andy had called back. "Thank god you called. The boss is going bonkers, mate. You need to get back here fast. The bloody air marshal has been here looking for you. He wanted to wish you good luck for the big fight at the weekend. Tell me you have been training for it while you have been up there, tossing cabers and fighting grizzly bears with your bare hands. When can I tell the old man you will be back?"

Andy took the usual banter well. He was used to the southern sense of humour after working with them for a year. "Pete, you are a bit confused, pal. Timber and fighting grizzlies? That's our Canadian cousins you're thinking of. Scots don't do that anymore. The bears were too scared of us and emigrated to Canada, where it is safer for them. I will be back tomorrow around teatime. See you then, Pete."

Andy decided this was not the time or the place to call Cammy. He needed to get home, pack, and say his goodbyes to his parents, Andy looked longingly at the entrance to the home, willing Lisa to appear. He did not want to go back in and disturb her, but he did not want to leave this way either. Eventually his heart gave way to his head, and he pointed the Fiesta south towards his family home.

Andy arrived home to find the house deserted. His mother and father had left for a dinner date later that evening. All that remained was a note on the dining room table telling Andy that there was a steak pie in the fridge for him if he condescended to return home for a change.

Andy smiled at the note. His mother had a knack for being sarcastic even in a short note. After raiding the fridge and devouring a pint of milk and some leftover chicken, Andy headed for his bedroom, calling Cammy on the way.

The phone rang for some time before his old pal picked it up. "Oh, so finally you decided to call me back, Paxton. OK, I have found out a bit about your flygirl. Take notes if you want to. Jean Maria Bruce was born in the parish of Kirkliston on March 11, 1920. She was the second daughter of a wealthy shipping merchant. Jean emigrated to Canada in 1935 to stay with relatives. In 1939, she returned to England via America. This was around the time of her parents' deaths in Europe. She was recorded living with her uncle in London and both worked for the Hawker aircraft company. They were both reported missing presumed dead during an air raid on August 12, 1940."

Andy listened while Cammy confirmed what old Jan had already told him. "Listen, mate, that's brilliant, but I need another favour from you. I know I already owe you big, but can you find out everything you can about a Second World War Polish fighter pilot called Artur Krol? Not just the well-known stuff. Anything that you could find would be good."

Andy waited for the barrage of abuse that was bound to come from his old friend. "What the hell are you up to, Paxton? Have they moved you to the RAF archives section or something?"

Andy smiled to himself. He knew Callum McPherson too well. "Cammy, just get me the info, and I promise—the next time I am back in Scotland, the food is on me."

Andy mind was spinning after Cammy's phone call. Everything the old man had told him about the girl had checked out. Andy decided to kill two birds with one stone—he needed to clear his mind, and he badly needed to get ready for the weekend. He was still turning things over in his head as he pulled the Fiesta off the road. Andy pulled a fifteen-kilogram-weight vest on over his T-shirt, locked the car, and started jogging up the gentle incline that led to Scotland's only functioning race circuit. Knockhill Racing Circuit was aptly named as it nestled at the bottom of a hillside some ten miles from Andy's home. Andy picked up the pace where the ground levelled off as it passed the main gate of the circuit. He then joined a dirt track that wound its way up the hillside finally stopping by the radio masts at the summit of the hill.

Halfway up the climb, Andy stopped jogging to drop down and execute twenty press-ups before continuing up the hill for another fifty metres before dropping and repeating the press-ups. This torture continued as Andy completed three climbs to and from the circuit to the masts before he finally collapsed at the summit, pulling a bottle of water from his weighted vest. He wiped the stinging sweat from his eyes as he was treated to the sun setting behind the miniature Wallace monument some miles away to the west. Behind him, the Knockhill course resembled a Scalextric track, while the view in front of him was the Fife coastline with the Forth bridges to his left and Edinburgh in the misty distance.

Andy's head had cleared as he concentrated on his body. He was going to need every bit of stamina if he were to take on the army opponent he had been drawn against this weekend. He was well aware how much it meant to his RAF colleagues as it had been many years since the RAF had won the inter-services championship. Andy had breezed through the RAF selection unbeaten, and with a few serious KOs to his name, he was the new hope of the RAF. It only proved how mind-blowingly serious the meeting with Jan Powlak had been to make him forget about his boxing commitments. Again, his mind was drawn to Jan Powlak and Jean Bruce. How was it possible that they had managed to pull the wool over the eyes of their RAF superiors? One thing was for sure. Jan would never be able to tell him. If only he knew the whereabouts of Jean Bruce. That in turn raised another question. Where the hell did she vanish to in the middle of the war...if she had stayed alive?

Andy shivered as a cold blast of wind cooled his sweat-covered body. It was time to return home. He needed to call Lisa and get his packing done for tomorrow. On arrival at his car, he was disappointed to find he had missed a call from Lisa. He decided to wait until he was home before calling her back so he could spend a decent amount of time talking to his favourite nurse.

Back at his parents' home, he was dismayed when Lisa's phone rang out without being answered. On the third attempt, he left a message for her to call him when it was convenient. Andy spent the time waiting for Lisa to phone packing for his trip down south the next day.

A bit later, Andy collapsed on his bed. His packing was finished. He had showered, and still there was no sign of his parents or a return call from Lisa. Andy tried Lisa one more time, but the call went straight to answer phone. Andy checked his bedside clock. He should be tucked up in bed, but he was still hoping Lisa would call him. He decided he would spend the time looking through Jan's things while he waited for Lisa to call.

Many of the pictures Jan had taken were of Merlin engines in various states of repair or Spitfires and Hurricanes with heavy battle damage recorded for posterity. There was no mistaking from the pictures that Jan was an engineer. He seemed to be more interested in the machinery than the brave people who flew them against a numerically superior enemy. Andy stopped at one picture that seemed unusual in that it did not feature a part of a fighter. It was a picture of the corner of a workshop with a storeroom door. Pinned above the door was a handwritten Polish sign. Andy had seen this word before, but it took him a few seconds to realise where. He checked the letter he had found in Jan's possessions. *Tygrysek* was mentioned in the letter. Andy Googled the word to find out what it meant and came up with "baby tiger." Suddenly Jan's words came back to him about putting Jean Bruce up in her own room in the workshop. This picture was of Jean's room. She was Baby Tiger. It made perfect sense. Any British officers conducting an inspection would probably think Tygrysek was Polish for storeroom.

A few pictures later, Andy was inspecting a picture of a terribly damaged Hurricane. Most of its tail had been shot away, and its canvas fuselage was peppered with bullet holes. Andy noted from the swastikas painted by the cockpit that the lucky pilot had chalked up nine kills. Then his eyes moved to the engine cover. Andy almost dropped the picture with excitement. Painted on the engine cover next to the Polish Air Force insignia was a leaping tiger cub.

Things were starting to fall into place. This was a picture of the Hurricane flown by Jean Bruce, also known as Baby Tiger. She had been the lucky pilot who had brought the badly damaged plane home from what Andy could only imagine must have been a living hell. Andy carefully replaced all Jan's precious photos in the shoebox before once again reading the letter he had received. Without noticing, he fell asleep

The sun streamed through the window of Andy's room the next morning, waking him from his slumber, Andy checked his bedside clock, cursing when he discovered he had overslept. He would need to get a move on if he was to be back in the office for teatime.

Andy checked his phone, but there had been no call from Lisa. As he was loading the car, his mother returned from an early shopping trip to find her son packed and ready to leave. Andy said his good-byes to his mother and promised to call his father, who had left earlier for a morning golf date with his pals.

Andy was making good time and had just passed Manchester on the M6 when Lisa called him back. He quickly checked around him for any sign of police cars before using one hand to answer Lisa's call. He did not want to miss her again and was prepared to risk the wrath of the law to speak to her.

"Oh, so you haven't left the country after all, Mr. Paxton? I thought you had done a runner and didn't want to speak to me anymore."

Andy winced. He was going to have to be very diplomatic with his answer if he did not want an unhappy nurse to deal with.

"Well, where do I start? Probably with a grovelling apology would be best. You're not wrong. I kind of have left the country, and you could say it was a runner, but please hear me out before you decide on my fate. With all that's been going on over the past few days—changing history, meeting a gorgeous, sexy nurse, that kind of thing—I forgot that this weekend I will be representing the Royal Air Force in the inter-services boxing championships. I was told to get my arse back down here by the powers that be. I did try to call and tell you, but it's been ships passing in the night, I think. Sorry, Lisa. I really mean that. Sorry."

For a few agonizing seconds, the line was silent. Andy's heart began to sink. Until then, he had not realised how much he would miss her if she said enough was enough now.

"Oh well, that's a pity. I could have done with a bit of company. Things are not going well up here. Not to worry, you can give me a call later. That's if you want to, of course."

Andy's smile returned. She had given him a second chance, one he would not muck up this time. "If I want to? You just try stopping me, girl. Lisa, I am so sorry. If there was any way of getting out of this, I would. I am on the motorway, but I will call you this evening. I promise."

Again silence. "OK, Andy. Grovelling apology accepted. Speak to you later. Bye, Rocky."

After he ran the traffic gauntlet of Birmingham, the rest of Andy's trip proved uneventful. On arrival at Northolt, Andy went straight to the office to find that everyone other than Pete had left for the evening.

Pete took the opportunity to hand the office over to Andy and head out for a hot date with a local girl, leaving Andy to answer calls for the last hour of duty. Andy used the time to draught a report to his CO explaining the events that had unfolded in Scotland. He placed this in his top drawer, ready for the inevitable meeting with his boss in the morning. This done, Andy closed the office, putting the calls on night service and heading to his digs for a quick bite to eat before heading to the gym. Andy reckoned he could get a couple of hours in before he would head back home so he could call Lisa.

Andy walked into the gym to be greeted with a roar from the far end of the gym. It was the last person Andy wanted to bump into tonight—Ben Reynolds, his trainer and the RAF's hardest PT instructor.

"Hi, Ben. How good it is to see your happy smiling face again."

Reynolds got right up to Andy's face, getting right into his personal space before replying. "Where the fuck have you been hiding, pretty boy? I hope for your sake you have been training because if you haven't, it's going to be a pretty short visit to the ring. They have a big Welsh squaddie lined up against you, and you can bet your fucking life on it—he will be built like a brick shithouse. You had better be ready for the session from hell tonight because I won't let you or any other pen-pushing prick drag the reputation of my boxing team through the gutter. Do we understand each other, Paxton, sir?"

As an officer, Andy outranked Ben Reynolds, but when you entered the gym, Ben Reynolds was the ringmaster. Away from the training environment, speaking to an officer like that would have fatal consequences for your RAF career.

Reynolds was a man of his word, starting with a barrage of one-arm press-ups, star jumps, skipping, and four minutes at a time of the plank, then punch-bag training. Next, Reynolds placed Andy in the ring.

"Sarge, I need to go in ten minutes. I have someplace I need to be tonight. Sorry."

Reynolds regarded Andy's sweat-covered face with cold eyes. "Put the fucking gloves on, pretty boy. The only way you are getting out of here in ten minutes is if I knock you out, or you knock me out because that is the only way you get past me before midnight. Do we understand each other?"

Andy had promised Lisa he would call. He did not want to risk missing her again. Reluctantly, Andy let one of the other trainers fit his headgear and gumshield. He had watched Reynolds spar before. The best part of his technique was his feet. He was light and fast, totally opposite Andy who used his upper-body power to great effect.

During the first two rounds, both men tested each other for weaknesses before Ben Reynolds's speed allowed him to land the first telling punch, high on the side of Andy's head. For a second, Andy thought he was going down, and if it was not for the dulling effect of the head guard, he might have ended up on the canvas, but as his senses came back, so did a determination to show Ben Reynolds he was more than just a pen-pusher. Reynolds was getting more daring as the bout continued. In the fourth round, he darted in, but Andy had watched a pattern form and was waiting. Andy was a natural left-hander, and his real power was in his left. At first, he countered the charge with his right, opening a gap for his mighty southpaw.

The punch was inch-perfect, catching Reynolds on the side of the jaw. Ben Reynolds was unconscious before he made contact with first the ropes and then the canvas. Andy removed the gloves and headgear to a stunned silence from those present as two fellow trainers tried to bring Ben back round.

Andy arrived back at his digs around eight thirty and made a beeline for the phone. Lisa must have been waiting on his call as she picked up her phone on the first ring.

"Hello, is that the RAF version of Henry Cooper?"

Andy wiped the sweat from his eyes before replying to Lisa. "I wouldn't go there at the moment. I got a wee bit carried away tonight and knocked out my trainer when we were sparring. Anyway, enough of my problems. How are you doing? Did you manage to get rid of those two goons at the home?"

There was a marked silence from Lisa's end of the phone. "Hmm, I have a bad feeling about them, Andy. They were asking some really weird questions. I don't know what they were trying to do. They kept asking questions about me.

They were there to wrap up Jan's affairs, for god's sake, not quiz me. Although they were polite enough, they seemed very hostile to me."

Andy frowned as he listened to Lisa. He could make no sense from a law point of view why Jan's lawyers would be remotely interested in Lisa's affairs.

"Oh, I almost forgot, Andy. It's Jan's funeral next week, and I was wondering if there was any chance of you making it to the funeral? It's just that it's so sad when there is no one there to see the old ones off. And I could really do with the company, truth be told."

Andy tried to think if he had anything planned for the week in question. "I can't think of anything on my diary. I will speak to my boss and ask for the time off. I can't see it being a problem. What time is the funeral?"

There was a pause as Lisa checked her diary. "We are having a service at the home Wednesday at 11:00 a.m. and then the burial around 11:45 a.m. Have you found out any more about Jan's mysterious girl pilot?"

Andy once again had to wipe the sweat from his tired eyes before replying to Lisa. "Only to confirm most of what Jan told us about Jean Bruce. Lisa, I am going to have to love you and leave you. I am shattered and soaking in sweat. I need to hit the shower then bed. I will see you on Wednesday. You call me if those asshole lawyers give you any more grief, and I will have words with them."

Once Andy had rung off, he sat for a second thinking over what Lisa had just told him. He was worried for her. He had witnessed at firsthand how Lisa took everything to heart, and this latest saga with Jan's lawyers seemed to be no exception. Lisa seemed friendly enough, but although Andy had only known the girl for a week or so, even over the phone he could tell she was not her normal self.

Ten thirty the next morning arrived far too fast for Andy Paxton's liking. He was summoned to the office of Squadron Leader Hardy, who was the officer in charge of overseeing the smooth running of the Northolt division of the RAF legal machine, the overall command of which fell to Air Marshal Harrington-Smith.

The two exchanged the usual pleasantries before Hardy got to the point of the meeting. "Andy, you can submit your written report later, but I would like you to take me through your findings of the meeting with this fellow Powlak, just in case Air Marshal Harrington-Smith asks me about your whereabouts again. Come on then, lad. Spill the beans."

Andy took a deep breath before beginning. He was still not sure how he was going to play this. He was not sure what his commanding officer's reaction would be since he was in uncharted territory. "Sir, I had a number of meetings with Jan Powlak. Initially, I wanted to assess his mental state. I needed to know if what he was going to tell me was worth hearing. After assurances by the staff that Jan Powlak was mentally fit to give testimony, I questioned the old man and came to the conclusion that there was a point of interest concerning the Royal Air Force. I feel that if this inquiry were to continue in any shape or form, it would be to find evidence of Jan's accusations, as there is currently little to go on bar a few photographs and testimony from a now-dead witness."

Hardy butted in impatiently before Andy could go any further. "Yes, yes, Mr. Paxton, but what was his reason for calling? Get to the point, man. You are beating about the bush. Spit it out."

Andy could hear Jan's words ringing in his ears. "And so it begins." Andy moved uncomfortably in his chair. It was show time.

"Jan Powlak stated that one of the Polish fighter aces during the Battle of Britain was in fact a woman. When one of the Polish pilots deserted, she took his identity and fought in his place. Jan wanted the record put straight and a woman called Jean Bruce recognized for her part in the war."

It did not take long for Andy to find out what Hardy thought of his revelation.

"Paxton, are you telling me it has taken you over a week to investigate what would best be described as poppycock? The delusional ramblings of a dying man? For god's sake, you don't actually believe any of this nonsense, do you?"

Andy knew he was treading on dangerous ground. This was his opportunity to bail out and agree with Squadron Leader Hardy, but he had promised the old man he would do his best, and pulling the plug now wasn't even close to his best, so Andy dug his heels in. "Sir, I know it seems farfetched. I was of the same opinion as yourself, but Jan convinced me that there is more to this than an old wives' tale. I looked into the matter, and there was a woman by that name who matched everything Jan said about her." Andy placed the shoebox with Jan's pictures on the table. He then proceeded to place a series of pictures in front of his commanding officer. "Sir, in the first picture, you can clearly see one of the returning pilots is a girl. Here she is again with Jan Powlak. This picture shows her makeshift accommodation in the workshop. The word above the door says 'Baby Tiger' in Polish. I believe this was what the Poles called her. In this picture you can see what is supposedly the Hurricane of Artur Krol, but if you look at the engine, it has a baby tiger painted on the cover. I know this is not enough proof, but I feel that it at least warrants further investigation."

Squadron Leader Hardy's face resembled a ripe tomato. He wanted to dismiss Andy Paxton's theories, but Paxton's pictures backed up his ridiculous story. He decided the decision was above his pay grade and dismissed Andy before calling Air Marshal Harrington-Smith for advice.

Andy did not return to his desk but instead hovered outside the door of the squadron leader's office, trying to pick up the conversation over the phone. The conversation was short and sweet, and Andy was summoned back into the office within minutes.

"Air Marshal Harrington-Smith is concerned that your head is not where it should be two days before your big fight. He has ordered me to tell you to drop the Powlak case forthwith and concentrate on your training. You have been relieved of duty until next week to allow you to train, so I would get yourself along to the gym right away."

Andy stood up to leave, holding his shoebox. "Sir, would it be possible to request leave next week to attend Jan Powlak's funeral in Scotland?"

The reddish tinge was returning to Hardy's face as he struggled once more to control his temper. "Paxton, pin your ears back, lad. If you think you can get away with anything you want because you are the air marshal's golden boy of boxing, think again. You have been told to drop the

Powlak thing. That includes the funeral. You are lucky not to be on a charge for fannying about in Scotland when you should have been back here working. Leave the Powlak evidence you collected. It will be reassigned. Now get out of my sight until Monday. Have I made myself crystal clear?"

Ten minutes later, Andy was just wrapping up a few loose ends with Pete before he left when he spotted Hardy leaving the office carrying Andy's shoebox. Andy watched unobserved from the office window as Squadron Leader Hardy headed across the lane to one of a number of huts containing filing systems. Andy watched with interest as Hardy bypassed the records hut and then entered the waste-storage facility. Andy said his good-byes to Pete and left from the opposite side of the building, taking the long way round and arriving at the waste storage ten minutes after Hardy left. It didn't take Andy long to find his shoebox. It had been placed in one of the bags marked for shredding and covered with some old papers. Andy removed the majority of pictures, leaving a few in case anyone checked, and then retraced his original route, keeping well away from his offices. If Andy hadn't been sure earlier how his superiors would react, he had no doubts now. If he wanted to keep his word to Jan, he would have to do it on his own.

CHAPTER 6
THE BIG FIGHT

Andy spent the next two days training. His head was not in a good place, and he took his frustration out on the punch bag. After his little mishap with the trainer, he had found it hard to find anyone willing to step into the ring to spar with him, so he concentrated solely on physical fitness.

On arrival at RAF Cranwell, Andy discovered that his was to be the final match of the event and that both Squadron Leader Hardy and Air Marshal Harrington-Smith had ringside seats for the event.

Andy was busy having his hands and wrists strapped up in preparation for his bout when a big blond-headed giant of a man appeared by his side. Both men looked each other up and down before the giant spoke to Andy. "You, Paxton? The boy from Scotland then?"

The giant spoke with a Welsh accent, and by the shape of his nose, he was a well-seasoned fighter, having taken more than his fair share of punches to the face.

"Yes. I take it you are Lloyd, my army opponent?"

Lloyd had a dead look in his eyes, and Andy Paxton found it difficult to suss the guy out. He was difficult to read. "You never been beaten, jock. I'm goin' to change that tonight. Mark my words, boy. You are goin' down tonight."

Before Andy could reply, the Welsh giant turned and walked away. Andy Paxton had boxed at his local club in Stirling and had been involved in a few matches in Glasgow before joining the RAF, but this championship was the biggest test in terms of quality opponents he had ever faced. Andy entered the ring with his stomach churning. All his RAF colleagues expected him to win, but Andy was not so sure. His plan was to try and survive the first round and then take it from there.

The ref, a tiny tattooed Yorkshire man, spoke to them as once more Andy Paxton looked into the eyes of his big Welsh opponent—still no sign of any emotion. It was like looking into the eyes of a zombie.

Round one started, and right away, Blondie was on the attack. Andy Paxton blocked everything Blondie threw at him, but it was taking all his time and quite a bit of energy to soak up the punches. Towards the end of the round, Blondie got just a bit too confident, and Andy let his left go, catching Blondie on the side of the head. Luckily for him, it was just before the bell, and he managed just to deflect the blow high, taking a lot of the power out of the punch, but even so, Blondie sat down for the minute's intermission with his head ringing and a clear warning that to let this Scotsman have a clear shot with his left hand would be a fatal mistake.

In round two, the Welshman started a little more cautiously, but as the round progressed, he started to fling everything into it again. Andy had survived the first round, and his nerves had steadied as he found his target. He knew the blond giant would push again, and when he did, Andy would be ready. Sure enough, the Welshman lunged forwards, but this time, Andy anticipated his move beautifully. He used the whole twisting momentum of his torso to add power to his left glove, and it contacted perfectly with the side of Blondie's head. Andy felt the shock of the contact travel up his arm and into his shoulder, and he knew no man could remain standing after a blow like that. Andy was proved correct as the towering Welshman landed on his knees, grabbing for the rope to stop himself falling further to the canvas. Blondie staggered to his feet while the ref continued the count.

For the first time, Andy was aware of the crowd going berserk around him. Blondie had been the favourite to take the title, and he had been stopped firmly in his tracks. The crowd sensed a major upset was on the cards, and suddenly the arena had come alive. The Welshman managed to beat the count—just—but was still in a bad way. Andy knew he had to get in there and finish him before he recovered. One good punch now, and it would be all over. Blondie knew that as well and backed away, his chewing gum legs struggling to keep him upright. Andy could not believe the giant Welshman was still conscious. He had never hit anyone so hard and have him stay standing. Andy Paxton moved in for the kill, hitting Blondie hard in the stomach with his left and his right and knocking him sideways as the bell went for the end of the second round.

Blondie collapsed onto his stool in the corner, his seconds working feverishly to repair the damage Andy Paxton had inflicted on him. Andy sat calculating what the score was. He reckoned the Welshman had taken the first round, but he knew the second was his by some margin. If he knocked him down or held his own in the final round, he reckoned he had him fair and square.

The third round got underway, and right away, Andy was astonished by how much the big Welshman had recovered from his pounding. It was as if he had never hit the canvas. Andy conceded a heavy blow to the stomach and knew he must come back at his opponent or risk losing the match. Both men traded blow for blow. The big blond Welshman was very scared of Andy Paxton's left and defended heavily. Andy had stepped up his attack and was landing some good body shots but couldn't find a way through with his left. His arms were like lead. He just wanted the bell to go and this hell to be over, and then Blondie caught him napping and hit him high on the forehead, knocking Andy backwards. He followed up with a lightening-fast right that caught Andy under the chin. The lights went out for Andy Paxton. He was just coming round as he heard the ref count him out.

The next day, Andy did not make it to the office. His right eye was almost closed, and he felt he had the mother of all hangovers. Andy had just returned to his bed after a trip to the kitchen to take some anti-inflammatory pills when his house phone started to ring. Andy listened to Pete explain that Squadron Leader Hardy had requested his presence. Andy threw his uniform on and headed to the office to find Hardy installed in his office, awaiting his arrival. Andy knocked and entered, wondering what today's meeting would bring.

"Ah, there you are, Paxton. Bad luck last night. You were unlucky. We thought at one point you had him. Still, never mind. I am sure your time will come. The reason I have called you here is to let you know that from next Monday you will be working out of our office in RAF Akrotiri in Cyprus. Time for you to get a bit of sun, quite a lot of sun actually. Akrotiri have agreed to a three-year posting, so you better get your kit together, Paxton. You will be leaving on a Hercules from Brize Norton tomorrow."

Andy was not in the best of moods to start with, but this had just put the icing on the cake. It was out before Andy could stop himself. "All very convenient, Squadron Leader. Pack me off where I can't get in your hair. Don't think I don't know what your game is. Just remember—perverting the course of justice also applies to RAF officers, and you are going to get your fingers burned over this Powlak affair. Be very careful."

Andy watched as Hardy went purple with rage before exploding. He got up, leaning over his desk. "How dare you speak to your commanding officer like that? One more word from you, just one out of place, and you will be on a charge. Do you hear me, Flight Lieutenant Paxton?"

In Andy Paxton's eyes, he had already gone too far to turn back, so he decided it was time to put his cards on the table, knowing it would mean the end of his RAF career.

"No, Squadron Leader, that will not happen for the simple reason that I know the truth. There never was going to be any further investigation of Jan Powlak's testimony because a few small-minded individuals with far more power than brains had already decided that it was not possible that a woman could fight for her country, and you sure as hell were not going to lift a finger to find out. That is why the air marshal told you to dispose of the photographic proof

I gave you. Unfortunately for you, I retrieved it from the shredding bag, and along with the taped conversation we had, it will stay in my possession until needed. So let's cut to the chase here. You will see to it that I am released from my RAF contract immediately, and in return, I will promise not to drag yourself and the air marshal through the courts for dereliction of duty and perverting the course of justice. Do you hear me, Squadron Leader Hardy? I am going to get packed up. When I return in two hours, have the paper work ready. Oh, one more thing, if you lean aggressively over the desk at me one more time, I will knock your teeth so far back your throat that you will need a toilet brush at the other end to clean them."

Andy marched from the office before the urge to smash Hardy in the face became overwhelming. The rage had been building in Andy since he found the discarded photographs. Losing his match had not helped, but to be punted off to a foreign country just for doing his duty was the final straw. Pete had been trying for months to get posted to Cyprus with no luck. There was no way this was anything other than an attempt at a cover-up.

Andy didn't so much pack as throw all his gear into his suitcase and holdall. Getting home was another problem, but a call to the nearest hire-car company proved fruitful. His one-way hire would be dropped off in one hour at the main gate, just in time for him to say good-bye to his pal Hardy.

Andy made one more call to the local TV station. "Hello, I am Squadron Leader Hardy from the legal department of the Royal Air Force. I am calling to let you know that in forty-five minutes at the main entrance to RAF Northolt there will be a very important announcement and press conference. I am sorry it is such short notice, but we have only just been given the nod by Number Ten to release the statement. No, sorry, I can't divulge anything to you at this point. The only thing I would say is miss it at your peril, chaps."

Andy hung up the phone and, for the first time that day, broke into a smile.

Thirty minutes later, Andy stood in his office waiting to be summoned to the headmaster's office. Pete was chalk white. Whatever had happened after Andy left was not good.

"Jesus Christ Andy, what have you done, murdered the queen or something? His lordship is going mental in there. Why are you not in uniform, you mad bastard? He will kill you!"

Hardy's office door was thrown open, and Hardy growled at Andy Paxton to get his arse in there. Andy strolled in, leaving his cases with Pete.

"Paxton, the air marshal is beside himself with rage. After all the things he has done for you, you know—"

Andy cut in before Hardy could continue. "Cut the bullshit, Squadron Leader. Where do I sign to get out? That is all I am here for." Andy watched as Hardy's face again turned a deep purple.

"What makes you think that you can dictate terms to us? You are only just in the door and still wet behind the ears. You should show some respect to people who have been doing the job for years."

Just then the phone started to ring. Hardy picked it up while Andy Paxton studied his expression. A look of utter horror appeared on Squadron Leader Hardy's face. He stuttered and stammered down the phone before slamming it down on the desk.

"I take it from the look on your face, Squadron Leader, that the press have arrived. I hope for your sake you have my discharge papers ready because if you don't, it will be your resignation you will be writing and sooner than you think."

Hardy rose from his desk and opened the top drawer of his filing cabinet. Without saying another word, he placed two documents in front of Andy, handing him a pen before explaining them through gritted teeth.

"One is your immediate discharge from the RAF, but it contains a clause saying it is only valid if you sign the second document stating that you cannot discuss or bring to the fore any evidence gathered while working under the auspices of the Royal Air Force and that failure to do so will invoke section 5, subsection 5a of the 1989 Official Secrets Act, resulting in your immediate imprisonment at Her Majesty's pleasure and, it has to be said, my pleasure also."

Andy stared at the paper work in front of him. It was checkmate. He was caught between a rock and a hard place. He had come too far to turn back now, but they had won in the end. They had Andy tied in red tape.

Andy signed the paper work, lifted his copies, and marched out of the office with his cases. He winked at Pete with his good eye and left, heading for the main gate and freedom. By the gate, a frustrated-looking reporter stopped him as he was leaving.

"Excuse me, mate. Do you know anything about the press conference?"

Andy turned and pointed to Hardy, who had watched him leaving. "No, buddy, but that bloke with the purple face is the man you want to speak to."

Andy waited until he cleared the bottleneck of the Birmingham M6 before pulling into the motorway services for a break. Andy's head was spinning. His headache was worse, and he felt sick. His conscience told him he had done the morally right thing, but he had just trashed his career in the Royal Air Force to keep a promise to dead man. He was busy thinking of how much to tell his parents when his mobile started ringing. Andy checked the screen and was glad to see that it was Lisa calling. She had never been far from his thoughts, but for the last day or two he had other things on his mind. He was surprised by how much his gloomy mood lifted as he saw her name appear on the phone screen. "Hi, Lisa. Boy, am I glad to speak to my favourite nurse! I could do with a friendly voice to cheer me up. What's been happening in sunny Dundee since I left?"

For a second, Andy thought he had lost the call, but then he realised he could hear background noise and Lisa breathing.

"Andy, I am in trouble. I need to have a talk with you when you come up for the funeral. Do you think you could meet me at my flat before the funeral? I am sorry to bother you, but I need your advice." Again there was silence on Lisa's end of the line.

"Lisa, I can do better than that if you like. Do you think you will be in tonight? I am on my way back to Scotland as we speak. If you're not working, I can come straight up and see you. How does that sound?"

This time Lisa's reply was much quicker. "That would be great, Andy. I will be in. I don't have much choice, Andy. You see, they have suspended me." Lisa's voice trailed off as she started to sob quietly, trying hard to hold herself together but failing miserably.

Andy was in shock. He had watched at firsthand Lisa caring for her patients. In the short time Andy had known the girl, the one thing he knew for certain was that Lisa's life was her work. He could only imagine what torment she must be going through. He wanted to ask her so many questions, but the one thing he knew Lisa needed right now was not someone hundreds of miles away firing questions at her when she could hardly speak for crying. He needed to be with her.

"Listen, girl, I will be there as soon as I can. Whatever has happened, we will sort it out. Now go and take advantage of the time off, and put your feet up until I get there, OK?"

Again there was a long silence before Lisa eventually replied. "OK, Andy."

Andy abandoned his planned trip to the restaurant for a bite to eat, instead filling the Ford Focus hire car to the brim, grabbing an energy drink and a sandwich, then launching the Focus northwards at the speed of many antelopes.

Andy pulled up outside Lisa's flat and checked his watch just as the BBC announced the start of the nine o'clock news. Andy was totally drained. He had woken up feeling terrible, and by lunchtime, his career in the RAF was over. He had then set off on a marathon drive to Scotland. All he wanted to do was to go to sleep and wake up to find out it was all just a bad dream. The only thing keeping him going was his need to make sure Lisa was OK and then find out what had happened while he was away.

Lisa opened the door on the second knock. She gasped at her first glimpse of Andy's battered and bruised face. "Oh my god, what have they done to you, Andy? You should be in bed, not driving up here to see me. Don't just stand there, man. Get in here until I have a proper look at that poor face of yours."

Within ten minutes, Andy was positioned on the couch, his wounded face treated with various creams and being cooled by a large ice pack around his eye. Lisa fired question after question at him about his face, but Andy brushed off her questions with ones of his own.

"Forget about my ugly mug. I will be just fine. Let's hear about your problems first. Come on. I didn't just drive up here for the scenery. Spit it out, Lisa."

Lisa's mood changed almost instantly. Andy's arrival had taken her mind off her problems and lifted her mood, but now she had to once more return to her torment.

"I have been suspended pending a hearing tomorrow to look into my conduct concerning Jan's stay at the home. His lawyers have put in an official complaint that I coerced their client into changing his will. Andy, I swear to you, it's not true. Those bastards have got it in for me for some reason, and I don't know why."

Andy went over a few legal things in his head before speaking to Lisa. "Lisa, it would be helpful if you could answer a few questions for me. Who suspended you? Did they give you any warning before the meeting, and were there any witnesses present during the meeting?"

Lisa sat down on the couch by Andy's side, turning so she could watch Andy's expression as she answered him. "It was Sir Antony Moorehouse himself who suspended me after coming out of a meeting with Jan's lawyers. It was in the reception area and one of the girls was on the desk, if that counts as a witness."

Lisa watched as Andy shook his head in disbelief. "OK, Matron, don't worry. I will come with you to the meeting tomorrow. In any disciplinary situation, the person in question is allowed to have a witness with him or her. Tomorrow we will get this nonsense sorted out once and for all. Now is there any chance your favourite lawyer can have a cup of coffee to keep him awake?"

Lisa returned from the kitchen a few minutes later with two steaming mugs of coffee and found Andy fast asleep. Lisa gently leaned across Andy, finding the lever to let the back of the couch drop into the bed position. She lowered it slowly so not to wake him. She untied his shoes and placed a blanket over him before gently kissing him on the forehead and putting the light out. She headed for her bed although she knew she would not sleep with the hearing hanging over her head.

Andy came to with a splitting sore head and made his way to the kitchen where the sounds and smells of breakfast had alerted him to the fact that once more, Lisa had woken up before him. In fact, she had been up for some time as she had not been able to sleep and had raided his hire car, removed his clothing, and proceeded to wash and dry most of Andy's clothes. Now, along with making breakfast, she was busy ironing one of Andy's white shirts for the dreaded meeting.

"Good morning, sleepyhead. Did you have a good sleep?"

Andy, still half asleep, rubbed his eyes, forgetting about his swollen eye. He winced, but the pain that shot through his head woke him up instantly. "What the hell happened last night? Did you drug my coffee? I feel terrible. My head is pounding."

Lisa finished ironing his shirt and hung it on the lounge door handle as she replied. "Chance would be a fine thing, squadron leader. You were dead to the world when I arrived with the coffee. It's your boxing catching you up, and don't bother whinging about it to me. If you use your head as a punch bag, what do you expect? It's a mug's game, and I thought you would have had more sense."

Lisa handed him a plate with toast, jam, and butter and a large mug of coffee and pointed him in the direction of the lounge.

"I didn't hear you complaining about my six pack or my boxing when you removed my shirt, Miss Preston."

Lisa sat opposite Andy as he tucked into the toast. "I would have expected a better argument than that from you. After all, you are a lawyer. You can have a six pack without getting your head knocked off."

Andy conceded he was not going to win the argument and contented himself with polishing off his toast and coffee before being hustled into the bathroom to shower and shave for the big meeting in an hour's time. Normally, Andy would have protested at being manhandled, but he had to admit to himself, he quite liked Lisa giving him the bossy-nurse treatment. It made him feel part of Lisa's life, like he was more than just a passing stranger. While he showered, he thought about the meeting and what he needed to tell Lisa. He knew some of it would not go down well with his favourite nurse.

Twenty minutes later, they had left the flat early, giving them time for a leisurely stroll along to the nursing home.

Andy took the opportunity to prime Lisa on the way he wanted things to go and saved the worst until last.

"OK, Lisa, here is how we are going to play it. I will do all the talking. If you are asked a question and I want you to answer, I will give you a nod. Otherwise, just sit and listen. I really don't know the best way to tell you the next part, so I am just going to go for it. When we are finished in here today, I very much doubt that you will ever work here again, no matter what the outcome. I know this place was pretty much your life, so I am sorry to be the one to break it to you."

Lisa stopped to wipe a tear away from the corner of her eye before looking into Andy's eyes. "I know, Andy, and thanks for trying to break it to me gently. I had already made my mind up that I don't want to work for anyone who would take the word of a person they had only just met over mine. All I want is my name and reputation cleared so I can move on."

On arrival, they were both ushered into Lisa's office. Four men sat on the far side of the desk. Sir Antony Moorehouse took centre stage with the general manager on his left and the two lawyers from Brentford Brothers on his right. Before Andy and Lisa had even sat down, Sir Antony Moorehouse's deep voice broke the silence.

"Nurse Preston, who is this person you have brought to the meeting? No one said anything about spectators being allowed."

Lisa was about to reply, but Andy caught her eye and frowned. Lisa looked at the carpet directly in front of her without speaking. Andy paused for effect, studying the faces of the four men in front of him. Moorehouse looked unhappy while his manager seemed like he wanted a hole in the ground to open up and swallow him. One of the lawyers sported a surprised look while presumably his brother had the ultimate poker face. Andy reckoned that he would be the more dangerous of the two.

"Gentlemen, as I am sure you are all aware, in the case of any disciplinary proceedings, the accused is allowed to bring a witness. Luckily for Lisa, her witness is also her lawyer. I can only assume that even though there are two lawyers and a manager involved, it slipped your minds that you should have informed Miss Preston of this fact.

"And while we are on the subject of incompetence, why was my client interviewed in a public place with no warning of the meeting, without proper witnesses present?"

Sir Antony Moorehouse had had enough and exploded before Andy could continue.

"You, sir, are out of order. I will speak to my staff when I want and where I want, and if I want, I will damn well sack them too, and you, sir, will not be able to do a damned thing about it. You are a jumped-up little upstart."

Andy smiled inwardly. He had them well and truly on the back foot. He watched as the general manager tried in vain to reign in his wayward boss before he completely blew the contract. The lawyer with the poker face knew Moorehouse had made a major mistake and attempted to divert the argument.

"I believe, Flight Lieutenant Paxton, you have no jurisdiction here as a lawyer, only a witness, as you work for the Ministry of Defence, and they have no interest in the proceedings here today."

Andy had been correct. He was dangerous. He was probably the one who had tried to get Lisa into trouble.

"Well, well, the lawyers do have a voice after all. I have some bad news for you…it is Mr. Brentford, I presume? You see, I have resigned my commission, which leaves me free to represent Miss Preston and you with a big problem. You see, as a witness, you and your sidekick can't be in here, so I am requesting that you and your sidekick both—how do you say it in lawyer speak, oh yes—sling your hook while you have the chance to walk away without ending up in court for all the wrong reasons."

Poker Face stood up he was shaking with rage, but his brother grabbed his arm and ushered him towards the door, telling him to stay calm. Moorehouse told them to wait in reception while he sorted things out. Andy was smiling at that comment when Moorehouse exploded at him one more time.

"You can wipe that grin off your stupid face, young man. You can't come in here trying to throw your weight around. I have friends in very high places, and I will make sure your career as a lawyer will be a very short one."

Andy had had enough abuse from the knighted windbag and decided it was time to stop this nonsense. Andy reached into his pocket, removing the Dictaphone and placing it on the table in front of Moorehouse and his manager. All eyes in the room were drawn to the flashing light on top of the little recording device. The general manager was first to recover from the shock that the proceedings were being recorded.

"Nice try, Mr. Paxton, but as a lawyer, you know that this recording would be inadmissible in court."

Andy nodded in agreement. "For once, you are correct, but who said I was going to use it in a court of law? Listen carefully, and don't interrupt me. This is what is going to happen here today. Lisa is going to hand you her resignation, which you will accept. You will also agree to pay any money she is owed and supply a glowing reference to any future employer who should enquire about her work. In return, Lisa will agree not to sue you for slander, and I will not let this recording fall into the hands of our tabloid newspaper reporter friends, who would love to hang a real live knight of the realm out to dry.

"Oh, one last thing. Sir Antony "Windbag" Moorehouse is going to apologise to Lisa for treating her so badly."

Andy stood up and snatched the recording device from the table. He was finding it hard to resist the urge to smack Moorehouse in the mouth. "I will wait outside while you sort things out. Lisa, don't leave this room without an apology. See you outside."

Andy caught Lisa's eye as he left, giving her a wink while the two men sat in deathly silence.

Andy was not finished. Once he got outside, he spotted the Brentford brothers hovering by the reception desk and made a beeline for them.

"Tell me, gents, was there any real evidence—other than hearsay, probably from a jealous member of staff? You expected to string this out until you extracted a big, juicy fee for sorting out the affairs of a dead man who could not give evidence. In short, you were quite happy to ruin the life of a young woman to increase the size of your wallets. You just didn't count on her bringing a lawyer. Well, guys, cat got your tongues? Here is your chance to present the evidence, so let's have it."

Poker Face pushed past Andy, heading for the door and followed closely by his brother. "You haven't heard the end of this, Paxton." Poker Face made a show of slamming the door as he exited.

Andy spoke under his breath as he watched the pair leave. "Oh, I think I have heard the last of you pair. Good riddance to bad rubbish."

He was aware of someone standing by his side. He turned to find Lisa watching him quietly.

"Well, Mr. Paxton, that was impressive. Where did you learn that?"

Andy laughed as they walked out the front door of the home. "Would you believe my mum? She is a retired lawyer who, between golf matches, is an advisor for the Scottish office."

Lisa took Andy's arm and walked him out of the door towards the car park. "I must meet her sometime. She must be quite a woman."

Out in the car park, Andy had a brain wave. "Actually, Lisa, could you excuse me for a second until I make a quick phone call?"

Lisa walked a few paces behind Andy in the general direction of her flat. As Andy made his call, Lisa took the time to study Andy's rear view. He had no backside to speak of, but what he lacked in hips, he made up for tenfold in shoulders. His rear view resembled an American football player, not the shape you would naturally associate with a lawyer. Lisa looked away as Andy turned back towards her after his call. She did not want to get caught eyeing up his rear view.

"Right, Miss Preston, that's all sorted then. You are going to get your wish. I need to drop off the hire car in Stirling, and my mum has agreed to pick us up. We can kill two birds with one stone—you can meet my mum, and I can sort out the hire car."

Lisa had not seen this coming and was at a loss as to what to say. Andy sensed her hesitation and jumped in before she could think of a polite get-out clause.

"Lisa, I have to confess, I have an ulterior motive. I need your help to deflect my mother's wrath. If you are presented to her, it might take the heat off me. Please come with me. We need to stick together on this. I help you in the morning, and you return the favour in the afternoon. What do you say?"

Andy put on the best puppy-dog expression that he could muster in the hope that Lisa would feel sorry for him. Lisa had a puzzled expression.

"I don't get it, Andy. What have you done that will incur your mother's wrath, and what makes you think dragging me along will help?"

Andy stopped outside Lisa's flat as she spoke, still sporting the puppy-dog expression.

"OK, OK, Andy. Let me nip up and change. Then we will go. You can explain what the problem is on our way to Stirling."

Andy could not hide his relief at Lisa's decision, grabbing her by the shoulders giving her a playful shake. "Ya wee beauty, thank you, Lisa. I will wait in the car."

Andy sat in the car, waiting for Lisa. His mood had improved drastically. He had had a good morning, he had helped Lisa, and she had not rejected his suggestion that they spend a little more time together. He knew his mood would not have been good if he had to deal with Lisa's rejection as well as losing his job. All he needed now was his mother and father to be cool about his employment hiccup, and he would be a relieved (if not quite a happy) man.

They had only travelled a few miles before Lisa decided to question Andy. "Well, come on then. Why are you so scared of your mother that you need me to back you up?"

Andy shot Lisa a sideways glance as he negotiated his way past a slow-moving cattle truck in the slow lane. He could tell from Lisa's expression she was somewhat amused by his predicament. "I'm not that scared, really. Well, maybe just a wee bit. I needed an excuse to see more of you, if I have to be brutally honest. I am sure Mum will be fine. After all, she wasn't that sold on me joining the RAF anyway."

It took a few seconds for it to sink in before Lisa clicked to the last comment. "Oh my god, I thought you were joking in the meeting about resigning. You mean you actually did it? What the hell happened to trigger that?"

Andy shrugged his shoulders, keeping his eyes firmly glued on the road ahead. "Where do you want me to start? Betrayal by my superiors, being sent too far away from the people I am fond of, and my word to an old man who put his trust in me."

Andy spent the rest of the trip telling Lisa about the last days of his RAF career. Lisa sat quietly, not interrupting Andy until he had completed his tale of woe.

"So in a nutshell, Andy, you sacrificed your career to keep your word to an old man."

Andy was half expecting Lisa to call him an idiot, but to his surprise, she reached out and held his hand as he changed gear.

"Don't worry, Andy. I will help you talk your mother round. After all, I don't know what would have happened today if you hadn't been there to sort out the men in suits."

CHAPTER 7
ANN PAXTON QC

Lisa and Andy were sitting on the wall outside the hire-car building, enjoying the calm before the storm, when Andy's mother pulled her car up directly in front of them.

Over the years, Ann Paxton had came to know the body language of her only son all too well. His drooping shoulders told a tale that Ann was not sure she wanted to hear. Instead, she focused on the pretty blonde perched next to Andy on the wall.

"Hello, I take it you must be the Lisa Andrew has been referring to in our conversations. Andrew, don't just stand there. Get your things into my car so we can get a move on. Come on. Chop, chop."

Andy loaded his bits and pieces into his mother's car while the two women regarded each other cautiously. Ann was not sure what to expect as Andy had very rarely introduced his lady friends to her. Lisa had expected a straight-to-the-point lawyer, and Ann had pretty much lived up to her expectations so far.

Once on the move, it was Ann who broke the ice. "I hope you have brought your pyjamas with you, Lisa. I have supper arranged, and the spare room linen has been changed, and the heaters are on to warm the room for you. You won't want to be travelling all the way to Dundee again today, surely?"

Lisa tried to catch Andy's eye, but he was looking out of the window at the view of the Ochil hills in the distance. Lisa was sure he was trying hard not to laugh at the situation Lisa had found herself in.

"Sorry, Ann, I didn't bring my PJs. I didn't know I was going to be staying. Not to worry, though. I am sure Andrew will have a T-shirt I can borrow for the night. Andy, I think it is about time you told your mum your news don't you think?"

Andy had been outmanoeuvred and had no option but to spill the beans. "I was going to wait until supper, but I suppose now is as good a time as any. I have resigned from the Royal Air Force and am at the moment out of work."

Lisa held her breath, waiting for the explosion, but it never came.

"Oh, well, it looks like you will be able to get a real job, one that pays proper wages. Your father won't be happy, but you are lucky. He is away for a few days with his pals playing golf. We will work on him when he gets back. At least Lisa still has her job. Maybe she can look after you until you get sorted."

Lisa had not expected the spotlight to be turned back on her just so quickly and took a few seconds to respond. "Actually I am not much better off than Andy. I resigned this morning, so we are both in the same boat, I'm afraid."

Ann Paxton shook her head but remained calm, saying nothing as she threaded her way through the evening traffic in the busy city of Stirling.

An hour later, Lisa and Ann chatted as Ann made the final preparations for supper. Ann dispatched Andy to wash and check her car over so she could spend some time alone with the girl to get to know her better. Ann had just discovered Lisa's reason for resigning and Andy's part in helping steer her through the debacle at the nursing home when Lisa's mobile phone started to vibrate on the kitchen worktop. Lisa excused herself and stepped outside to answer the call from the unknown number. When she returned, Ann could tell that something was troubling her but decided to let Lisa tell her in her own good time. The rest of the meal preparation was done more or less in silence, and then Ann asked Lisa to find Andy and bring him in for his supper.

Andy had just finished washing the last of the soap from his mother's little Volvo when Lisa appeared by his side, putting her arm round his waist without speaking. Andy turned the hose off and was about to give Lisa a cuddle when his mother appeared around the side of the building.

"Come on, you two. Let's go before your supper gets cold. Andy, find out what Lisa drinks and sort her out, will you? That's a good lad."

Andy shook his head as his mother disappeared round the corner again. "That's a good lad! She forgets what age I am. You wait and see because I have brought a girl home, she will be trying to tell me about the birds and bees before the night is out!"

Lisa was giggling at Andy's last comment but steered him towards the dining room before his mother came looking for them again.

After supper, Lisa brought up the subject of her mysterious phone call while Andy poured them coffees.

"I am sorry to be a pest, but would it be possible for someone to give me a lift to Edinburgh tomorrow or to the train station? I had a call earlier from the lawyer vultures dealing with Jan's will. They want to meet at their offices at eleven tomorrow. Would that be a problem?"

Andy was nodding in agreement. "I am sure Mum will let me borrow the Volvo. We can go together. Someone has to keep an eye on those guys."

Lisa had lost a bit of her colour as she caught Andy's eye. "You can take me through, but they have told me you are not welcome in their offices and to come alone. Sorry, Andy."

Ann Paxton had been listening without comment but decided to intercede before her son lost his temper.

"Don't worry, Lisa. We will all go on a trip to Edinburgh. I haven't met the Brentford brothers. It will be interesting to find out why they have barred my son. When I have finished with them, we can have lunch in the capital, make a day of it so to speak. Andy can look in the job centres for you both while you and I have a quiet word with the lawyers."

Lisa realised the Brentford brothers had just bitten off more than they could swallow. She was pretty sure Ann Paxton was not going to miss them and hit the wall, not where her son was concerned.

The Brentford brothers were busy sucking up to their American guest when the secretary announced over the intercom that Lisa Preston and her lawyer, Ann Paxton, had arrived for the eleven o'clock meeting. The two brothers made eye contact but said nothing in front of their guest. Poker Face was calm on the outside, but his mind was racing. If this was who he thought it was, they had underestimated the nurse. Ann Paxton was one of Scotland's leading prosecution lawyers. She was the main advisor to the first minister and had been instrumental in bringing the Lockerbie bombing to court. She spent most of her time these days in Brussels fighting for British interests and law. Poker Face was finding it hard to believe this legend in Scottish law would be interested in the goings-on of a simple nurse.

Poker Face's hopes of a mistaken identity faded along with his plan to take control of the meeting as he watched the legend that was Ann Paxton enter the room dressed in her trademark white Armani business suit and carrying her matching white-leather attaché case. His brother made a quiet choking sound but could not get any words out, leaving Poker Face to deal with the situation unfolding in front of him.

"Miss Preston, there was no need to bring a lawyer with you. This meeting is no more than a reading of the late Jan Powlak's will. There is no need to involve a second lawyer."

Ann Paxton never gave Lisa the opportunity to reply to Poker Face. "Mr. Brentford, please forgive Lisa for being overly cautious where lawyers are concerned, especially after her last meeting where her professional etiquette was questioned without good reason. While we are on the subject of Mr. Powlak's will, can you tell me, as you are here at his request, where in the will it barred my son from attending this meeting, or is this another failure by Brentford brothers to carry out the duties required by the law society of Scotland to provide full and fair legal services to the public? I am fairly sure you have no relevant answer to that, so unless you want to make a fool of yourself, please get on with the business at hand."

Poker Face did not enjoy his first encounter with Ann Paxton and decided any further comments he made would toe the line. He did not want to pour petrol on the fire.

"Very well, Mrs. Paxton, we will continue. You may or may not know that Jan had no living relatives. His will simply states that he leaves all his worldly goods to Miss Lisa Preston. At this point, I would like to introduce our other guest, Mr. Jake Shelton, managing director of Powlak Air and executor of Jan Powlak's will."

Jake Shelton was a giant of a man, his weather-beaten face giving away the fact that he had spent much of his life under the rays of a hot sun. Ann and Lisa studied him as he shook their hands in turn. His warm smile did not hide the fact that he was a very streetwise character, and when Jake started speaking, his deep American voice reverberated around the room. "Miss Preston, I know this will have come as a shock to you, but I am here to hopefully help make things a little easier for you. Please call me Jake, and if I may, I will call you Lisa.

"What I would suggest, folks, is that now we have been introduced, Mr. Brentford can forward on the boring paper work, and we can go and grab some lunch while we go over business. Does that sound OK to you, ladies?"

Jake Shelton stood up as a signal to leave, and Lisa followed suit. Lisa was about to agree to Jake's suggestion when Ann stood up, giving Lisa's arm a little squeeze.

"Mr. Shelton, we would be glad to meet with you, but unfortunately, we already have a lunch appointment. We would be happy to meet you for dinner this evening. Would that do?"

Jake Shelton was not used to people saying no to him, but he had watched Ann Paxton in action and had no doubts she was not a woman to cross. He needed the Preston girl on his side, so he decided to comply with their wishes. "No problem, ladies. Say where and when, and I will be there."

Ann thought for a moment before replying. "We can eat where you are staying, say eight o'clock? Lisa's partner will be joining us, so if you can make it a table for four that would be good."

Jake nodded in agreement. "Consider it a date, ladies. I am shacked up at the Sheraton. See you at eight."

Andy had parked the Volvo in a side street facing the lawyer's offices and was somewhat surprised to find Lisa and his mother walking towards him less than half an hour after he had watched them enter the premises. As usual, it was his mother calling the shots.

"Andrew, can you drop me at Holyrood? I need to go over some legal papers with the fisheries minister. You can treat Lisa to some lunch. I suspect later she may be in for a bit of a surprise. I will get a taxi later and meet you at the Sheraton at eight for dinner. Lisa can fill you in over lunch."

Andy dropped his mother outside the Scottish parliament, then made his way to Lothian Road, where he dropped the car and headed on foot to a little Italian restaurant where he knew they could have a quiet meal and a chat. Andy was a bit worried as Lisa had not said a word since they dropped off his mother. He couldn't make up his mind if she was in a mood or just deep in thought.

"Come on then, Lisa. Has someone stolen your tongue? What happened with the lawyers? Why the sudden decision to frequent the Sheraton tonight?"

Lisa was facing out on to the street, and for a few agonizing seconds, she watched the pavement procession outside without answering. "Andy, I'm sorry. My head is not with it at the moment. It's hard to explain. It's like my life is changing before my eyes, and I have no control any more. It's a weird feeling."

For a moment, their conversation was interrupted while the waiter took their lunch order.

"Sorry, Andy, I haven't been very forthcoming. Jan has left everything to me, whatever *everything* might be. There was a man in the lawyers with them, Jake Shelton, the boss of Powlak Air. He also seemed to be in charge of the lawyers. We are meeting him tonight, I presume to discuss Jan's estate. I don't know why the lawyers didn't do that. What do you think?"

Andy sat thinking for a few seconds. He played with the cutlery before coming to a decision.

"One thing is for sure. This Jake guy didn't fly halfway round the world out of the goodness of his heart to help you. There must be something in it for him. Maybe Jan still had shares in his company, and he hopes to buy them from you, or maybe Jan stored his gear with him, and he wants rid of it. It looks like we will have to wait until tonight to find out for sure."

Lisa watched as Andy picked up his phone and clicked on a predialed number. "Hi, Callum. Guess who? Listen, bud. I need some info, and I need it like yesterday. Honestly, Cammy, it is really important. I need you to find out about an American company called Powlak Air. Can you help me, mate?"

Lisa could hear the voice on the other end of the call, but it was too weak for her to make out the conversation.

"Andy Paxton, if you keep calling me like this, you are going to have to get me a job working for you. How quick do you need the information?"

Andy smiled at the last comment. If only Cammy knew how close to the truth he was. Andy had already pencilled Cammy into his team for when he started working for himself one day.

"How does yesterday sound, mate?"

Cammy rang off, promising to phone as soon as he had something.

Lisa took Andy's hand and squeezed it. "Andy, I don't know what I would have done without you. Really, I'm not joking."

It had all been too much for Lisa. Andy could see the tears welling up and attempted to lighten the mood. "Don't worry, Miss Preston Remember, I am an out-of-work lawyer. You can put me up for a few weeks free of charge until I get a job and repay the rent."

Lisa was smiling, but tears were still not far away. She fought them back valiantly, sniffing and blowing her nose. "Nice try, Andrew, but we both know you don't need someplace to stay. Your mother wouldn't want to lose her only son that quickly. No, you will be just fine at home."

Andy lifted the napkin from his lap and wiped away a solitary tear that was welling up in the corner of Lisa's eye.

"Don't cry, Lisa. It's not fair. It's hard enough to resist cuddling you at the best of times without you being all cute and vulnerable. It's me who should be crying anyway. Stay with my mum? Come on, girl, please. Have you not seen how bossy she is? Why do you think my father has bailed out on a golf trip? It's not fair. I don't even play golf. You were supposed to save me. Some girlfriend you turned out to be."

Lisa looked directly at Andy. His last comment struck a chord with her. He was sure of it.

"Andrew Paxton, what makes you think I am your girlfriend? We have been on one date, we haven't made love, and the only kiss we shared was the result of a bet! In my book, that falls short by some way of girlfriend status."

Lisa beckoned Andy towards her with her finger. Andy was trying to read Lisa's expressions to see if he was about to receive a slap for his girlfriend comment, but instead Lisa got hold of his shirt, pulling him closer and kissing him seductively full on the lips.

Andy's first reaction was to pull away. He was not used to getting up close and personal in such a public place, but his resistance quickly collapsed. All Andy wanted to do was hold Lisa. It was Lisa who broke the embrace, smiling at Andy's obvious discomfort at having to display his affection in public. Then Cammy saved the day, timing his phone call to perfection.

"OK, Andy, here is the lowdown on Powlak Air that you asked for. Luckily for you, I have a mate in the States who is seriously into aeroplanes. Here we go then. Powlak Air is based in Reno. It started life in the late forties and since then has grown into a bit of a monster. From its first days as a repair shop for old ex-military planes, it reinvented itself as a race workshop for the craze that swept America using highly tuned piston-engined single-seaters in air races. In the eighties, it changed tack again, heading down the military-aircraft route, doing bits and pieces for McDonnell Douglas and Grumman. Last month it hit the big time. It was awarded a multibillion dollar government contract to service, overhaul, and upgrade its fleet of F22 Raptors. The company employs 122 engineers and designers and is privately co-owned by two men. Jan Powlak founded the company and is the joint owner along with his one-time foreman and test pilot, Jake Shelton. There are rumours that Lockheed Martin is actively trying to acquire Powlak Air to add to their portfolio. Analysts have valued the company at six point one billion dollars. At short notice, Andy, that is about as much as I can do. I hope that helps you, pal."

Andy thanked Cammy before hanging up. His head was spinning at the news. God knows what Lisa was going to do when she found out. Andy looked upon Lisa with new reverence and more than a pinch of fear. He was possibly looking at a very beautiful blond billionaire. In his mind, if this were true, the world was her oyster. Why would she bother with an unemployed loser like him?

Lisa could tell from the look on Andy's face and his pallor that he had been told something profoundly disturbing to him. She decided to concentrate on lunch and only engaging in small talk until Andy felt able to tell her what was wrong. After lunch, the pair headed for the Princess Street gardens. Lisa attached herself to Andy's arm as they walked off their lunch.

"You must be wondering what my mate found out about Powlak Air, Lisa. I think this evening, if my info is correct, you are going to be pleasantly surprised. I don't want to jinx things for you, so for the moment, I think we better leave it at that. Just keep your fingers and toes crossed that Cammy is right. That's all I'm going to say."

They found a vacant park bench and sat down to enjoy the late-afternoon sun and each other's company. Andy's mind was full of doubts over their relationship.

Then Lisa reached once more for his hand. "Andy, are you remembering that it is Jan's funeral tomorrow? Are you still OK to come with me?"

Andy squeezed her hand gently. "No problem, Matron. I'll be there. It might prove rewarding. Who knows? Some of his wartime buddies might turn up to say their last goodbyes. I might get the chance to speak to them about Jean Bruce."

Lisa was shaking her head slowly. "Andy, would it not be better to just let it go and get on with your life? It's been too long. The trail is cold."

Andy frowned. Lisa had still to find out how stubborn he was. Once Andy started something or set his mind to it, he was like a dog with a bone. He would not let it go.

"Sorry, Lisa. I gave the old boy my word that I would do everything in my power to uncover the truth. The RAF might have gagged me, but it won't stop me finding out what really happened in 303 Squadron all those years ago. I don't know how I will do it, but I will do it."

Lisa smiled and cuddled into Andy's side for warmth as the sun dropped in the early evening sky, causing the temperature to fall quickly in the shade of the gardens.

"OK, Sherlock, but for the record, I think you would have more chance of finding the Loch Ness monster."

Andy stood up, pulling Lisa to her feet. "For your information, Miss Preston, the Loch Ness monster is next on my list, and that hunt will begin just after I find Jean Bruce and figure out a way to tell the world about her story. But for now, it is getting late, and it's just about time for us to head back to the Sheraton for dinner. I hope they have decent grub. I am starving, none of that à la carte crap."

Andy and Lisa bumped into Ann Paxton as she stepped out of a cab in front of the Sheraton foyer. As they entered the foyer, they were met by Jake Shelton and ushered into a private function room where a table for four had been arranged in the middle of the room. Drinks and food orders were taken before the four settled down to the business at hand. Unusually, Ann Paxton was not the first to speak. The stage was taken by the booming voice of Jake Shelton.

"What I would like to do, folks, if it is all right with yourselves, is give you a rundown on the situation we all find ourselves in tonight. It will probably go quicker without interruptions, so if you can hold back with the questions, I will answer anything you want once I have finished my little speech."

Jake looked round the room at his silent audience before continuing. "OK, folks, here goes. Jan started the business after the war, sorting up flying circus planes. I joined him as a test pilot when he stepped up to building and modifying planes for air racing. We had a sweet thing going back then. Powlak was to air racing what Cosworth was to Formula One. If you wanted to win, you needed a Jan Powlak Merlin engine in the nose of your machine. By the eighties, things were changing, and Powlak Air won a few small contracts, development work with other aviation firms. Jan was getting on a bit and had lost interest. His Merlin engines were not sought after any longer, and he had no interest in modern avionics. Jan decided to do a bit of travelling, and we agreed that I would run Powlak Air in his absence. That was the last time I set eyes on Jan Powlak. After that, it was phone calls initially, and then, when he settled in Scotland, our business was carried out through his lawyers. Although I was not surprised when Jan's lawyer contacted me to say he had passed away, I was shocked to discover he had bequeathed his share of the business and all his assets to his nurse." He turned to Lisa. "You must have made some impression on the old guy. He was as hard as nails.

"So on to the next part of the evening. When Jan left on his world tour, Powlak Air was a company ticking over with fourteen employees. Since then, its fortunes have exploded. Only last month, Powlak Air was given a government contract to look after the maintenance and development of its F22 Raptors and the advanced development of its future replacement. In short, Powlak Air is batting with the big boys. We currently have 130 employees, but that will increase with the completion of our new service hangars, maybe to as many as two hundred employees. Jan Powlak owns 60 percent of the business, and I own the other 40 percent. What I would like to do is propose that I make you an offer for Jan's share of the business, as clearly you would not be interested in running it yourself. Due to the massive investment being undertaken, the banks will only allow me to offer you five million dollars for your share of the business. On paper, it is worth more admittedly, but my commitments to the banks mean I am financially stretched to the limit. I think for the moment I have talked enough. I see our food is here, so why don't we eat, and you can ask me questions after dinner."

During the main course, Lisa sat quietly, but Ann Paxton could not contain herself and fired the first question at Jake.

"Jake, how much money have you had to invest to bring the government contract on board?"

Jake smiled at Ann, laying down his fork and knife while he answered her. "You sure know how to put a fella off his chow, Ann. You see, this is why I think Lisa should take the money. The worry is not worth it for her. Powlak Air has invested three million dollars, and the bank has invested twelve million dollars in new buildings and tooling. That is why they will only advance me a further five million to buy out Lisa."

Andy joined in with a question of his own for Jake. "Jake, haven't respected analysts valued Powlak Air at sixt point on billion dollars?"

Jake had a grin the width of Texas on his face as he answered Andy. "Yeah, and Donald Trump could be president one day. Those guys that make the figures up throw everything in the pie, including future profits. Son, if everything goes perfectly, then maybe some day it will be true, but life isn't as easy as those bean counters think."

After they'd dispatched with dinner, Jake ordered drinks for everyone, proposing a toast to Jan's memory. This completed, Jake once more took centre stage, everyone else content for the moment to listen to him.

"OK, Lisa, as Jan's executor, I have to ask whether the next part of the evening should be between just us two, or should I go ahead with all present? It's entirely up to you, honey."

Lisa blushed but let Jake go on.

"As Jan's executor, I have a few bits and pieces here for you. These are the keys and papers to Jan's home in Reno. It has been cleaned and kept serviceable in his absence, and all bills are up to date. This is the contents of Jan's bank account. The funeral and his bills from the home have all been deducted from the account, and it has been shifted into your name. The account stands at eight hundred and thirteen thousand, four hundred and ninety-five dollars.

Jan was also the registered owner of three aeroplanes. They are stored at our workshops, and for the moment, they need not be moved until you decide what to do with them. Two are racing Mustangs, and one is a restored Spitfire Mk IX. There are also eight overhauled Merlin engines and two Griffon engines."

Andy was trying to calculate in his head the rough value of the things Jake had just listed when Lisa cleared her throat and started speaking for the first time. "Mr. Shelton, thank you for doing all this. If you don't mind, I have a few questions to ask you. If you were to pay me five million for my share in Powlak Air, would it not place the company in a dangerous position with no reserve left in case of unforeseen problems?"

Jake nodded silently in response to Lisa's first question, unsure where she was going with this angle.

"That being the case, and as at the moment Powlak Air can't afford to buy me out for the correct value of my share of the company, I would like to remain a sleeping partner. It is clear to see that you have a great passion for the company you have built up over the years. In my opinion, it can't be in any safer hands. Would that be acceptable to you, Jake?"

For a few seconds, Jake Shelton didn't answer. No one was sure if he was thinking over the implications or he was just gobsmacked that he was in partnership with a nurse.

"OK, Lisa. Let's do this together, but you must tell me if anyone tries to get you to sell your shares in the company. That is my only request. Do you have any other questions, or should we wrap it up for tonight?"

Lisa glanced across at Andy. He was sure he could see devilment in those beautiful eyes. "Just one more thing,

Jake. I would like you to fire the lawyers you have been using in the UK and employ my lawyers—Paxton and Paxton."

Ann and Andy Paxton looked at each other, but for once, Ann Paxton was speechless. Jake rose from his seat, smiling and extending his huge hand across the table to Lisa.

"Lisa, it is a pleasure to know you and do business with you honey. Consider your request granted. I will put things in motion right away. I am sorry, but I have an early flight tomorrow and an important meeting with the Department of Defense, so I will not be able to attend Jan's burial. I will speak to you, say Monday morning? We will do a tour of Powlak Air. I will send our private jet to pick you up from Edinburgh Airport on Saturday morning. Feel free to bring our new legal team in the UK with you for the tour. Good evening, folks. Got to go."

Andy, Ann, and Lisa watched as the big American strode out of the room, his long legs carrying him at a fast pace. Jake was still turning things over in his head, for some unknown reason, his head was telling him to trust his instincts. The little blond nurse was no dummy. She seemed to be a genuine person. Jake hoped so because if she wanted, she could sell her share of Powlak Air to the big guns for considerably more than five million, and he couldn't do a damned thing about it.

Andy threaded the little Volvo through the late evening traffic as he picked his way out of the Scottish capital, heading for home when Lisa interrupted his train of thought.

"Andy, could I be a real pest and ask you to take me to Dundee tonight? I know it's late notice, but we have the funeral tomorrow, and I really need to get home and sort out my clothes."

Andy was about to reply when his mother beat him to it. "That's not a problem, Lisa. Andy can just take the Forth Road Bridge and head up that way. Do you have an outfit? If not, I am sure I can dig up something of mine. It might be a tiny bit loose on you, but it would do for a funeral."

Lisa needed time alone to think things through. Her life had just turned a corner, and she was struggling to take it all in. She needed to iron her clothing for tomorrow, but more than that, she needed peace and quiet to think.

"Thanks, Ann, but I have a wreath being delivered as well. It would be better if I was there to pick it up."

Ann waited for a few minutes before bringing up a subject that she felt Lisa needed to be sure about. "Lisa, I know it is none of my business, but I just want to make sure you are doing the right thing for you. Are you sure you don't want to sell your share of the business? You do know that if Jake can't afford it, there would be nothing stopping you selling to the highest bidder. I am not saying you made the wrong decision. I just wanted to make sure you take everything into account. If you like, you could call that your first piece of advice from your new lawyers."

Andy and his mother made eye contact. It was an idea neither of them had contemplated, but Lisa had put it on the table, and now it didn't seem like too far-fetched an idea.

On arrival at Lisa's flat, there was an awkward moment as Lisa climbed out, saying her good-byes. Andy wanted to do more than just fling her out, but his mother's presence put a twist on the situation. Lisa was about to walk away when Ann stepped in.

"Andrew Paxton, where are your manners? Get out and show Lisa to her flat door. These days you never know who is lurking about."

Lisa was about to object, but Andy jumped out of the car and grabbed her hand, leading her towards the flat. Lisa opened the front door, and Andy stepped inside, ready to follow Lisa up to her flat door, but Lisa stopped him just inside the front door.

Andy was about to ask Lisa why she had stopped him but before he could, she pulled him down towards her, kissing him passionately, dropping her handbag, and wrapping her arms around his neck to make sure he couldn't pull back from the embrace. After what seemed like minutes, they both came up for air. Lisa had relaxed her frame completely and was hanging onto Andy, who was supporting her light but firm torso.

"Wow, now that is what I call a good-night kiss. Where did that come from, Lisa Preston?"

Lisa recovered, pulling herself together and retrieving her handbag. She still made body contact with Andy, the warmth of her body radiating through Andy's clothing, stopping him from releasing his grip on her petite waistline. Lisa looked up into his eyes. Andy sensed she was trying to make up her mind about something. He just wasn't sure what that was.

"Andy, I better go. Your mum is waiting for you. That was just a wee thank you for being such a nice guy. Will you come over early tomorrow? I don't want to be late for the old boy's funeral." Lisa pulled back gently from the embrace and headed for the stairs, turning back just as Andy reached the outer door.

"It's a pity you weren't here alone. I was kind of in the mood to go the next step down the road to real girlfriend status tonight. Not to worry—all good things are worth waiting for, my mum always says."

Lisa winked at a bemused Andy, and she launched herself up the stairs before Andy could form any kind of coherent reply.

Andy climbed back into the Volvo, and his mother pointed the car back in the direction of home. For the first few minutes, they both sat in silence, deep in their own thoughts. But it did not take long for Ann Paxton to start talking. She was not a woman who stayed quiet for any length of time.

"You took your time seeing Lisa to her door. I take it she is taking the Powlak Air situation in her stride. When you fly to Reno, Andy, you keep an eye on her. She is a clever girl, but Jake Shelton is also clever. He did not get his company to where it is by accident, and he will stop at nothing to keep control of it, so you need to look after her."

Andy was smiling to himself in the darkness of the Volvo cabin. His mother has obviously taken a shine to Lisa, and he was going to wind her up.

"So, Mother, I take it from that little speech you have taken a liking to Lisa?"

Andy should have known better than to tangle with his mother, but the cork was out of the bottle, and he couldn't put it back in.

"Oh, I have a taken a liking to Lisa? That is rich coming from you, young man. You can wipe that grin off your face along with Lisa's lipstick. Your old mother can see in the dark, you know, and as I am pretty sure Lisa Preston is going to be my daughter-in-law at some point. I am looking out for you both."

For the second time in the last thirty minutes, Andy had been struck dumb. First Lisa's comment and now his mother's latest comment had just knocked him for six.

"Now hang on a minute, Mother. A good-night kiss doesn't mean wedding bells by anyone's standards. You are well off the mark there."

Ann Paxton smiled at her son's denials as she headed home along the M90. "Andy, you are in love with the girl. It's as plain to see as the nose on your face, and as far as I can tell, I think the feeling is mutual. Now enough of that subject. What are we going to do about Lisa's request that we be Powlak Air's lawyers? I have no objection to it, and you are out of work anyway. It will save us both an ear-bending from your father when he gets back."

Andy thought for a second before replying. It was time to air his idea about Cammy working with him.

"It might be an interesting proposition, but I want Cammy to work for us. That is the deal breaker for me."

Ann Paxton drew her son a withering stare before replying. "Andrew, you are hardly in any position to demand anything, but I suppose Callum can be our paralegal. I receive a retainer each year from the government for my services. We can put that towards his wages, and Callum can help me collate figures for the government when he is not helping you. Agreed?"

Andy decided to quit while he was ahead and agreed to call Cammy the next day and offer him a job in the new family business. That night, sleep would not come for Andy. He had so many things tumbling around in his head—his new business venture, his relationship with Lisa, the funeral—but one thing in particular burned in his brain. Jean Bruce. He had promised Jan he would do everything in his power to see justice was done and that Jean and not some faceless deserter received the recognition for her heroism. With the restrictions imposed on him, however, he had no idea how to go about it. First things first. Before he started his new job, he was going to have a go at finding this woman...if she even existed. Paxton and Paxton would just have to wait until he had exhausted all avenues of investigation.

Andy was just finishing his breakfast when his mother handed him the house phone.

"Ah, you are up! I have been trying to get you for the last twenty minutes. Did you fall asleep on your phone again, Paxton? I have news on the Artur Krol front, old son. Didn't turn up much more about him than you can find on Google, but a study of the electoral register proved fruitful. Although Mr. Krol was posted missing presumed dead by the Royal Air Force, he did, according to the register, leave behind a younger brother who was evacuated from London to our very own Kilsyth, where he lives to this very day. Maybe a wee visit from yourself could turn up a bit more about his brother. Sorry if my info is a bit sketchy, mate, but I do much better work with present day, not history."

Andy decided it was time to take the bull by the horns. "Cammy, answer me one question. What would it take for you to come and work for me? No joking, an honest answer, please."

For a few seconds, the line was silent as Cammy tried to decide if this was a Paxton windup or if he was being serious. Then he blurted out, "Oh, I think thirty grand and a company car would swing it, mate. How does that grab you?"

Andy smiled to himself. Just a bit more coaxing, and he would have his man. "Callum, mate, I have seen your driving. Thirty grand and no company car, thirty days leave a year, and the pleasure of having me as your boss. What do you say?"

Cammy was chuckling down the other end of the line. "OK, Mr. Paxton, you have a deal. You better not be kidding me though."

Andy was glad his friend had agreed to join his team. He checked his watch. The last thing he needed was to be late for Lisa.

"Listen, mate, I need to fly. I have a funeral this morning. Can we meet at the usual Indian in Stirling tonight? Say sevenish? I have someone I would like you to meet, and we can sort out the fine details of your new job."

"Sounds good, Andy. Just as long as you are buying, I will be there."

Andy arrived at Lisa's flat at ten thirty and was dismayed to find Lisa still wandering around in her PJs, Lisa greeted him at the door with a peck on the cheek, then led him by the hand to the living room and pulled him down to sit by her side.

"Andy, I am going to skip the service at the home. I don't think I will be welcome there. If you don't mind, we will go straight to the cemetery for about twenty to twelve. I was going to call you and tell you, but I thought we could both use some time to ourselves. Things have been so mad lately." Lisa snuggled into Andy's side, and then, just as the pair were getting comfortable, Lisa jumped up like a woman possessed and headed for the bedroom.

"Andy, wait there. I almost forgot—wait until you see this. You won't believe it."

Andy's mind was running riot as Lisa returned after a few minutes, her hands behind her back and her face positively beaming with excitement. Lisa sat down again by Andy's side, flourishing a scrap of paper between her fingers.

"Read it, Andy, I had to read it five times before it sank in."

Andy removed the paper from Lisa's finger and read it to himself. The paper was an ATM account summary in Lisa's name. It stated her account held £572,955. Andy smiled and handed her the slip back.

"I can't believe it, Andy. I am officially half a millionaire."

Andy was chuckling at Lisa's naïveté. "Lisa, you own two airworthy Mustangs and a Spitfire and 60 percent of a company, not to mention a house in Reno. Don't you get it, girl? The two Mustangs alone make you a multimillionaire."

Lisa was shaking her head at Andy in mock disgust. "My mother told me not to count my chickens before they were hatched." Lisa changed the subject before Andy could pursue it further. "Here is a map of the city so you can plot us a route to the cemetery. It's not far from Ninewells Hospital, so you can use that as a reference point. I will go and get ready."

Andy was about to pick up the map when Lisa leaned over and kissed him softly on the lips. Then she headed for her bedroom.

CHAPTER 8
LAST RESPECTS

At around eleven thirty, Andy and Lisa arrived at the entrance to Balgray Cemetery near the centre of Dundee. Andy abandoned his mother's Volvo by the gates and, after asking directions from a worker by the cemetery buildings, headed to the right along an access road that climbed steadily uphill towards a wooded section of the sprawling graveyard. By the trees at a junction in the access road, a small number of people were gathered by an open grave. Lisa spotted Susan from the nursing staff talking with Reverend Black, the local minister, who was a regular at the nursing home. Andy stood quietly observing the mourners while Lisa made her apologies for missing the service at the home just as the hearse appeared, gliding silently to a stop by the graveside. Andy watched as the well-oiled machine of the undertakers' team placed the coffin above the grave, ready for one last journey to its resting place. Andy looked at the assembled body of people, wondering who would take Jan's cords. Reverend Black answered his question for him as he addressed the people present, stating that due to the age of most of the mourners and lack of numbers, the cemetery staff would lower the coffin.

Lisa stepped forwards, placing a solitary wreath on the old man's coffin. Reverend Black used this as a signal to start, and after saying a few words about Jan, he asked the small group to pray with him. Andy watched out of the corner of his eye as all around prayed and the staff slowly dropped the coffin out of sight, never to see the light of day again.

Andy did not pray but instead squeezed one of Lisa's cold hands in a reassuring manner. Andy was not listening to the words of Reverend Black. He let his mind wander. He found it difficult to understand how a man of Jan's standing, who had lived a full and interesting life, could end up so alone, buried in a graveyard far from his homeland. In the future, people would read his gravestone and have no clue as to the stature and remarkable life story of the man buried here. Andy found this unbearably sad and vowed to himself to fulfil his promise to Jan.

As the mourners broke up, heading back to the home for tea and sandwiches, Lisa said her good-byes to the people from the home. Andy watched as the ground staff covered the grave with boards and artificial grass to stop anyone from falling into the grave until the staff filled it in at a later time.

Andy and Lisa were standing alone by the graveside when they were approached by the head undertaker. He apologised for the interruption but explained that by law, someone other than the person buried must own the plot. As Jan had no one, it was up to her to sign a document stating she would be responsible for the upkeep of the grave. Lisa signed the paper work while Andy studied the area around Jan's grave. As silently as the hearse arrived, it departed like a huge black ghost, making its way back down the hill towards the main road. Andy and Lisa were left alone by Jan's final resting place.

Lisa had not shed a tear although Andy could tell by looking at her that the service had taken a lot out of her mentally. She was pale and silent. Her usual glowing complexion was gone, and in its place were sunken red eyes and goose bumps.

Andy wrapped his arm around her, turning her away from the grave and taking in instead the view of the Tay Estuary, which lay below them, and the blue misty hills of Fife stretching away in the distance. Andy spotted a bench three or four rows of graves below them and started strolling down the hillside towards it, towing Lisa along by the hand.

Lisa sat by his side without objection, still holding onto his warm hand, Andy watched as a tear found its way to the corner of her eye. As Andy watched, she blinked, and the tear escaped, tumbling down her pale cheek and coming to rest on her blouse before soaking into the material.

"Andy, that was so sad. Please god, don't let me die alone like that."

Andy used his finger to gather up another tear as it made its break for freedom. "Don't cry, Matron. If you don't stop, you will start me off, and that won't be a pretty sight, I can assure you."

Lisa was just about to reply when the rumble of a big car approaching broke her concentration. Andy and Lisa watched as a large white Rolls Royce pulled up and stopped in front of Jan's grave. The pair watched with interest as first a large Asian gentleman dressed in a suit climbed out.

He was followed by a second Asian man, also dressed in a suit. Both men took up positions at each side of the rear wings of the big limousine, studying the surrounding area. Andy observed the closer Asian man tap on the back wing of the car. Seconds later, an elderly lady dressed in black stepped from the rear of the Rolls Royce carrying a wreath of red roses. Andy and Lisa watched mesmerized as the old lady knelt in front of the grave, kissing the roses before placing them on the covering board. The woman bowed, then made her way back to the limousine, followed by the two men. Andy was sure they were her bodyguards. The big car did a three-point turn then started back down the hill.

Something clicked in Andy's head, and he took off like a gazelle, leaping over headstones in his mad rush uphill to the graveside, Lisa trailing in his wake. Andy arrived at Jan's grave and stared down at the roses. The card attached to the new wreath said only two words, but they made Andy's head explode.

LOVE, JEAN

Lisa had just reached the path when Andy exploded past her, throwing himself down the road towards the rapidly vanishing Rolls Royce.

By the time Lisa had stopped and read the card, both Andy and the Rolls Royce were gone.

Lisa headed down the hill towards the main gates of Balgray Cemetery. She was almost at the entrance before Andy reappeared, climbing back up the hill towards her.

"Sorry to just leave you like that. Did you see the writing on the wreath the old lady placed on Jan's grave?"

Lisa nodded without saying anything. She was looking at the sweat beading on Andy's forehead.

"Jesus, Lisa. I think we have just seen Jean Bruce. She was so close, and she slipped through my fingers."

Lisa used her handkerchief to dab away the sweat that was threatening to make its way into Andy's eyes. "I take it from that, Mr. Paxton, that you did not catch the Rolls?"

Andy shook his head in disgust, but he had a glint in his eye that told a tale. "No, they were too quick for me. All is not lost quite yet, though. One of the gardeners saw me trying to catch them, and when I gave up and returned, he called me over. He knew the car. It belongs to a local wedding hire company, Caledonian Carriages. I will give them a call when we get back to the flat. With a bit of luck, we can find out who hired the car and where they are staying."

It only took a few minutes for Andy and Lisa to reach the flat. Lisa retired to her bedroom to change out of her funeral gear while Andy busied himself on the Internet looking up Caledonian Carriages. The gardener from Balgray Cemetery had been correct. There was indeed a wedding firm based in Broughty Ferry, a mere stone's throw from Dundee. Not only did this match, but also the car that was advertised on their web page was the exact double of the car that had visited the cemetery. Andy only waited seconds before the phone was picked up by the limo hire reception. Andy let the man on the other end of the line go through his usual spiel before making his request.

"Hello there, I am Andy Paxton from Paxton and Paxton solicitors. I believe one of your Rolls Royces was hired today to take an old lady to Balgray Cemetery. I am in need of your assistance. You see, the gentleman who was buried today was my client. He died leaving everything to his best friend, a lady called Jean. Unfortunately, we have been unable to trace her. The lady you took to the cemetery left a wreath signed 'Jean.' You would be doing myself and your client a huge favour if you could tell me where you picked up or dropped off the old lady so we can get in contact with her about the contents of my client's will."

For a few seconds, there was no reply. Andy had his fingers crossed that the man on the other end of the line had not seen through his deception.

"Well, I suppose telling you will do no harm, probably my good deed for the day. I will tell you, mate, but I don't think it will do you much good. It was myself who picked up the lady you are asking about and the two gorillas she arrived with. I picked her up from Dundee Airport and dropped her back off at the same place immediately after she visited the graveside. One of her gorillas paid me in cash. The hire was arranged over the phone, and I am pretty sure the receptionist said it was an overseas call, but my mind could be playing tricks with me. Looks like you need to speak to someone at the airport, mate."

Lisa had just emerged from the bedroom when she heard her front door close. She wandered into the living room to find it deserted, but on the coffee table was a hastily scribbled note. "Gone to Dundee Airport. Back shortly. Love, Andy."

Shaking her head, Lisa headed for the kitchen to put the kettle on. She had only been in the bedroom for a moment. The man was unbelievable, like a dog with a bone. She could see now that no one was going to get any peace until this Jean Bruce matter was settled once and for all.

One way or another, if she wanted Andy to calm down, she was going to have to help him find out the truth.

Andy's trip to the airport was not as successful as his call to the limo hire company. Nobody seemed to know anything about an old lady who was dropped off by Rolls Royce. His yarn about the will did nothing to help his cause, and thirty minutes later, he left the airport, his hopes of finding Jean Bruce almost as bruised as his battered face.

Lisa was waiting by the window when Andy arrived back at the flat. Andy was not sure what reception he was about to receive after his rapid departure and entered Lisa's lounge expecting the worst. To his surprise, she was calm and somewhat quiet.

"The wanderer has returned. Well, Sherlock, did you find out anything at the airport?"

Andy sighed, shaking his head. "Sorry Lisa, but I had to check it out. There might have been a chance that I could catch her at the airport, hence the note. I didn't want to disturb you. I failed miserably, I'm afraid. No one remembered her, a waste of time, sorry. Anyway grab your gear. We have a dinner date with Cammy tonight in Stirling, and I have something lined up to recharge our batteries after the low of this morning's proceedings."

Lisa had that worried expression on her face again. "Can I get a clue as to the dress code for this evening? I know what you are like with your surprises."

Andy was beaming all over his face. He loved keeping Lisa in the dark for as long as possible, and today would be no exception.

"Casual clothing tonight—it's just an Indian and a chin wag. Got to show you off to my mates. You will need a warm jacket, jeans, and outdoor footwear for this afternoon though."

Lisa narrowed her eyes at him before replying. Although Andy was still getting to know Lisa, he had seen this look before, and it told him she was up to something.

"OK, Andrew Paxton, I will play your little surprise game, but I have something you have to agree to in return. Tomorrow, I want you to come with me on one of my own little surprise trips. It's only fair, don't you think?" He agreed, and she grinned at him.

Andy stopped at his home in Muckhart only long enough to change his clothing, grab a couple of bottles of water, and rejoin Lisa in the Volvo for the last part of the road trip. Ten minutes later, Andy turned off the main road in the little town of Dollar and threaded his way through the housing. Lisa watched as the little Volvo reached the edge of the town, and Andy turned onto what could only be described as a coach road, winding its way up into the hillside into the Ochil hills behind Dollar.

Lisa read the signpost as they passed. It would appear that they were going to look at an old castle. The road finally came to an end, the route barred further by a heavy gate. Andy grabbed the water, locked the car, and headed off in the direction of Castle Campbell. To Lisa's surprise, Andy bypassed the castle, joining a track that wound its way over the hillside in a westerly direction, climbing as it went. Lisa could see that the summit was still some way off. She was having to push hard to stay with the long strides that Andy had set as the pace. She had just steeled herself for the final push to the summit when Andy stopped. In front of him stood a stone cairn.

Andy studied the cairn while Lisa attempted to regain her breath. Andy was first to recover and break the breathless silence.

"This is as far as we go, Matron. This is what I wanted to show you."

Lisa studied the cairn, which had an engraved plaque built into it. The cairn marked the spot where three Spitfires had tragically crashed while on a training exercise during the Second World War. Lisa finished studying the writing, then removed her jacket, placing it on the ground as a makeshift cushion. Andy was about to follow suit, but the stiff breeze that racked the hillside, flattening the grass around them, changed his mind. He joined Lisa sitting on the edge of her jacket and used his jacket as a quilt, cuddling into Lisa and pulling the jacket over them both in an attempt to share body heat and keep out the wind.

"Lisa, I didn't just bring you up here for the exercise or the view. I wanted to show you the cairn. I wanted you to understand where I am coming from. I thought showing you this might explain my train of thought. This cairn was built by an army major and a group of volunteers. These people went the extra mile. If they hadn't built this cairn, these brave airmen, two of whom made the ultimate sacrifice, would in time be forgotten. No one told them to do it. They just knew it was the right thing to do. Lisa, no one is telling me to find Jean Bruce, but I too know it is the right thing to do.

"When Jan Powlak found out she was still alive, he knew it was the right thing to do also. People have to know the truth. I don't know how I am going to get the message out there, but I will do my best. I owe Jan that at least. After all, he has changed the course of my life, and thanks to him, I met you, Matron."

Lisa had been sitting quietly, taking in what Andy was saying but the *matron* comment was too much to bear. Andy received a punch to his shoulder from his coat-sharing partner next to him.

"Nice try, Paxton, but you are not in this alone. I was Jan's nurse, and he left me everything. Do you really think I am going to let you swan off into the sunset looking for this mythical woman pilot? No, Andy, you are not gong to find her alone. We are going to find her. We are a team, whether you like it or not. Also, it may have escaped your notice that I am no longer a nurse, so you can cut the matron nonsense before I give you another black eye to replace the one that's almost recovered!"

The pair sat for some time, taking in the stunning views from high above the Forth Valley. In front of them, the little town of Dollar nestled at the foot of the hill, and in the distance, the sun glinted from the Forth Estuary as it transformed into a snaking river, working its way across the landscape until it vanished from sight in the Stirling area.

"Andy, I kind of already guessed you were not about to let the pilot thing go. You didn't really have to bring me up here to convince me. I get it, I really do!"

Andy did not make eye contact instead choosing to look in the direction of Stirling, away from Lisa.

"Lisa, I think what I was trying to say is that I don't expect you to have to get involved in this hunt. After all, you are now a rich woman. You can do what you want. You don't have to hang around with me—that is, of course, unless you wanted to."

Lisa laid her head on Andy's shoulder. He had not been ready for that reaction and was unsure what to say next. There was a moment of silence between them. Lisa was thinking through what Andy had just said, and Andy waited quietly for her answer.

"My turn to put my cards on the table, Andy. I am not about to charge off into the sunset with some male model. For one, how would I know if he loved me or just my bankbook? I was kind of hoping we could keep getting to know each other. At least I know you were interested in me before I had money. We seem to get along OK. We just need time together to find out if it's just a passing attraction, or if there is more to it than that. I will do everything I can to help you find this woman. Jan would have wanted me to help, and who knows? Maybe it will strengthen our relationship. I am happy to go the extra mile with you if you want me to."

Andy pulled Lisa to her feet, giving her jacket a shake before holding it out for her to put on. "Come on, partner. Let's get you off this hill before you catch a cold."

Andy looked back at the cairn as Lisa slipped into her jacket. "One of the pilots survived the crash, you know. The poor bugger had to drag himself off the hill in the middle of winter to get help. He was too injured to walk. Now that is determination for you. Lisa let's hope our determination to find Jean Bruce can live up to that example!"

CHAPTER 9
CAMMY

Later that evening, after a quick pit stop at Muckhart, Andy and Lisa headed to Stirling for their rendezvous with Callum McPherson. En route, Lisa decided to quiz Andy about his friend.

"So how long have you known this Callum guy?"

Andy did not reply at first as he was busy navigating around a parked bus. "Callum and I met at Edinburgh University. I can't actually remember what he was studying. We just knew each other socially. There wasn't a bar or a club that Cammy couldn't get you into. He knew every bouncer or doorman in the capital. He now works for a company that mainly researches family trees, but he also finds lost relatives for law firms who are dealing with wills and that type of thing, a sort of electronic detective, if you like."

When they arrived at the Indian restaurant, they found Cammy waiting by the door. "Well, if it's not Andy Paxton. I thought I was going to have to send out the search parties for you."

Cammy stopped talking as Lisa appeared around Andy's side and for the first time came into Cammy's line of sight."

"Well, well, Mr. Paxton. I must say your taste in girlfriends has improved drastically since we last met. Don't just stand there like a big idiot. Introduce me to your blond friend."

Lisa had only just met Cammy, but already she could see why he was so successful at what he did. His tongue was made of pure silk. No wonder he could talk his way around people. Lisa stepped forwards before Andy had time to string a reply together.

"Hello, Callum. Andy has told me all about you. It's nice to put a face to a legend. I'm Lisa. You must be starving. I know I am. Let's go in and spend some of Andy's money on good food."

Cammy was chuckling as he held the restaurant door open for the new arrivals.

"Well," said Lisa, "I hope Andrew hasn't told you *everything*. I am sure he will have censored some bits, if for no other reason than to spare your blushes."

Callum had already picked the table, which was situated at the back of the room in its own little booth. They ordered food before the conversation continued. This time Cammy directed his remarks to an unusually quiet Andy Paxton.

"Right. Let's get down to business, Are you serious about this job? If you are, I am due holidays. If I take them, I can be with you by the end of the week."

Andy nodded agreeably to this suggestion. "Deadly serious, mate. I have one client already, a business partner, and a list of things needing checked, mate."

Cammy was chuckling to himself again. "Who would have thought it? Cammy and the Paxman ride again! Mad, man, pure mad!"

Cammy was smiling but Andy Paxton had a straight face. "Cammy, pin your ears back. We need to bring you up to speed on things that have been happening."

Cammy sat enthralled as Andy explained Jan Powlak's story and the hunt that was about to begin for Jean Bruce. He explained Lisa's involvement in the affair and his former employer's stance on the situation.

The meal was well into the dessert course before Andy finally stopped talking. Lisa had said very little, preferring to let Andy explain the situation they now found themselves in. Callum had asked various questions as the story unfolded, but now he sat quietly for the first time that night, thinking to himself.

"OK, Andy, only one thing puzzles me, and I am going to need clarification. Lovely, blond, bubbly billionaire Lisa here seems to like you for some unknown reason. Why for the love of god have you not married the poor girl? Is there something I am missing here? Did you turn gay and not tell me?"

Andy looked crestfallen, but Lisa was finding the banter between the pair of old mates very amusing.

"Lisa, honey, look at him! Black eye—he would have you think he is the strong, silent type. Nope, just too slow to keep up with my youthful yet wise banter. You ever get fed up with this big punch bag, give me a call. I am your man, sweetie."

Lisa was smiling, and she reached under the tablecloth to give Andy's thigh a squeeze before replying to Callum's assault on Andy's character. "I will bear that in mind,

Cammy. First things first, though. We have an offer I don't think you can refuse."

Before Lisa could finish, Cammy interrupted. "Lovely Lisa, I doubt there is anything I would refuse you. Please continue."

Andy was shaking his head at Cammy's antics, but he was also puzzled about this offer Lisa had mentioned. Lisa knew she was taking a bit of a risk sticking her nose into Andy's business, but she had a feeling that Cammy would go the extra mile if there were something in it for him. She made her mind up and voiced her idea.

"Andy was telling me you requested a company car. If you pull this off and we find Jean Bruce, there will be a company car in it for you, isn't that right Andy?"

Lisa gave Andy the best puppy-dog eyes she could muster as Andy stared at her for the moment, lost for words. Callum was watching Andy waiting for his response to Lisa's proposition. Andy had been well and truly backed into a corner by the pair of them. As the silence started to turn awkward, Lisa started to panic. She was starting to think she had gone too far when Andy finally broke the silence.

"Well, Cammy, it would appear that my new business manager here has altered the terms of our contract. I suppose I can work with that—*if* we find Jean Bruce. It's a deal."

Lisa clapped her hands with pleasure and some relief at Andy's decision. "And what do I get for being so clever and brokering the deal between you both?"

Andy had a wicked glint in his eye and the hint of a smile as he stared into Lisa's puppy-dog eyes. "Lisa Preston, you read my mind. What you get is the pleasure of telling my other business partner about the company-car thing."

Lisa took a noticeably sharp intake of breath at the suggestion while Andy broke out in a smile at the thought of Lisa telling his mother.

Callum had watched Lisa's reaction and was intrigued by it. "Well, spill the beans, folks. Who is your other partner?"

Andy knew exactly what the reaction would be and took great pleasure in the announcement. "It's my mum. Come on, mate. Paxton and Paxton—the clue is in the name, no?"

Andy watched as a look of horror appeared instantly on Callum's face. "Wow, wow, wow. You never told me about that, Paxton. What the hell are you doing going into business with the wicked witch of the west? She still hasn't forgiven me for dragging you into that lap-dancing bar, like you needed dragging. Lisa, that woman is evil. You can't make me work with her. Come on!"

Callum looked perplexed as Andy and Lisa killed themselves laughing at his sudden transformation from cool dude into gibbering wreck.

"Come on, Cammy! Thirty grand and a company car!"

Callum said nothing, shaking his head and staring into space. Andy and Lisa also said nothing, waiting for Callum to decide his future. Suddenly Callum sighed and leaned across the table towards Andy, holding out his hand for Andy to shake on it.

"Paxton, you are lower than a snake's belly. Just keep the old battle-axe away from me. You have a deal, by the way."

Just as they were leaving the restaurant, Andy's phone went off. He stopped while Lisa and Cammy strolled along the street at a leisurely pace to allow Andy to catch up when he finished his call. While they were alone, Lisa decided to bring up a point with Callum McPherson that had been troubling her all night but that she had so far refrained from mentioning.

"Callum, you know Andy will get into big trouble with the authorities if they find out he has been talking about Jan Powlak after signing his gag order. You will look out for him? I wouldn't like anything happening to him. Do we understand each other?"

Lisa was staring into Callum's eyes to gauge his response to her request just as Andy reappeared, leaving Callum no time to reply to Lisa.

Callum took the bull by the horns on Andy's arrival, announcing he had no desire to be a gooseberry and that he was heading for the nightclubs and he would speak to them in the morning.

The car was cold, and Lisa used this as an excuse to cuddle into Andy's shoulder on the return trip. An attempt to keep warm as the car heated up, she said. Andy was first to break the silence in the little Volvo.

"Just to let you know, that was my mother on the phone. She has turned down the bed in the spare room and put the heater on for you. Hope that is OK with you, boss."

Lisa slipped back across to her seat before continuing. "Oh, so I have graduated from matron to your boss now? Andy, listen. You need to be careful what you say. I don't want my lawyer ending up locked away in a military jail for breeching the Official Secrets Act."

Andy shrugged his shoulders without looking in Lisa's direction. "I hear you, but in my defence, I told Cammy about Jan before I signed anything."

Lisa shook her head as Andy glanced over to see her reaction. "I may be a nurse, Andy, but I am not stupid. You are treading a fine line, and you know it. Getting yourself locked up to prove a point is madness. We will find a way to tell Jean Bruce's story and keep your word to Jan without getting you in trouble. Anyway, change of subject, today we did it your way. Tomorrow you have to keep your word. It's my turn for surprises, so if you want to tuck me in tonight, you better get a move on. We are running out of time for a cuddle if we have to be up early tomorrow."

Lisa smiled to herself as the little Volvo seemed to find a new lease on life as Andy negotiated the twisty road only a few miles from the village of Muckhart.

Lisa and Andy arrived at Muckhart to find the house in darkness. Andy breathed a sigh of relief. His mother had obviously headed to bed, allowing Andy to escort Lisa unhindered to her bedroom. Andy followed Lisa into the bedroom, hopeful that she would make good on her promise of a good-night cuddle. Lisa did not object to his presence and kissed him before removing her jacket. He watched mesmerized as she tossed the quilt to one side and patted the bed, inviting him to join her. Andy genuinely thought this was going to be a night to remember until his mother put a dampener on his plan for the remainder of the evening.

"Andrew, when you have finished tucking Lisa in, please come to the kitchen. We have business to discuss."

To Andy's dismay, Lisa seemed to find this very amusing. Andy's face said it all. His disappointment bordered on despair as he dragged himself of the bed. Lisa pulled him back for a second, giving him a peck on the cheek while whispering in his ear, "Poor Andy, just when you thought you were going to have your wicked way with me, Mummy drags you away. If you are quick, you never know. I might still be in the mood. Now go before your mother comes looking for you."

Andy dragged himself dejectedly to the kitchen where he found his mother. The light above the kitchen table illuminated a mountain of paper work. Ann Paxton studied her son over the top of her reading glasses as he entered the kitchen, Andy didn't need to say anything. His body language said it all.

"I take it you were on a promise, and I have just burst your bubble, young man."

Andy shrugged but said nothing, not sure that he should be discussing his sex life—or rather, his lack of it—with his mother.

"Sorry to spoil your evening, Andrew, but I promise you, this is important. I have a taxi booked early to run me to the airport, so I will not see you for a bit, and this needs sorted tonight. Grab a seat while I go over some legal things with you."

Andy sighed and looked at the kitchen clock longingly.

"OK, young man, I had the papers drawn up and registered for our new law firm, and I need a few signatures from you. I have marked the areas with a cross." Andy patiently signed the documents as his mother explained what he was signing and why. To Andy's dismay, this took a very long time, and all he could think of was Lisa waiting for him in the guest bedroom.

Finally Ann Paxton came to a part that held Andy's attention. For a short time, it even took his mind off the beautiful blond girl waiting for him in the bedroom.

"OK, Andrew, this is very important, so pay attention. Here is a cheque for Callum's first month's salary. Please see that he gets it and ask him to fill in these documents so we can set up a wages account for him. Finally, this is your company account. Your wages will be paid into it, and your father and I have deposited fifty thousand pounds into the account. We were going to give you the money for a house or wedding gift, but we both feel that you need it now. Do what you want with it. Put some of it down as a deposit on a house, or keep it until you need it, but it will get you off the ground."

For some time, the pair sat discussing ways to attract work before Andy checked the clock. It was 2:30 a.m. Andy kissed his mother on the forehead, thanked her, and said his good-byes before heading along the hall to his room. En route, he stopped at Lisa's door, but the light was off, and Andy sensed she was sleeping. With regret, he headed past her door to his own room.

Andy was awoken the next morning with a start as someone forcibly swept the duvet from the bed. He opened his eyes just in time to see Lisa's cheeky grin as she left the bedroom, leaving him lying on his mattress as naked as the day he was born and shivering with the sudden cold of the morning air.

Andy found the duvet thief busy making coffee and toast in the kitchen, dressed in her own jeans but sporting one of Andy's old Scotland rugby tops. Andy joined her at the breakfast table, still trying to recover from the little sleep he had managed to get. Lisa was obviously a morning person while Andy was the exact opposite. A large mug of coffee later, Andy started to feel half human. Lisa bustled about, cleaning up the breakfast dishes, not wanting Ann Paxton to come home to a mess.

"Come on, Andy Paxton. Get a move on. We have a busy day ahead of us. We are going to get you a car first, and then we need to do a bit of shopping. You are remembering that we fly to America tomorrow. Oh, and later this afternoon, I am taking you to meet my mother."

Andy Paxton stopped midbite. He had raised his eyebrows at the car thing and winced at the shopping thing. He had forgotten about the American thing, but the mother thing stopped him in his tracks.

"My god, woman, you are unbelievable, I wonder if Powlak Air know what they have let themselves in for. The least you could have done this morning was give me a cuddle before ripping the covers off. I think you owe me that if you are going to drag me all over Scotland and then present me to your mum."

Lisa had that twinkle in her eye again. Andy sensed before she even opened her mouth that it would be a retaliatory comment. "Andrew, from what I saw when I removed your bedding, I think it would have been more than a cuddle. Unfortunately, we don't have time this morning. So stop mucking about, get your jacket on, and let's get a move on."

Lisa waited by the kitchen door as Andy grabbed some paper work, keys, and his jacket. As Andy went to step past Lisa, she stopped him, kissing him seductively before stepping back.

"You do realise that tonight we will not be able to continue where we left off last night. We have got to get to Edinburgh Airport early, so that means an early night for both of us. No hanky-panky. Just warning you, big boy."

Andy groaned as he made his way past Lisa to the car. For the moment, it seemed to him the physical part of their relationship was stuck in the mud.

Andy decided Stirling was as good a place as any to hunt for a car and headed in that direction. En route, Lisa tried to quiz him on what type of car he wanted. Andy had to admit to Lisa that he hadn't really thought about it and that Cammy was the expert when it came to cars.

Andy pulled the Volvo in at the first garage he came across, but one look at the price of the Land Rovers for sale told him he was going to have to set his sights a bit lower. He did not think his mother and father would be impressed if he blew all his money on one car. While Andy studied the Land Rover prices, Lisa made her way across the road to a SEAT garage opposite. Andy stopped window-shopping and followed her, The SEAT prices were more suited to his pocket and twenty minutes later, after an argument with Lisa as to who was paying for the car, Andy won and arranged to pick up the ex-demonstrator after lunch. Next on the list was shopping.

Lisa had sensed that Andy was not a shopper and dispatched him to the local tailors to check out the suits while Lisa sorted out her own shopping. To Andy's surprise, Lisa met up with him as he left the tailors, announcing that she was finished. Having finished shopping so quickly, they had time to kill before the car was ready, and the pair found themselves tucking into coffee and cake in a garden-centre café opposite the SEAT garage while they waited for the agreed-upon time to pick up Andy's new car. Andy had just finished his cake when his mobile phone started to chime. A quick check of the screen showed that Cammy was calling him.

"Afternoon, boss. I have been a busy little bee, and I have a bit of interesting news for you, so I thought I would check in with you. After your story last night, I called the

Dundee Airport and after a bit of arm-twisting, I have found a bit about your vanishing granny. It has to be said, something is going on here. I am not surprised you had no luck finding anything out the other day. The management was tight-lipped. Eventually, after a few phone calls, I got lucky. I talked to an engineer called Gordon who was based at the airport. I arranged to meet him at the service gate. Since I don't have a company car, and at vast expense to myself I may add, I used my motorbike to get me up to the meeting in Dundee. The long and the short of it is, Gordon confirmed an old lady and her entourage stayed only long enough for their Falcon 900 to be refueled and take off—about an hour. After slipping Gordon a hundred pounds to ease negotiations, he let me into the office, and after a bit of digging through the fuel receipts, I found the fuel bill for the Falcon 900. The bill was settled over the phone by the owners of the Falcon 900, a Swiss bank called PSS, or to give it its full title, Premier Strasse Suisse. I took the liberty of giving those awfully polite Swiss bankers a call and was ever so politely told to mind my own business. For the moment that is it, but never fear. Cammy is working on a way to loosen the lips of those tight-lipped bankers, so to recap, you owe me a hundred pounds, and I am in need of a company car. How has your day been so far?"

Andy was busy going over what Cammy had just told him. "We are in Stirling, waiting on my new company car, which I may add, you may be able to borrow as I am going to America tomorrow. If you crack the Swiss bank, it is yours to use."

Lisa looked puzzled at the mention of a Swiss bank but was content to wait until the phone conversation was over before questioning Andy.

"Andy Paxton, you, sir, are a gentleman. Where do I pick up the keys? What have you bought me, and I take it *we* means the lovely Lisa is still with you. Tell me, Paxton. Have you bedded her yet, or are you pissing about as usual?"

Andy smiled to himself. As usual, Cammy had gone straight for the jugular. "It's a ex-demo Leon FR. I will text you where the keys and car are after you get a result in Switzerland, and as for the last question, wouldn't you like to know!"

Cammy was chuckling down the phone as he answered Andy. "Sweet, an FR, nice choice, mate. I will need to get to work on breaking down the Swiss silence so I can get the keys. And I was right about you and Blondie—you bottled it, mate. I hope you are a better lawyer than a lover, or my new job won't last long, I fear. Later, mate. I have work to do."

As promised, the car was ready on time, and Lisa gave Andy her mum's address so Andy could find it on the sat nav. En route to Lisa's mum's, Andy filled Lisa in on the phone conversation with Cammy, only omitting from his update Cammy's comments about Lisa. The trip went quickly, and Andy's new mode of transport purred along like a Swiss watch. Lisa took over from the sat nav as they entered the village of Errol just north of Perth, guiding Andy through the streets until they came to a little white cottage on the far side of the village. Lisa pointed to the cottage and then sat quietly as Andy manoeuvred his new vehicle into a space just down the road. Andy was about to get out when Lisa grabbed his wrist. Until then, Andy had not been aware of the change that had come over Lisa since she entered the village. She was visibly pale and was looking worried.

"Andy, just a bit of background info before we go in. My mum is cared for by her lifelong friend Mazie. My mum has dementia, so we will just see how it goes. Just to warn you before we go in. Sometimes she can be hard work."

Lisa led the way in through the front door, shouting a greeting as she entered. Andy followed at her heels and had to let his eyes adapt to the gloom of the room as all the curtains were pulled shut. Two high-back chairs sat either side of a roaring fireplace, and each chair was occupied by a grey-haired old lady. Lisa spoke first to Mazie, and then turned her attention to the old lady on the right.

"Hello, Mum. How are you doing today? You're looking lovely. Has Mazie had you at the hairdresser again?"

At first, Hanna Preston did not alter her stare into space. Then Mazie barked at her from the opposite seat. "Hanna, it's Lisa come to see you. Are you no speakin to the lass?"

Mazie's outburst seemed to bring Hanna back to the real world. First she looked at Lisa, then back to Mazie.

"Hush you. Of course I am speaking to Lisa. Do you think I would nae speak to my wee lassie. Hello, honey, how are you doing today?"

Lisa pulled a chair across the table and signalled Andy to do the same. "Mum, I have brought someone with me to meet you. Mum, Mazie, this is Andy." Lisa hesitated for a second, looking up into Andy's eyes before continuing. "He is my boyfriend. I thought I had better bring him across so you can cast your eye over him."

Mazie was the first to react to Lisa's news. "Hello, son. You must be special. Our Lisa is fussy when it comes to boys. There are not many who measure up to her high expectations. Nice to meet you. Hanna, speak to the laddie. Don't just sit there like the queen, woman."

Again, Hanna seemed to come out of a dream when badgered by her old friend. Lisa was sitting closest to her mum, holding her hand.

"Mazie, I am no stupid. Hold yer tongue, woman. Sorry, son, nice tae meet you. Andy, is it?"

Andy nodded and was about to speak, but Hanna continued where she had left off. "And who is this bonny lassie you have brought with you?"

Andy glanced across at Lisa, but it was hard to tell her thoughts. Her face was cast in stone.

Mazie was about to explode, but Lisa caught her eye, putting her finger over her mouth to signal Mazie not to speak.

"Mum, it's me, Lisa. I was here last week. Have you forgotten me already?"

Hanna's face burst out into a beaming smile as she studied Lisa's face in detail. "Lisa, love, of course, I'll no forget you. I remember you now. People think I'm losing my marbles, but I'm just getting old. How could I forget you? You do my hair every Friday, and Mazie's too!"

Andy made his way back to the car. His heart was heavy for Lisa. He had seen at firsthand the torture Lisa must go through with every visit. Lisa had never spoken about her mother, and Andy had not realised Lisa was nursing a broken heart. Andy waited patiently as Lisa went through a few things with Mazie in the relative sanity of the kitchen. She left the usual envelope with spending money for Mazie's and her mother's needs, only this time the envelope was bursting at the seams. She explained her trip to Mazie and the extra money and reiterated to Mazie that she could still get her day or night on her mobile even if she was in America.

The return trip was quiet. Andy was not sure what to say to Lisa, who was obviously still hurting from the visit. As Andy passed Auchterarder on the motorway, the sign for Gleneagles loomed up. Andy cut left off the motorway and then headed left again, away from Gleneagles, through Glen Devon, the road winding its way up the hill before dropping down on the southern side of the Ochil hills. It was still relatively early yet, and Andy pulled his new car off the road at the head of the Glen Devon reservoir. To her surprise, he pulled Lisa out of the car.

"Come on, Lisa. We need to blow away the cobwebs with a walk to stretch our legs and raise our spirits."

Lisa said nothing but followed Andy onto the path that led to the dam at the head of the valley. The path was usually used by fishermen and water-board staff, but today they were alone.

Andy slowed the pace to allow Lisa to catch up with him, and as she drew near, he put his arm around her. They strolled the short distance to the dam head arm in arm and stood mesmerized as they watched the water from the overflow cascade down into the depths of the valley on the far side of the dam.

Andy did not break his gaze from the depths, and he was first to break the gloomy silence masked only by the distant thunder of the water as it made contact with the valley floor far below them.

"Lisa, how long has your mum been suffering from dementia?"

Lisa looked up from the depths, her cheeks wet from her tears. She wiped the tears away with the back of her hand before replying. "Five years now. I swear it was the shock of my father's death that brought it on. She was fine before that, a real smart cookie."

Lisa dabbed her eyes with a hankie, smearing her immaculately applied mascara and making her look even sadder than she clearly already was. Andy took charge of the hankie, using it to do a temp repair on Lisa's eye makeup.

"Has your mum's condition always been as bad as today?"

Lisa was watching a bird of prey hovering above the choppy surface of the water at the far side of the reservoir. "She has got worse this last year, that is for sure. You never know what you are going to get when you arrive. It is hard to explain. Dementia is like the sun on a cloudy day. Nothing is going right, and it seems the clouds will never lift, and then suddenly, she will be fine for a few fleeting minutes, just like the sun finding a chink in the clouds. When this happens, it's the mum you have always known, but then the clouds return, and a stranger sits where your mum was only a few seconds ago. I visit hoping for the chink of sun through the clouds, for one day soon, the sun will be lost forever. You see, Andy? I have more money than I will ever need, but as they say, money isn't everything. It won't give me back my mum. Life can be so beautiful and yet so cruel."

Andy was lost for words. He was not sure if the words existed that could do justice to the situation. Instead he pulled Lisa to his chest, cuddling her as they both watched the osprey dive from a great height as it thundered into the water in search of its prey. As if on cue, the clouds moved, bathing the surface of the water in sunshine as the osprey lifted off, dragging an unfortunate fish in its dripping talons.

Lisa and Andy stayed glued to the spot, both realizing they had just been treated to one of most breathtakingly beautiful displays of Scottish wildlife you could wish to see. It was made more special by the fact that the sun had just appeared at the very second the osprey broke the surface of the water. They waited by the dam for a few minutes, hopeful that the osprey would return, but Lisa brought them back to reality with a bump, remembering that she was due to fly to Reno in a few hours and most of her gear was still in her flat in Dundee.

The next few hours were spent travelling to and from Dundee with only a quick stop en route to visit a chip shop to grab a quick bag of chips. Back in Muckhart, with the time fast approaching witching hour, Lisa helped Andy pack his bags for a quick getaway in the morning. Their task was not made easy as no one had told them if they were going for a couple of days or a couple of weeks. Packing finished, Andy was surprised to find Lisa climbing into his bed rather than heading for the spare room. Andy made a quick call to Cammy to arrange for him to come to the airport with them so he could remove and use Andy's new car. On returning to the bedroom, although he had been away for only a few minutes, he found Lisa tucked up in bed wearing one of his -shirts. She was fast asleep. Andy was no better. No sooner had his head hit the pillow then he was also in the land of dreams.

CHAPTER 10
AMERICA

The next morning turned into a mad dash as neither of the sleepyheads had set an alarm. Lisa was first to waken and raise the alarm that they were late. No breakfast and a spirited piece of driving got them more or less back on schedule as they stopped in Stirling to pick up Callum McPherson. Twenty minutes later, they were on the one-way system that surrounded Edinburgh Airport. Lisa was the only morning person in the car and had made most of the conversation during the drive, receiving (for the most part) one-word answers.

She tried one more time to liven up proceedings. "I wonder if our plane has arrived yet?"

Andy Paxton smiled at his mate Cammy as he replied. "I wouldn't get your hopes up. We will probably find two tickets for an economy airline waiting for us."

Cammy was busy studying the tail of the jet that was parked closest to the perimeter fence of the airport. "Care to take a wager on that Paxton, old chap? Look at the tail of that jet!"

Emblazoned over the full tail fin were the words POWLAK AIR POWER. Lisa's taxi was here.

Jed Turner stood by the check-in desks. Although he was one of the three aircrew who manned the Powlak Air Jetstream aircraft, his attire was somewhat different from that of your run-of-the-mill aircrew. He had no pilot suit or cap, but instead he wore khaki chinos and a shirt and sported a leather flying jacket. He looked more military than civilian. The card that he held in front of him simply stated one name: LISA PRESTON.

The airport terminal was pretty quiet, and as Andy and Lisa entered the terminal, they spotted Jed and his out-of-place uniform instantly.

Jed had obviously done this before and whisked them and their luggage through a entrance marked PRIVATE. Ten minutes later, after Jed had introduced them to the rest of the crew, the Jetstream's engines were fired up, and the plane was allowed to taxi out onto the main runway, ready for takeoff. Lisa and Andy were left alone in the cabin, and Lisa searched for Andy's hand. The jet's high-pitched engine whistle turned to a roar as the pilot increased the engines to full power for the takeoff. Andy watched as the Forth bridges appeared on his left for a few seconds, then vanished as the jet climbed into the white billowing clouds above the capital.

The flight took just over ten hours, and Jed had to wake his sleepy passengers as the Jetstream made its final approach to Reno-Tahoe airport.

On arrival at the airport, Jed once more ushered his guests in through a side door where they were interviewed in a private room before being herded into a waiting limo.

By the time they had navigated Reno, it was late afternoon. Paul, their driver, stopped outside one of Reno's huge hotels. He turned, addressing his comments solely to Lisa. "Miss Preston, this is the accommodation that has been arranged for your legal team."

Paul then stepped out of the vehicle, opening the door open for Andy to get out. "Sir, your reservation is under Powlak Air. I believe your suite is the directors' suite. I will return for you at 7:00 p.m. as Mr. Shelton has arranged an evening meal to welcome you to Reno."

Andy Paxton and Lisa had not expected to be split up. Andy gave Lisa's knee a squeeze before stepping out onto the walkway. Paul handed Andy his case and ducked his head back inside the limo before the door closed.

"Well, that was unexpected. I will go and check out my digs. See you at dinner, 'Sue Ellen.' You better go and check out South Fork."

Lisa was giggling at the *Dallas* pun. Andy watched her power down the side window just as the limo was about to pull away.

"Well, if you are going to be my JR, you better get yourself a Stetson." Lisa blew him a kiss as the limousine pulled out into the traffic. Andy turned his attention to his hotel accommodation, checking out the outside of the large building before heading inside. The letters GSR were emblazoned on the outside walls, and once he was inside, Andy noted that this was short for Grand Sierra Resort. The young woman on the reception desk was pleasant, and when advised that a room had been booked under Powlak Air, she called on a member of staff to escort Andy and his bag up to the directors' suite.

After the opulent outside and the fancy lobby, Andy was expecting a nice room, but when Andy was left alone to wander round his accommodation, he was shocked by the size of it. Judging by the suite, Jake Shelton must have been expecting a team of lawyers for Lisa, not just him.

Andy had just decided to grab a shower to pass time while waiting on his limo to come back and was fiddling with the controls when his mobile went off, the screen showing that Lisa was calling him.

"How's the posh hotel room looking, JR? I have just been dropped off at Jan's, or should I say *my* bungalow on the outskirts of Reno. You will need to get yourself over here tomorrow. I have more pictures from the Second World War for you to look at, and I have found that I am also the proud owner of two old piles of junk in the garage."

Andy was just about to reply when the hotel phone started ringing. Andy let Lisa go, knowing he would see her shortly at supper, and he answered the hotel phone. He was surprised to find that there was a call waiting for him from Callum in the UK.

"Hello, boss. How are you getting on in the wild west? Sorry to bother you, but I have a bit of an update for you."

Andy could tell from the excitement in Cammy's voice that he had something new to add to the investigation. "OK, Sherlock, let's have it, but first, tell me how the hell you found me. I didn't even know I was coming here."

Cammy chuckled to himself at Andy's lack of faith in him as an investigator. "Andy Paxton, why did you employ me? I called Powlak, and they gave me the phone number. It's not rocket science, is it, old boy? Anyway, enough of that. I have two new pieces of information for you. I am not sure where they fit into your jigsaw puzzle, but maybe you can make more sense of them than me. Remember I said I had traced Artur Krol's brother? Well, I did a bit of digging with a Polish friend of mine, and he managed to find the Krol family in their archive. It would appear that in the confusion that surrounded the Second World War, the authorities never carried out a proper check on Artur Krol's family. I wasn't happy with what I found, so I borrowed your old RAF uniform and paid his brother a visit. It got the reaction I was expecting. The old man just about had kittens when he saw the uniform. Not the reaction you would expect from the proud brother of a war hero. More the reaction you would get from a deserter trying to hide his real identity.

"My suspicions were correct. You see, Artur Krol had no brothers or sisters in the UK. For that matter, he was an only child. The old man in Kilsyth has been living a lie since the Second World War. He is the deserter Artur Krol himself. I would bet my new company car on it.

"My second bit of information is another mind-bender. I decided that the Swiss bank PSS was probably too tough a nut to crack, so I decided to attack the problem from a different angle. I had taken a picture of the mystery jet's fuel receipt. Although it was paid for over the phone, the pilot had to physically sign for the fuel, so I thought I might be able to trace him, and I was correct. I did manage to trace him. His name is Frederick Le Combe, and he was not that hard to find.

"As I have stated previously, there is something strange going on here. Frederick Le Combe is also a fighter pilot. He served with the French Air Force before joining their much acclaimed display team, Patrouille de France. Le

Combe retired from the air force some time ago but has a one-man flying school in the South of France. I think when you get back from your American trip, a second trip to France might not be a bad thing. I don't want to call him as it will give him time to cover his tracks. We need to meet him face to face, so we can quiz him and watch his response to our arrival and questions—that is, if you want to carry on. Andy, something isn't right about this. I spoke to Dundee Airport again and the Civil Aviation Authority. Someone high up is trying to cover the tracks of this flight. There is now no record of that jet ever landing or taking off from Dundee.

"You have got to ask yourself who has the clout to pull off a stunt like that. I'm a bit worried we are going to end up at the bottom of the River Forth wearing cement shoes!"

Andy Paxton had been listening intently to Cammy's report. He had a few points to bring up but waited until Cammy was finished before responding. "How the hell did you get my spare uniform? Tell me you didn't use my name when talking to the old man!"

Callum McPherson was killing himself laughing at Andy's obvious horror at his actions. "Don't worry, mate. I kept your name out of it. By the way, if your old dear asks how the fancy-dress party went, just go with the flow. It was the only way she would have handed over your uniform. So do we keep going or call it a day?"

There was silence at the American end of the line as Andy weighed up the situation. "Cammy, brush up on your French. I don't know how long I will be here, but I am sure my mother has a few things you can be doing for her until I get back."

Andy could hear the groan at the other end of the line but ignored it.

"OK, Paxton, but hurry back. I don't know how long I can be nice to the old battle-axe."

As arranged, the limo returned and delivered Andy to Jake Shelton's ranch some 12 miles from Reno and situated at the foot of the misty mountains that were the backdrop to the Reno skyline. Andy and Lisa were wined and dined by their host, and the evening passed pleasantly, with all parties getting to find out a bit more about each other. Jake seemed to have the wrong end of the stick. He seemed to be under the illusion that because Andy had been in the Royal Air Force, he knew aircraft inside out. Andy agreed with some trepidation to join Jake the next morning for an aerial sight-seeing tour of the area. Lisa refused the opportunity to join them and instead announced to them both that she was going to visit the offices of Powlak Air. Jake had let slip to her that the sudden growth of his company had left his office team struggling to cope with the increase in paper work, in particular the military documentation, which seemed to be never ending and was threatening to bring the office to a grinding halt.

Next morning, after a call to Andy to wind him up about his impending flight with Jake, Lisa got Paul to pick her up from Jan's bungalow. Paul was Powlak Air's driver and general handyman. Lisa used the opportunity to quiz Paul about Jake and his business. Paul confirmed what Lisa already suspected—Jake Shelton was a hard but fair boss who was committed to the business that he had run since Jan had left years ago. He was single although he did have a soft spot for blondes, but when they found out that Jake showed little interest in them after the initial attraction, they left him to his aircraft business.

Paul explained as they pulled up at the Powlak offices that they had only moved into the bigger building six months ago in expectation of winning the military contract. Paul dropped Lisa at the door, handing her his card and mobile number and telling her to call him when she was ready to leave.

Lisa walked into the lobby to find the reception desk unmanned. She followed her nose to the end of the hall where she entered a large room and a scene of what could only be described as mayhem.

At the head of the office to her left, a large African American lady sat surrounded by phones. She was generally trying to organize chaos. Six women of various ages were fighting their ways through mounds of paper work stacked on the floor by their desks, while all around the office, cardboard boxes lay, some open and unpacked, others still sealed. Lisa could see that a further room separated by a small office sat at the back of the building. Jake had not been kidding. Lisa had completed an office-management degree as part of her supervisor training for the home in Dundee, but it did not take a degree to see things needed changing.

Martha had just taken her third call in the last ten minutes from Jake's foreman in the workshops. He was looking for job sheets for the latest shipment of aircraft parts. She was on the edge when she spotted the slim blond girl standing by the door, observing the goings-on in the office.

Martha should have been more observant, Lisa was wearing a designer suit, Jimmy Choo shoes, and a matching handbag—not the type of attire a office temp would be kitted out with, but she had other things on her mind. If this was the girl from the temp agency, she needed to get her doing something.

"Honey, don't just stand there. Did Bill from the agency send you down to look at everybody working? Pam over there will give you filing to do for her. Don't stand there, girl. Jump to it!"

Lisa was surprised at her introduction to Martha and, truth be told, a little amused at the situation. Lisa walked over to Martha, reaching to shake hands with the big woman.

"Hello, sorry. I think we have our wires crossed. I am Lisa Preston. Jake Shelton said it would be OK for me to pop in and see how things are going here."

Martha was staring at Lisa, looking her up and down without speaking. Suddenly and without warning, she turned back to her desk, speaking to Lisa as she walked away from her. "So you are the English girl. Jake did say you might appear. Feel free to look around, but don't disturb my girls. As you can see, we are very busy."

Lisa had hoped for a smoother introduction. She did not like to be dismissed like a naughty schoolgirl, and the red mist started to descend.

Lisa could feel her cheeks starting to flush as all the eyes in the office watched her follow Martha to her desk. Martha had just sat down when Lisa made her presence felt by standing in front of Martha, blocking her view of the office. Lisa looked down at the name plaque on the desk, and then addressed her full attention to Martha. Lisa kept her voice low and under control, not wanting to cause a scene on her first visit to the office.

"I feel, Martha Smith, that we need to get a few things sorted out here before we go any further. Here is a nice easy one for you to start with. I am not English. I am Scottish. Secondly, when I give someone the courtesy of my name and offer to shake hands, I expect a polite reply whether I am the office junior or your new boss. Which brings me to that very point. We need to sit down and find out what is going wrong here, so your polite cooperation would be appreciated."

Lisa watched Martha's eyes widen as she was speaking. She could tell her first attempt at speaking to Martha had not gone down well with the big woman. Martha stood up, almost hissing as she replied to Lisa.

"I have only one boss, and that's Mr. Shelton, not some jumped-up Brit who thinks she knows better than a supervisor who has worked for Powlak Air for twenty years. You are not my boss. You just inherited some shares and think you can fling your weight about. I am going to call Mr. Shelton, and then I am going to fling your ass out of my office, girl!"

Lisa put her hand on the phone to stop Martha lifting it to her ear. "By all means call Jake, but do it in the office, not here in front of your staff."

Lisa and Martha marched to the office, avoiding eye contact with the girls in the office. Lisa knew before the call was made that Martha was doomed. She did not want her to completely lose face in front of her girls.

Lisa listened to Martha put her case to Jake. Then she defiantly thrust the receiver at Lisa. Lisa put the phone to her ear, knowing what was coming. She had planned for this confrontation and was ready.

"Jesus Christ, Lisa, what are you doing? You have Martha wound up something terrible. This won't help things. I think you had better back off until we have a chat about things."

Lisa had been expecting this, but now was the time to sort it, not over drinks at dinner. "No, Jake, let's sort it now. Your office is a disaster, and it will bring down the company. A chain is only as strong as its weakest link. And as I am the major shareholder in the company, I have an interest in looking after my future, our future. You will let me sort it, or I will sell my share in the company to someone who will sort it. Jake, trust me. I have had business management training. I can do this with or without your help!"

Lisa waited for Jake's reply, but only a low groan came from the other end of the line. Eventually, Jake answered. "OK, Lisa, you win. Put Martha back on the line, will you?"

Lisa watched Martha's face as she was told in no uncertain terms who was now in charge of things in the office. Martha hung up without saying a word, but before she left the office, Lisa stopped her.

"Martha, I am sure in the back of your mind you are thinking of leaving. No one likes handing over a job, so please, before you decide on your future here with Powlak Air, hear what I have to say.

"This is no witch hunt. I need you to keep doing what you have been doing for the company for years. I would like you to handle the non-military side of the business. I know from what Jake has told me you know it like the back of your hand. I would like you to take four of the girls and concentrate on that side of the business. You can take the other room and pick your four staff. For the moment, I will concentrate on the military side with the two other girls. Do we have a deal?"

Lisa once again held out her hand for Martha Smith to shake on the deal. Lisa had her fingers crossed that Martha would agree to help. The last thing she wanted to tell Jake Shelton was that the first thing she had done was lose his longest-serving member of staff on the first day of her re-shuffle. Martha looked at Lisa's hand, eventually shaking it unenthusiastically.

"You do know you will never be able to run the military side with only two people, young lady."

Lisa nodded at her new supervisor. "I know, Martha. I am just about to get on the phone and sort that out hopefully. Young lady is OK, by the way, but I would rather you called me Lisa."

Lisa called a contact number at the Pentagon who in turn put her in contact with Major Tim Harper of the DMAG unit. DMAG was short for the US Air Force Depot Maintenance Activity Group. Lisa's conversation with Major Harper proved fruitful. Lisa needed staff who were familiar with US military paper work, and the DMAG group was the perfect place to look. Major Harper had a number of staff who were coming to the end of their terms with the military and were looking for jobs in civvy street. Lisa arranged for two of Harper's demob staff to attend Powlak Air the next day for interviews. Lisa picked up Paul the driver's card and called him. To his dismay, it was not to pick up Lisa. Instead he had been summoned to come and help move paper work to the appropriate offices.

Jake Shelton arrived at the offices with his co-pilot for the day, Andy Paxton, in tow. Jake was almost frightened to enter the office. He feared the worst.

Martha had vanished from her preferred position at the head of the office. Instead he found Lisa hovering over two of the staff, while in the background, he could see Martha in the office on the phone, while four girls worked in what used to be his boardroom. The clutter had almost vanished, all but some neatly stacked boxes in the corner, and these were being moved by his driver, Paul.

The mayhem that he had become accustomed to when he entered the office was gone, and in its place was a calm he had not seen since the military contracts had arrived. Lisa spotted the new arrivals and walked over to them, smiling at the expression on Jake's face.

"Hello, guys. I hope you have come to take me to dinner. I could eat a horse. We are just about to pack up for the night. What do you think, Jake?"

Jake was still busy looking at Paul and his boardroom. "Lisa, they did tell you that is my boardroom you have stolen. I mean, where are we going to have our big meetings now?"

Lisa waved as a couple of the girls slipped away for the evening. "Jake, if you don't get your accounts sorted out, the only meetings you will be having will be with the banks, and I am sure they will supply the offices. Come on. I am ready for supper. Let's talk over some food. I am starving."

Lisa said her good-nights to Martha and the rest of the remaining girls, leaving Martha to shut up for the evening. Jake headed for a good steakhouse, and since he was a regular, he was welcomed in by the headwaiter. They were shown to his usual booth, where they ordered and were left in peace to discuss the day's goings-on. Andy was very quiet, and Lisa picked up on this almost immediately.

"Andy, you are very quiet tonight. Has the cat got your tongue?"

Before Andy could speak, Jake jumped into the conversation. "Andy may be a touch delicate this evening. I think it was the loop that put him off. Must be too much G for his RAF stomach."

Jake's humour had improved drastically since he found that Lisa had not destroyed his office. In fact, he was rather impressed by the improvement that Lisa had managed in only one day, and he guffawed at the thought of Andy's face as he performed his aerobatics. Andy wanted to reply to his host's comments, but his brain told him to shut up. He did not want to insult the man. Lisa sensed Andy's mood and waded in before Andy could put his foot in it.

"I thought you were taking Andy for a sight-seeing tour of the area, not trying to kill him in a stunt plane. Jake, he is a lawyer, and he was a lawyer in the RAF, so no wonder he isn't saying much. Do you think you will be able to manage your steak, Andy?"

Andy nodded and winked at Lisa to let her know he was fine and just holding his tongue for the moment.

Lisa decided it would be safer to change the subject. She moved on to a subject closer to her heart. "Jake, I called the Pentagon today and got put in touch with a nice gentleman called Tim Harper. He is flying two members of his team to Reno tomorrow morning for job interviews. Do you think Paul can pick them up and bring them to the office?"

Jake Shelton almost swallowed his beer glass as he listened to Lisa. "What in the name of all that's holy did you think you were doing, girl? No one just phones up the Pentagon. Shit, I hope you didn't piss them off. We need the contracts. I can't go back now. I wish you had talked to me first. We are maxed out on staff. We just can't afford more people."

Lisa had half-expected Jake to pull her up, but the fact was, they badly needed help, and she was ready for him. "Jake, before you go flying off the handle, hear me out. One, employing ex-military staff strengthens the bond between us and the military. Two, we need people who work the military systems and can follow them up quickly. Your workshops, so full of new staff and equipment, were doing nothing today because your office could not figure out what needed to be done or raise worksheets for the workshop to carry out the repairs. Like I said on the phone, the weakest link—sort the office, and the rest will follow. Trust me. It will work. Increase the productivity, and we will have the extra money to pay for extra staff."

Lisa was watching Jake for any sign that hinted at what Jake was thinking of her suggestion. His brows were down, and he was purposely not making eye contact with her—not a good sign. Lisa did not want to fall out with Jake, but she knew in her heart she needed to drag Jake's office into this century before it brought down the company. She needed to do something to get Jake on board.

"OK, Jake. I hear what you are saying, but we need the staff, so we need to balance the books until the government cheques start flowing in. I want you to sell Jan's planes and his stock of engines. I would imagine that will keep an extra two staff members paid until the cash flow improves."

Jake had never contemplated this outcome, and it took him a few seconds to compute how much money Lisa was talking about sinking back into Powlak Air.

"Lisa, honey, that is a lot of cash you would be putting back into the company with nothing really to show for it. If I were you, I would take a moment to think about it."

Andy did a quick calculation in his head. He reckoned Lisa was probably suggesting pumping five million dollars back into Powlak Air, if his math was close to the mark. He watched his fellow diners, still keeping his mouth shut. This was between two company directors and really none of his business. Although his head told him he should be concerned that Lisa might be getting into things she had little knowledge of, his heart told a different story. He was very proud of the wee blonde Scottish nurse who had taken more than her fair share of knocks and was still game for a huge new challenge that had been thrust upon her with no warning. Lisa was having none of Jake's suggestion that she think about it.

"Jake, the extra money will get me my new staff and help the company, which is 60 percent mine anyway. Let's do it."

Although Jake said nothing, he was beginning to rethink his view of this new business partner who had been forced on him. Any ideas he had had that she was baggage to be tolerated were melting away. She was proving to be quite a savvy business partner. By the end of the meal, Lisa had made Jake promise he would get onto selling her inheritance as soon as possible. Although Lisa told Jake she was going to get a taxi back to the bungalow, Jake refused to let her, bundling them both into his Jeep Cherokee and heading for her house. En route to Lisa's bungalow, Jake offered to drop Andy at his hotel, but Lisa made it clear she needed Andy back at the house to go over some things that she had found. Jake had something to attend to, so he dropped off the pair, arranging to pick up Andy in an hour or so.

Lisa's first port of call was the double garage, the up-and-over door creaking into action after years of inactivity.

In the gloom of the evening, two shapes stood out from the back wall of the large garage. Lisa groped her way along the wall, searching with her hands for the light switch. Andy's eyes were just beginning to get used to the gloom when the overhead light burst into life, blinding him for a few seconds. Lisa first looked at the two dust-covered cars and then turned her recovering eyesight towards Andy who was standing just outside the garage, staring at the two filthy old machines, his mouth wide open but saying nothing. For a second, Lisa thought something was wrong. Suddenly Andy recovered his senses and walked into the garage to stand in front of the two old cars.

"There is no doubt in my mind that this is Jan's house, Lisa!"

Lisa was puzzled. She looked again at the two old cars, one of which looked as if it had played the part of Chitty Chitty Bang Bang. The other was more modern but sitting on four flat tyres. Lisa, by her own admission, knew nothing about cars and was relying on Andy to give her some idea what she should do with the old heaps. This was the reason she had brought Andy to the garage first before he immersed himself in the things Lisa had found inside the house.

"Well, Mr. Paxton, what should I do with them? Do you think Jake will know a scrap yard that can pick them up?"

To Lisa's surprise, Andy Paxton started to laugh at her suggestion as he walked round the old cars. "Remind me to show you a bit about cars some time. I am no car expert, but that one with the flat tyres is a Ferrari Dino 246 GTS, I used to have a poster of one on my bedroom wall when I was a kid, and the old one is an Alfa Romeo of some description.

It might be a 1750SS, but I am not sure, Callum would know for sure. It's old though. Pre-war. Nineteen twenties, I think."

Lisa looked over the old cars, but what Andy had said meant little to her. "Oh, well, I suppose Jake can add them to his list of things to sell."

Andy wanted to object but toned it down to a mere suggestion. "Don't sell everything of the old boy's, or you will have nothing to remind you of him."

Lisa shrugged her shoulders without saying anything and led Andy through the adjoining door from the garage into the house. Andy looked around the living room but found little of interest. Jan had obviously had little time for home comforts. His house was sparsely furnished. Jan's idea of decoration was a row of different types of heavy machine-gun bullets, presumably from the guns of the Spitfires, Hurricanes, and Mustangs he had worked on in the war years. They stood up on end from one side of the large fireplace to the other, looking almost like a row of metal teeth. The decor was pure seventies and showed nothing of the wealth the old man had accrued over the years. Andy smiled to himself as he checked out Jan's deep shag-pile khaki-green carpet in the living room and lemon-and-gold-striped curtains held back with khaki tiebacks. Andy decided that Jan must have been a bachelor—no wife would have allowed that colour scheme in her house. Andy reckoned Jan had picked it because it reminded him of his beloved warplanes. Andy wandered into the dining room where Lisa had stopped. On the dining room table were a number of photographs that Lisa was poring over, rearranging their positions while she waited for Andy to finish his one-man tour of the house and join her at the dining-room table.

Lisa said nothing as Andy joined her, and together they gazed at Jan Powlak's memories captured in black and white. More than a few of them portrayed the same young woman who was present in the pictures that Andy had rescued from the nursing home and then again from the RAF.

One picture in particular struck Andy. It portrayed the girl, presumably Jean Bruce, reclined on a deck chair in glorious sunny weather in front of the dispatch building. She was decked out in full flying gear and surrounded by her fellow aircrew. Although it seemed to have been taken in a rare moment of peace, away from the horrors of air combat, the pale face of the young girl said it all. Her haunting eyes stared at the camera lens and showed the incredible stress she must have been under. Every sinew of muscle seemed ready to respond to the next squadron scramble that surely must come. Another picture that caught Andy's eye was Jean standing like a naughty schoolgirl while Jan inspected the damage inflicted to the tail flaps of her Hurricane, turned to Swiss cheese by the guns of an unknown enemy. The last picture on the table was probably the most chilling of all. It was of the operational readiness board displayed in one of the hangars. It listed the operational status of the flight crews and the status of their aircrafts on that particular day. Andy noted that five pilots' names had a line through them, three followed by the letters MIA and two with KIA. A further three aircraft were scored out and marked as unserviceable. Andy noted that one of these belonged to Tygrysek. It looked to Andy like Baby Tiger had had a busy day at the office, and 303 Squadron had taken a pounding that day.

Although the pictures had been taken decades ago, looking at them caused a sense of atmosphere in the quiet dining room. For some reason, Andy could almost feel Jan looking over their shoulders as they studied his pictures. Lisa sensed that the old photos had struck home with Andy and quietly slipped her hand into his.

Lisa whispered quietly, "MIA and KIA mean missing in action and killed in action, am I right?"

Andy nodded without speaking, still caught in the spell the pictures had cast over them. Lisa squeezed his hand, turning her eyes away from the pictures and looking at Andy.

"She must have been a very brave woman, don't you think?"

Andy nodded again, this time dragging his eyes away from the pictures. "Yes, she was a brave person. They all were. They put their lives on the line day after day to ensure Adolf Hitler's plans for Great Britain never came to fruition. For the first time, his mighty Luftwaffe was defeated and Hitler was forced to cancel his invasion plan—the proudest moment in RAF history. Why is it so hard for them to admit they got a helping hand from a wee Scottish lassie with a fire in her belly? It's a decision taken by short-sighted bigots using red tape to cover their tracks and hide the truth. I can't let what we have discovered be lost. Call me an idiot, but I need to find out if Jean Bruce is still alive. I need to tell her story, so Jan can rest in peace. I know until the matter is resolved, I will have no peace knowing I gave Jan my word."

Lisa was starting to read Andy better, and she knew that look. She was worried he might do something stupid and end up needing a lawyer rather than being a lawyer. Lisa took his hand, leading him into the kitchen and away from the old pictures in an attempt to take his mind off the matter for the moment.

"Andy, promise me that before you do anything regarding Jan's story you will run it past your mother. To you she is maybe just your mum, but she is a smart cookie. I know she won't let you get into any legal trouble. Come on. I need to hear you promise me."

Andy could tell that Lisa was worked up about it for some reason and used it to tease her. "So what's it worth, Matron?"

Lisa pushed Andy in mock disgust against the kitchen worktop. Andy had expected a slap for his matron comment but was pleasantly surprised when Lisa kissed him gently on the lips, then pulled away before Andy could continue the embrace.

Lisa had a wickedly seductive smile on her face as she moved to the far side of the kitchen. "Andrew Paxton, I would be more worried about what you won't get if you don't promise me. Enough said?"

Andy was about to answer Lisa when the kitchen door opened, and the large frame of Jake Shelton filled the doorway.

"Evening, folks. Lisa, honey, I have just sold your planes and all the spares to a friend of mine who has been after them for years, so go ahead with your staff and anything else you can think of that is needed."

Lisa turned her full attention to Jake, walking past him and out into the garage. "Jake, do you think you could do the same with these old wrecks? No point in them sitting here any longer gathering dust. If we can turn them into some cash for the company, so be it."

Lisa was not expecting what happened next. Andy marched into the garage standing between Jake and Lisa. "No, this isn't right. Lisa, you have gone too far this time. If you sell everything the old man worked for, pretty soon his memory will vanish. The only thing left will be his name over some corporate monster that bears no resemblance to anything Jan Powlak stood for."

Andy turned to Jake pleadingly. "Surely, Jake, you knew the man better than both of us. Am I not correct? We need to keep some of the things the old man treasured."

Andy Paxton avoided looking at Lisa, instead turning his attention to Jake Shelton. Jake was treading on egg-shells, but he could see both parties were expecting him to adjudicate on the matter at hand.

In his heart, Jake knew Andy was right, but Jake had little time for his heart where his business was concerned. He needed to keep Lisa sweet, and if that meant making a deal with the devil, so be it.

"I hate to say it, Andy, but Lisa gets my vote. No point hanging onto old relics when the money could be spent strengthening the company Jake founded. Sorry, son."

Andy Paxton needed to get out before he said some-thing he regretted, so before anyone could object, Andy walked out of the open garage door, heading in the general direction of his hotel.

Lisa was about to chase after him, but Jake stopped her.

"Leave it be, honey. Sometimes a bit of space isn't a bad thing, I am just about to leave. I will have a word with Andy and drop him at his hotel. You had better get some shut eye if you are interviewing in the morning. I will get Jan's old cars sorted for you. Sweet dreams, honey. Paul will pick you up in the morning ad then head to the airport to pick up the people for the interview."

Jake gunned his Jeep down the road in the direction he had seen Andy take, finding him on the sidewalk ten minutes from Lisa's house.

Andy had calmed down a little and accepted a lift from Jake without needing too much persuasion. Jake decided to take the bull by the horns before Andy started on him again.

"Andy, hear me out before you lose it again. I understand where you are coming from, but Lisa is the major shareholder, and if you think you are having a hard time, buddy, you ain't seen nothin. Put yourself in my shoes. I have been running things for years, and now a little Brit nurse is calling the shots. I have had to change the way I look at things, but you know, so far she has been right. So for the moment at least, I will do what Lisa needs done. You should too, son. Doesn't take a NASA scientist to see the girl is sweet on you. Don't be an asshole and screw it up for yourself. You could do much worse than dating a pretty little blond billionaire."

Andy knew Jake was correct, but if things were to work between Lisa and himself, there would need to be more than just looks and money. Andy decided that if Jake was in a say-it-like-it-is mood, he was going to have a few searching questions of his own for the big American. There was one question that had been floating around in Andy's head since they had first met Jake Shelton.

"Point taken, Jake. As we are putting our cards on the table, answer me a couple of questions. Did you ask Jan's lawyers to discredit Lisa professionally to try and get her to drop her claim on her inheritance?"

Jake took a deep breath before replying. "Son, business is business. I may have nudged them in that direction, but that is water under the bridge. We are a team now, for better or worse."

Andy nodded and went onto his second question. "Jake, you said a few seconds ago, and I quote, 'Lisa is a pretty little blond billionaire.' How much is Powlak Air worth, and none of that horseshit you spouted back in Scotland."

Jake rubbed his chin as he pulled up outside Andy Paxton's hotel. "When I first met Lisa, I didn't want to tell her the truth, not all of it anyway. I was telling the truth when I said all I could offer was five million for her share. I was maxed out on my credit, and that is all I could get my hands on.

"What I neglected to mention was that the aerospace company that lost the military contract to us approached me the day after the contract was signed and offered six point nine billion dollars for the entire business." The big man shook his head and chuckled. "Any sane person would have jumped at the offer, but I hated the way they just thought they could whore me out of the game. It gave me huge satisfaction to tell them to stick the money and watch their reaction as someone flung their billions of dollars back in there smug faces.

"I was worried that Lisa would do a deal with them and freeze me out. Andy, let me tell you. I now know that will never happen. I have been studying her. She has the bug. I would bet my last buck that if they approached her, they would get the same result as I gave them. She wants Powlak Air to succeed. Hell there is more chance of her trying to buy me out than of her selling me out.

"As for Jan's legacy, leave that with me for the moment. I know a dealer in Vegas who will buy the vintage Alfa Romeo. The Dino I will leave at the office for the moment. It was Jan's guilty pleasure. I am with you when it comes to that car. I can still see Jan running about in it yet. It was his baby. We will see if we can talk Lisa into sparing the Ferrari, you get some shut eye and I will see you tomorrow."

Lisa was up early the next morning. Showered and fed, she sat waiting for Paul to pick her up. From the moment she got up, she had wanted to call Andy but resisted the temptation, hoping that he would call her. She had been feeling slightly guilty since waking up. Andy was probably right—the company was not in a bad way. There was really no need to get rid of all Jan's things.

She went over her reasoning in her head. She would never use the old cars or the planes for that matter, so why have them clutter up a garage that could be put to good use? It was silly that she and Andy had fallen out over such a trivial matter. No, she would wait on Andy calling her.

Andy had woken early and tossed and turned before deciding he could sleep no more. He needed to clear his head. He left the hotel before seven with no real idea where he was going. His lack of boxing training was showing, and he decided that he would go for a run to help his fitness levels. Andy pointed his nose towards one of the hills in the distance. Using this as a focal point, he set off at a slow, steady pace, crossing a few roads but steadily working his way out of civilisation and towards the country. Finally, he found himself on a dusty trail that wound its way towards the distant mountains. Andy had wanted to call Lisa and apologise for his behaviour last night, but his stubborn nature had stopped him from calling. He wanted to be in a better frame of mind before he called her.

Deep down, Andy Paxton knew what was bothering him, but he did not want to admit it to himself. He wondered what Cammy was getting up to back in Scotland. He smiled to himself as he pictured Cammy being bossed about by his mother. Andy's brain wandered as he ran. Things had turned upside down in his life in the last six months. He had lost his job, been knocked out in the ring, and found a girl whom he had real feelings for, not to mention finding out from an old man that history was wrong and needed to be rewritten.

Andy had been running for four hours when he came across an old shack by the side of the dirt track he had been following.

Andy stopped, giving himself a minute to catch his breath. He had helped himself to a few bottles of mineral water from the hotel bar, and now he gulped down two greedily. It was then that he noticed the man watching him from the back of the old wooden shack.

Andy shouted a welcome to the old man, who made his way out to the roadside to size up his unexpected guest.

"Good day, young man, are you lost? Ain't no one comes out this way unless they are lost."

Andy extended his hand and shook hands with the old guy. "I hope I haven't disturbed you, sir. No, I'm not lost. I just needed to go for a run and followed the track here. I am Andy Paxton. Nice to meet you."

The old man broke into a smile as he shook hands with Andy. "The name's Isaac, Isaac Beddam. Can't be too sure these days. Lots of undesirables wandering about. Follow me round to the backyard. I have some cold lemonade for you. Better than that bottled horse piss you are drinking there."

Isaac's backyard was guarded by Zara, a huge, pure-black German shepherd who eyed Andy up and down before returning to her resting position, safe in the knowledge her master had allowed the arrival of the stranger in her yard.

Propped up against the wall of the shack was a pump-action shotgun, presumably left there just in case Andy was not a friendly.

"Forgive the hardware, son, but thirty years in the Reno police department makes you careful and probably a bit paranoid, truth be told."

Isaac ambled across to his Chevy pickup truck, sliding the shotgun behind the driver's seat before returning to Andy via Zara to give her a pat on the head.

Andy watched as the old man readjusted his baggy jeans, pulling them up as he walked. He sat down next to Andy, filling two tall glasses with cloudy lemonade from a large condensation-covered pitcher.

"Nice to have a guest with us, ain't that right, Zara? Usually I just enjoy my own company. Been quiet out here the last couple of years since my wife passed away. Have got out of the way of conversation. So what are you running for, son? Is it a fitness thing, or do you have something on your mind? In my experience, that's usually the case. You don't look like no tourist either. What brings you to Reno?"

Andy took a sip of the ice-cold lemonade. Its bitter-sweet flavour awakened his taste buds, and he took another mouthful before replying.

"Wow, now that is how you make proper lemonade. The running thing is a bit of both. I am a bit of an amateur boxer and haven't trained for a while, and I am here on business at Powlak Air, so I have a few things going through my head."

Isaac studied his boots for a few seconds before continuing his gentle interrogation of Andy. "Powlak Air, Powlak Air...of course. Jan the Ferrari man! Ain't seen that old buzzard in years. Is he still kicking about in that red Ferrari?"

Andy was amazed he had stumbled on someone who knew Jan. "No, sadly, that is why I am here. Jan passed away a short time ago in Scotland and left his share of the company to my friend, my girlfriend, so here I am drinking lemonade in Reno. Strange old world, isn't it? Andy stared into the distance, he wondered what Lisa was up too"

Lisa's interviewees arrived from the airport around eleven, and after coffee, Lisa took the first candidate into Martha's office.

Anne Marie Harper was her name, and via a few searching questions, Lisa found out that she was the daughter of Major Tim Harper, the person she had contacted at the Pentagon. Anne Marie did not seem to be particularly bothered about the interview but after a bit of interrogation, Lisa discovered the girl had wanted to take a year out and visit Europe before continuing with her career. It had been her father who had talked her into the job interview.

Lisa was not slow to realise that a connection like this to a serving officer in the Pentagon could be good for Powlak Air and went about trying to change Anne Marie's mind on taking a year out. It took a bit of goal-post changing, but eventually Lisa achieved her target.

She hired Anne Marie to be the new military-operations supervisor. She would stay with Lisa in Jan's old house until she found her own place. Lisa had doubled her salary to get her, and the only way she could justify it was to make her a supervisor.

Lisa's second candidate was a middle-aged man called Chris. He had served in the military all his working life and had decided it was time for a change.

Lisa's most important question was whether Chris would have a problem working with Anne Marie as his supervisor.

He seemed OK with the idea although they both knew he was far more qualified to fill the supervisor post.

Lisa spoke to her two new arrivals, arranging a working lunch with them both before introducing them to the team in the afternoon. While Paul was summoned to take them to lunch, Lisa gave into the thing that had been at the back of her mind all morning and called Andy's number. To her bitter disappointment, the call went straight to his answer machine. He obviously didn't want to speak to her.

Paul delivered the trio to a newly opened restaurant that had been spoken highly of and advised Lisa to call when she needed to be picked up.

Over lunch, the three of them devised an operating system that would sort Powlak Air's weak links in the chain of command. Anne Marie and Chris would gather the repair orders from the various air bases and pass them to the two girls already in the team to dispatch the work orders to the workshops. The two girls would then collect the finished job sheets and total the invoice before passing it back to Anne Marie and Chris for them to pass to the military for payment. Anne Marie would be responsible for making sure the invoices had been paid to Powlak Air. Lisa was particularly happy that Anne Marie would be in charge of payments as she knew if she were having problems, she had her father on the inside to help unpick the logjam. It had also become apparent in the conversation that there was a military-software application that would make life much easier for them all. Before Lisa could ask the question, Anne Marie volunteered to call her father and ask if it could be given to a civilian contractor to speed up the process. All in all, the morning had been a huge success, but to Lisa, it didn't feel like it. Lisa excused herself from the table. First, she called Andy's number again to find it still diverting to his answer phone. Lisa hung up without leaving a message. Then she called Paul and asked him to pick them up and take them back to the office.

Back at the office, Lisa introduced the new pair and laid out the plan they'd discussed over lunch. It was late afternoon before she tried Andy again and then, in a fit of frustration, called Paul and asked him to go and find Andy and bring him to Jan's place. Lisa excused herself for the day, telling Paul to find Anne Marie and Chris a hotel for the night and to drop them off after (and only after) he had delivered Andy to Jan's house.

This done, Lisa called a cab and headed home. If she was going to straighten things out with Andy, she wanted to do it in private, not at the office.

Isaac Beddam had offered to give Andy a lift back into town, but although in the short time Andy had spent with the old man, he had come to like him, Andy refused. He needed to sort things out in his head, and Isaac giving him a lift would only serve as a distraction. Andy said his goodbyes to the old man and started back on his long trip towards Reno and a hard decision he knew he had to make.

Andy had to admit to himself that he had misjudged the distance he had covered in the morning. The last couple of miles to the hotel he ran on empty tanks, but his head was sorted. He knew what he must do and was determined to go ahead with it although most people would say he was mad.

In the lobby of the hotel, he met Paul the driver who told him that Lisa wanted to meet him at her house. Andy was open to the idea but informed Paul he needed to shower and change. Paul was dispatched to the lounge and plied with coffee and newspapers while he waited for Andy's return.

Lisa paced up and down, uncertain how to handle Andy when he arrived. She wanted to clear the air between them, but she did not want to fuel an argument. She was very conscious that since their paths had crossed, they had been close friends with no bad feelings between them. Lisa passed the time by giving Jake a call to tell him how things had gone at the office today.

Jake was missing in action, apparently out on the workshop floor, sorting some piece of broken equipment. Lisa left a message with Carol, Jake's PA, and returned to pacing up and down waiting on Andy's arrival.

Lisa's plan of a quiet chat with Andy fell at the first hurdle as both Jake and Andy arrived at precisely the same time. Jake was the first to speak. "Well, if it isn't Andy? We need to stop meeting like this, son. People will start talking. Lisa, my girl, I hear you pulled another rabbit out of the bag. Girl, you are proving to be full of good surprises. Get you coat on. I am taking you both out for dinner, and it's going to be a double celebration as I sold that old Alfa over the phone for half a million dollars. Turns out the dealer knew Jan and the car."

Lisa was shocked by Jake's statement. "I can't believe that dusty old thing is worth that much money. Listen, guys. I have had a busy day. Would you mind if I gave it a miss tonight?"

Andy Paxton said nothing, but Jake Shelton was having none of it. "I wouldn't mind, but the chef at Le Grande might be unhappy. I have booked our table. Now get your coat on, young lady, or we will be late. Come on, Andy. Has the cat got your tongue tonight, buddy? Tell her, son. Life is for living. You're a long time dead, young lady. Enjoy it while you can."

Reluctantly, Lisa gave in and followed them both out to Jake's Jeep, where Andy held the door open for her to climb in the back. He then joined Jake in the front, leaving Lisa sitting by herself while Jake chauffeured them to Le Grande for dinner. Jake did all the talking while his two companions said nothing, both far away in their own thoughts.

Lisa had secretly wanted Andy to get in the back beside her. She wanted to hold his hand to reassure herself they were still OK as an item.

As the meal progressed, Andy tried to find the right time to speak, but it never seemed appropriate. Lisa had been watching him closely and knew something was up. It was Jake who gave Andy the opportunity he had been waiting for.

"Andy, I was thinking of loading the old Ferrari on a trailer tomorrow and getting it out of Lisa's hair. How about giving me a hand to move it?"

At first, Andy was like a rabbit caught in the headlights. His time had come, and he wasn't ready for it. "Guys I went for a run today to clear my head, and I have decided that it is time for me to head home. Please, before you guys say anything, hear me out. Lisa is busy with her new project, and truth be told, there is nothing here for a British lawyer to do. I have just started a new business, and I have a few things in Europe to tie up. I am booked on a BA flight early tomorrow morning. I am sure Paul can take my place moving the Dino."

Jake wasn't sure what to say but looked across at Lisa who had gone chalk white. Lisa felt as if she had been struck by lightening. She had been so busy with the office, she had not seen this coming, and it took the wind out of her sails. All three had lost their appetites, and Jake drove them home in silence, pulling up at Andy's hotel first. Lisa jumped out as the Jeep stopped, telling Jake she would find her own way home. Jake put up little argument to this, glad to be free of the silence that had enveloped the Jeep on the way to the hotel.

The pair watched Jake leave before Lisa broke the silence. "It would have been nice to have been kept in the loop. You certainly know how to ruin a meal. What time do you fly tomorrow?"

Andy could sense the anger in Lisa's voice and was unsure what he could say that would defuse the situation. "I need to be at the airport for 8:30 a.m. Would you like to come up for a coffee? I need to talk to you before I go."

Lisa's temper boiled over. She could hold back her feelings no longer. "Oh, so you want to talk now, do you? After you decided what you were doing? Nice of you to let me know. It would have been nice, from a girlfriend's point of view, to have had some input into your decision."

Lisa had started to sob but continued with her reprimand. "I didn't expect that from you. It's the act of a selfish bastard, not a boyfriend."

Lisa had had enough and ran to a taxi stand at the entrance of the car park. Andy shouted after her, but she paid him no heed, looking away as the taxi passed him on the sidewalk.

Andy had known he was going to have a tough time with Lisa, but he had not expected so severe a reaction. She had succeeded in making him feel like a scumbag for leaving, but he had made up his mind, and nothing was going to change that. Dejectedly, he headed for his room to pack and get ready to leave in the morning.

Lisa had just about managed to hold it together in the cab. Only the occasional tear escaping down her flushed cheeks gave away her state of mind.

One hour later, Lisa sat in her bed. She had just drained the last drops from a bottle of white wine and was in no mood for sleep. Her head was spinning, but it wasn't the wine. Although her anger had subsided slightly, it had left an ache that would not go away. Lisa kept asking herself if she had caused the situation by her headlong charge into the management side of Powlak Air.

She had not noticed Andy's mood change until it was too late. She knew perfectly well that Andy's mood and stubborn nature were to blame just as much as her mishandling of the situation, but it did not help the empty feeling she had inside.

Lisa did not want to be here all alone. Now that Andy was gone, she wanted his company more than ever. She had all the money she would ever need, but at that moment, the thing that she wanted most, money couldn't buy.

Something in her head told her to sort it right then or risk losing Andy for good. Lisa sprang into action, calling a cab and then heading for the shower before applying make-up while she waited for the cab to arrive.

Her mind was wandering as the doorbell rang to announce the arrival of the cab. Lisa gave the mirror a quick check to make sure her makeup was perfect before flinging on a raincoat and flat shoes.

Andy Paxton had finished packing some time ago and was watching his curtains gently sway from side to side as the air conditioning moved them. He could not sleep. His stomach was churning. He knew he had made a bad mistake not talking to Lisa before making his decision, but it was too late now. All he could do was try to call Lisa when he got home and apologise to her.

Andy just about jumped out of his skin when the doorbell went off. He had organised an early-morning call, but surely, this wasn't a member of staff at this time of night.

Andy opened the door cautiously to find Lisa standing there. His heart leapt when he saw who it was, and he had trouble keeping his delight hidden from her. Before Andy could say anything, Lisa got in first. "I need to know one thing, Andy, and don't lie to me. Does you going back to Scotland mean that we are finished as a couple?"

Andy wanted to scream "No!" at the top of his voice but managed to contain himself. "Never, Lisa. I only wanted to give you a bit of space. I could see how seriously you were taking sorting out the Powlak office. I misjudged things, and I upset you, and I am truly sorry. I can cancel the flight and help Jake tomorrow. Just say the word."

Andy stood like a condemned man before the judge, waiting on his sentence. Lisa thrust her hands into the pockets of her raincoat, clearly deep in thought but making no attempt to enter the room. While Andy waited on her decision, which to him seemed to be taking an eternity, he studied Lisa. He had only missed her for hours, but she looked stunning. Her hair had just been washed and glowed like silk. Her makeup, although slightly heavier than usual, was still expertly applied, and she had almost a glow about her.

"No, Andy, I think you are right. You should head home. You have a new business to get going, and I am holding you back."

Andy's heart started to sink, and he could not keep the despair from showing. Lisa was telling him to get on his bike, and he deserved it for treating her so badly.

"There is one last thing before you go that I would like to sort out if we are still going to be dating."

Lisa walked past Andy into the room without being invited. She turned in the middle of the room to face Andy and unbelted the raincoat, letting it drop to the floor. She was completely naked save her shoes, which she kicked off. Then she walked past Andy, who had been struck dumb by the insanity of the situation.

"Andy, I would shut the door if I were you. It's not a spectator sport, you know!"

Lisa strolled into Andy's bedroom, climbing into bed as Andy reached the bedroom door. "Lisa what the hell? Have you been taking drugs?"

Lisa smiled seductively as she tucked herself into the bed. "Andy, just shut up and make love to me, for god's sake. I would like to think that little show was enough of a hint, don't you think?"

Daylight streamed through the curtains as morning fast approached, but neither Lisa nor Andy had slept a wink. Both were drenched in sweat, and Lisa had curled up in a ball, wrapped tightly in Andy's arms. A beautiful calmness had finally descended on the pair after a frantic night of passion. The sound of Andy's early alarm call broke the spell around the pair as Andy crawled across the bed to reach the phone and acknowledge the call.

Lisa would have tagged along to the airport to say goodbye to Andy, but her lack of clothing made her rethink her situation. Lisa called Paul to come and pick her up from the hotel, then joined Andy in the shower for a last embrace before her chauffer arrived to take her home.

Andy promised to call her as soon as he got home, but there was little time left for chatting as Andy's taxi was waiting, and he was running late.

Lisa found Paul waiting for her in the lobby. He wore a smirk that said he knew what she had been up to.

"Hello, Paul. Thanks for picking me up. Can you drop me off at the house and then wait until I change for work? By the way, just to set the record straight in case you were wondering, yes, I am sleeping with my lawyer. He also happens to be my boyfriend."

This caught Paul completely off guard, and he stuttered a reply, falling in behind Lisa as she marched out of the hotel lobby heading for the car.

Twenty minutes into the flight, Andy fell fast asleep. His marathon jogging session combined with his marathon bedroom session and no sleep had taken their toll on him, and he was dead to the world.

CHAPTER 11
ROAD TRIP

On arrival at Edinburgh Airport, Andy found Cammy waiting by the baggage carousel for his arrival.

"Boy, you look like you had the flight from hell, old son. Let's get you home to Mommy. With any luck, it will take the heat off me. She had me doing bloody filing yesterday. Thank god you are back, my friend."

On the way home, Andy gave Callum a rundown on the events that had taken place in Reno, leaving out the falling out between himself and Lisa and the consequent making up last night. Andy informed Cammy about the two old cars that Lisa had found in her garage and almost had to grab the steering wheel as Callum almost crashed the car when he found out Lisa had just about put an original Ferrari Dino to the skip. It was the mention of the old photos that brought Cammy back to his senses regarding the Jan Powlak situation.

"Bloody hell, Andy, I almost forgot to tell you the new bit of information I have managed to unearth for you." Cammy delayed telling Andy as he negotiated around a wide load on the motorway. "OK, the Frederick Le Combe guy that I traced from his signature on the fuel receipt? I did a bit more digging, and I have found a bit more about his location.

"Le Combe is usually based at Bourg-Ceyzériat airfield on the outskirts of the French town of Bourg-en-Bresse near the Swiss border. His Cessna aircraft is registered to that airfield. I think this should be our first port of call when the investigation team of Paxton and Paxton hit the streets of France."

Andy Paxton sat quietly thinking things through before passing comment on Cammy's latest piece of information.

"OK, Cammy, this is what I want you to do. Get a travel plan together for us, but don't book anything tonight. I need to run it by my mother and Lisa before we vanish into Europe. Take the car back to your house, and I will drop you off."

Cammy was grinning from ear to ear at Andy's suggestion. "No, mate, I take it your mother hasn't spoken to you lately. You can drop me off at our office in Stirling. While you were away living the high life in America, your mother has been busy. Why do you think I have been filing and moving furniture all week? I was hired as an investigator, mate, not bloody Pickfords!"

Andy chuckled away to himself while Cammy negotiated the motorway off-ramp for Stirling. He had wanted to get home for a sleep, but Cammy's revelation had changed his mind. Now he wanted to have a look at his new working environment.

Five minutes later, Cammy pulled up outside a smart-looking modern office block on the Castle business park on the outskirts of Stirling. Cammy showed him round the office then left, leaving Andy to shut up and promising to get back to him tomorrow with his travel plan to their French destination. Andy watched as Cammy headed away on his motorbike before reaching for the office phone.

Andy called his mother, who had just left a meeting in London and was on her way back to her hotel. Andy explained that he was taking Cammy over to France for probably a week or so. To Andy's relief, his mother didn't put up too much of a fight, only telling him to be careful, Andy said his good-byes then decided on one last call before heading for home and bed.

It had only been a day since Andy left, but Lisa was already missing him badly. She was daydreaming when her mobile phone started to vibrate in her pocket. Her heart missed a beat when she read Andy's name on the incoming-calls screen.

"Hello, Matron. Just checking in to let you know I got back OK. How is the Powlak-Preston business empire getting on?"

Lisa was so glad to hear his voice, she decided not to scold him for yet again winding her up. "Nothing much to tell you, but it's good to hear your voice. What has Cammy been up to, left to his own devices?"

Andy had planned to break it gently to Lisa that he was heading to Europe, but her searching question had left him no option but to bring up the subject now.

"Cammy has traced the pilot of the plane who landed at Dundee Airport to a little airfield in France, so Cammy and I are making plans to head over there to see if we can find out anything from him about his passenger that day. It is a pity you are so busy. A few days in France would be so much nicer if you were with me."

It was a spur of the moment thing, but it was out before Lisa could stop herself. "You're on. Give me a week until the office gels and we get our first return payments from the government, and I will join you on your detective trip. How does that sound?"

Andy was dead on his feet, but this bit of good news woke him up and changed his mood instantly. He had been worried that it might be months until he saw his girl again, but now, with a bit of luck, he would see her next week.

"Way to go, Lisa! Cammy is arranging everything as we speak, so when I get the details, maybe Jake will let you use the company jet to meet us at some point along the route."

Lisa was bouncing up and down with excitement at the thought of the impending trip. "There will be no maybes about it! I will be taking the company jet, and Jake will just have to like it. Call me the minute you get the details, and I will put things in motion at this end. I can't wait. Paris is so romantic. We need to stop in Paris. We will stop in Paris. Tell Cammy to put that on his list of things to organize."

Lisa wanted to talk more, but Andy's jet lag had returned, and he needed his bed badly.

The next morning Andy awoke to hear voices coming from the kitchen. Pulling some clothes on, he made his way there to find his father and Cammy in deep discussion about the merits of golf buggies on a golf course. The discussion came to an abrupt stop on Andy's arrival in the kitchen.

"Hi, Dad. Long time no see. How are you doing?"

Andy's father was a tall, silver-haired gentleman whose looks had started to fade slightly, mainly due to his activities at the nineteenth hole at many of his local clubs. Andy could tell looking at him that he was having to hold back his real feelings. His face had flushed, and it now matched his nose, which was red from drinking too much.

"So you bailed out of the RAF without discussing it with your old dad. Going to work with your mother and dragging this poor chap with you? Frying pan into the fire, lad, mark my words. Let me tell you, working with your mother will be hard work, son. I know. I have the T-shirt!"

Andy had expected worse from his father. Obviously his mother had told him to lay off. Andy knew how much it would have hurt his father's feelings, and he had taken this into account before throwing in the towel.

James Paxton, or to give him his full title, Squadron Leader Paxton, had been based at Leuchars Airbase in Fife until he retired. He had been instrumental in shaping Andy's career path since Andy left school.

Andy was acutely aware that it was a massive slap in the face to his father that his son had dropped out of the service at such an early stage in his career. Callum could sense the tension between the two and, for once, kept his mouth firmly shut.

James Paxton had said his bit and decided in the interest of family relations it was time for him to head for the Muckhart golf club and the company of his golfing buddies.

Andy watched the Volvo leave the drive before flicking on the kettle and joining Callum at the kitchen table.

"You do know your father is still ragging with you for leaving his beloved air force, mate."

"Oh, yes, I think that one will take him a long time to forgive me for. Right. More to the point, how are the French plans looking? Have you got things lined up?"

Andy could tell from Cammy's face that he had once again jumped the gun but waited for him to lay out what he had sorted.

"You know how you said not to do anything yet? Well, I might have bent the rules on that slightly, mate."

Andy sighed, shaking his head. He should have known better. When it came to Cammy, it usually ended up being a white-knuckle ride. "OK, I am bracing myself. What have you done this time?"

Cammy leaned across to pat Andy's back as he started explaining his plan. "OK, we fly to Bristol. I found a company in Bristol that rents fully restored Volkswagen Doormobiles. We pick that up, then head for Portsmouth and then Cherbourg. I have plotted us a course across France, mate. It will be magic! We leave tomorrow morning. Seriously, mate, this will be brilliant!"

Andy's first reaction was to laugh. Cammy had to be kidding. "Tell me you are joking. You haven't booked any of this nonsense, have you?"

Andy's rebuff took the wind out of Cammy's sails. "Yeah, kind of, well actually, yes. It's all booked."

Andy's second reaction was to start considering belting Cammy in the mouth. "You idiot! Did I not tell you just to look into it and not to book anything? Jesus, Cammy, it will take us forever to get to the South of France in one of those old heaps. Can you get the money back?"

Cammy was shaking his head before Andy stopped talking. "Sorry, mate, no can do. It's not refundable. The flights and ferry are booked as well. In fact, it's totally sorted. All you need to do is turn up at the airport tomorrow. Your father is going to drop us off."

"Oh, that's bloody brilliant. Thanks, Cammy. Let me recap. We are going to drive across Europe in a camper designed in the Second World War with no hotels booked, and we are to be driven to the airport by my father who thinks I am the spawn of Satan. You have thought it out carefully! You're a twat! Right, get your ass out of here before I sack it. I will see you here tomorrow morning for the trip from hell. Good-bye!"

Cammy left with his tail between his legs while Andy, fuming once more, went to pack his bags for the trip.

Andy left it until late in the evening to phone Lisa in America, letting her get back from work before interrupting her evening.

To Andy's surprise, Lisa thought Cammy's camper trip was a good idea.

"Andy, I don't see why you have a problem with it. It will give me time to get finished up here, and maybe taking things a bit slower isn't a bad thing. I hope there is room for three in the camper? Looks like you and I are going to have to behave ourselves. We can't continue where we left off in the hotel. You will just have to practice celibacy for a bit until we can get some time alone. I will call you when I get finished up and find out where you are, and then we can arrange to meet up. It must be late across there, Andy. You need to get to your bed if you have a lot of travelling to do tomorrow."

The trip from home to Edinburgh Airport went without a hitch, although things were still frosty between Andy and his father. Andy was last to leave the terminal at Bristol, and he spotted Callum making a beeline across the car park towards an elderly gentleman standing beside a bright orange-and-white 1968 Volkswagen camper van complete with whitewall tyres and spare tyre mounted on the nose. Callum was like a kid in a sweetie shop. Andy shook his head in dismay and ambled unenthusiastically across the car park to where Callum was slavering over the old camper.

Paper work sorted, Callum asked if he could drive to Portsmouth, which Andy had no problem letting him do.

Andy did note that Callum had had the good sense to hire a left-hand-drive model. Most of the driving was going to be in France, so it made sense.

With the old camper stowed safely on the ferry, Cammy and Andy headed for the ship's café and a meal before getting some sleep. After the meal, their thoughts turned back to the real reason for Callum's tour of France.

"Listen, Andy. I know you are sore at me for dragging you out in the old camper, but there was another reason I picked it as our way of getting about. Something about this whole business smells wrong. OK, this might or might not be the woman you are looking for, but look at the facts, Andy. She arrived with two bodyguards in a private plane registered to a bank. Then, when someone starts looking into the flight, the flight plan is wiped from any records. You just can't do that. Call me paranoid if you like, but I am sure in the past week or so I have been watched. Also, I didn't tell your mother, but the caretaker for the offices says he let BT into the office to check a line fault. He had the correct credentials, but when I checked with them, they had no one working overtime when the visit occurred. I have been working from home. I don't trust the office. Hence, the old camper—no tickets or airport security to check, just take the back roads and pay for fuel with cash. Harder to be traced."

Andy had kept his face straight as long as he could but burst out laughing when he could hold it in no longer. “Come on, Cammy. We all know you have been dying to get your hands on an old camper. You don’t have to justify it with wild stories. You will have us wearing bullet-proof vests next. Time for some shut-eye, mate, or do you want to take turns at standing guard?”

Andy carried on laughing, but Callum said nothing. He knew what he knew, and nothing was going to change his mind on the subject.

Next morning was spent gathering some provisions and fuelling up the camper van with Cammy insisting on almost a full service before venturing onto the French roads. Andy took his first shot at driving the camper and remarked if they were indeed chased by Cammy’s faceless enemies, they would be as well to surrender, as the camper exhibited the speed and acceleration of Sammy the snail. Cammy’s plan to take the back roads might well be defeating surveillance, but it was not fast. By lunchtime, they had only travelled half as far as expected.

Andy handed the controls back to Cammy after a lunch of baguettes and ham washed down with bottles of mineral water. A major effort on Cammy’s part to pick up the pace resulted in them travelling about three-quarters of the planned route that day. After stopping for the night in a gateway to a farmer’s field, Andy took control of the map, and Cammy headed off to explore the area around them. Andy calculated the route to Paris from their present position. Then he called Lisa, who seemed to be sitting on the phone as she answered it on the second ring.

"Hi, Lisa. It's the French expedition here. How are things in Reno?"

Lisa had been waiting all day on Andy's call. "Good, things at the office are just about sorted. I am just waiting for our payments to start flowing, which they promise will happen before the end of the week. Jake knows I am requisitioning the jet to get me to France. He says when I get back, he will have a surprise for us both, so it looks like another trip to Reno for you. How is France?"

Andy checked that Cammy was not around before replying to Lisa.

"Oh, we are on a Cammy back-road tour of the French countryside. We will be in Paris by Friday, so we can meet you there. Call me when you know when you will arrive, and the flower-power mobile will pick you up. It's good to hear your voice. I am missing you."

"You will be fine, Andy. You have Cammy to tuck you in."

Andy Paxton made a groaning noise before replying. "Friday can't come quick enough. I would rather you tucked me in, please."

Peace in the camper was shattered as Cammy returned, pulling off a wet jacket as he had been caught in a rain shower while out scouting. Andy explained Cammy had just arrived and said his good-byes. Cammy tried to wrestle the phone from him, but he was too late, and Lisa was gone by the time he gained control of the phone.

"So what did your girl want? I bet she would love a shot in the camper you know."

Andy was watching Cammy closely for the eruption as he replied. "We will find out if she does on Friday, mate. We are changing course to Paris and picking her up from the airport."

Andy watched as this registered with Cammy. "No way! Did you not hear a thing I said about someone keeping tabs on us? For sure, if we waltz into the airport in Paris, we will have our mug shots all over Interpol, and whoever else is looking. It's a bad idea, Andy. Don't do it."

There was no way Andy was going to go back on his word to Lisa, but he knew from listening to Callum's fears, he would not be happy.

"You will just have to like it, Callum. I have already promised Lisa we will be there. You need to stop being so paranoid. No one is following us. It's your mind stuck in overdrive. Get some sleep. We have a lot of driving ahead, mate."

The next morning did not begin well as Callum's dream machine was not for starting. To Andy's amazement, Callum, far from being annoyed, pulled out a tool kit and started taking the old Volkswagen to pieces, looking for the fault and clearly in his element. While Cammy took the ignition system apart to find out why the spark was missing, Andy pondered what might have been if only he had arranged the transport instead of Callum.

He would have been sitting talking to Frederick Le Combe instead of sitting in a field watching his mate slowly losing his cool with the antique camper van.

Eventually after of two days travelling and patching up the camper, they arrived in Paris with Cammy fretting about losing their cloak of invisibility by showing themselves to the many CCTV cameras of Paris.

Cammy's mood brightened slightly when, en route to pick up Lisa, they stumbled across a VW camper specialist. Andy dropped Callum and continued on to the pickup point arranged outside the main terminal while Cammy scoured the VW specialists for a few new electrical components that had been found to be well past their best but which he had cleaned up to keep the old girl moving.

The second Lisa spotted the old camper, she was in stitches. "Oh my god, Andy! I take it Cammy has turned your quest for the truth into a remake of *Carry On Camping*. I am impressed you made it this far. Well done."

Andy took the ribbing from Lisa in good spirits. He was glad to see Lisa. It had seemed like months that they'd been apart, not just a week or so. Lisa grabbed Andy, giving him a longer-than-expected hug, confirming in Andy's mind that she too had been missing their friendship. Andy launched Lisa's case into the back of the VW and retraced his steps to the shop where he had dropped off Cammy. They found Cammy sitting on the kerb with a carrier bag of electrical spares for the old camper van.

"Hi, Blondie! How was America? Have they nominated you for president yet, or are they waiting until you conquer their aircraft industry?"

Lisa was getting used to Callum's sharp tongue and decided it was time to inject a bit of her own wit into the proceedings. "They tried to keep me in America, Callum, but I said no and abandoned my jet-set lifestyle, not to mention my own private jet, to be here in romantic France with a pair of half-wits in a prehistoric VW camper trundling across the Continent. Second thoughts, I must be mental, but hey ho, here we are anyway."

Lisa winked at Andy as Cammy busied himself unloading his bag of camper goodies into one of the lockers, ready for the next breakdown emergency.

After leaving Orly Airport south of Paris, Cammy pointed the camper van south on the A6. It was late afternoon, and they made the joint decision to leave the final part of the journey until the next day and to find someplace to stop for the night and sample some of the local cuisine for supper.

Some time later, Cammy pulled the camper off the A6, heading for the town of Auxerre. On the outskirts of the town, they came across an old whitewashed converted mill sporting a bed-and-breakfast sign. Lisa, the only one of the three who spoke a decent level of French, was dispatched to find out if breakfast could be stretched to an evening meal. Some time later, Lisa returned sporting a beaming smile.

"OK guys, we are sorted. Juliet, the lady who runs the B and B, is happy to serve us an evening meal as long as we are all OK with mint lamb and roast potatoes."

Andy and Cammy had been living on a diet of bread, cheese, and ham since arriving in France, so a proper evening meal was just the ticket, and both agreed wholeheartedly that mint lamb and roast potatoes were just fine.

"Oh, there was one other thing, boys. Juliet has only one single room left, but she is happy for you to park the camper in her courtyard. You both can get cosy there, as I have booked the single room for myself."

As they ate the excellent evening meal, the banter continued over Lisa's room, Callum leading the debate.

"I think it is only fair that because I am doing the lion's share of the driving, I should have the single room so I can get a good sleep. Anyway, it would be far better for you two lovebirds to share the bed in the camper, would it not?"

Andy was in two minds about the situation, but Lisa had a different idea. "Nice try, Callum McPherson. I didn't sign up for the *Carry On Camping* thing in the first place, and now that the initial fun of driving a VW camper van has worn off, don't expect me to swap places with you just so you can get a comfy bed."

Andy smiled to himself. Cammy's camper-van idea was not turning out quite the way he had planned it.

Next morning, Andy was first up and his kit packed away. He was keen to get to the airfield to hear what the pilot had to say about his passenger and his unusual flight to Dundee Airport. Cammy was still trying to wake up after a rough night in the cabin of an overheating camper van as Lisa appeared, flinging her bags into the back of the camper.

By lunchtime, they were approaching the town of Bourg-en-Bresse. After refueling the old camper van, Andy called them together to decide how they were going to handle talking to the pilot. Andy wanted to talk to him personally, and after suggesting this, he was surprised that Cammy put up no objections to this course of action.

After a few missed turns and a stop to consult the map, the camper van finally pulled up outside the main buildings of Bourg-Ceyzériat, a reasonable-size aerodrome on the outskirts of Bourg-en-Bresse.

Callum contented himself by going for a wander round the airfield while Andy and Lisa went in search of their target, Frederick le Combe. Andy entered the little café on site and asked behind the counter for Le Combe. They were directed past the main building towards a hangar that stood alone towards the end of the single runway. As they walked, the hangar grew in size until they arrived at the half-open folding doors. Inside, a white Piper Cherokee 180 sat dwarfed by the huge hangar. On the far side of the hangar, a light glowed from an office in the gloom of the hangar. Andy and Lisa could see no one in the hangar so made their way across to the small office. A sign in French on the door proclaimed it was the property of the Blue Line flying school. Andy knocked on the half-open door and entered to find a distinguished middle-aged man sitting at his desk, neatly piled files either side of him.

Lisa introduced them in French, asking if he were Frederick Le Combe. When the gentleman nodded, Lisa asked if he spoke English as her partner was not so good with the French language.

"But of course, English is not a problem. Please call me Fred. May I ask whom I am speaking with and what I may do for you today, my friends?"

Andy felt much happier now that he could talk to the man without having to guess half the conversation.

"Thank you, Fred. I am Andy Paxton, and this is my girlfriend, Lisa Preston. We are from Scotland and are here looking for some information that you may be able to help us with."

Fred had a puzzled expression on his face as he listened to Andy. "I cannot think why I could help you, but if I can, I will do my best. Please tell me what you need from me."

Lisa said no more, instead spending her time studying the Frenchman as he spoke, ready to help if her translation skills were required.

"Fred, we have come a long way from Scotland, so I am hoping you can unravel a mystery for me. Last month, I believe you piloted a jet that landed briefly at Dundee Airport, dropping off an old lady and two Asian men for an hour or so. Is this correct?"

For a second, there was silence. Frederick Le Combe studied the papers on his desk rather than making eye contact. "You are very well informed, my friend. May I ask how you came upon the information that I was the pilot of this aircraft?"

Andy was not sure, but he sensed a subtle change in the atmosphere between them. "One of my investigators found your signature on the fuel receipt when you had the jet refueled for its return flight.

"Investigators? Are you investigating me, Mr. Paxton?"

Lisa stepped into the conversation as she could sense a standoff approaching. "Fred, no one is investigating anyone. Andy is a lawyer, and I am a nurse. Andy made a promise to an old patient of mine that he would find an old friend of his. Unfortunately, he died, and we think you may have flown this old lady to his funeral. All we are trying to do is get in contact with her. No one is in trouble. We just need to find her. Andy and I would be very grateful if there is any information you could give us."

Frederick Le Combe turned what Lisa had just told him over in his head before finally replying. "Yes, my friends, you are perfectly correct. It was me who was chartered to fly the old woman to Scotland. I don't know if there is much I can tell you that you don't already know. The flight was arranged through the Swiss bank PSS. I believe the jet belongs to them. I was not informed of the nature of the old woman's business, only that the stay in Scotland would be a short one and that I should have the plane refueled and ready to leave as soon as she returned from her business. She was picked up from here and brought back here. That is as much as I can tell you, sorry."

Andy was not satisfied with the answers he had been given. Fred was right. He had said nothing that they already didn't know.

"Fred, do you know the woman's name or where she is from? Have you ever taken her anyplace before? Is there anything else you can remember that could help us trace the old lady?"

Before Andy stopped speaking, Fred was already shaking his head. "Non, my friend. She was surrounded by her minders. I briefly spoke to one of them, but they were not the type who chatted to you. I may have flown her somewhere before, but I am not sure. For sure, if I did, it was a long time ago. I feel if you have come this far, the bank PSS may be able to tell you more than I can. Now, if you do not mind, I must prepare my aircraft for a flight. Is there anything more I can do for you today?"

Andy and Lisa said their good-byes and headed back to the old Volkswagen in search of the missing Cammy.

They found Cammy wandering along the main road away from the airfield, Andy stopped the camper and picked him up. While Cammy took over the driving, Andy plotted a new course for Switzerland and Geneva, the home of Premier Strasse Suisse, the bank who had paid for Frederick Le Combe to fly Jean Bruce to Dundee. On the way, Lisa and Andy discussed their meeting with Fred.

"There was something odd about our friend Fred. When he found out about his signature, just for a fraction of a second, he dropped his guard. I don't know, Andy. It was as if he expected us to have no proof of his flight and faced with the fact we did have proof, he had to rethink his story."

Andy was not so sure that was the case. "He probably just didn't like being questioned like that."

Andy hadn't finished his sentence before Cammy joined in the debate. "I never met the guy, but I was poking about the canteen asking about the old woman, and one of the engineers having lunch told me that he has seen the old woman on more than one occasion and always with Frederick Le Combe, so I tend to agree with Lisa. I wouldn't trust what he told you today. Let's go and have a crack at the bank before we jump to conclusions.

By the time the old camper van trundled its way into the streets of Geneva, it was too late to attempt speaking to anyone in the bank. Cammy had other ideas anyway, and he dropped Andy and Lisa outside a large supermarket before going in search of an Internet café three blocks away. Cammy found it. He dumped the camper van in a side street and headed into the café. Callum wanted to know a bit more about the bank they were going to visit in the morning. He wanted some ammunition. Andy had done the interviewing today, but Callum fancied a crack at the bank staff in the morning.

He had a good idea that he would end up flung out on the street, but he was going to give it his best shot. He always loved a challenge.

Unfortunately for Lisa, they had arrived in Geneva too late to hunt for any hotels or guesthouses. The best Callum could manage was a twenty-four-hour supermarket car park. It had the basic essentials—toilets, food, and a place to park for the night. Over a meal in the back of the camper van, the three conspirators went over the plan for tomorrow's assault on the Swiss bank.

"Listen, guys. You hired me to find out things, and I let you have a go at the pilot yesterday, but the bank will be a whole different kettle of fish. These guys don't give information out to just anybody, so by all means come in and have a look around the bank, but let me handle it, and don't let on that you know me. I have been doing a bit of digging on the Internet, and Premier Strasse Suisse are not squeaky clean. There is a lot of chat on the conspiracy sites that they are quite happy to do business with anyone, and when I say anyone, I do mean anyone. We need to be careful here. I would imagine they have some friends in very low places."

The next morning, Andy and Lisa left the camper hand in hand, having decided a wander through the streets of Geneva would be the best way to get to the bank. Callum shaved then pulled out a suit bag from the back of the camper. He needed to look the part if he were to be believed by the bank staff. At 10:15 a.m., Callum marched with some authority into PSS Bank and straight up to a reception desk on the left.

"Good morning, madame. Please may I speak to your bank manager or whoever is in charge here today."

The blond girl behind the desk gave a curt response. "We have no appointments booked for our manager today, sir. Can I make an appointment for you to see our manager?"

Callum had been expecting this response and went into full acting mode, removing his wallet and flashing his identity card over the desk at the receptionist.

"Young woman, this matter is of great importance. I suggest you get me your manager here now. Tell him Rod Halliday from the Civil Aviation Crimes Unit is here to speak to him, and if you do not want Interpol arresting you for obstruction, I would do it now!"

The young woman has went pale but asked him to take a seat at a leather-clad desk just behind her while she went in search of her superior.

A few minutes later, she returned with a small, suited man resembling Agatha Christie's Poirot.

"Good day, sir. Annette tells me you need to speak to our bank manager. I am the duty supervisor. May I be of some assistance?"

Callum stood up, pulling himself up to his full height and looking down on the smaller man. "Yes, you can go and find your manager and stop wasting valuable time."

"You must understand, sir, that our manager is a very busy man. May I ask what this matter is about?"

Callum gave the little man his very best death stare as he spoke, leaning down and getting right into the little man's face and personal space. "You can tell him that he is being investigated for breach of civil aviation laws. You can tell him that his Falcon 900 will be impounded pending investigation of allegations made that the aircraft was used to smuggle drugs into Great Britain, and you can tell him that if I do not have his full cooperation today, he will be answering these questions at a police station of his choice."

The little man was about to go in search of his boss, but he stopped in his tracks, turning back to Callum. "Before I go in search of my manager, do you have documentation of who you say you are?"

Callum removed his identity card and handed it to the little man who studied it before handing it back and scuttling off in search of his boss.

As Callum sat waiting on the manager, he noted from the corner of his eye Andy and Lisa entering through the side door. The PSS building was not like any normal high-street bank. It was housed in a seventeenth-century town house. The main foyer had two ornate staircases leading to the first floor and could have been mistaken for the entrance to a museum rather than a bank. Only the presence of desks and computers gave away the fact that this was a working building. Ornate tapestries adorned the walls along with oil paintings from hundreds of years ago. Even the desks that housed the computers were oak and green leather and did not look out of place in the grand hall that was the foyer.

Callum did not have to wait long before he was joined by Poirot, the girl, and a tall, thin, elderly man who looked far from in the best of health, probably having spent most of his life trapped behind a desk.

"I believe you want to speak to me about our company jet."

Callum did not waste any time as he wanted to keep the bank staff on the back foot.

"You own a Falcon 900 registration number Yankee Kilo Oscar 4533. Can you explain to me why last month it flew into Dundee Airport in Scotland but its logs have been deliberately removed from civil aviation computers, rendering the flight invisible? Furthermore it has been alleged by a reliable source that this flight delivered a consignment of drugs destined for the streets of the Scottish capital. What I need from you, sir, is the flight log, including passengers and any cargo that was transported, also permission from you to have customs officers search the plane with sniffer dogs to detect if drugs have been present."

Callum was watching all three closely. Both Poirot and the girl were genuinely shocked and looked to their boss for his take on the situation. The tall man said nothing for the moment, thinking things through.

He seemed as cool as a cucumber, but Callum could see beads of sweat starting to form at his hairline, betraying the fact he was under enormous pressure to comply with Callum's wishes.

"My dear Mr. Halliday, I know nothing of altered records, but I can confirm that a lady and her security staff did use the jet to travel to Scotland last month. PSS Bank is more than happy to allow customs to check the aircraft, but I can assure you this lady has nothing to do with drug dealers. I can tell you no more until you can supply me with the appropriate warrant as you must understand, my client has her right to privacy, and I for one will not break that code until ordered to by the authorities. Tell me Mr. Halliday, do you think the Civil Aviation Authority will be able to produce the warrant today, or should I not hold my breath?"

The bank manager had put the ball back firmly in Callum's court, and he had run out of tricks, so it was time to sound the retreat while he still could.

"My dear sir, I will leave you for the moment to arrange for the warrants to be raised, but knowing Premier Strasse Suisse has a reputation for holding some unsavoury groups as clients, I don't think it will be long until we meet again. Good day, my friends."

Callum would have given his right arm to have monitored the calls that were leaving PSS Bank five minutes after he left the building. He had tried every trick in the book and pushed his luck to the maximum with, as he suspected, little to show for his efforts.

Back in the camper, the three amigos discussed the lack of headway they were making. Andy was deeply depressed that so far, they had found out very little and was for heading for home, but Callum was not for giving up.

"Listen, Andy, I want a crack at the pilot again. He is the weak link here. I have a feeling about him. Listen. We have to go back that way anyway. We have nothing to lose. Let's give it one more go."

Andy nodded dejectedly while Lisa tried her hardest to lift the mood in the camper by offering to buy supper once they reached Bourg-en-Bresse.

Outside the airfield again, Callum asked Andy and Lisa to stay put in the camper while he worked his web of deceit once more.

As Callum walked into the small café, he spotted Fred sitting by himself, drinking coffee and deep in thought. Callum had studied his picture from the Internet, and apart from a few more grey hairs, he was just the same as his pictures. It was time for act two. Callum approached the counter without looking back, speaking in a loud voice for all to hear.

"Hello there, do you speak English? I am looking for Frederick Le Combe. I am from the Civil Aviation Authority and need to interview him."

Callum watched in the mirror above the counter as the assembled customers looked in Fred's direction. He watched the half-hidden hand signal for them to keep quiet, and not a person stirred. The shop owner answered Callum with a shrug of the shoulders as Callum ordered a coffee to go.

After a few seconds, Fred stood up and headed out back in the direction of the toilets. Callum waited a few seconds and followed him as if making for the toilet also.

At the far end of the hall, Fred was on the phone with his back to the café, looking out of the window as he spoke to the person on the other end of the line.

Callum did not let the door close, since that would have alerted Fred to his presence. Instead he stood deathly still, listening for any juicy bits of conversation.

"You were correct, madame. He is here, yes. No, I have not spoken to him, and no, I think until this is sorted, you must stay at Nantua. They will not know about the château. You can fly down to the Camargue later, once they have been dealt with and the coast is clear. To come here now would not be wise."

Callum quit while he was ahead and closed the door silently, heading back to the counter to pick up his coffee and leave quickly.

CHAPTER 12
HUNTED

Andy and Lisa were sitting in the camper when Callum came into sight, running from the airfield café. Out of breath but exited, he relayed what he had heard between gulps of the strong coffee. Andy didn't like the "dealt with" part of the conversation one little bit and fired up the old camper, determined to put distance between themselves and the airfield before any unwanted visitors arrived to have a word with them.

They had just made the motorway, when Callum collapsed from the passenger seat across the steering wheel. Andy managed to push him off with one hand as he fought the old camper for control.

Lisa dived from the back seat, pulling Callum backwards away from the van controls, giving Andy a chance to correct the swerve that had taken control of the van. Two minutes later they had found a slip road and stopped, fearful for their collapsed friend.

Lisa's nursing head kicked in, and she barked orders to Andy as she opened Callum's shirt, making sure his airway was clear.

Lisa was puzzled. Callum was not unconscious. He seemed to be awake, but his body would not respond. He could not speak, and Lisa noted that his pupils were dilated, like someone out of his face on drugs. She made him comfortable in the back and kept a close eye on him while Andy negotiated the back road, finding a large tree-covered grove to try and hide the camper from prying eyes.

Andy was first to air his thoughts. "What do you think, Lisa? Should we get him to hospital before he gets worse?"

Lisa had not lifted her head. She was busy reexamining Cammy's pupils.

"I'm not sure, Andy. I have never seen this before. I suspect the coffee Callum came back with was drugged, but I have never seen a drug have this effect before. He appears to be stable, but he seems to be paralyzed. Even his pupils do not react to light. I think we take things hour by hour. If he has been drugged, the people who did this will be waiting for us to take him to hospital, and it could be a trap. Remember what Callum said about the clientele at PSS Bank."

Andy thought about it for a second before replying. "I agree with you. Before you arrived, Cammy was adamant he was being watched. I told him he was talking rubbish, but I take it all back. I think we will shack up here for a bit and keep an eye on Callum."

For the next four hours, Lisa never left Callum's side, checking his pulse and temperature every twenty minutes. Andy passed the time by looking through the road maps Callum had brought with him.

He found what he was looking for. Halfway between Bourg-en-Bresse and the Swiss border, the town of Nantua was situated on the banks of Lake Nantua. Andy wondered to himself how many châteaus were situated in Nantua. It would take all three of them to check the surrounding area. Cammy, for the moment at least, was more important. Andy needed to think and decided it was time to stretch his legs and left Lisa tending to Cammy, who was still comatose. Andy promised to be back shortly with some provisions to keep them going for the moment.

Andy had walked for fifteen minutes and was entering the outskirts of a town called Macon when he saw something that immediately gave him an idea. Andy walked on into the town and decided on a plan of action. He had seen a car for sale outside a house on the outskirts of the town. He stopped at the bank, withdrawing four thousand euros and then heading back to the car, putting some final details to his plan on the way.

Luckily for Andy, the French gentleman selling the Peugeot 505 estate car spoke more English than he did French, and after spinning him a yarn that he and his wife were here on holiday and their car was sick and needed a garage, but he needed transport. The gentleman accepted the four thousand euros and attempted to go through the paperwork for the car with Andy, Andy nodded in all the correct places, but he had no clue what the French man was on about, and after driving off in the car, he stuffed the offending paper work in the passenger glove box. Andy knew they could trace his bank transactions, but because he'd bought the car with cash, and he had no intention of sending the paper work away, for the moment, they were invisible again. Soon they would be gone and on their way to Nantua, which considering what had just happened, was not a bad thing. Andy's master plan to evade whoever was after them was not complete. After arriving back with the car, Andy explained to Lisa what he was doing, helped her drag Cammy into the back of the estate car, transferred a few things, then headed off back to Macon and a garage he had spotted on his visit to the town.

The owner of the garage only spoke French, but after a few minutes, his wife arrived on the scene, and Andy explained to her that he wanted to leave the camper to be checked over as it had problems starting. Andy handed over the bag of bits Cammy had squirreled away and left, taking one of the garage's business cards and promising to phone next week to see if the camper was ready to collect.

On the way back, Andy went over in his head what he planned next. A lot depended on Callum. Andy had his fingers and his toes crossed that his mate would come to soon. He did not want to go near a hospital if possible.

Back at the grove where the Peugeot was hidden from prying eyes, Andy and Lisa decided it was better to move away from the town due to his bankcard transaction. Andy turned back on his original route and plotted a course towards the border town of Nantua, stopping a few miles short for the evening and allowing Lisa to have one more check at Callum before getting some sleep.

Andy was woken in the morning by a foot touching his shoulder. For a second it did not register that it could not be Lisa as she was curled up next to him on the passenger seat. Then Andy was wide awake, peering over the back of his reclined seat to check on the condition of his mate. For a second, it seemed nothing had changed. Then Andy noticed Callum's right leg twitching. Andy grabbed Lisa, waking her from a deep sleep. Lisa was awake instantly and checked Callum over again before speaking.

"I think whatever Callum was given is starting to wear off. His pupils are starting to react to light, and I can feel muscles beginning to react to stimulation. We might just be in luck. I need to stay awake to keep checking on him. Who knows what the side effects might be."

Andy started the big Peugeot and toured around the little village closest to where they had stopped until he found what he was looking for.

Andy pulled the car up outside the shop marked *boulangerie* and vanished inside returning after a few minutes carrying paper bags full of croissant, pain au chocolat, chassoun aux pommes, and cakes and polystyrene cups brimming with strong black coffee. Andy was for trying to feed Callum some coffee, but Lisa stopped him.

"No, you don't. I know you mean well, but you will only choke him, and in the state he is in, you could actually drown him, cutting off his oxygen, and he wouldn't be able to tell us, I know you want to get on with the search, but be patient. He is coming back to us, slowly but surely."

Andy was not about to argue when Lisa was in matron mode, instead finishing his coffee then trundling the big old Peugeot along at a sedate pace, not wanting to spill Lisa's coffee or upset his old mate in the back of the estate car.

Midmorning Andy pulled into a parking space on the south side of Lake Nantua, parking the Peugeot while Lisa checked on their patient.

Although to Andy there didn't look like much improvement, other than Callum sweating badly, Lisa assured him that Callum was making good progress. Andy decided to stretch his legs and check out the surrounding area. Andy walked along the stone wall by the roadside, admiring the view of the lake. Above and behind him, a large house stood on the crest of the hill overlooking the lake. Andy changed his attention to the house and its silhouette dark against the pale blue sky above when suddenly he became aware someone was speaking to him. Andy looked down, letting his eyes adjust from his skygazing to find a tiny, weathered old woman hunched over her walking stick, smiling at him as she spoke. Andy tried to understand what she was saying, but his limited vocabulary and her strong accent stopped him from understanding a word she said.

Andy found himself apologizing to the old lady for not understanding her when there was a voice he did understand and recognise behind him.

Lisa had walked up behind him while he was trying to understand the old woman and had been listening to the old lady repeating herself.

"The old lady is telling you that the house you have been staring at was where she used to work in the kitchens years ago before she married. She wanted to know if you were here to visit the house and to warn you that there was no one at home if you were visiting."

Andy looked again at the big house. What was the chances that the first château they looked at was the one they were after? Andy decided it was worth a try. They had to start someplace, and here was as good as any.

"Lisa, can you ask the old lady who owns the house on the hill?"

Andy waited patiently as Lisa chatted with the old woman.

"The house belongs to the Chemolie family. It has been in the family for six generations."

Andy's heart sank. This was a family house, not the home of the old lady he was looking for. Andy turned his attention away from the house and back to the unattended Peugeot, checking for any movement inside it.

Lisa chatted to the old lady for a while before saying good-bye and following Andy back to the car. Callum looked as if he were in a sauna, not a parked car. Sweat was pouring from every pore.

Lisa was looking up at the château as she spoke. "I bet the château has a magnificent view of the lake from that height. No wonder you need to be a Swiss banker to afford a pad like that. How much do you think it is worth, Andy?"

It took a second for what Lisa had said to register with Andy. "What do you mean by Swiss banker? Did the old woman tell you it was owned by a banker?"

Lisa nodded as she ducked inside the car to check on Cammy.

Something clicked in Andy's head, and he set off up the road to find the entrance to the château, He found it and then followed it, a winding track up the hill to the front of the house. As Andy arrived at the front door, he noted the absence of any vehicles. The old woman was correct—no one was at home, Andy circled the house, looking for an open window, but the château was locked up securely. It was then that Andy spotted an old man working away in a field a few yards from the front door of the property. Andy called to the man and to his surprise, he spoke perfect English.

"I am sorry to bother you, sir, but is the old lady at home?"

Andy had taken a guess that if he started the conversation showing that he knew nothing about the owner of the château, there was a good chance the old man would tell him nothing.

The old man stared at Andy for a second, trying to remember if he had seen him here before. He had seen many strangers at the house in recent years, but he was not sure about this one.

"No, my young friend. You have missed her. She left yesterday afternoon."

Andy's heart leapt into his mouth. His gamble had paid off, but he needed to know if this old lady was the old lady he was looking for.

Andy racked his brain, pulling together all the tiny pieces he knew about the woman before his next searching question.

"That is a great pity. I have some bank papers she needs to sign. You don't happen to know when she will be back, do you?"

The old man had swallowed the story hook, line, and sinker, Andy was from the bank. It was making perfect sense, and he dropped his guard completely.

"No, my friend, she did not mention when she would be back. Maria has gone down to the vineyards to visit her family, I believe, so it may be some time until she returns."

Andy threw another few things into the conversation to gauge the reaction from the old man. "Oh well, PSS will just have to wait until Madame Chemolie returns from the Camargue. I guess the papers will just have to wait."

The old man was smiling as he turned away, heading back to his work in the field, leaving his final comment as he walked. "My son, when you own the bank, you can do what you want. I am sure one of her directors will sign your papers. Good day to you, and safe journey back, my friend."

Andy strolled back down the hill towards the car park, turning over in his head what he had found out. It was not conclusive proof, but there were far too many coincidences for this to be the wrong woman. The old man had not corrected him when he mentioned the PSS Bank or the Camargue area, so if he were correct, this old woman was Maria Chemolie who owned PSS Bank and was headed to a vineyard to visit family in the Camargue region of France. Not a bad morning's work. Cammy would have been proud of him.

Andy was not ready for what greeted him as he arrived back at the car. Callum was outside the car on his knees, throwing up into the long grass while a concerned Lisa looked on, making sure he was not choking on his own vomit. After some time, a sweat-covered Cammy dragged himself from the grass, resting his head on the back wheel of the Peugeot and letting his shattered body rest for a few minutes before Lisa presented him with a bottle of mineral water to help flush the toxins out of his body. Andy helped his mate to his feet and walked him round to the back of the big Peugeot, sitting him down on the edge of the boot. While Callum poured water down his throat, Andy explained what he had found out that morning. Andy looked at his two companions and came to a decision that they needed to stop and recharge their batteries before going on any further with their search. None of them had seen a bed or shower for a couple of days. Callum was still a long way from full recovery, and Lisa was dead on her feet from looking after Callum. They needed to stop and rest for a day at least. Andy checked his map and found a hotel about ten miles to the west of them. He bundled the weary troops back into the Peugeot and headed to the hotel.

Andy was the first to awaken the next morning. He slid off the side of the bed quietly, letting Lisa sleep. He dressed and checked on Cammy, who had an adjoining room. Cammy was still asleep, but Andy could tell from the loud snoring that he was out of trouble. A quick rake through Callum's gear found the laptop Andy was looking for.

He adjourned to the bar of the hotel and ordered a pot of coffee while he waited for his colleagues to wake up and join him.

After a slight communication problem with the staff over Wi-Fi access, a kind waitress took his laptop and entered the required code, handing it back with a smile.

Coffee cup in hand, Andy spent the next hour surfing for any information about Maria Chemolie, but he soon found out that she was not the most outgoing person where the Internet was concerned.

Eventually his perseverance paid off when he discovered an article posted by a magazine for horse enthusiasts. The image at the top of the page showed white ponies running across a hillside, but the caption underneath was what Andy had been searching for: "Camargue horses bred by Maria Chemolie on her farm, Cheval Blanc Le Vignoble."

Andy entered the farm name into the search engine and immediately came up with an ad for red wine that showed the vineyard and farm complex and the address where the wine could be bought from the farm shop.

There were no pictures of the woman to confirm for Andy that it was the same woman from the graveside, but it ticked all the right boxes.

Andy was about to order a second pot of coffee when he spotted what could only be described as the walking dead entering the bar.

In all his life, he had never seen Callum in a state like this, and he had seen him in a few states. The man was struggling to walk, his body still recovering from being drugged.

Gingerly, Cammy sat down next to Andy. He sat quietly while Andy ordered more coffee for them both.

"Jesus Christ, Andy, what the hell happened to me?"

"Lisa thinks that you were drugged. She has never seen a drug with the same symptoms, but she is pretty sure someone doctored your coffee at the airfield. It looks like someone was going to grab you when the drug took effect. Luckily, you made it back to the camper before it hit you."

Callum sat sipping his coffee and shaking his head. "Talking of campers, where did our transport disappear to? I can't see it in the car park."

Andy went over what he had done to hopefully throw whoever had drugged Callum off the scent and explained his discovery of the woman's house in Nantua and his conversation with the old gardener, which had led him to his Internet search. Cammy nodded as he described his deductions then tutted as he looked at the open laptop.

"OK, Andy Paxton, you used the laptop to search for this Chemolie woman? Did you not think that whoever is watching us will not be looking for someone doing Internet searches for her name? I think you need to get Lisa up, and I will order breakfast, and then we need to get out of here before someone turns up to check on the hotel Internet and who has been using it."

When Andy returned to the table with a sleepy Lisa in tow, he found two cooked breakfasts waiting for them. As Lisa and Andy tackled breakfast, Cammy, whose head seamed to have cleared, was using the laptop to search for something.

"Oh, so I shouldn't be surfing the net, Cammy, but it's OK for you to do it?"

Callum stopped what he was doing and looked over the top of the breakfast menu at his mate. "Well, the cat is out of the bag as far as that is concerned, thanks to you, so I thought I would see if I could top your investigative skills by checking a few things you might not know about."

Lisa finished her breakfast first and excused herself to go and shower and pack up. Callum watched her as she left, then turned his attention back to his mate.

"I am still amazed at you, Paxton. How could you, with all the chat-up skills of a plank of wood, manage to land a drop-dead gorgeous blond billionaire, while I, the silk-tongued stud of Scotland remain single? I just don't get it, man. Life is so unfair."

Andy did not want to hurt his mate's feelings, so he stifled the laugh that was building inside him. Callum suddenly stopped talking, concentrating on the page on the screen in front of him.

"Right then, smart arse, you were good, but as suspected, I am better. Maria Chemolie is the widow of Manfred Chemolie, who died leaving his banking fortune and business to his wife. Manfred Chemolie was her second husband. Her first husband was Henri Chevallier, the owner of the White Horse Vineyard chain. Did you get all that stored in your lawyer brain? I know it's hard to believe, but we have found a woman that is richer than your Lisa."

Callum tapped a few keys and then gave a snort. "That all ties up nicely, but there are a few unanswered questions. Why is somebody hell-bent on stopping us? Also, this may be the woman we are looking for, but how can this be your Spitfire woman? Nothing ties up with a British fighter pilot. You have got to face the fact that we could well be barking up the wrong tree here, mate!"

Andy was shaking his head and having none of it. His notorious stubborn nature was rearing its head once more. "No, Callum, this is the woman who flew to Scotland to put a wreath on an old man's grave and signed it 'Jean.' I am sure of it. And as you pointed out yourself, the bank she owns does business with some pretty nasty characters. That could explain why somebody doesn't want us to mess with the boss."

Callum was not convinced by Andy's attempt to persuade him.

"So, lawyer boy, tell me, where in that warped mind of yours can you connect a French or Swiss banker with an alleged Scottish female fighter pilot from the Battle of Britain? It's a fairy story, one you would tell your kids to get them to go to sleep. No one will believe you, Andy. I am not sure you believe it yourself."

As the heated conversation went on, Callum and Andy did not notice Lisa coming up behind them, ready to leave.

"I believe him, Callum. You forget, I was there when Jan Powlak told the story to us, end of discussion. Come on. Where are we headed this fine morning?"

Callum was about to speak, but Andy cut him off. "Thanks, Lisa. You see, Cammy, you are outnumbered. We are going vineyard hunting today, and before you start, Cammy, I will not stop until I meet this woman Maria Chemolie face to face and ask her why she visited Jan's grave."

Callum threw his hands in the air in mock despair. "OK, boss. Let's do this. She is probably the head of some drug cartel, and we are all going to end up at the bottom of a river with cement shoes, but hey—as long as you get to ask her the question, that's fine!"

Andy and Lisa were smiling at Callum's antics, but there was doubt in the back of their minds that he might be closer to the truth than they wanted.

Andy drove for the best part of the day with Lisa filing in as map reader while Callum spent his time fighting off the last effects of the drug—cold sweats and cramps almost made him cry as he fought to control his body in the back seat of the big estate car. Four hours of driving brought them to the outskirts of the town of Arles. Andy finally stopped in a lay-by to let Cammy exercise his seized legs while Lisa plotted the final part of the trip. Their surroundings had changed drastically as they travelled farther south into the Camargue region. The sandy ground and increased temperatures made this part of France look markedly different from the rest of the country. Lisa plotted a route to the southwest of Arles, skirting along the top of the Camargue national park before dropping down towards the Mediterranean coast and the famed areas where the white Camargue horses were to be found, along with their target—Cheval Blanc Le Vignoble and hopefully, the mysterious Madame Chemolie.

The big Peugeot's air conditioning had given up completely, and the three amigos were just about to call a halt. They had been travelling along the D6572 for too long, Lisa was double-checking her map reading to see where she had gone wrong. Andy was checking how much fuel he had left when Lisa let out a squeal. She was pointing to an entrance to their left that sported a full-size statue of a Camargue horse. Mounted on the fence next to it was a signpost that read "Cheval Blanc Le Vignoble."

Andy swung off the dusty road onto the drive of the estate, following the road slightly uphill past a meadow on their right that had a few of the Camargue horses dotted around. Andy passed a stable complex on their left, but he spotted the big house further on and headed directly for it, parking the dust-covered estate car at the front door. He headed straight for the door without waiting for Lisa or Callum to follow.

To Andy Paxton's frustration, there was no reply. Andy and Cammy headed round the back of the big house to try and find someone while Lisa strolled down towards the stables. Andy and Callum failed to find anyone, but Lisa had better luck.

Just as Lisa approached the barn door, a woman in her thirties walked out. Lisa looked round for the boys, but they were nowhere to be seen. She decided to introduce herself.

"Good afternoon. I am Lisa Preston. My friends and I have come all the way from Scotland to speak with Maria Chemolie. I am sorry to bother you, but could you tell me if she is here, and if not, where we can find her?"

The tall distinguished brunette regarded Lisa with searching big brown eyes. "I am Oriane Pascal. The lady you are searching for is my grandmother. I am afraid that you have came a very long way for nothing. You have just missed Grandma. She left yesterday."

Andy and Callum had heard the voices and appeared by Lisa's side just as Oriane finished speaking.

"Hello there. This is Callum, and I am Andrew. I couldn't help overhearing you say that we have just missed your grandmother. Would you mind filling in some details about your grandmother for us?"

Oriane smiled, studying the two new arrivals with interest. "Of course, but I must warn you that Grandma is a very, how would you say, private person. She says very little about herself. Maybe it would help if you could tell me why you have come so far to see Grandma?"

The three of them looked at one another, not sure who should speak or how much they should tell Oriane. Andy decided he would speak wording his question cautiously. He did not want Oriane to clam up on him.

"Oriane, we believe your grandma visited a grave in Scotland recently to pay her respects to a friend of ours. Can you confirm whether your grandma did this? Also our friend who passed away was friends with a woman called Jean Bruce. Have you ever heard that name or heard your grandma mention it?"

Oriane shrugged her shoulders, looking away, trying to remember, but her look was blank, and Andy knew before she spoke she did not know anything.

"I am so sorry. You have all come so far, and I cannot help you. What was the name of your friend who died? Maybe I know that name."

Callum had wandered behind Oriane and was looking at picture frames with hundreds of pictures pinned together, mostly of show-winning horses with names and dates written on them.

Andy was watching Callum out of the corner of his eye as he replied to Oriane. "Our old friend who died was a Polish man called Jan Powlak. Does that ring any bells, Oriane?"

Again Oriane's face was blank. It was Callum who spoke first, saving Oriane from a further apology.

"Oriane, these pictures are fabulous. Tell me. This picture here taken in 1961. Would this be a picture of your grandma?"

Oriane's face lit up at the mention of the picture. "Well spotted, yes. Grandma doesn't like her picture taken. That was her first show-winning horse. She does not know that I have smuggled that one out of her scrapbook."

Callum continued to check out all the pictures while speaking to Oriane. "I can see your grandma had a good eye for horses. I bet these three horses were all show winners, am I correct?"

Oriane checked the three horses that Callum had pointed out to her. She was surprised and turned, studying Callum more closely. "I see it is not only Grandma who picks good horses. Well done! Not only did you pick winners, but you picked her first three winners. I am impressed."

Andy had watched the pair checking each other out and decided it was time to break up the mutual-admiration society.

"Oriane, can you tell us were we might be able to find your grandma?"

Oriane broke her gaze away from Callum, turning back to Lisa and Andy with a beaming smile.

"But of course, this I can answer for you. Grandma loves racing cars. She left yesterday after picking up her passes for the Monaco Grand Prix. She never misses it. You know her bank sponsors one of the race teams—Williams, I believe—but you will not find her there. She always stays at the Hôtel de Paris. She has her own balcony to watch the race from. She took me when I was younger once. This is how I know she will be there. I think after the race she has meetings abroad, but she did not say where. I hope this helps you."

Andy and Lisa thanked Oriane and were about to leave when Cammy stopped them. "Oriane, I have one last question. Do you like Volkswagen camper vans?"

Oriane was like a rabbit caught in the headlamps. "Well, I don't know. I have never been in one. Why?"

Callum lifted her hand and kissed it before backing away, still talking to her. "Well, Oriane, never say never. If I turn up here with one, you can give me your opinion. Au revoir, Oriane."

Andy and Lisa were splitting their sides laughing as they left the estate. Lisa repeated Callum's last words. "*Au revoir, Oriane.* Callum McPherson, did nobody tell you less is more? You were putting it on too much. Take it from a girl. That type of approach scares girls away."

For a second, Callum said nothing, letting things calm down and pausing for effect. "Andy, Lisa, I apologise. You were both correct. This is no fairy tale. We have just visited Jean Bruce's home, and wait for it…here comes the Sherlock Holmes bit that you employ me for.

"The three horses that I picked from the wall were called Hurricane, Spitfire, and Baby T. Who but Jean Bruce would name her horses that way? Yes, people, sit back and stare. You are in the presence of greatness. Changing the subject, I think I am in love. How hot was Oriane? Drop-dead gorgeous, rich, and available. We need to find Jean Bruce, so I can come back here and sweep her granddaughter off her feet."

Andy was still taking in what Cammy had just found out while Lisa was shaking her head at the Oriane comments. "Cammy, what makes you think Oriane is available, or is that a Sherlock moment as well?"

Cammy tutted at Lisa's naïveté. "Lovely Lisa, why do you think I kissed her hand? No rings or marks where rings have been. No boyfriend pictures. Trust me—she is up for grabs, and what a catch that would be!"

Lisa changed the subject back to the reason they were all here. "So, Madame Chemolie, where do we go from here?"

CHAPTER 13
MONACO

Andy pointed to the map in Lisa's lap.

"Don't just sit there, map reader. Plot me a new course for Monaco. We will swap drivers and keep going. We need to get to Monaco before Madame Chemolie does another runner."

Lisa was thinking about what Andy had just said but she was concerned. "Correct me if I am wrong, but won't we need tickets or some type of passes to get into Monaco when the racing is on?"

Cammy joined the debate in his usual style. "Don't you worry about that, missus. I am sure I can come up with something that will get us into the Hôtel de Paris."

The big Peugeot pulled up for a refuel at a motorway services early the next morning. After a stop the previous night for some much-needed rest, Callum had decided to change the game plan slightly.

"I have been thinking, team. We can't go waltzing into Monaco unprepared. When we head off again, I am going to change direction. We are going to Nice Airport. I have a bit of shopping to do, and you pair don't want to be around just in case it all goes pear-shaped. You can both put your feet up in one of the airport cafés and order breakfast while I go hunting."

Andy was looking at the time. He was concerned. It was early Sunday morning, and time was fast running out for the trio to find their target.

"Cammy, are you sure we need to take this detour? This is race day, and we need to be in the right place before Madame Chemolie does one of her runners again. The chances of finding her after that are slim."

Cammy pulled on a pair of sunglasses to take the glare of the sun coming up in his windscreen as he pulled back onto the slip road before replying to Andy. "Trust me, old son, this is important. We don't do this, and we won't get within a mile of the old lady."

Andy decided to ask no more. He was going on the principal that the less he knew, the better.

On arrival at Nice Airport, Cammy abandoned the car in the short-stay car park and headed into the airport alone, arranging to meet Lisa and Andy in the coffee lounge when he had completed his mission.

It didn't take Callum long to zone in on his prey. It was race day, and Nice was the closest airport. Race fans who hadn't arrived for the whole weekend were pouring off flights ready to be ferried to the Monaco race circuit and their seats or hospitality areas.

Callum watched as three well-dressed men made their way across a packed hall towards the gents. He watched as one man handed his friend their hand luggage as a pair of them entered the toilet area, Cammy noticed the folder protruding from one of the bags at the man's feet. Cammy made his way towards the unfortunate candidate, judging his move to perfection.

As he passed the back of the man, he slipped his foot into the loop of the hand luggage and kept walking, causing the bag to be pulled from the man's feet, sending the bag flying and Callum diving to the ground, pulling an unsuspecting passenger with him for good effect. The move was perfection. Any premiere league footballer would have been proud of his dive. The man was horrified that he had caused chaos in the hallway and first tried to apologise to the passenger Callum had pulled down with him. Suddenly he realised that the contents of his bag were scattered all over the hallway. Callum instantly became the good Samaritan, helping gather the belongings together in the busy corridor.

The man thanked Callum for his help, and Callum was delighted to find that the gentleman was a fellow Scot. Work done, Callum deposited the folder in a bin and gave his newly acquired Formula One tickets a quick once-over as he walked towards the coffee lounge and breakfast with his friends.

Andy was just adding sugar to his coffee when Callum appeared with a beaming smile. He sat down while Lisa handed him half of her toast.

"Yet again the legend that is Callum McPherson has come up with the goods."

Callum handed Andy and Lisa a lanyard each complete with Monaco pass and a ticket each and passes for a balcony viewing area.

Lisa and Andy examined the passes while Callum continued with his self praise.

"Not only have I got us passes, but they are for three members of a Scottish racing car team. How is that for genius! We will even sound like we are the rightful owners of the tickets. Now eat up, and let's get the hell out of here before I get arrested, we need to get to the Grand Prix before the real owners of the tickets find them missing and report them to the authorities."

On the outskirts of Nice, Callum pulled the Peugeot in behind a taxi and to Andy and Lisa's surprise shot out to talk to the parked cabbie. Five minutes later he was back, hustling both of them out of the Peugeot and into the taxi.

"Come on. We need to move. The cabbie will get us as close to the hotel as possible, but we need to move before the roads get totally clogged up with traffic."

Although the plan was good, unfortunately the traffic was terrible, and as the driver gave up and dropped them off, Andy could hear the Formula One cars in action in the distance. Andy was not worried about missing the race as long as he could get to the Hôtel de Paris before the old lady decided it was time to leave.

In the foyer of the Hôtel de Paris, David Pender was a worried man. He had been given the task by his section leader at MI6 of finding out why someone had taken an unhealthy interest in PSS Bank's owner, Madame Chemolie.

His first instinct was that there was little to worry about. The three people he had been tracking were not on any wanted list, and David could find no reason why they should have an issue with the owner of PSS Bank.

As time had gone by, things had started to worry him. The three suspects had crossed to Europe and had actively started searching for the head of the bank. David Pender at that point had sanctioned his team to apprehend one of the three for questioning.

From there, things had gone drastically downhill. The tracker they had fitted to the camper van in Switzerland to tail the trio had been rendered useless when they switched cars after a failed attempt to lift one of the three at the air-field. This was not the act of three innocent citizens. MI6 had been too slow and had failed on two other attempts to apprehend the trio as they had been always one step ahead. The latest info from Madame Chemolie's granddaughter was that they were heading for Monaco to intercept the banker at the Hôtel de Paris. Pender was awaiting further instructions from headquarters, but the behaviour exhib-ited by the three suspects could not be ignored, and if need be, he would shoot first and ask questions later. PSS was far too important to let anything or anyone get in the way. It had to be safeguarded at all costs.

Madame Chemolie watched the final laps of the Monaco Grand Prix on her private balcony on the top floor of the Hôtel de Paris. Only Fred, her pilot, sat by her side while outside her door, her two bodyguards waited for the old lady's next move.

Chemolie was not in the best of moods. Both race cars her bank sponsored failed to even get into the points, and to add insult to injury, the new race cars were a quiet shad-ow of Formula One cars of past years. Madame Chemolie asked Fred to make his way to the plane and prepare it for the flight to Washington. Madame Chemolie informed her two guards that she would be visiting the bar for a drink and to say her good-byes to the staff of the Hôtel de Paris.

The Formula One cars were on their final lap as Andy, Lisa, and Cammy arrived at the rear of the Hôtel de Paris, Lisa's phone had rung already, but she had ignored it as she followed Andy through the streets of Monaco. Now, the phone was ringing again. Lisa checked the screen and then shouted over the engine noise to Andy to keep going. She knew where she was now and would catch them up inside. The caller was Jake Shelton. Lisa was worried that something was wrong back at the office and decided to take the call.

Andy was on a mission now. His target was in sight, and nothing was going to stop him. Andy entered from the side and made his way along the veranda of the big hotel. Although the race had finished, fans were still milling about the front of the packed hotel.

David Pender's senses were still concentrated on the crowd of people at the entrance to the hotel. He spotted Andy and Callum heading for the front door of the hotel. Pender wasted no time, nodding to his colleague Ben standing by the steps. The pair didn't seem to be armed, but Pender was taking no chances. He picked up a copy of the race programme left outside by a guest and used it to conceal his Glock 19 as he fought his way through the mass of bodies to intercept the pair before they entered the hotel. Pender waited until Ben was in position by the second male before stopping the lead suspect and ramming the muzzle of his pistol firmly into his ribs.

He spoke into his ear. "Put one foot into the hotel, and it will be the last thing you ever do. Turn round now and retrace your steps. Do it, and do it quickly, my friend, if you know what is good for your health."

Andy said nothing but looked down to find a handgun was being pressed hard against his side by a very serious-looking individual. Andy caught Lisa's eye as she hurried to catch up with her friends but then ducked in behind a couple of race fans heading to the bar for after-race refreshments. Callum had suffered the same fate and was being led away in front of Andy by another man decked out in a Ferrari T-shirt. Andy had a sinking feeling. He had been so close. God knew what was going to happen now.

Lisa was in a blind panic. She had caught a glimpse of the gun pressed against Andy's side, and as he was led past her, his complexion was chalk white.

She had done nothing, knowing that if she had tried anything, Andy would have tried to come to her rescue and would probably now be dead from a gunshot wound.

Lisa's mind was racing. Should she contact Andy's mum or call the police? She was not sure the police would believe her story. Lisa forced herself to calm down. What was it about this woman they were looking for that had caused them to be drugged then abducted? Lisa decided to find the woman and confront her before involving the police. Lisa needed to know what she was up against before involving the authorities.

Lisa wandered into the busy bar, looking around for some clue as what to do next. Then she spotted the big Asian-looking guard standing just inside the door. She followed his line of sight to the end of the bar where a little old lady sat alone. Lisa's heart jumped into her mouth. This had to be Madame Chemolie. Lisa stopped a waiter and asked the question. He confirmed Lisa's suspicions. It was Madame Chemolie—in the flesh at long last.

Maria Chemolie stirred her club soda, deep in thought about her meeting with the CIA director the following day. She was tired of all this cloak-and-dagger stuff. She was too old for it. At her age, she should be taking things much more slowly. Maria Chemolie hardly noticed the pretty blond girl who had pulled herself up onto the closest bar stool until she spoke.

It took a few seconds for it to register that the girl was speaking to her. Then the girl repeated in a low and nervous voice, "Hello, Jean, or should I just call you Baby Tiger?"

Maria Chemolie was in shock. For a second, her brain was numb. Then she recovered, turning her full attention to the pretty blonde nervously waiting for a reaction from her.

"My dear girl, I must say you have succeeded in rendering me speechless. Tell me—what you expect to gain from calling me these names. Money? Blackmail, maybe? I have to tell you that you do not know what a dangerous path you are walking. If I were you, I would walk away now while you still can, my dear."

Lisa had not expected this reaction, but she pressed on with her voyage into the unknown. "Maria, if you are Jean Bruce, Jan Powlak would have wanted you to help me. I was Jan's nurse, and I think you may be able to help me. All I ask is you help my friends. If you can, then maybe we can have a chat—no money, no blackmail, just a chat. Is that too much to ask, Maria?"

Maria Chemolie studied the face of the young woman, trying to make up her mind where to go with this unexpected confrontation. It would have been easy for her to deny the girl any further audience. One look in the direction of her bodyguards would trigger the girl's removal. If there was one thing Maria Chemolie prided herself on, it was her ability to judge people's characters, and it was this that stopped Maria from calling her guards. She wanted to hear more from the girl before she committed herself in any way to the young woman.

"May I ask why you seem to think I can help your friends?"

Lisa moved closer along the bar towards the old woman before speaking, making sure they were not overheard by any race-car fans who were still milling around in the bar.

"My boyfriend, Andy, and his colleague, Callum, were coming here to try and meet you. Andy was Jan Powlak's lawyer, and Jan made Andy promise to try and set the record straight regarding you. I just watched as they were led away at gunpoint from the front door. I don't know what is happening here, but I do know that it has to do with you. I don't care what you or your organisation are up to. I think you may have the power to get my friends released. Like me, Maria, they only want to have a harmless chat with you. We have been followed, drugged, and abducted, and all we wanted to do was speak to you, so please, Maria, if you can do something to help, it would be appreciated. After all, we were only following Jan's last wish. Please, Maria, can you help?"

By then, Lisa was holding Maria's hand and gazing into the old lady's eyes as the first tear splashed down onto the counter by their hands. Lisa removed her hand from the old lady's and brushed away a second tear before it made a bid for freedom.

Even before the tear had landed, Maria Chemolie had made up her mind. Maria signalled to her closest bodyguard, and he made straight for the bar, parting the crowd as he came. Maria whispered in his ear for a few seconds before he nodded and headed towards the back of the hotel to carry out his instructions.

Ten minutes later, Lisa and Madame Chemolie were being whisked through the streets of Monaco in a convoy of three black Mercedes limos. Barriers and policemen stood aside as the cars flashed past. Inside the middle limo, the two women were separated from their driver by a bulletproof curtain of glass.

"We are heading to the airport, where you will be reunited with your friends. You may leave at that point if you wish, or you may accompany me on my flight to America, thus giving us the chance to have that chat you wanted en route. I will need two things from you for this to go ahead, though. First, I need your permission to let my guards search you all for weapons—tedious, I know, but they insist on it if you are to travel with me. Secondly, I don't know your name, my dear."

For the first time since meeting the old lady, Lisa broke out into a beaming smile. "Thank you, Maria. My name is Lisa, and yes, you can search us. It's no problem."

"Lisa, you don't have to thank me. If doing this would have pleased my friend Jan, it is the least I could do. After all, I owe Jan more, much more than that. I take it that you found me as a result of my visit to poor Jan's grave?"

Lisa nodded, relaxing for the first time in hours. There was something about being in the presence of the old lady that was comforting. Although Lisa had no proof, she knew in her heart that this woman was no gangster or drug kingpin. She was the type of woman who did not make false promises. She knew in her heart that Andy and Callum would be safe, and this lifted a great weight off Lisa's shoulders. Suddenly, she remembered her conversation that afternoon with Jake Shelton.

"Maria, I almost forgot in all the drama of this afternoon that Jake Shelton, Jan's old business partner, is unveiling some sort of tribute to Jan at Powlak Air headquarters in Reno the day after tomorrow. If you are flying to America, I am sure Jan would have loved you to be there, along with his friends and business partner. Do you think you could fit that into your trip?"

The Falcon 900 was refueled and ready to go. Fred waited patiently as the black Mercedes pulled up. He was ready to help his old friend and boss onto her private jet but was surprised to find that Maria Chemolie had arrived with a second passenger in tow—and then knocked completely off his game when Maria announced to him that she wanted to change destinations from Washington to Reno. Fred helped the two ladies on board then excused himself while he did the maths for the fuel needed and tried to sort out a flight plan.

Andy and Callum arrived at the Falcon 900 in the back of a Renault Espace and were dragged out of the back seats unceremoniously, hands cable-tied behind their backs. They were led to the steps leading to the Falcon's door before their captors released their arms, handing them over to the big Asian bodyguard standing by the steps. The guards were still frisked them when Lisa sprinted down the steps, flinging her arms around Andy's neck. Madam Chemolie watched the two lovebirds from the Falcon's side windows, smiling to herself.

Once the boys were searched, Lisa led Andy and Callum up the steps and into the plush leather cabin of the Falcon to meet the person who had been the centre of their universe for the past few months.

Andy was speechless as he was introduced to Maria, but Maria had no such problem and launched a verbal assault on the trio.

"Hello, Andy and Callum. Lisa has been putting me in the picture while we were waiting on your arrival. Please bear with me. I feel that the least I should do is explain what the hell is going on."

There was a pause as the big Asian guard climbed on board and closed the hatch while Fred warmed up the engines waiting for his departure slot from Nice airport.

"Saroj, can you give Fred a hand in the cockpit while I talk to my new friends?"

The big guard nodded but said nothing. He vanished into the cockpit, closing the cabin door behind him. Maria waited until Saroj had left before continuing with her speech, her voice lowered to stop the cockpit crew hearing what she was about to say.

"I don't think that the authorities would want me to tell you any of this, but you have been through a lot and deserve an apology and an explanation. I think we can keep this a secret between the four of us.

"In a nutshell, my bank is not what it seems. I was approached by MI6 and then the CIA to let my bank be used in a sting operation against first Al Qaeda and then the Russian mafia, the Columbian drug cartels, and basically now any scum who need to hide their money and transfer it without their enemies finding out. For years now, we have built a reputation with the criminal underworld that their money is safe with us, which it is. Unfortunately for them, they have not grasped the fact that my bank is staffed with British and American undercover analysts who track where the money goes. It is such a simple thing, but none of them have twigged that they are being tracked through my bank.

"Guns, drugs, bombs, bribes—we know it all. Unfortunately, with this knowledge comes great risks, hence my ex-Gurkha bodyguards and why MI6 got very jumpy when you three started tracking me. Don't worry. Agent Pender, who abducted you, has been told to back off, and MI6 have been told to stand down as I have vouched for all three of you."

There was a pause in the proceedings as Fred announced over the intercom that the Falcon had been cleared for take-off and that they should hold onto their seats as he was in a hurry to get into the air. He did not want to miss his slot as the airport was very busy today.

Once airborne, Madame Chemolie produced glasses and a bottle of chilled Champagne from a cabinet next to her big leather reclining chair. Lisa did the honours and passed the filled glasses around until they all held one. Maria Chemolie raised her glass, making eye contact with each one of her shell-shocked guests.

"I think that as Jan has brought us together, it is fitting that we should honour him with a toast. To Jan Powlak, the best flight engineer that I have ever known. Jan."

The four new friends toasted Jan, and a silence fell upon the cabin, no one quite sure what to say next.

Andy was desperate to ask Maria about her past but somehow managed to contain himself. It was again Maria who made the first move.

"I can tell that you are all desperate to find out about me, but humour an old lady and tell me about yourselves first. It is a long flight, and we have many hours ahead of us to talk about me before we reach Reno. Ladies first, so Lisa, I think you should start. Then we will hear from Andy, and last but not least, Callum."

Lisa went over her career and how she came to know Jan. She told about meeting with Andy, how Andy had came to her rescue over Jan's will, and the subsequent aftermath leading up to today's encounter.

Andy explained his career in the RAF and how it had come to pass that he had been sent to Dundee to interview Jan Powlak and in the process bumped into Lisa at the nursing home. After that his story pretty much mirrored Lisa's, as they had been joined at the hip from then on. Maria interrupted the conversation before Callum could start.

"Excuse me, Callum. I just wanted to say something to these two before the notion fades. Lisa, Jan was not an easy person to get to know. For him to leave you everything and trust you to look after him, I feel in my heart you must have made his last few years happy ones, my dear.

"As for you, Andrew, I can see that you worship the ground Lisa walks on. Take it from an old lady who has seen and done almost everything in this great world of ours—don't wait! Life is too short. Take fate by the throat. What I am trying to tell you is Lisa loves you. For goodness sake, grab the opportunity with both hands while you can. Marry her. She will say yes. I know it!"

Andy and Lisa made eye contact but said nothing, struck dumb by the old lady's words. Callum found this extremely funny and chuckled away as he sipped his Champagne. Maria realised that she had embarrassed her guests and turned to the chuckling Cammy.

"Well, Callum, I think it is your turn to take centre stage. Please proceed, my friend."

Callum emptied his glass then leaned forwards, making eye contact with Maria. Callum went over his career from university, where he had met Andy, to his job researching family trees, to his recruitment to try and find Maria. He went into great detail about all the clues that he had turned up in the hunt for her. Then he could not help himself and brought up the visit to the vineyard and how he had found the three horses, adding that he thought Maria's granddaughter was enchanting. Lisa cut in before Cammy went any further.

"Maria, I think what Callum is trying to say is that he took quite a shine to Oriane, and I think we should leave it at that before you decide to fling Callum out without a parachute."

Again Maria was ahead of them. "To answer the question that you were about to ask me, Callum, Oriane is single, yes, but she is a complicated girl, and as yet no one but her horses have won her heart. Many have tried, but you never know, Callum, my friend. You may be the one. After all, you found me, and you for the most part stayed one step ahead of MI6, so you may find a way to Oriane's heart. I will see to it that I put a good word in for you."

There was a pause as Lisa topped up their empty glasses. The attention of the three new arrivals was firmly on their host. For Andy, the tension was at screaming level. Maria sensed the anticipation and cleared her throat.

"Very well, but before I go any further, I must insist that anything spoken about on this aircraft stays among ourselves. You may tell whomever you wish once I am dead and buried, but until then, I do not want to be in the limelight. I have only a little time left on this planet, and I wish to live it in peace and quiet, so we understand one another, yes?"

CHAPTER 14
ONE OF THE FEW

Jean's Story Begins

My name is Jean Maria Bruce. I was born on March 12, 1920, in the village of Kirkliston, Scotland. I was the tomboy of the family. My mother and father had travelled in Europe and seen the future, and so they sent me to Canada to work on my uncle's farm. In truth, my uncle was not a pleasant man, and my only real pleasure was learning to fly his old Waco INF crop sprayer. Eventually his bad temper drove me to leave and seek a new life in America. My love of flying burned deep inside me, and I joined a flying circus, wing-walking at first before eventually getting to fly the biplane in the show. One thing led to another, and I became their stunt pilot, even getting myself into the American papers as the female daredevil of the sky.

America was slow to follow events in Europe, and just as things in my life were looking good, I got the news that my parents had gone missing while skiing. I packed up and returned to England to seek more information from my father's youngest brother, my uncle Bill.

By this time things were getting really nasty between Germany and Great Britain, and no matter how hard I tried, I could not get permission to travel to the continent to search for my parents. Uncle Bill was my rock. He found me work in the Hawker company where he worked and helped me write letter after letter to my MP or whoever would listen. Eventually the Red Cross listened to me and promised to try and find out more from their contacts in Europe.

One morning, a little man with a bowler hat arrived at my uncle's door with terrible news from the Red Cross. My mother and father had been apprehended on the Swiss border and accused of spying for Britain. There was no trial, only the firing squad. The gestapo executed them where they stood and left the locals to bury them.

I was beyond devastated. My uncle managed to pull some strings, and I joined him delivering spares so that he could keep an eye on me.

This is when I met the flight crews from 303 Squadron. They had just arrived in England and were trying hard to impress their RAF officers so they could have a chance at revenge.

I remember on one particular visit, one of their Hurricanes did a tight loop of the base, the pilot using the power of the Merlin engine to pull the airframe against the g-force of the turn. The engine noise of the hard-working Merlin made the hairs on the back of my neck stand up, and at that point, I knew somehow, someday I would fly one of those beasts.

My uncle knew of my love of flying and let me wander about the bases while he sorted out his deliveries.

The aircraft I had just watched do the turn taxied up to the dispatch building, and as I approached the fighter plane, its pilot jumped to the ground, smiling at me. That was the first time I had met Tomasz Zajac. He was a squadron leader with the Polish squadron and had arrived with his men, battle weary from exile in Romania.

Over the next few weeks, Tomasz and I became friends. At first, Tomasz did not believe that I was a pilot and invited me into the cockpit of his precious Hurricane to see if I knew what to do with the controls. After I proved my point, Tomasz showed me some of the features and layout specific to the Hurricane. I did not know at that time that the little tuition he gave me would save my life in the near future.

On August 23, 1940, Uncle Bill and I were delivering engine spares to 303 Squadron. As we arrived, the base was empty, but the hum of aircraft engines was not far away. I watched three Hurricanes approaching the far end of the base, skiffing over the boundary fence before touching down and taxiing to a stop in the usual spots., Tomasz was first out of his craft while his wingman, Peter Kalinowski, crossed the airfield to speak to his comrade Oskar, if my memory serves me correctly.

Suddenly all hell broke loose. The first wave were Messerschmitt Bf 109 fighters. They attacked at low level, strafing the runways and buildings with machine-gun bullets in preparation for an attack by their bombers. Poor Peter started to sprint for his machine but was cut down by a hail of bullets. I was frozen to the spot in terror, and it was Tomasz who brought me back to my senses, screaming at me. At first I thought he was telling me to take cover, but then it dawned on me that he was climbing into his Hurricane and bellowing at me to follow suit and climb on board Peter's pilotless machine. Tomasz had decided to risk me flying the valuable fighter plane rather than leave it to the mercy of the Nazi fighters and almost certain destruction. As I clambered unladylike into the fighter, a man appeared, pulling headgear over my head and helping me start the big Merlin engine. This was your friend and mine Jan Powlak.

I don't recall him speaking to me. Maybe he did. Who knows? I was in a blind panic, trying to remember what Tomasz had told me about the Hurricane.

As I followed Tomasz in the lead Hurricane, the sky started to rain bombs down on us. Even over the noise of the Hurricane the terrifying scream of bombs dropping was clear. I watched as Tomasz increased power for takeoff, and I followed him. My first mistake was the throttle. It was stiffer than I had expected, and I trundled down the runway on half throttle, watching first Tomasz then Oskar lift off while I was still taxiing. At that point, I realised something was wrong and applied more pressure to the throttle. Then I remembered Tomasz telling me the throttle had a locking mechanism for landing. I found it on the left just below the throttle and slackened it. The Merlin roared like a bull and leapt forwards, the torque of the engine causing the machine to veer off line. I corrected the drift and started to feel the fighter come to life as its wheels left the ground. There was no time to loose. The airfield boundary was rushing towards me at an alarming speed. Luckily I remembered where Tomasz had told me the landing gear controls were, and I pulled my wheels up as I gently started to lift the nose of the Hurricane. Just as I thought I had it sorted, only yards in front of me a Messerschmitt appeared on a collision course. It was heading for the airfield to strafe whatever had survived the bombing run.

What happened next was pure gut instinct. I had no feel for the aircraft yet, so the manoeuvre was seat-of-the-pants stuff. I sat the Hurricane on its wing tip, banking hard to port and levelling off to allow the engine all its power and torque to deal with the instant change in direction. I knew even in my stunt planes in America, I would have stalled the engine with such an aggressive move, but it had to be done. I waited first for the crash of metal as the two planes collided and then, after surviving this, I turned my attention to my altitude. My wing tip could only have been two or three feet from the ground. I levelled off and started to climb, looking for Tomasz in the lead Hurricane as I rose to safety. My first instinct once safe was to play with the Hurricane and get the feel of it, but I knew I had already chanced my luck, so I concentrated on finding Tomasz and Oskar and following them. We effectively flew in a big loop until the Germans left. I later discovered that 303 Squadron had still to be cleared for action. We landed, and for a few minutes, I was floating on a wave of adrenalin. People were shaking my hand and patting my back. Then I noticed Tomasz change. He was the first one to realise Uncle Bill's lorry had been destroyed by a Luftwaffe bomb.

In a fraction of a second, my elation was plunged into earth-shattering despair. That evening with more than a little vodka in my system I agreed to take the place of the deserter Artur Krol.

I had nothing to lose. I did not have anything in Scotland to go back for, and my Uncle Ted in Canada was not my cup of tea. Tomasz explained that he did not want to lose face with his RAF commanding officers. We were united in a common cause. We all wanted revenge. I had lost my family, and the pilots had lost even more—their families, their homes, their country.

Tomasz promised me if I joined, he would teach me everything he knew about killing Nazis. Full of vodka and a burning desire for revenge, I thought it sounded like the only way forwards. From that moment on, I became Artur Krol.

The next day, while Jan and the other ground crew tried to repair the damage the Luftwaffe had caused, Tomasz Zajac, myself, and a few of his pilots helped bury Peter Kalinowski and the body of the dead German pilot who, I learned after the air raid, had crashed trying to avoid colliding with my Hurricane.

In the truck on the way back from the local cemetery, Tomasz informed me that he had claimed the German plane as a kill for Artur Krol, and that in the afternoon, we would head off on my first training flight.

The weather that afternoon was not good, so I spent a bit of time talking to Jan Powlak, who had been assigned to me as my aircraftsman. I had a feeling that Tomasz had picked Jan to babysit me and try and keep me out of sight in a damp cupboard in the workshop, well away from the watchful eyes of the RAF officers leading 303 Squadron.

The afternoon was spent trying to get flying gear to fit me as I was on the petite side for a fighter pilot. Tomasz appeared later that afternoon to say that due to the bad weather, no flying was allowed, and we would see how the weather was tomorrow.

I was gutted. I had been buzzing at the thought of spending some time getting the hang of flying a fighter plane. It was then with nothing to do and no vodka to cloud my thoughts that the enormity of what I had agreed to hit me.

I was a civilian woman masquerading as a RAF pilot. It was nothing short of madness, but as I considered pulling out while I still could, the faces of my mother and father and his little brother, Uncle Bill, filled my head. I had nothing left in this world. So what if they flung me in jail? I was prepared to pay this price for just one chance to pay the Nazis back for destroying my family and ruining so many lives.

Jan, I think, sensed what I was thinking and sat passing the time with me, trying to take my mind off things. We talked about life before the war—Jan working for Alfa Romeo, his racing days, and his life as a boy in Poland. I told him all about America and my bonnie Scotland. We must have listened to each other. Jan ended up in America and then Scotland, while among other things, my great passion is motor racing.

That night I could not sleep. I could say it was the loss of my family or the position I found myself in, but truthfully, it was the promise of flying the Hurricane the next day.

The camp was just waking up the next morning when Jan and Tomasz arrived at the storeroom door with strong coffee and my flight suit.

The morning mist still clung to the runway as Tomasz lifted his tail wheel then pulled the nose of his Hurricane up followed by his new wingman—me!

Tomasz turned to port on a northwest route, taking us away from any potential encounters with enemy aircraft. Today was all about learning to fly the Hurricane, not about using its potential to go chasing Germans. Tomasz patiently showed me some evasive manoeuvres that would help if I ended up with an enemy fighter on my tail. All the time we were flying, Tomasz was drumming into me not to fly level in a combat zone and to always look up, as German fighter pilots used altitude to their advantage and were normally to be found high above their bomber formations. My flight that day went without a hitch. On our final approach to the airfield, we could see in the distance great swarms of German aircraft and British fighter planes darting among them. More than a few of the invaders were having a bad day. Some bombers were trailing black smoke across the azure sky of the south coast of England.

It was blatantly apparent that although they were doing a good job, the RAF were massively outnumbered. Tomasz I think was having the same thoughts, and I could hear him cursing in Polish as we turned away from the battle to land our fully armed fighter planes, denied combat because of ludicrous air force red tape.

My flight debrief took place in my cupboard by Tomasz and Jan. I had done a good job apparently, and things had gone well, but secretly in my head, I had been on a leash today. I had followed orders, but I knew instinctively that the Hurricane had so much more to offer. Its big Merlin engine had hardly broken a sweat today, and its manoeuvres were cautious. In my heart, I knew that given time, I could make the Hurricane dance and dance to my tune.

Tomasz left to get some food and then annoy his commanding officer about the operational status of 303 Squadron.

Jan brought me some breakfast and stayed to cram more information into my head about the Hurricane. While the rest of the unit stripped the crashed Messerschmitt Bf 109 for souvenirs, Jan brought the broken engine of the enemy fighter into the workshop and dismantled it, examining every nut and bolt for weaknesses that could be exploited to our advantage. Jan warned me of the dangers of engaging one of these fighters at high altitude as it had a superior fuel system and would dangerously outperform the Hurricane. Jan recommended that any dogfight, should it occur, be kept below twenty thousand feet to give the big Merlin engine enough fuel to perform correctly. Also, he told me that when using the machine guns, I should keep the firing to only very short bursts as there was a limit to how much ammunition the Hurricane could carry.

My next flight was as part of a group. The whole Romanian section of 303 Squadron, as they had become known, took off heading northwest again, away from the action.

Tomasz Zajac, Oskar Piotrowski, Eryk Sawicki, Jakub Kowalski, Krytian Duda, Janek Vawenska, and poor Peter's brother, Marek Kalinowski—these men had flown as a fighting unit before and really only needed to get used to a girl flying in their midst. At first, there was little talk, but as things settled down, the Polish chatter over the radio grew louder until Tomasz Zajac told his men to shut up in English.

That evening, when Tomasz and the rest of his men were sure the English officers had retired to the local pub, I was invited into the canteen to meet the rest of my new team. I sat mesmerized. I had picked up a few Polish words, but in a group, the voices melted together, producing an impossible collection of speech and dialect that I could not understand. Marek Kalinowski came and sat down beside me. He told me that Peter would have been happy knowing that his Hurricane would not be wasted and that he knew I would help avenge his death.

Next morning I was fast asleep when the storeroom door was flung open by Tomasz. He had a crazy look in his eye as he told me that day 303 Squadron had been granted operational status, and I needed to get dressed and fed as we were probably going to get our first taste of action.

That day was August 31, 1940, and it will stay in my memory until I die. Tomasz marched up and down while I watched proceedings with Jan from the workshop door. It was late afternoon before the phone call came to scramble our fighters. There was a nervous excitement in the air as we left Northolt, this time turning southeast. Our unit was led by one of the RAF officers guiding us to our target area, where bandits had been sighted crossing the channel in strength.

Over Kent, we spotted the enemy dead ahead, mainly fighter planes escorting a few Messerschmitt 110 fighter-bombers. Any hope that the RAF officer had of a controlled attack went out the window in the first few seconds as the Poles broke formation, every man intent on sending the enemy to oblivion.

My call sign was Polish for "Baby Tiger," a name that I had been given by the men after my first flight in the Hurricane. Shouting *Jean* over the airwaves would have been a bit of a giveaway that all was not as it should have been.

Tomasz screamed my call sign over the radio, telling me to stick to his tail like glue. The German formation broke up as the German fighters picked their targets and broke away, leaving the bombers to try to defend themselves. Tomasz picked a fleeing 110 bomber and plotted a course to intercept with my Hurricane in close pursuit. Suddenly I was aware of flashes from my starboard side. Then a couple of dull thuds unsettled my Hurricane. This was followed suddenly by the belly of a 109 cutting across my nose in a power dive. I was so scared I forgot to fire at a target that was right in front of my nose. I cursed at myself for not looking around, Tomasz had broken contact with the 110 after he discovered me missing from his tail. He came looking for me but found himself being chased and fired on by the same 109 that had attacked me. I eventually found Tomasz well below me, being chased by the 109. To my great relief, Oskar had been watching and intercepted the Messerschmitt Bf 109 as he closed on Tomasz. At first, I thought Oskar was going to ram the fighter, he was so close. Then I saw his machine guns speak, tearing great lumps from the port wing of the Nazi fighter and sending it in a spiral towards the ground, its wing all but torn off. I watched fascinated to see if the pilot escaped, but the fighter ploughed into the trees before the canopy opened and exploded on impact.

Suddenly I realised I had been sight-seeing in a war zone and again cursed at myself for my stupidity.

Checking above me before starting a spiral climb while looking for possible targets was strange. A sky that minutes ago had been full of warplanes was empty, the fighters scattered all along the Kent coast, all involved in their own little battles.

Tomasz and Oskar found me before I found them, and the three of us headed back in the direction of Northolt keeping a keen eye out for the enemy.

On the ground, the mood was one of elation. Tomasz was initially grumpy because he had failed to score a victory, but when it became apparent that his Romanian section had all returned alive, his mood lifted. He patted Oskar on the back for saving his neck and scoring the Romanian section's only kill of the day.

I on the other hand was furious with myself. The Hurricane's guns were taped over to protect the guns, and this tape was only broken when the guns were fired. To my horror, my machine was the only one in the Romanian section whose gun covers were still intact. Worse than that, I had lost my position on my leader's wing and allowed an enemy fighter to first have a go at me and then to attack my leader's plane. I had not covered myself in glory. In my mind, I needed to get my head out of my arse and do it pretty bloody quickly before it was me crashing into the trees with my wing hanging off.

In the evening, Jan arrived at the storeroom and asked me to follow him into the main hangar. My Hurricane sat to one side, a section of the tail panel cut away where two cannon shells from the German had punched through the canvas-and-wood outer skin of the Hurricane. Jan pointed to the section, bringing my attention to the damaged metal inner section and the frayed control cables to the rear tail section. He did not say anything. He didn't have to. I was lucky to have made it back in one piece.

That night, Jan and two others worked through the night to change the cables and patch up my Hurricane for our next scramble.

The next day, Jan's work was not put to the test, and an uneasy stillness settled over Northolt as pilots mingled about, trying to calm their prebattle nerves. We had all been in action now, and the stress was clear to see on the faces around the dispatch building as men waited to see what hand fate was going to deal them.

I spent the day with Jan, helping him tidy up some tail ends with my machine, removing the covers one by one to inspect my unfired Browning machine guns. We should have enjoyed the day off more because September second made up for it. On our first scramble of the day, I lost Tomasz when we exited cloud cover to find three Messerschmitt 110 fighter-bombers directly in front of me. I opened fire on the centre bomber, but I had again made a mistake.

I was too far away to cause any damage to the bombers, and instead, my shots served as a warning to the fighter-bombers, who broke ranks heading their own ways. I followed the middle aircraft but again opened fire too far behind. To my dismay, my guns stopped firing, I thought that they had jammed, but later I found out that I had emptied my guns. A quick look round told me that although the Germans were gone, so was 303 Squadron, so I turned dejectedly for home before German fighters found me with no way of defending myself.

I arrived back at Northolt first and trundled up to the hangar where Jan was waiting anxiously for his machines to return from battle. Luckily, all the RAF commanding officers were still in the sky. Jan scoffed at my idea that the guns were jammed, stripping the inspection plates off while the aircraft was being refuelled. As Jan expected, the guns were out of ammo. Again our luck was with us. All members of 303 Squadron returned safely—no kills to shout about but safe. That afternoon, we were scrambled two more times. The first time, we were beaten to our target by three Spitfires who broke up the bomber formation. By the time we got in on the action, the bombers were scattered to the four winds, and the Spitfires had their hands full with the fighter escort, but they seemed to be coping well enough, so Tomasz turned our flight to starboard, hunting the coast for more German raiders. We were out of luck and ordered by ground control to return to base. Like a few of us, this was the first time I had witnessed the Spitfire in the flesh, so to speak. It was a graceful-looking machine that was already making a formidable reputation for itself in the skies over England.

Our third squadron scramble of the day was again mistimed, and we arrived in the designated area to find that the enemy had already been engaged. I was determined to stick to Tomasz this time and tucked in at his back as he went into a shallow dive. Tomasz had noticed a Hurricane in trouble. Its engine was smoking, and it was being harried by a Bf 109 fighter. The Nazi pilot was intent on his kill and was unaware of Tomasz until it was too late. His Hurricane opened fire right on the tail of the Maesserschmitt, blowing the tail ailerons clean off. His second burst was at a slight angle, and I watched as the shells exploded along the fuselage, smashing into the engine and cockpit, causing the fighter to turn belly up, flames pouring from the engine cover, before the plane went into a steep dive and vanished below the low cloud, never to be seen again.

I watched as the damaged Hurricane's cockpit was thrown back and the pilot bailed out of the smoking machine. I got a glimpse of the engine cover as it started to lose altitude. The maple leaf told me that this lucky Canadian would live to fight another day, just not in that machine.

On returning to base, I was happier with my performance. I had not put a foot wrong this time and was given a hug for my efforts from Tomasz, who was in a great mood after scoring his first kill.

Next morning was September 5. I will always remember that day. We were scrambled fairly early, and this time we arrived above the German bomber formation. I was shocked at how many bombers were in formation and started scanning the heavens for their fighter escort. It was inconceivable that this number of bombers would have no escort. Sure enough, the fighters were high at one o'clock and coming down on our position. Tomasz judged the distance and decided that we could be among the bombers before the fighters were on us. I followed Tomasz with Oskar on my port wing. As expected, the bombers started to break formation as they spotted us, but today, they were too late. At the last minute, Tomasz banked hard to starboard, ducking gunfire from one of the bombers and heading straight for one of the attacking fighters. I could not make the turn without hitting the bomber and instead ducked under its wing, which presented me with a perfect target—a Junkers JU 88 bomber just below the first bomber. It was so close I could make out the expression on the co-pilot's face as I gave my guns a quick burst. I was over and past it before I could blink, but standing on the tail rudder brought me back to port just below the bomber. Smoke and flames were billowing from the port engine as I fired a second burst into the starboard wing. Smoke started to pour from the second engine, and the big bomber dropped like a stone. I followed it down and watched it crash and explode without seeing any parachutes. I clenched my fist and punched the air. I had at last struck a blow for my parents' murder. Far from having remorse, I was elated. This was only the start.

I was determined Germany would pay a heavy price for taking my family from me.

The mood was good as we arrived back at Northolt. Our Romanian section had done its bit. Oskar again had a kill, and Marek joined the scoreboard along with myself. In total that day 303 Squadron shot down five fighters and three bombers. The celebrations were overshadowed slightly as the other section of 303 was missing a Hurricane, its pilot posted as missing in action. That evening we rested. Most of our group thought that three scrambles was as busy as it could get, but we were so wrong. The following morning was a beautiful start to the day. Sitting out on our deck chairs, you could almost believe you were in a park somewhere enjoying the summer.

Our scramble came eventually, and we turned south after leaving Northolt, then started to climb towards our target zone.

Marek's scream in Polish to break was the first indication something was very wrong. Our bomber formation turned into twenty-plus bandits and all bloody fighters coming down on us from a high altitude.

The fighting was bloody and desperate. Every one of us had a Bf 109 on his tail. I felt the dreaded shudder as bullets tore into my fuselage. I put my Hurricane belly up, kicking the tail rudders at the same time. The chasing Messerschmitt could not live with the turning pace of the Hurricane and had to fly past on the port side. I had a fraction of a second to bring my guns to bear on my enemy. I was lucky and clipped his tail with the Brownings as he passed, sending him into an unrecoverable tailspin. No sooner had I stopped shooting than the dull thud came again. This time

I could feel that I was damaged. The Hurricane was not responding well to my efforts. I decided to try to get low, away from the hell that was all around. Bullet tracers passed over my nose as I struggled to lift the nose of the Hurricane as the ground loomed up in front of my cockpit. I watched in horror as a Hurricane fell from the sky, its cockpit ablaze. I felt like a traitor limping away, but to turn back to the fight would have been certain death. I told myself it was better to live and fight another day.

I managed to limp my Hurricane back to base, thanking god when the wheels touched down. I was not the first to return. Two battle-scarred Hurricanes sat wearily outside the hangar as mine joined them. Jan ran forwards, a look of relief on his face, and he was joined seconds later by Tomasz and Janek.

Jan and the others were looking at the back of my machine as I climbed down to join them. The hole in the rear fuselage was so big you could have climbed through it, and the top half of the tail fin was gone.

I was still pulling my gloves off as my machine was wheeled into the workshop. Jan had vanished. I stopped and blew my machine a big kiss before turning to see Tomasz and Janek looking at me. I told them I would blow a kiss to my aircraft every time she brought me back alive from that day onwards.

After the dust settled that day, we realised we had taken a beating. Oskar, myself, and Janek had scored three kills in the Romanian section, and the others had somehow managed to shoot down another four enemy planes, but we had lost six Hurricanes and two pilots, including our English RAF commander. Wounded, he had managed to crash-land, but he was out of the equation now. Jan and his team worked through the night, with Tomasz urging them on to try and get as many machines as possible back in the air for the following day.

I had gone to sleep shattered but woke up drenched in sweat. I had dreamt that I was trapped in a burning Hurricane. I did not want to go back to sleep and joined Tomasz fretting over our broken machines as Jan never stopped. By eight o'clock the next morning, we had twelve serviceable machines for whatever Jerry was going to throw at us that day.

The next day was September 7. That day, the German war machine made a fatal error, switching its attack to the London docks. Its fighter cover was limited due to low fuel, and our fighters had longer in the air as we were closer to the action now.

Midmorning, we were scrambled and vectored towards a formation of bombers headed for London. Ground control had got it spot on. The sky was full of them with very few fighters to help. Tomasz was a man possessed. He wanted payback for the previous day and led the formation in without checking for fighter cover. The Dornier Do 17 was a German heavy bomber and had little chance of outrunning a fighter. They were for the most part unprotected. By the time my guns were empty, I had watched three go down by my hand, and others were falling from the sky.

With no ammunition left, there was little point hanging around, and like others from the squadron, I turned for home and a chance to refuel, rearm, and get ready for the next wave of bombers.

The second wave never returned that day. Adolf must have been licking his wounds as 303 Squadron shot down fourteen enemy planes that morning with a loss of two Hurricanes.

That evening it was clear to see that our lot were starting to feel the strain. Poor Eryk could not keep food down, while Marek was pale and withdrawn. I noticed while Tomasz was speaking to us, he was having problems holding his tea, his hand shaking badly.

I seemed to be OK as long as I was awake. When sleep came, so did the nightmares. Secretly I prayed that when my time came, it would not be in a burning Hurricane, I made a pact with myself if I caught fire, I would find the biggest German bomber I could and ram it before the fire did the job for me. I was giving my Hurricane Baby Tiger, now complete with tiger motif on the engine cowling, the once-over in the hangar when Oskar Piotrowski appeared by my side. He was having a bit of fun, joking with me that I owed him one. Unknown to me, he had dealt with the second Messerschmitt that had filled my Hurricane full of holes. He told me he expected me to pay the compliment back if he ever was in trouble. On that note, we both headed our separate ways, Oskar to find some vodka, and I to try getting some nightmare-free sleep.

The next day, the Germans tried London again with much the same result. Although I arrived back empty-handed, 303 Squadron chalked up another ten enemy planes. Still, we lost two Hurricanes, both pilots killed in action from the other flight. The jubilation of scoring victories had worn off as men collapsed, waiting for the next scramble to come.

September 16 was another day that was burned into my memory for all the wrong reasons. We were busy in the morning. Tomasz, Oskar, and I all shot down a 109 each. Our flight was just finishing rearming, and our tea was brewing when we were scrambled again. As we got up to combat altitude, the sight in front of me was hard to describe. It looked to me like the whole of the Luftwaffe were engaged with every RAF fighter we had over London. No matter where you looked, dogfights were going on. We had joined the battle late and soon were scattered to the four winds. That day, it was every man for himself. A Messerschmitt 110 fighter-bomber made the mistake of trying to get on my tail, but I stood on my tail rudder, flinging the back of my machine round in his path, forcing him to break off and go high. He presented me with his underbelly, and I obliged by sending my bullets into it with precision. I am not sure if it was his fuel tank or his bomb load that exploded, but the shockwave threw my machine over to starboard just in time to see Tomasz and Oskar pass me on the starboard side, heading for a formation of nine Dornier bombers headed unimpeded towards the centre of London. A quick check all around was clear, so I decided to join the party and followed at a slight distance as Tomasz attacked first from the port side of the bombers. I watched as the lead bomber started to drop out of formation as its port wing caught fire, Oskar picked the rear plane and started firing before falling away from the attack. At first it looked like he had just switched tactics, but then it became apparent something was wrong. He dropped his nose, and his fighter went into a shallow dive. I broke off the chase, following him in the dive. I screamed at Oskar to pull up but there was no response, Oskar never pulled out of the dive. I watched horrified as his Hurricane ploughed into a railway siding, exploding on impact.

By the time I pulled myself together and climbed back towards the bombers, Tomasz had dispatched a second bomber in flames. I was in a foul mood and didn't bother with tactics, picking one of the bomber's undersides and waiting, waiting. Then I opened fire at point-blank range, stupidly emptying all my remaining ammunition into the German bomber, only pulling away at the last second as it started fall towards me out of control and doomed.

I made the return flight to Northolt with a heavy heart. Oskar had become a good friend, and he had saved my skin into the bargain. It was hard to believe he was gone.

Once on the ground, things did not improve. Tomasz had landed a few seconds ahead of me and was waiting for me to confirm that we had lost Oskar. The bad news was not over yet. Tomasz informed me that Eryk Sawicki had also been killed in action. The pilots of 303 Squadron had shot down sixteen enemy aircraft that day. Three were my kills, but that night there was no celebrating. The Romanian section had paid heavily. In my little cupboard, I cried myself to sleep.

The next day, the 303 Squadron was scrambled, but with two aircraft shot down and three badly damaged, the remainder of the Romanian section was stood down for the day to repair the aircraft and receive replacement pilots.

That day, I was in the main hangar helping Jan check a faulty landing-gear mechanism on my machine. A few of our flight had left the base to drown their sorrows the night before and were licking their wounds as the sound of Merlin engines arriving broke the peace and quiet.

I popped my nose round the corner of the main door. The Canadian squadron that shared Northolt along with the remainder of 303 had left only a short time ago. I wanted to know if it were battle-damaged machines arriving home.

Three shiny new Hurricanes were parked in front of dispatch. I was about to wander across to them when Tomasz sprinted past me, signalling me to follow him. Tomasz grabbed a shell-shocked Jan Powlak and dragged him into my little cupboard. There was a lot of frantic, garbled Polish shouted as Jan started to undress, Tomasz turned his attention back to me, grabbing me and dragging me across to an empty engine crate.

He explained as he half-helped half-flung me into the crate that Group Captain Vincent had arrived with two new pilots and had asked to congratulate Artur Krol as he had heard that he had shot down three enemy planes yesterday.

Poor Jan had been press-ganged into playing the part of Artur Krol while I was ordered not to leave the crate until someone came for me.

And so it was after that first time, whenever visitors arrived, I was dumped in a crate while Jan played the part of me.

Later that evening, Marek called at my cupboard, asking me to go to Tomasz's room. On entering, along with Tomasz and Jan, I found the two new pilots who regarded me wide-eyed.

Tomasz introduced the new pilots: a Czech called Ondra Malenov and a Pole called Frank Wozniak. To my surprise, both Ondra and Frank spoke good English. Frank was a godsend. Before the war he was a translator for the Polish government, just what we needed in the camp.

Tomasz made a comment that was obviously aimed at me as the Polish contingent in the room cackled to themselves, leaving Ondra and myself none the wiser.

Frank translated for us. Tomasz had told them that I would be their flight leader, and they were to stick to me like glue. Baby Tiger would show them how to kill Nazis. The only thing more dangerous than a Polish fighter pilot was a crazy Scottish girl, he said. Frank later told me in confidence that Tomasz had threatened to cut their throats if it ever got out that their flight leader was a girl.

I had put on a brave face that night. In truth, I did not want to babysit new pilots. Life above England was dangerous enough without having to try and look after novices.

On September 27, 303 Squadron took to the air, and I assumed the role of nanny to my two novice pilots. Frank had eleven hours training, while Ondra had nine. Neither had ever seen a German fighter, but such was the need for pilots that they were pressed into service to fill the gaps in fighter command, South of London. Contact was made with a large bomber formation with fighter escort heading for London. Tomasz and two others ran the gauntlet of fighters, breaking through into the midst of the bomber formation, splitting them, and in the process, causing chaos. I held my two apprentices back, waiting for the inevitable stragglers to make a run for it. Just as I spotted a Heinkel HE111 dropping from formation, Ondra peeled off to starboard as a Bf 109 passed, I screamed at him to leave it, but the airwaves were full of screamed orders as battle commenced and Ondra was gone, lost in the chaos of battle. Frank had the good sense to follow me in on to the tail of the Heinkel and waited as my first shells thundered into the port wing of the big bomber. The German rear gunner tried to fend me off as bullets thudded into my machine, but I was damned sure he was going no further and again fired on him, setting the German machine alight. I guided Frank and myself upwards in a spiral. I saw the first chutes appear from the German bomber as its crew bailed out. I looked back just in time to see three Bf 109s heading our way. Somewhere in the middle of my evasive manoeuvres, Frank had gone missing. For the next ten minutes, I had to keep my Hurricane dancing to keep it from being hit by the two 109s that would not give in. Luckily for me, they must have been low on fuel and eventually broke off the dogfight, heading for home.

I was trying to get my bearings when just in front and below me, a ME 110 fighter-bomber emerged from the clouds. He was heading for home and sleeping. I put the Hurricane into a dive, waiting until I was almost touching him before opening fire. Both his engines and his cockpit were hit by the Brownings as I swept past, pulling my machine out of the dive to assess if I needed a second bite at the cherry to finish him off. One engine had stopped while his second engine was on fire. He was in a shallow dive, and I watched from his rear starboard area.

Just as I decided he was finished, from nowhere, the fuselage of the ME 110 was hit by cannon shells. On my port wing, a Spitfire roared in, all guns blazing.

The 110 ploughed into a field a few seconds later, but this was not the object of my attention. I was raging at the idiot in the Spitfire. By the look of his flying, he was straight out of the box. He had to have been a new boy. Nobody in his right mind would have emptied his guns into a plane that was already going down. It was the waste of equipment on a fool that irked me. The idiot could have got another German instead of wasting bullets. I pulled my Hurricane alongside him and gave him a few universally known hand signals before turning and heading for Northolt.

My aerobatics had taken longer than I thought and for the first time, I had been marked up as missing. I was the last to make it home that day. Four of 303 Squadron's pilots never made it that day, and only six Hurricanes were serviceable for the next day.

Ondra Malenov was one of the four killed in action. I vomited when I was told. Ondra had been left in my care, and I had failed to save him. Frank had made it back, but his Hurricane was badly shot up, and he had been taken to hospital with a bullet wound in the leg.

On the plus side, that day our squadron alone had shot down fifteen enemy aircraft with other squadrons scoring big. Adolf's men had taken one hell of a beating.

I was not in a good mood when Tomasz appeared to tell me that I was only credited with one kill. The 110 had been claimed by a Spitfire pilot. I was incensed, and Tomasz had to physically restrain me as I tried to leave the hangar heading for the commanding officer's quarters to give him a piece of my mind. Tomasz had to remind me our commanding officer would have no idea who I was, I returned to my cupboard where I remained for the remainder of the evening.

There was one last air battle that springs to mind. On October 5, ground control vectored us to a large bomber formation making its way up the Thames Estuary, and 303 Squadron fell upon them like a pack of starving hyenas. I had just dispatched a ME 110 to a watery grave at the bottom of the Thames when I noticed far below me a Hurricane trailing smoke and being harried by a pair of Bf 109s. As

I closed on the trio, I deliberately fired from too far away to let my German friends know they were not alone, hopefully taking their mind off their pursuit so the wounded Hurricane could make good its escape while I tangled with its pursuers. I lost sight of one Messerschmitt. The one I was chasing was good, very good, but he was too cocky. He could have outrun me, but he chose to tease me by staying just out of the range of my guns. I waited patiently for him to make a mistake, and on one of his diving turns to port, he was just in range of my Brownings. I fired a burst, removing a section of his tail, and from that moment on, he was history. As his damaged machine struggled to manoeuvre, I brought my sights on to his cockpit and fired a long burst, peppering the German machine's fuselage and sending the machine into a spin. Eventually, it exploded on the mud flats that bordered the River Thames.

Upon landing at Northolt, I was plucked from my cockpit by Tomasz Zajac and hugged like his long-lost daughter. It turned out that the stricken Hurricane had been Tomasz. Eventually I had come good in his eyes, his wingman, and actually saved his life. Unfortunately, Marek Kalinowski was not so lucky, and he was killed in action. Like his brother Peter, he never saw his homeland again.

For myself and also 303 Squadron, this was the end of our Battle of Britain. The squadron was withdrawn from frontline service to rest, recover, and repair the squadron's aircraft. We were transferred from Northolt to Leconfield in Yorkshire, where I moved up in the world from a cupboard to an oil store. Poor Jan was tasked with cutting my hair to make me look more like a male pilot from a distance.

Early in 1941, I finally got my hands on a Spitfire as 303 Squadron was reequipped with Spitfire Mk Is and tasked with escorting bombers on raids into France. Although the Spitfire was undoubtedly the thoroughbred of the RAF, I never felt at home with the fighter. I had grown to used to my Hurricanes habits, and the Spitfire was a much more nervous aircraft to fly. I continued to occasionally notch up the odd Nazi scalp, but compared to the Battle of Britain, things were more controlled and the German pilots less willing to go up against the formidable Spitfire.

By the end of 1941, only three of the original Romanian section from 303 Squadron were still flying. We had returned to our old haunt at Northolt where yet again, I was confined to my cupboard. We were now equipped with the superior Spitfire Mk V, and in my opinion, not a minute too soon. German pilots had a new toy to play with, and it came in the form of the Focke-Wulf 190. If rumours were correct, it was a formidable aircraft, possibly even the new king of the sky.

Summer of 1942 saw our squadron patrolling the English Channel, giving cover to our ships as they ran the gauntlet of the channel.

August 12 started like any other day. We climbed into our machines to give us a tactical superiority. We encountered heavy cloud cover over the coast, and after a few minutes, I broke through the cloud to find myself all alone. My radio was not picking up transmissions, so after a good look around up top, I decided to duck below the cloud again to look for my flight. They were nowhere to be found, but below me and to my starboard side, two small aircraft stood out above the background of the grey sea. My heart skipped a beat as my eyes made out the sleek shape of two German Focke-Wulf Fw190s making there way towards a merchant ship in the distance.

I had the chance to duck back up into cloud cover and go looking for my buddies before the Germans noticed me. Although my head told me to do this, my heart knew I couldn't leave the freighter unguarded. I was about to find out exactly how good the Focke-Wulf really was.

In a vertical dive, I opened fire on the two Focke-Wulfs, hitting the rear of the two aircraft with devastating effect. The Spitfire's cannons ripped the aircraft apart in midair, causing it to explode before I was fully past. The shrapnel from the German's plane cannoned into my Spitfire, causing an unknown amount of damage. Before I could react, the second Focke-Wulf pirouetted in midair, and almost before I knew it, he was on my tail as I tried to outmanoeuvre him with my stricken machine. No matter what trick of the trade I tried, the German machine was a match for my Spitfire. Eventually I climbed into the cloud cover in an attempt to lose my German friend. After a few manoeuvres in the cloud, the gunfire from behind my position stopped. I turned to starboard one more time, and out of the cloud, the Focke-Wulf appeared, on a collision course with my Spitfire. Neither of us was willing to break first and give the other a clean shot. At the last minute, the German pilot flinched, but he was a fraction too late, and our aircraft touched for the briefest of seconds.

The Focke-Wulf fell in a spiral motion away from my aircraft, but I could feel a vibration from my engine, so I pointed the nose downwards, relieving the stress on the sick Merlin engine. Just as I cleared the cloud, my engine started to destroy itself—terrible grinding noises, oil, smoke, and vibrations were coming from the engine covers. I looked around to try and get my bearing. Over my shoulder, far away in the distance stood the white cliffs of Dover, and only a mile ahead of my position was the French coast. I made a split-second decision. There was no way the sick Spitfire was going to make it back. All I had to my advantage was height, and landing near the coast in France would have meant instant capture as it was patrolled heavily by the German army.

If I were going to land this thing in France, it would have to be far enough inland to give me a chance to get away before the Germans found the Spitfire. To the north of my position was a forest, but in the middle was a large clearing. I kicked the tail rudder round, pointing the smoking engine in the direction of the forest clearing. Trying to lower the landing gear proved fruitless. My wheels were locked up solid. My landing was going to be fast and sore.

As my wing tips came level with the tops of the trees, I pulled the nose up, bracing myself and going in belly first. The tail hit first, throwing the nose of the doomed machine downwards. The propeller blades dug in and shattered, causing the Spitfire to summersault, landing belly up.

I had hit my head and was dazed. I could smell fuel, but I was trapped upside down in the wreck. I managed to get my parachute straps off, and although the canopy was smashed, I was jammed between the seat and the ground. I could hear the hiss of fuel hitting hot metal. I was waiting for the roar as the fuel ignited and had given up any hope of escape when the side door was ripped open and strong hands pulled me through the gap and into the sweet air of freedom away from my Spitfire funeral pyre.

I was still reciting the Lord's Prayer to myself as I was carried into the woods and placed with my back to a tree. Such was the concussion, I could not tell if I had been captured or not.

CHAPTER 15
FRANCE

Jean's Story Continues

My head was splitting. As I started to come round and recover from the crash, I noticed a young man sitting opposite me and watching me like a hawk. Henri Chevallier was part of the French resistance group working in the area. Luckily for me, I picked the very clearing that the RAF were going to use that evening to drop supplies for the French resistance. I had landed my Spitfire right in the middle of a covert operation.

The clearing would soon be crawling with Germans looking for the enemy fighter pilot. I had ruined their plan, and Henri Chevallier was not slow in letting me know.

After I had got my act together, Henri led me away from the crash area, eventually coming to the edge of the forest. We travelled across fields by the hedgerows, away from roads that could contain German troops, until we came to a whitewashed farmhouse. Henri led me into the barn and pointed to the hayloft. I got the message and climbed up into the loft to await my fate. Henri vanished, returning much later with crusty bread, slabs of cheese, and a dress that had almost lost its flower pattern, it had been washed so many times. Henri waited by the barn door as I changed into the dress, taking my RAF gear and burying it in the field behind the barn. Over the next few days, Henri appeared with a young lad who spoke good English.

He taught me some French and Henri some English. I was informed after asking about getting back to England that it was too dangerous at the moment, but I would be told when it was possible.

Henri had moved north from the Camargue region where his family had a vineyard. He was a fugitive on the run from the Germans. Young Alan explained that Henri had been out hunting for ducks with his father's shotgun when he came across two German officers who had decided that for fun they would stampede a herd of the local Camargue ponies down to the water's edge, where the German army had mined the beaches in case of Allied invasion.

Henri watched in stunned horror as the lead pony was blown to pieces, much to the amusement of the Nazi officers.

Neither of the sick individuals were paying attention to the young man as he approached them from the rear of their vehicle. Henri could not control his rage. He shot the closest officer at point-blank range with his father's old shotgun, blowing a hole in his chest the size of his fist, and then he shot the second soldier as he spun round to defend himself, sending him tumbling over the side of the Kubelwagen.

Henri fled without checking whether the second Nazi was dead. It was a mistake that saw him hunted for days before he managed to escape the region and join up with the French resistance in the north of France.

A month later, Henri and Alan arrived to tell me that I was going to a meeting with someone from the resistance in the town of Wimereux. They wanted to meet me and talk to me as they had never seen a woman pilot and were suspicious of my credentials.

Henri and I were taken some miles by the farmer's horse and cart before being dropped off by the roadside where we were to wait for a contact at the crossroads. After a cold wet wait hidden in trees by the roadside, a man on a push-bike arrived and talked at some length with Henri before heading off up the road, Henri and me following at a distance.

While we walked, Henri explained to me that Wimereux was a costal town, and it was fortified and guarded by a German garrison against assault by the British. Over the weeks spent with Alan and Henri, I had mastered the French language if spoken slowly. I did not like what Henri was telling me. To me it seemed we were marching right into the hands of our enemy.

Some time later, our guide stopped and waited for us to catch up. In low, whispered voices, the two men discussed what was going to happen next while I waited for their next move. A few fields from the town, we arrived at an old ruined barn where Henri placed me behind a wall next to the road. He told me to stay there until he was sure the coast was clear, and then he marched off to meet the resistance.

I sat with my back to the wall, deep in thought. How the hell was I going to get back to 303 Squadron without being found out once I arrived back in England? My train of thought was suddenly interrupted by a loud arrogant

German voice very close to where I was hidden. He was shouting in stuttering French at unknown people to raise their hands.

For a second, there was silence, and then gunfire, screaming, and explosions. I was frozen to the spot with fear, not knowing what to do next. The shooting must have only been a few seconds, but it seemed like an eternity.

Suddenly there was a deathly silence broken only by the occasional muffled moan from close by.

I plucked up every last ounce of courage and turned, popping my head up slowly above the top of the wall. On the road just in front of me two German soldiers lay motionless. They had been shot were they had been standing, I had a quick look around, but in the gloom of the night I saw no one. I jumped onto the road, removing a Luger handgun from one dead officer and picking up a grenade that the other had been about to throw before he was gunned down. Just as I straightened up, there was an order barked in German from the darkness. I froze, rooted to the spot with fear. Out of the darkness marched a German SS officer flanked on either side by a German soldier. From the handle of the German grenade I was holding something dangled against my hand. My brain registered that it must be the way of arming the unfamiliar German grenade.

I pulled down on the chord and then dove for the ground. At the same time, I lobbed the grenade towards my enemies' legs. My aim was off, and the grenade bounced off the left wall before landing just behind the SS officer's legs. He was fast and threw himself away from the grenade. One soldier watched in horror, frozen to the spot, as his colleague stooped down to grab the grenade and get rid off it.

There was a loud thump as the grenade detonated, decapitating the first soldier and sending fragments of metal in all directions, catching the second soldier in the throat. My first thought was that I had got the three of them, but as I watched, the SS officer stumbled to his feet, dazed, his cap blown off in the blast. He started groping about on the ground. Then I realised he was looking for a weapon of some description. I screamed in French at him to stand still, bringing the Luger up and pointing it at him. We both spotted his sidearm lying just to his left. I screamed once more for him to stop, but he did not pay any attention to me as he scrambled for his pistol.

I took aim and squeezed the trigger. Nothing happened, and the German was about to grab his gun. I squeezed again—nothing. The SS officer stood up, dusting down his tunic while pointing his pistol at my head.

He growled at me in German, but I had no idea what he was saying. I decided I had to try and get away and made for the wall. I heard a loud crack as his pistol was discharged and expected to feel the force of the bullet smash into me. There was nothing, only silence. I reached the wall and glanced back as I leapt onto the wall. The German SS officer was face down a large dark stain was forming around his torso.

Henri appeared by my side, smiling at me before removing the Luger from my hand and fiddling with it. Then shooting the SS officer with it again, just for good measure. Henri handed me back the Luger, pointing to the grip and the little lever above it. I had tried to fire the weapon with the safety catch engaged, much to Henri's amusement.

A few seconds later, another person appeared out of the darkness, heading our way. I lifted the Luger, but Henri stopped me as a tall man hobbled up towards us, clearly in some pain. His right shoulder had been hit by a bullet. The man was chalk white and shaking badly.

Henri introduced the man to me. He was Jean Paul, the head of the resistance in the Wimereux area of northern France. Jean Paul spoke excellent English and addressed his comments to me while Henri listened, trying to make out the conversation. Jean Paul had been betrayed by one of his men and explained that with this person still at large, it was suicide to try and get anyone across the Channel. He was worried that now that the resistance had killed the German soldiers sent here to ambush us, there would be a witch hunt in the area. The gestapo would leave no stone unturned in the region until they were sure they had killed or captured any resistance fighters involved in tonight's ambush. He explained that he was going to tell Henri to take me south to his aunt's farm where I should be safe until the gestapo had finished their investigations in Wimereux.

Jean Paul talked at length with Henri, giving him instructions as where we were to head for. Jean Paul wished us a good trip before vanishing into the night, promising to come for us when the coast was clear.

It took the best part of two weeks to navigate our way past German checkpoints and roadblocks before we reached the little village of Lignac in central France. Jean Paul's aunt lived on the outskirts of the village by herself. Her husband had been killed in the Great War, leaving Clara Dupre to run the farm by herself.

Aunt Clara, as she became known to us, was at first hesitant to take us into her care, fearing the wrath of the German gestapo if they were to find us, only doing so because Jean Paul was her family. After a few awkward days, Henri threw himself into repairing barns and fences, work that Aunt Clara had found beyond her as age was fast catching up with the old lady, leaving Aunt Clara to show me how to cook, a pastime that was alien to a tomboy like myself. As the weeks passed, and Aunt Clara watched her farm returning to a good working condition, our presence was accepted by the lonely old lady. The arrangement gave her a ready-made family that she had been denied by her husband's untimely death.

Weeks turned to months, and we heard nothing from Jean Paul. Lignac was relatively quiet. Living in the country on the farm, it was sometimes easy to forget the war. I was no longer the pale, rake-thin, short-haired tomboy that Henri had dragged from the wreckage of the Spitfire many months ago.

The food on the farm was plentiful and nourishing. My figure had filled out to that of a young woman in her prime. My ginger mop, which had once been cut by a mechanic with greasy old scissors, had grown into an auburn mane styled by Aunt Clara, and my washed-out dress was replaced with new clothes from the local seamstress in Lignac and paid for with fruit and vegetables.

Henri had taken on the farmer role well, as his previous life in his father's vineyards had prepared him for the task. The summer sun had baked him a golden brown, and his flat belly had turned to taut, rippling muscle. There was no real surprise that in that type of situation, romance flourished turning a tomboy into a woman.

Months turned to years, and as love flourished between Henri and me, my hatred for the Germans faded. Gone was the urge for revenge, replaced with a longing for this war to end so Henri and I could come out of hiding and settle in a home of our own and get on with our lives.

I remember one summer's day when I returned to Aunt Clara's kitchen after taking lunch to Henri, who was harvesting in the fields some distance to the north of the farm. Aunt Clara had a guest. As I entered the kitchen, my heart almost stopped. Sitting opposite Aunt Clara was a German soldier. Before my mouth betrayed me, Aunt Clara explained she had already told the lost dispatch rider that I was her daughter, Maria, and I had been out in the fields helping my husband harvest the crops.

Bern had stopped at the farm because he was lost and looking for directions to the town of Lignac, where he was to meet the commanding officer of the southern defences. It was clear that Bern was disillusioned with the war. He was not at all guarded with his comments. I felt sure that if a gestapo or SS officer had heard him, he would have been court-martialed for his insubordination. His orders were to inform the commanding officer that his panzer divisions were to travel east to join the Fourth Panzer corps. He then let slip that he had heard that there had been a great battle at Kursk and that the Germans had been driven back by the Red Army. He had a bad feeling that Germany was going to lose the war.

For the first time since the beginning of the war, I felt that there was light at the end of the tunnel.

Bern stayed for a second glass of Aunt Clara's homemade lemonade before heading on his way, clutching a jar of Aunt Clara's strawberry jam to his chest, a far more important item than the orders he carried for the panzers.

I watched the young motorcyclist leave with a sense of confusion in my heart. I wanted to hate him, but all I felt was sorrow that people like us had been set against each other by the actions of a power-hungry lunatic.

Time seemed to stand still on the farm as season followed season. Winters in France were mild compared to my distant memories of Scotland and its frozen winter mornings, huddled close to the fire watching the snow falling outside. Summer was once more upon us as Henri checked the progress of his beloved crops, fretting when the weather would not do as he hoped. On one such wet day, we had just finished feeding the pigs and hens when a familiar voice called to us from Clara's house. Jean Paul had travelled through the night to reach us at the farmhouse. My first thought was one of dread. He had come to take me across the Channel to a world I had forgotten. I had fallen in love with Henri and the last thing I wanted was to be separated from him and sent back to a country where all my relatives were gone, left on my own while my lover and future husband was on a different continent.

Jean Paul was not here for that. He explained that certain trusted members of the French resistance had been told that an invasion was imminent and that he had been tasked with destroying the railway lines leading to the coast to hamper any German troop movement into the coastal area. The information was top secret. He could not trust his colleagues from the north with such important news. One slip of the tongue could be catastrophic for the Allies' invasion fleet. That left him with a shortage of manpower. He could not do the job by himself; he needed help.

The only people he could trust were the people who had survived the German ambush that dark night so long ago.

Henri was cautiously in agreement with Jean Paul, but I was not so sure. It was at that point that Jean Paul dropped the bombshell on us that changed our thoughts on the situation. During the gestapo manhunt for the killers of their soldiers, Henri's young friend Alan had been betrayed by a Nazi informer and had been beaten before being paraded before the locals in the town square. The SS officer had proclaimed that unless the murderers who had killed the brave German soldiers handed themselves over by twelve noon, the young traitor would be executed by firing squad. No one came forwards, and at twelve, the fourteen-year-old was placed for all to see in the middle of the square. The boy's distraught mother tried to plead with the SS officer but was knocked to the ground by the incensed SS colonel. Then he shot her in the head as she tried to get to her feet.

Her son struggled to free himself as he watched his mother's last breaths. Fearing further intervention by the outraged locals, the officer gave the order, and the young boy was cut down in a hail of bullets.

All the hatred that had faded over the last few years came flooding back with a vengeance. This Nazi plague had to be stopped once and for all. The Allies must invade and wipe this disease from the face of the earth, no mercy given to these animals, and Henri and myself would do what ever Jean Paul needed. Death to the Nazis. We did not need any further persuasion. If we did this properly and the invasion were successful, the war could be over by Christmas, and we could move to Henri's father's vineyard to settle down and have our own family life.

Reluctantly, we left our safe haven with Aunt Clara and found ourselves being whisked away north in the hastily arranged mayor of Lignac's official limousine, complete with French and German wing-tip flags borrowed by Aunt Clara who promised the mayor his pick of that year's produce from the farm in return.

During the journey north, Jean Paul explained that Operation Vert was one of the measures planned prior to the invasion of France. Jean Paul had been given the task of putting the rail line from Paris to Rouen out of action. It was a vital link for the Germans who would need this rail link to send reinforcements to the German troops in the event of an invasion.

Just south of Paris, our luck ran out as Jean Paul negotiated a tight bend. Slowing the car down, we spotted the road ahead blocked by a big black saloon car. Standing in front of the car were two men dressed in civilian clothing and a French police officer waving us down.

As Jean Paul slowed down, Henri removed the Luger I had taken from the ambush and placed it by his side, ready for what might happen next.

Jean pulled up next to the three men as they looked into the now-stationary car.

The tallest of the civilian-looking strangers stepped forwards just as Jean Paul kicked the driver's door open, catching the policeman in the chest and knocking him backwards. Such was the force Jean Paul used that at the same instant, the tall stranger went to pull a weapon from under his raincoat, but he was too late.

The car was filled with the chatter of machine-gun fire as Jean Paul emptied the Sten gun which lay across his lap into the two unsuspecting strangers, knocking them over like skittles.

Jean Paul stepped out of the driver's seat, ready to finish off the pair just as I screamed a warning to him. He turned to find the policeman taking aim with his sidearm. There was a loud crack and the officer folded, his knees buckling under him, his gun slipping from his fingers as blood starting dribbling from the corner of his mouth.

Henri had seen him draw his gun and had reacted a fraction of a second before Jean could bring his machine gun to bear on the police officer. Henri had shot him through the heart, killing him. He was dead before his body hit the ground.

On inspection, all three men were very dead. Jean Paul pulled papers and IDs from the two dead men. Both were German gestapo.

Henri stood looking dejectedly at the dead French policeman, but Jean Paul told him to snap out of it. The policeman knew the score before he drew his weapon.

We loaded the dead bodies into the mayor's limo and pushed it into a forest clearing, covering the vehicle in branches before transferring four heavy crates and the Germans papers into their big black Mercedes Benz.

Jean Paul handed me a Walther pistol taken from one of the dead Germans, tucked the second German's weapon in his belt, and reloaded his Sten gun before continuing his trip northwards, avoiding Paris at all costs.

As the dawn fast approached, Jean Paul finally reached the position that had been designated as our target. The road travelled parallel with the railway track. High above on the top of a railway cutting, Jean Paul and Henri dragged the four cases from the rear of the black Mercedes Benz, forcing the tops from all four cases to reveal dynamite stolen from a French quarry.

The plan was to mine the rail track and also the walls of the cutting, waiting for a train to arrive and derailing the train, then blowing the embankments, making the recovery of the train a huge task, buying the Allies time to get their troops ashore.

The plan was good, but there was a big problem. The dynamite had no detonator or wiring, only short fuses pushed into the end of the charges. After a lot of head scratching, Jean Paul came up with a risky plan that we both reluctantly agreed to.

We were going to dig two deep holes in the embankment, one on either side. Then we would pack the rails with dynamite. When the train could be heard in the distance from a point further down the track, we would blow the rails. Jean Paul and Henri would then scramble down to the holes packed with dynamite, and as the train came into view, they would light the fuses and run for it. If they got the timing right, the banking would blow just as the train was derailing. We would the get the hell out of there and move on to Jean Paul's next target.

For an hour, we dug down like demented rabbits, placing the dynamite in bundles at the bottom of our excavations, leaving only a few sticks for blowing the rails. I was dispatched with my Walther along the embankment to the south, tasked with waving my hands above my head when I was sure a train was coming.

It was a cold, dull morning, and I stamped my feet, trying to get some heat into my legs as I waited for the doomed train. I wondered who would be in the train that we had condemned to destruction. If it were Germans, good, but what if it turned out to be a passenger train? Innocent people would die. I wondered if this was too high a price to pay to stop the Germans sending reinforcements to the coast.

My thoughts were interrupted by the noise of a steam train in the distance. My eyes followed the path of the noise, and I could see the steam rising against the backdrop of the grey sky some distance away. I gave the signal and started walking back along the embankment. In the distance, I watched Henri and Jean Paul set the charges on the track, then climb the embankment to the charge holes. There was a dull thump and a cloud of mud as the track exploded, leaving both rails in a mangled heap. The train was closer now, and as I looked back, I could just make out the eagle and the swastika on the front of the engine. I breathed a huge sigh of relief. This was a camouflaged troop train, probably bringing troops back from leave in Paris to their posts on the coast.

My heart was pounding as I watched Jean Paul and Henri set the charges and run. Henri had to clamber up the embankment, but Jean Paul had much further to cover, running down the far embankment, then up the other side.

At that point, it was clear to see that we had misjudged the speed of the train. As it passed my position, young soldiers hung out of the windows, blowing me kisses and wolf whistles. The tears started to run down my face as the driver spotted the mangled rails and tried to stop his speeding train.

Jean Paul cleared the rails just in front of the locomotive, but he was too close as the inevitable happened. The train derailed, burying itself into the bank directly below my position. For a second it looked like Jean Paul had escaped as the engine came to a thundering stop, its boiler exploding as metal folded in on itself. Then the first carriage catapulted over the engine, crashing down on Jean Paul's position just as both embankments erupted. I staggered backwards, almost washed away by the landslide caused by the explosion. Carriage after carriage tumbled over the top of each other. Screams, moans, and the hiss of escaping steam were all that could be heard from the dust-filled crater that was once a railway line.

I looked around in a dazed state, concussed by the explosion. In the hell and confusion that had just taken place, I had lost contact with Henri. I staggered along the edge of the crater looking for him. Out of the dust far to my right, a figure stumbled over the edge of the crater.

As the dust began clearing and the figure grew closer, I recognised this was not Henri but a dazed German soldier. He spotted me and started to raise his rifle, his face now close enough for me to see the confusion in his eyes.

I raised the Walther Jean Paul had given me and shot him in the forehead, watching as his body tumbled back into the pit.

I turned back, heading for the black Mercedes Benz, panic starting to grip me. There was no sign of Henri.

I needed to check the car. If he were wounded, he would have tried to make it to the car. Jean Paul was gone. I was praying that Henri had made it out of the embankment before the landslide swept him away.

I was so far gone that I had not heard the arrival of more unwanted guests. The first I knew about it was the chatter of the Sten gun as it fired from some distance to my left.

I looked to my left to find a German army motorcycle and sidecar, both soldiers trying to take cover from the machine-gun fire. The soldier closest to me glanced over at me before returning fire in the direction of the machine-gun fire. He had obviously ruled a girl out as no immediate threat.

I took aim, still in a dazed state from the blast, and shot the soldier twice in the chest.

His comrade had no time to notice that his partner had been killed. He stood up to get a better firing position and was cut down by the Sten gun fire. To my great relief, Henri appeared on the other side of the motorcycle, checking both German soldiers were dead before joining me by the Mercedes Benz.

There was no time to lose. Any thought of more sabotage was gone. Without Jean Paul, we had no idea what to do next. Our only objective now was to put as much distance between ourselves and the train disaster before the Germans discovered the wreck and closed everything down, looking for the saboteurs.

Henri drove southwest, keeping to the country lanes, while I reloaded the Sten gun and kept the Walther ready for our next encounter with the German army. Luckily our gestapo friends had left us a Mercedes Benz full to the brim with fuel. All day we drove without encountering one German patrol. Finally, in the small hours of the morning, we had to stop. With no fuel left, the big black German car was a liability. We pushed it into a fast-flowing river and watched in the moonlight as the waters pushed the floating car downstream before it finally vanished below the surface with a whoosh of spray.

All night, we walked, shattered mentally and physically The adrenalin that had carried us away from the railway line had long worn off.

Finally what we had been dreading happened. We were out in the open only fields on either side of the road with no cover for miles, and Henri spotted them—twelve heavy trucks packed with German infantry troops, only seconds from our position.

Henri made to remove the Sten gun from under his jacket, but I put my hand on his arm, stopping him from removing the weapon. We both knew if we opened fire, we would die. Henri was for going down in a blaze of glory, taking as many Germans with him as possible. I was not so ready to die just yet. Yes, if we were discovered, I had the Walther ready in my coat pocket, but only if we were discovered.

The tension was almost unbearable as the trucks thundered down on our position, As fast as they approached, they were gone, vanishing into a dusty cloud, heading north in a hurry. Only the officer in the lead truck gave us cursory glance as they passed.

We did not know at that point, but these troops were headed to the coast. The invasion was in full swing, and all available German troops were being rushed into the area to try to drive the Allies back into the sea.

Late that evening, we arrived back at Aunt Clara's, dropped off by one of Aunt Clara's neighbours who was returning to his farm from the local market. It was Eric, Aunt Clara's neighbour, who broke the news to us that the invasion of France had started.

Aunt Clara was overjoyed to have us both back safe from the clutches of the Nazis. A bit of explaining had to be done to the mayor about where his limousine had vanished to, but when he found out that it had been used to good effect against the German war machine, he let the matter go saying that the town had bought the car, and it was just the town doing their bit to free France from the Germans. A couple of months passed with reports coming in from all around of fierce fighting. Henri fretted at not being able to help, but I talked him out of doing any more, saying that we had done our bit for the war. The last thing I wanted was Henri going and getting himself killed just when an end to this horrific war was in sight.

One September evening, I was helping Aunt Clara set the table for our evening meal while Henri was sleeping by the roaring fire. Outside the rain was falling hard, and the rain masked the sound of the approaching vehicle arriving in the courtyard.

Henri was drowsy, just waking from sleep, as I leapt for my coat and the Walther resting in the pocket. Suddenly the front door was rattled by a stranger to the farm. I still had my hand in the pocket of my jacket as a tall soldier walked into the room.

Sergeant Lee Whitmore of the United States Seventh Army was not expecting what happened next as I released my grip on the Walther and launched myself into his arms in a release of pure joy and emotion. For us, at last, the war was over. Even to this day I remember the soldier's name, such was the enormity of that moment.

CHAPTER 16
PEACE

Jean's Story Concludes

Three months later, after arranging for a local lad to stay and labour for Aunt Clara, we travelled south to the Camarque and Henri's father's vineyard, Cheval Blanc le Vignoble.

Any thoughts of living a luxury life in the South of France were dashed the second we arrived. Poor Henri was devastated to find that the SS had sought revenge for the two soldiers killed on the Cheval Blanc le Vignoble estate and, as a warning to others, had executed Henri's father and mother for harbouring enemies of the Third Reich.

Only a couple of the workers remained, but their efforts were for naught as German troops regularly looted any wine produced by the ailing estate. It was clear to see that to return the estate to its former glory, a major injection of cash would be needed. In war-torn France, such a thing was only a dream. No one had a penny to spare, never mind lend to Henri.

After a few weeks making the house and surrounding buildings habitable again, Henri decided to take a big gamble and head to Switzerland, which had remained neutral throughout the war. He was hoping to talk one of the banks into lending him the money to get the estate back on its feet again.

The war still rumbled on in Germany, but Henri hoped that by getting to the bank now, he would beat the inevitable stampede to the banks for the funds to repair a shattered continent that would happen when Germany was eventually defeated and peace once more was the order of the day.

Henri wanted me to stay at the vineyard, but I persuaded him to let me accompany him to Switzerland to try and find a bank to lend us the money.

Premier Strasse Suisse was the first bank in Geneva that we tried, and after our initial enquiries, we were passed to a young man to take our details and start the ball rolling—or not as the case might be.

Manfred Chemolie was a junior manager with little experience and even less customer-handling skill. After taking down a few notes, he scampered off, presumably to talk to someone who could make a decision on the matter. Then he returned, somewhat flustered, with a fistful of paper work.

The good news was that we were granted the loan, but the bad news was we were not sure if we could afford it. The rates were eye watering, and the loan had to be repaid in full by the end of the third year. We had no idea how much profit the vineyard was capable of producing. Only a fool would have taken the money with the vineyard as collateral against the loan, but we had little choice if we wanted to make a go of the estate.

Papers signed, we bid farewell to Manfred, who handed us two large sacks of cash, proclaiming that he would visit the estate in person every six months to collect the bank's interest payments.

Henri and I were married at the vineyard the following month with only a couple of Henri's friends and workers from the estate present. The French records departments were in turmoil, so it was easy enough for me to tell them that Maria Zajac was a Polish refugee who had lost everything including papers. The Polish I had learned at 303 Squadron came in handy, and I borrowed my old squadron leader's name and town to complete the deception. The Camargue was my new home, and by vanishing into the system, I could start my new life here with my new husband, becoming Maria Chevallier, the wife of a vineyard proprietor.

There was no time for a honeymoon. The next day was spent in the fields assessing what needed to be done urgently and what could wait.

The months rolled on, and we spent the money sparingly. Some of it we used to pay Manfred his interest, as we were still not producing anything to sell.

There was one day around that time that I remember vividly. I had risen from bed, feeling unwell. Henri had already left for the fields with the other men. I eventually felt well enough to venture out, and it was a beautiful May morning. I decided it was time I explored my new home and headed off for a walk. On a narrow lane, I bumped into a local man who, among other things, informed me that the radio had just broadcast that Germany was to surrender today to the Allies. We were both delighted by the news, and I continued my walk with a spring in my step. As I approached the undulating fields that led to the coast,

I caught sight of a group of the famous Camargue horses grazing quietly in the morning sunshine. I was busy admiring them when something very familiar caressed my eardrums. I didn't need to look to know what it was—a sound that made the hairs on the back of my neck stand up, the glorious sound of a Rolls Royce Merlin engine. My trained fighter pilot's eye caught sight of the Spitfire just below the morning sun and heading my way. Before I knew it, I was on my tiptoes, waving my sun hat with all my might like a schoolgirl as the fighter approached.

To my delight, the pilot spotted my efforts and rewarded them with a victory roll as he passed my position, sending the ponies off in all directions.

Over the years, I have thought back on that moment as a very unique moment in my life. To me it was as if the Spitfire was signing off and the Camargue horses were taking its place in my affections. Coupled with the victory roll and the day the Germans surrendered, it was a special day. A week later, I realised I was ill for a reason. I was pregnant with our first child—all these things coming together in one day.

God works in mysterious ways, they say, and that day, I felt that he was definitely pulling the strings.

Over the next few years, with a lot of hard work and a good bit of luck, we cleared our debt to the bank. By this time, Manfred, whose uncle owned the bank he worked in, had stepped up to become bank manager, and he had become a family friend, continuing to visit every six months to sample our wine and to introduce us to his new bride, Ellen.

By the time we attended Manfred's wedding, our little family had grown to two boys and two girls. Any thoughts of my helping on the estate were for the moment put on the back burner as I had a pretty full-time job being a mother.

The next eight years were busy times but good times as Henri and I watched our family grow. Things had gone well for us since the end of the war. Two good years for our wines put the estate firmly in the black with a healthy bank balance in Switzerland to show for our efforts.

I had drifted into breeding the local horses now that my children did not need as much attention, and I attempted to get Henri to slow down and spend more time with his children.

One day, I returned from the stables with my youngest two to find Henri curled up on the toilet floor holding his head in agony, unable to move because of the headache. I did not know it at the time, but this was the beginning of the end. Over the next few months, Henri spent a great deal of time with doctors trying to find out why his migraines, and now nosebleeds, were so frequent.

Henri died in his own bed six months later, refusing to be taken to hospital, wanting to be with his family. The doctors carried out an autopsy to find that Henri had died from a brain tumour.

I was a walking wreck for months, but I had no option other than to get on with my life, however empty I felt. I still had four children to bring up without a father and a business to run. The first year was hell on earth. I cried myself to sleep night after night.

The second year was better, but then Manfred arrived alone one winter's day unannounced. Ellen had been killed in a car crash in Italy while visiting Lake Garda. We were both lost souls, and for the next year, we spent more time visiting each other in an attempt to stop depression taking control of our shattered lives.

Manfred and Ellen did not have children, so when visiting the vineyard to help with the bookkeeping for the estate, he took great delight in playing with the children. Manfred's visits became more frequent, and a year later, we were married, and I became Maria Chemolie. As time passed and the children moved to schools in Switzerland, I spent more and more time with Manfred, working with him in the bank while my trusted staff ran the day-to-day affairs of my vineyard.

Manfred inherited the banking business from his uncle five years later, and for a further seven years, Manfred and I shaped the bank to our liking, helping less well-off people get a start in life. Then once more my life was turned upside down when Manfred collapsed and died from a massive heart attack, leaving me in charge of a vineyard and a Swiss bank.

Overnight, I had moved from being a wealthy woman to being one of Switzerland's banking millionaires. From then until now, things have not changed. My family have grown up and flown the nest, but I still spend most of my time overseeing banking affairs, only stealing the odd weekend on the estate where my granddaughter now runs most things, following in my footsteps with her love of horses.

CHAPTER 17
WISE OLD LADY

As if on cue, just as Maria Chemolie was finishing her story, the cabin door opened, and Fred stepped into the cabin.

"Sorry to interrupt you, but we are approaching American air space, and I hate to rock the boat, but do we all have passports and paper work before we end up tied in red tape at the airport?"

Madam Chemolie thought for a second before replying. "Just out of curiosity, Fredrick, I take it Saroj is doing the flying while you are doing the worrying? If you call my good friend Bruce Ellis at CIA headquarters in Langley, I am sure he will smooth things over with the relevant people at the airport. After all, he owes me quite a few favours."

Fred was about to turn round and return to the cockpit when a thought occurred to him. "Listen, my friends, I apologise for lying to you at the airfield, but you see, I had to protect this old lady. You understand, I hope."

For a while, as the Falcon 900 made its approach to Reno airport, the occupants of the jet fell silent. Andy, Lisa, and

Cammy were deep in thought, turning the things Maria said over in their heads while Maria dozed, tired after her storytelling marathon. Later, Lisa, seeing that Maria was once more awake, passed her a glass of water that she had poured from a bottle of mineral water.

"Please take a drink, Maria. Between the air conditioning and the storytelling, your throat must be in need of some lubrication."

Maria winked at Lisa but took the water from her, swallowing it without coming up for a breath until she had drained the glass. Lisa said nothing. She was amazed by the old woman, who was in her nineties and remarkable for her age. Anyone who did not know the truth would have probably said she was in her early seventies. Although she had had a busy life, she looked remarkably well.

Lisa had seen in her previous employment that older people still retained a good memory for the past but usually had issues remembering what they had done that day. Maria exhibited none of those telltale signs of aging. Lisa had noted that her day-to-day memory and her long-term memory were pin sharp, probably because Maria Chemolie was still using her brain to its full capacity running her banking business.

Fred's voice burst into life through the cabin speakers, announcing that they were on their final approach to Reno and that they were about to start descending. This reenergized Maria, and she cleared her throat before her announcement.

"While I still have your full attention, I would like to clarify a couple of things with you. I do not wish to spend my remaining time fighting off reporters trying to get me to tell the story I have just relayed to you. Furthermore, the publicity that would bring would not be good for the covert operation taking place at my bank in Switzerland. Therefore I must ask you all to keep our little chat a private matter between ourselves. After I have passed away, if you still feel the need to tell my story, so be it. For the record, the RAF states that Artur Krol shot down sixteen aircraft, with a further three unconfirmed and five damaged enemy aircraft." She snorted. "Utter rubbish! I was never able to contest my record because of my gender. The truth is I shot down twenty-three enemy aircraft and damaged another eight of them. If someone writes about me, give him those figures because they are the truth, straight from the horse's mouth, not some bean counter that never got his backside off the ground."

On arriving at Reno airport, Maria Chemolie and her entourage were ushered from the Falcon 900 into a nearby customs office. Waiting for them was CIA Special Agent Bruce Ellis and two deputies who led the rest of the group into an adjoining room to sort out documentation while Ellis was left alone with Maria Chemolie.

"Well, Maria, I knew you were coming to see me, but I can't recall including a visit to Reno in our plans. I don't suppose you could enlighten me?"

Maria Chemolie smiled as she pulled up a chair and sat down at the desk. Maria loved to play cat and mouse with Bruce Ellis. He was a clever and cunning member of the Central Intelligence Agency, valued highly by the last president, and if rumours were correct, he had the ear of the current president also.

"Come now, Bruce. I am sure you could tell me better than I know myself what I am here for. I will explain my arrival in Reno, but you can fill in the blanks if I miss anything."

She smiled wickedly. "I was about to leave France for my meeting with your director when these three young people asked me to join them at Powlak Air in Reno to celebrate the life of an old friend of mine, Jan Powlak, who was the original owner of the company. I was going to call your boss to reschedule our meeting to allow me to complete my trip to Reno before visiting you a day or so later—nothing sinister, just an innocent party."

Bruce Ellis had that look on his face that said he knew something everyone else didn't. He paused for effect, making Maria Chemolie wait for his version of her trip.

"Yes, you were correct, Maria. We did know most of what you have told us. MI6 confirmed you were travelling with Andrew Paxton, who is a lawyer; Callum McPherson, a private investigator; and Lisa Preston, a shareholder and director of Powlak Air.

"I have to say, Maria, that the girl is causing us some concern. You see, Powlak Air is a government military contractor working with some very sensitive aircraft technology, and having a foreign director of the company was not in our plans. To check on the situation, as a precaution, I have planted a CIA agent in the Powlak team to monitor their operations. When you visit Powlak Air you may bump into your old bank manager, Frank Whitton. When he left the undercover post at your bank, I reassigned him to work undercover at Powlak Air. He goes by the name of Chris Morton, so if you bump into him, you never met him before, right?

"One last thing—your meeting was to be with me anyway. The president wanted me to convey his thanks to yourself and your bank team. To date, the banking trap has resulted in half of the terrorist activities all over the globe being foiled as a direct result of information gathered at your bank. From Bin Laden to Gaddafi and now ISIS, we can track them through their banking transactions. Because of your success, I must be blunt. Madame Chemolie, this operation is vital to the security services of the world. It must not be allowed to fail. You are an old lady, and no one can go on forever. Do you have a successor in mind to run the bank when you retire or die?"

Madame Chemolie had become used to questions about her ability to operate a bank at her age and was not phased by the comment.

"My dear Bruce, be assured that Swiss banks leave nothing to chance. As for myself, I wake up and thank god for every day he gives me. I do not wish my family to be drawn into your spy business. Although they will own the bank, I have left firm instructions that my replacement, when it comes, will give yourself and the British full cooperation in relation to terrorist activities. You have my word that your work at the bank will continue. In exchange, I want your word that you will never involve any member of my family."

Bruce Ellis avoided eye contact with Maria Chemolie. He knew he would try to avoid involving Maria's family, but he could not truthfully give his word on the matter. Instead, he changed the subject.

"MI6 tell me that they had great difficulty keeping a tail on your three guests. Are you sure that you trust them, Maria?"

Maria Chemolie stood, signalling that the meeting was about to come to an end.

"My dear Mr. Ellis, if I did not trust them, they would not have left Monaco. I may be old, but as yet I still have all my marbles. I will confess I did not know that Lisa was a director of Powlak Air, but I am sure she has nothing to hide. She is a kind-hearted girl. Continue to spy on Powlak Air, if you must, but I am sure you will have no problems, at least as far as Lisa Preston is concerned. Now, if you are finished with our meeting, I have a party to get ready for."

Lisa was first to finish with the red tape in immigration, and she used the free time to contact Jake Shelton, who dispatched a limo to pick them up from the airport and take them to hastily arranged suites at the Atlantis Hotel.

Madame Chemolie, Fred, Saroj, and Cammy all had suites while Andy and Lisa opted to head to Jan's old home.

Lisa and Andy had just been dropped off when Andy's mobile started ringing, Andy checked—it was Callum calling from the hotel.

"Hey, you guys need to come and rescue me. This crazy old dear wants me to take her out on the town tonight. You need to save me, man, or I am going to spend the night line dancing with a bunch of geriatrics. Come on, Andy. Help me out here, man!"

Lisa was listening into the call, and they both chuckled at Cammy's predicament.

"Sorry, Callum, you know normally I would be right there to dig you out, mate, but it has been a very long time since I had Lisa and a bedroom all to myself, if you catch my drift, mate.

"We will pick you up tomorrow for the Powlak Air thing—if Maria hasn't worn you out on the dance floor by then, mate. Have a good night. See you tomorrow."

Andy hung up before Callum managed to curse at him down the phone line.

The next morning while they once again showered together, Andy quizzed Lisa about what was to happen at Powlak Air that day, but his enquiries were of little use. Lisa was just as much in the dark as he was. Whatever Jake had organised since their last visit was a mystery. Jake Shelton was playing his cards close to his chest and had not hinted at the nature of the gathering arranged other than to say that it was to honour Jan and his contributions to the Powlak Air company.

CHAPTER 18
POWLAK AIR

At four thirty that afternoon, the Powlak Air limousine pulled up outside the main entrance to Powlak Air, which was draped with a cover. Jake Shelton and the complete work force, including a few invited guests, were waiting as the limo pulled up and stopped. Jake himself stepped forwards, opening the limo door to allow its passengers to disembark. Lisa offered to give Madame Chemolie a helping hand, but she was brushed away. Maria nimbly stepped out and shook Jake Shelton's hand as the rest of the limo passengers spilled out behind her.

"Good afternoon. I take it you must be Madame Chemolie. It's nice to put a face to a name at last. Welcome to Powlak Air. My name is Jake Shelton, and I am the managing director. Lisa has told me that you knew Jan."

Madame Chemolie studied Jake for a few seconds before replying. Lisa watched as she scrutinised her business partner as levelly as she had scrutinized Lisa herself in Monaco.

"Hello, Mr. Shelton. I see you have a few more grey hairs since the last time I saw you."

For a second, Maria Chemolie glanced past the puzzled Powlak boss, making eye contact with Bruce Ellis who was standing in front of the Powlak employees.

"I see by the look on your face, Mr. Shelton, you are at a loss as to where I have seen you before. I take it that Mr. Ellis there and the rest of your government are the ones giving you the grey hairs. We have never met, Mr. Shelton, but I did see you when you arrived at my bank in Switzerland to arrange a loan to finance your big jump into the military-contractors league. In fact, it was because of that and your company name that I ended up, after all these years, finding my old friend Jan Powlak. I regret now that I did not visit him before he died. A letter was poor substitute, I am afraid."

Jake Shelton was genuinely shocked. "You own PSS Bank! Wow! Now that is impressive. We must talk more, but I think we are keeping a lot of people waiting here. I will get on with it, and then we can have a chat over drinks in a few minutes."

Maria nodded, stepping to the sidelines and giving Jake Shelton centre stage. Now that all his guests were present, Jake wasted no more time. He thanked everyone for attending and explained that Powlak Air had decided to honour its founder, Jan Powlak, with a new reception and meeting area. Jake went on to add that he was handing the honour of unveiling the new extension to the building to Director Lisa Preston, who had been a close friend of Jan's and was with him in his final hours.

Lisa was shell-shocked at this but managed to hold herself together long enough to thank everyone for coming. Then, without further ceremony, she pulled the cord handed to her by Jake Shelton, and with a whooshing noise, the covers dropped on the new extension, revealing a glass-fronted atrium.

In true American bigger-is-always-better fashion, Jake's extension was huge, almost double the size of the old reception area, which had not been small to begin with. The next shock was what they could see through the glass doors. There, in all its glory, was Jan's restored Mk IX Supermarine Spitfire, complete with a new coat of camouflage paint depicting the aircraft's wartime role in the Royal Air Force. The small crowd poured in through the big glass doors to get a better look at the interior of the new extension.

Mounted on a pedestal next to the Supermarine Spitfire was the last Merlin engine Jan had rebuilt before retiring, an engine that had never been used since the rebuild and that had now been treated to a makeover by Rolls Royce as a display unit. Every nut and bolt on the engine had been chromed, and the big power unit sparkled under the new atrium lighting. A gold plate attached to the engine stated that the unit had originally been fitted to a Hawker Hurricane flown by the Polish fighter ace Artur Krol.

On a small stand next to the engine and protected by a UV glass frame was a RAF engineer's report to Rolls Royce. It stated that the engine had been replaced due to concerns with low oil pressure, and it was signed, "Jan Powlak, Head Aircraftsman."

In the corner of the glass atrium was the last piece of Jan Powlak memorabilia. Gleaming in Ferrari red, Jan's newly restored Ferrari Dino sparkled under the lighting. On the solid wall that now made up the back of the new reception area were blown-up copies of old photos. They were now life-size and decorated the walls of the building.

Lisa, Andy, and Callum moved slowly along the wall, studying the old pictures with great interest. A few of the pictures showed Jan working on Spitfires and Hurricanes. As the pictures progressed along the wall, they became more modern until they depicted Jan in America with his new venture.

Pride of place above the reception desk was a photo of Jan Powlak and Jake Shelton standing on a podium, holding a silver trophy above their heads. Both men were smiling and enjoying the moment.

The three of them were still looking at the picture as Jake Shelton quietly walked up behind them.

"That's a beaut, ain't it? That was Jan and I winning our first air race. There was no looking back from that day. Great memories, don't you think? I hope the new building meets with all your approvals."

Lisa listened as Jake entertained them with stories about air races until she noticed Maria Chemolie standing by the Merlin engine. She looked so small and frail next to the big Rolls Royce engine. It was hard to believe she had piloted one of these brutes.

Lisa strolled across to Maria and was surprised to find the tough-as-nails old lady weeping.

Maria looked up as Lisa approached and wiped away a tear. "Lisa, did you read this? All those years, and he kept my engine. I never even had the decency to visit my old friend. Instead I sent him that stupid letter. What makes it worse is I can't even say sorry to him now. I would give everything just to say good-bye to him. What a stupid old woman I was."

Lisa escorted Maria across to a seated area, urging her to sit down before fetching her a glass of water.

"Maria, don't be so hard on yourself. Your letter was not a stupid idea. Before you made contact with Jan, he was on his last legs. I have seen it so many times before. He was only going through the motions of living, treading water until it was his time to go. Your letter reenergised him. It gave him a will to live again. He wanted the world to know about you. He never said as much, but I think while he thought you were dead, he believed no one would believe his story, so he simply didn't tell it.

"But the minute he found out you were still alive, he knew you could back his story up, and he made it his mission to try and get the world to listen to an old man's tale. Sadly he died, but before he did, he managed to convince Andy and me that his story was not some delusion but a secret that had remained hidden for decades."

Maria Chemolie recovered her spirit a little and pointed to the third picture from the left. It depicted Jan being introduced to a high-ranking Royal Air Force officer.

"Lisa, cast your mind back to my story on the way here. That picture is Jan being congratulated for shooting down three enemy aircraft in one day. At the moment this photo was taken, I was getting cramp in an engine crate in the hangar."

Maria sighed. "My dear, all Jan would have needed to do was show the historians the pictures of Artur Krol and get them to compare them to the pictures of Jan Powlak. They would have found they were the same man, and there was no Artur Krol...although I suppose I would have been the final part of the jigsaw puzzle. I think I was afraid to meet Jan because I knew in my heart, he would want me to tell my story. Lisa, I am ninety-seven and a billionaire. I have nothing to prove, and all this story would do is cause me grief and heartache. I have told you and your friends the whole story. After I am gone, if you must, you have my permission to tell the story. I must warn you though, that you will be called liars and cheats. Your boyfriend has already lost his job over this. Before you do it, you must weigh up what the cost will be to your credibility."

As the party fizzled out and people drifted away from the building, Lisa and Maria found themselves joined at the seating area by first Bruce Ellis and then Jake Shelton. Maria had recovered her composure and was back on form. She regarded her seated entourage with a look of devilment in her eye. Lisa was only partially taking notice as she watched Callum and Andy taking turns to sit in the Spitfire cockpit. Then her attention returned fully to the conversation when she heard Maria Chemolie mention her by name.

"Lisa, Jake, I would like to introduce you to Mr. Bruce Ellis, one of the CIA's top men. Bruce told me not to tell you, but your company has been under surveillance by his department to make sure you are behaving yourselves. Bruce, I take it your man here has nothing bad to say about Powlak Air?"

Bruce Ellis was blushing and giving Maria Chemolie a death stare. "We have concluded that your company has a clean bill of health, and we will be withdrawing our agent immediately."

Maria turned her attention back to Lisa and Jake Shelton. "You see, working for the government can be bad for your health, especially if you don't toe the line. Luckily, I have a bit of leverage in that department, so here is what I propose to do.

"Bruce, Powlak Air are my friends, and as long as they have government contracts, my bank will remain at your service, if you catch my drift.

"Lisa and Jake, I am going to ask Lisa for a very special favour soon, so as a favour to Powlak Air, tomorrow my bank will remove any interest charges on the loan given to your company, and the loan period will be extended indefinitely to allow your company to invest in its future." Jake was too shocked to speak instead leaning across and kissing Maria's hand.

Bruce Ellis was the first to excuse himself, followed by Jake Shelton. Maria Chemolie took the opportunity to speak before Andy and Callum finished playing with the Ferrari controls.

"Lisa, that favour I talked about—do you think you could tear yourself away from Andy this evening to join me for dinner, just you and me in my rooms?"

Lisa arrived outside Maria Chemolie's room at eight and was ushered into the suite by Saroj. Maria had already ordered for them both, and as Lisa arrived, so did the food, a mixed platter of various dishes from steak to caviar. The choice was huge. Lisa reckoned there was enough food to feed the local football team, never mind two women.

"I hope you don't mind, my dear, but I cut a few corners so we can have our chat without any interruptions."

Maria handed Lisa a plate and joined her by the table, picking through the huge number of choices laid out before them. For a few minutes, as the women chose their food, there was no conversation. Then, their plates full, they returned to the table to dine and to talk.

"Lisa, you must be wondering what is on my mind. Our visit to Jan's old place of work got me thinking about planning my future. I did not want to discuss this with you until I had spoken to my family. This evening I talked at length to my children, and now I am ready to talk to you.

"Both my husbands chose to be cremated and their ashes scattered, so unless I follow their example, I have no plans for my funeral. This may seem a strange request, but would you do me the honour of arranging my funeral?

"I remember badgering Jan to go and visit Scotland whenever we talked between fixing planes and flying. Eventually, Jan did visit Scotland, and there he lies with no family in a Scottish cemetery.

"I have decided I would like to be buried in my own country. I may have hidden behind a Polish identity and lived in France and Switzerland, but when it comes down to it, I was born in Scotland, and I want to be put to rest in Scotland, so if this is the case, why not next to my good friend Jan Powlak. Lisa, I have not known you long, but already I see what Jan saw in you. Like Jan, I trust you. Do you think you could do this thing for me?"

Lisa did not need long to think about the proposition. She felt through Jan she already knew Maria Chemolie well. "Of course, I will do this for you, and it will be our secret. Now! We have talked enough of death. Let's celebrate life. Maria, tell me about your family and your horses." For hours, the two women discussed whatever came into their heads, both women drawing closer to each other as the evening progressed.

Lisa let herself into the house in the early hours of the morning after being dropped off by Paul. Her attempt to sneak into the bedroom was halted abruptly as Andy switched the light on. He could not sleep and was waiting up for Lisa.

"You didn't keep that poor old lady up until this time blethering, I hope?"

Lisa pulled off her clothing and collapses on the bed by Andy's side. "That poor old lady, as you put it, could talk the hind legs of a donkey while polishing off a bottle of wine. For someone her age, she is quite remarkable."

Andy's attention was starting to wander as he cast his eyes over Lisa's naked body on the bed next to him.

"So what did Maria talk about until this time in the morning?"

Lisa rolled on to her flat stomach making eye contact with Andy. "You have a choice—we talk about what Maria said, or you can give me a cuddle."

Two seconds later, the light was switched off. Andy had made his decision.

Over toast and coffee the next morning, Lisa went over a few things that she and Maria had discussed the previous night, leaving out the subject of her burial.

"Hurry up and finish your toast, Andy. I called Paul when you were in the shower. He will be here in fifteen minutes to take us to the airport. I thought you might want to say good-bye to your old pal."

Andy looked puzzled, and Lisa chuckled. "I take it Callum hasn't told you yet that he is hitching a lift back to France with Maria this morning?"

Before Andy could reply, the doorbell rang, announcing the arrival of Paul with the limo to take them to the airport.

When Andy and Lisa arrived at the airport, Maria Chemolie and her small band of travellers had already arrived and were waiting for Fred to give them the go-ahead to make their way to the Falcon 900. The minute Maria Chemolie spotted Lisa, she broke out in a beaming smile. Callum was grinning from ear to ear, and Andy stopped in front of him. "Sorry, mate," Callum said. "I was going to call you this morning, but I didn't want to disturb you two lovebirds. Maria has kindly offered to give me a lift back to France to pick up the camper. I suppose I can't talk you into another camper adventure, mate?"

Andy was shaking his head before Cammy had even finished his sentence. "Thank you, but no thank you. You knock yourself out, mate, and I will see you back in Scotland in a couple of weeks. It may have slipped your mind that we still have a business to get on its feet back home. But one thing is for sure—my mother will not have forgotten. I haven't called her in weeks, so I am in enough shit as it is without trying to explain why you are AWOL in France."

Callum assumed an expression of pretend hurt. "Aw, mate, and there I was thinking I was doing you a good turn by getting the camper back before we get charged a fortune for it. I suppose I am not getting overtime for picking it up, then?"

Andy chuckled to himself at Cammy's comments. "Cammy, you run that past my mother if you wish, but I don't fancy your chances of leaving the office with your scalp intact. Anyway, remember, I know you. There is more to this than just you getting the camper van back. I take it on your return trip, you might bump into a certain granddaughter called Oriane?"

Callum was about to reply to Andy's question, but he was beaten to it by Maria, who had strolled over with Lisa.

"Yes Andy, Callum will be seeing my granddaughter when we get back to France. In fact, I have already spoken to Oriane, and we have agreed that she will accompany Callum for a couple of days to navigate for him so he doesn't get lost on his way across France. I have no doubt Callum will be the perfect gentleman with my granddaughter. Isn't that right, Callum?"

Callum put his arm around the old lady, giving her a friendly hug. "You know me, Maria. Oriane is safe with me."

Maria looked up at Callum. "It would not be good if I had to send Saroj to the aid of my granddaughter. If you have never seen a Gurkha in action, it is a fearsome sight. Bear that in mind, Callum, for future reference."

Callum nodded without speaking just as Saroj, who was standing a few paces away monitoring the passers-by, caught his eye, smiling wickedly at Cammy before breaking eye contact and returning to scanning the people in the immediate vicinity for potential threats.

Maria, content that she had put a warning shot across Callum's bow, turned her attention to Andy and Lisa. "Lisa, darling, do you think you could go and get some coffees while this strong young gentleman helps an old lady find a seat?"

Maria watched Lisa head off in search of coffee before taking Andy's arm and escorting him over to a seated area.

"Andrew, I don't really need coffee. I just wanted a word alone with you before I leave. I would like to give you some good advice in private. From what Lisa tells me, you have taken to heart Jan's wish that my time at 303 Squadron be made public. I don't want the story to die, but I feel it is better told by families, passed down to others that way, not splashed all over the tabloids and hounded to death. I feel in my heart that if Jan were here today, he would agree to this. You now have the story in your head, and for me, that is all that matters. For myself and also for Lisa, don't go doing anything stupid with the information I have given you.

"The most important thing to come out of this, I feel, is that you have found Lisa, and she has found you. Jan has brought you both together, so here is the best advice you will receive today. Lisa is madly in love with you. Marry her, have lots of children, and tell them how you met and about the woman who was a pilot. Tell them to tell their children. That way I will live forever, and you will have done what Jan asked of you. Andrew, I am an old woman. I may never see you again. Do not treat my words lightly. So many of my generation gave their lives so your generation were free to live life, so live it, Andrew. Marry the girl."

Andy noticed the tears welling up in the old lady's eyes as she stood up and walked towards Lisa who was returning with a tray of coffees. He wanted to say something to the wise old lady, but no words came to mind. Instead he sat staring at his pretty blond girlfriend as she dished out the coffee. Maria was right. He did not know how he had survived without her, and the thought of going through life without her was too much to bear.

CHAPTER 19
ORIANE

The Falcon 900 touched down at Nice Airport in the early evening. Callum was thrilled to find Oriane waiting in the arrivals lounge for her grandmother. Callum watched as the women embraced each other warmly. It was clear to see that Oriane was the apple of Maria's eye.

While the two women chatted, Callum studied Oriane. Only tiny age lines around the corner of her mouth gave away the fact she was in her thirties. Removed from the stables, she had cleaned up well. Oriane was sporting a white-and-orange retro fifties three-quarter-length dress which hugged her trim figure and showed off her shapely legs. Callum had no doubt that the dress was a designer item, and Oriane showed it off well. Her shoulder-length brown hair had been scooped up into a bun, reinforcing that fifties look.

Suddenly Oriane was gone, leaving with a shy little wave to Callum. Maria turned her attention to Callum, and it was clear from Maria's body language, all was not well.

"Callum, this is where we part company. I have a meeting in Monte Carlo. I had planned for Oriane to accompany you to London, and then I would have sent Fred to Heathrow to pick her up, but Oriane has different ideas. She has driven here and will pick you up outside. She will take you to pick up your vehicle and then follow you to the ferry to make sure you get back OK. She is then going to a horse show in Paris. There is little point arguing with her. She is as stubborn as the horses she looks after. It is a pity you cannot make the full trip together. I think you would be good for my granddaughter. She needs someone to show her that there is more to life than horses. I hope you both get on well. Give her time to come out of her shell before you judge her. I know you will like her. I am late for my meeting, so I must say good-bye. I will see you again, but for now, good-bye, my young friend."

Callum walked outside to the pickup area to be greeted by the blast of a car horn. Callum turned to find Oriane pulling up to him in a stunning-looking sports car. For a few seconds, Callum could not help himself, doing a full three-sixty round the car before opening the trunk and depositing his bag next to Oriane's luggage. Callum had only ever seen a Monteverdi High Speed in magazines. They were a very, very rare breed of luxury sports car. The Swiss sports car was old but in immaculate condition. Callum jumped into the passenger seat and made his first mistake.

"Nice wheels. Does Maria know you have nicked one of her cars?"

Oriane regarded Callum with her big brown eyes, and she shook her head without saying anything as she pulled out into the busy Nice traffic.

Callum's second mistake followed rather quickly when Oriane asked where the camper van was parked. Callum had to admit that he had no idea. Oriane regarded him with wide-eyed disbelief, pulling off the road and into a roadside lay-by.

"So let's get this right. You came back to France to pick up a camper and you have no idea where it is. How can this be?"

Callum knew. He had not started the trip well and had to improve drastically before Oriane got the wrong impression.

"Oriane, I know you must think I am an idiot, but I do know that the car is in the vicinity of Macon, so if we start heading in that direction, I will try to explain why. At the moment, I can't be more precise."

Oriane had a look of thunder on her face, but Callum was not sure what he had said wrong this time.

"Macon? Very well, we will head for Macon. Grandma neglected to mention this to me. I was under the impression the camper van was near Nice, not halfway across France."

Oriane pulled out into the traffic, once more heading out of the Nice area. While she negotiated the road systems, she said nothing. Callum was content to listen to the big American V8 engine of the Monteverdi burbling away. Once Oriane got onto the motorway network, she was the first to continue speaking.

"Callum, now you can tell me your story. Then I have a few questions for you, but first, I think I should hear your story."

There was no way Callum could tell part of the story without telling the full story. Oriane listened intently as Callum relayed the story to her and how he had been drugged when the camper was left, resulting in him not knowing about it.

He explained that when they were nearer their destination, he would contact Andy for final directions to the garage.

Oriane finally threw the towel in and pulled into a hotel by the motorway intersection. She had been driving all day, and what's more, the big sports car's fuel gauge was telling her to stop.

Oriane thought she would simply pay for two rooms but was informed that the hotel only had one double room left. Callum could tell by the hesitation in her voice that she had not thought of this and did not know what to do. Callum came to her rescue, volunteering to sleep in the passenger seat of the car.

As the trip progressed, Oriane had warmed to Callum, and she would not let him sleep in the car. Eventually, she talked him into sleeping in the room but on the chair in the corner. After ordering room service, the pair talked well into the evening about Oriane's grandma. Oriane admitted she had heard about her grandparents' involvement in the resistance, but she knew nothing of Jean Bruce and was surprised to find that she was of Scottish blood.

The next day after breakfast, they continued their road trip. Callum had forgotten about the car and was finding it hard to resist the charms of Oriane. Only the thought of the big Gurkha beating him to death stopped him from exploring their relationship further.

While Oriane stopped for fuel and a lunch break the next day, Callum called Andy and received abuse and directions to the garage on the outskirts of Macon.

A further load of abuse in French by the garage owner followed before a large wad of cash calmed him down and paid for the extended stay of the VW camper van in his yard.

Callum gave Oriane the chance to cut and run for her trip to Paris, but Oriane had already missed the show and told Callum that her grandma would not forgive her for going back on her word to escort Callum to the ferry.

Over the next two days travelling north, the two became closer still, so much so that Oriane handed Callum the keys of her prized Monteverdi, which had been a twenty-first birthday present from her grandma. At first, Callum was overenthusiastic with the accelerator pedal, only slowing up when Oriane found it impossible to keep up in the old camper van.

That evening, Oriane was treated to the delights of sleeping in a camper van. She pretended enthusiasm to keep Callum happy, and that night, lying awake in her bunk, Oriane thought of more than just friendship with a member of the opposite sex for the first time in many years. Grandma had been correct—she liked Callum a lot.

Finally, the trip was over. Oriane and Callum were leaning on the seawall in Calais watching a ferry far out to sea heading their way. The old camper was booked on the evening ferry, which left Callum with a few hours to kill before he had to leave. He so badly wanted Oriane to come with him, but he was not sure of her feelings towards him. Oriane broke the silence that had sprung up between them as they studied the sea.

"Callum, my mother is worried for Grandma. Tell me. Has she spoken to you of her desire to be buried in Scotland? She called my mother out of the blue and told her she was thinking of being buried in Scotland and did my mother have any objections to this. My mother did not object, but she is worried about the state of Grandma's mind. Normally,

Grandma is such a positive person. It is not like her to be negative. She has never mentioned her death before. Have you any idea what is behind her thinking?"

Callum turned his attention from the sea, making eye contact with Oriane. "I suppose it will come to us all at some point. Your grandma is ninety-sevenish. With all the good will in the world, she can't have a lot of time left. This must be playing on her mind. She has never mentioned anything to me, but if she wants to come home to Scotland, why not?"

Callum's ferry was docking, and Oriane was just about to leave when he finally plucked up the courage to ask Oriane the question that had been on his lips all day.

"So now that you know you have Scottish blood in your veins, when are you coming to visit Scotland? I would love to see you again—that is, if you can get someone to look after the stables for a while."

Oriane leaned into the cab of the camper and gave Callum a peck on the cheek, handing him a scrap of paper before stepping back from the window, smiling. "You read my mind, and now you have my number. Call me, and we will discuss it. Bye, camper boy."

Callum drove from Dover to the airport with his head in the clouds. He knew instinctively that he was in with a shout. Oriane was indeed interested in him.

When Andy and Lisa arrived back in Scotland, it was to find that his mother had been busy with the new business. Ann Paxton was no fool. She knew her son too well. If she was to get his mind off the Jean Bruce episode and on to his new career, he was going to have to work on something that would inspire him. Within five minutes of entering the office on his first day back, Ann Paxton handed him a file, asking him to handle this case as it was right up his street.

Andy studied the file carefully. It was not lost on him that the case was against his former employers. This whetted his appetite for revenge, and he delved deep into the file, becoming engrossed in its contents. His mother's plan had worked.

Lisa had headed straight to her mother's house to check on her and rendezvoused with Andy at her flat in Dundee later that evening. The pair had only been apart for a day, but they chatted as if they had been separated for weeks.

"Well, how was your first day as a big-shot lawyer? Did your mother kill you for not calling?"

Andy smiled. "It went surprisingly well. I never even got a telling off from my mother, but she has been busy finding me lots of work. In fact, I wanted to speak to you about my first big case. I have a farming company up north that Mother has taken on as a client. They want us to look into the possibility of taking the Royal Air Force to court for unlawful damage to their property. Normally, when I was in the air force, I would have defended the RAF, but I have been pitched in on the other side of the court so to speak. It is going to be a lot of hard work gathering data and interviewing the people affected, but I am looking forwards to it. Sorry to waffle on. I will be working around the Inverness area a lot, and I wondered if you fancied coming with me. We could hire a cottage, and you could have a bit of a holiday while I do my bit. What do you think?"

Secretly, Lisa was relieved that Andy had finally dropped Jan's last wish and was getting on with his life. "Midges, rain, and probably no Internet—you know how to sweep a girl off her feet, don't you, Paxton?"

Andy looked crestfallen. He had hoped Lisa would keep him company while he collated the data required to build a case. Lisa couldn't keep her smile in any longer.

"Don't look so worried. I was pulling your leg. Of course I will come with you. Someone has to look after you."

Over the next few months, Andy planned his trip up north while Lisa divided her time among Dundee, Stirling, and Errol, spending vast sums on taxis when Andy was too busy to chauffer her around.

On his return from France, Callum was put to work collating flight paths, flight plans, and technical data on Tornados, Typhoons, and any other spurious aircraft that frequented the Lossiemouth Air Base in the north of Scotland. It was not hard to understand that the closure of the Leuchars Air Base in Fife must have had a knock-on effect as Lossiemouth had probably doubled its workload.

Andy and Lisa had taken up residence in a cottage in the village of Findhorn on the Scottish coast. Andy had picked this spot as it was only a stone's throw from RAF Kinloss and within easy reach of RAF Lossiemouth. Lisa had fallen in love with the picture-postcard little cottage and friendly village atmosphere of the little town on the coast.

Two weeks into the project, however, on a Saturday morning, their peace was shattered as Cammy arrived, suit-case in tow. It was not a huge surprise as Callum was working on the same case as Andy. What was a big surprise was his guest.

Oriane Pascal followed Cammy into the little cottage kitchen where Andy and Lisa were brewing coffee. Oriane seemed quieter since their last meeting but was even more stunning now that she had left her horse gear back in France and was modeling designer jeans and a blouse.

Andy watched the pair interact as they chatted in the cosy little kitchen. He was sure Cammy was a changed man. Andy wondered if the lovely Oriane had indeed tamed his wild friend and colleague.

Oriane was asked how her grandma was getting on, but Oriane had to admit that other than telling her grandma she was coming to Scotland for a holiday with Callum, she had not spoken to her for some time. Maria was a very busy lady.

That evening, the two couples dined out at a restaurant in Nairn. Lisa and Oriane chatted while Andy and Callum talked business.

"Cammy, tomorrow I have a meeting on the Black Isle with one of the company's shepherds and a local vet. I need to try to link the data you have been collating with sheep miscarriages in the area. It would be a help if you and your laptop could accompany me to the Black Isle tomorrow to try and tie the information up with local knowledge of sheep deaths—that is, if you can tear yourself away from your French lady friend?"

Cammy glanced across at Oriane, who was deep in conversation with Lisa, before replying. "No problem, boss. It will be hard, but for you I will do it."

Next morning Andy broke the news to the girls that Callum would be accompanying him north to meet up with some witnesses and take statements and data. The decision was met with little resistance as the girls decided to head into Inverness for a spot of shopping and lunch.

Andy and Callum met the shepherd and his vet in an out-of-the-way pub on the Black Isle and discussed the case over steak pie and chip. The meeting ran long into the afternoon and ended satisfactorily with the vet promising to get in touch with other vets in the area and pool any information they had on animal deaths and miscarriages linked to the airbase. Andy and Callum bid the men good afternoon, then headed back to the car. Andy decided to call the girls in the hope that they were still in Inverness and could meet for dinner in the capital of the north, but he had two problems: his phone was almost out of charge, and even when they switched to Callum's phone, there was no signal, Andy resigned himself to the fact that they would just have to meet the girls at the cottage.

CHAPTER 20

LEGEND

As Callum pulled up in the hire car, Andy caught sight of Lisa out of the corner of his eye coming from the cottage, alone and chalk white. Andy had that sinking feeling in his stomach. He had no idea what Lisa was about to tell them, but he had seen that look on her face before, and he knew it was not going to be good.

Lisa had been crying. Her eyes and nose were red, but she pulled herself together as Andy and Callum stopped in front of her. Callum was obviously thinking along the same lines as Andy and not seeing Oriane sent him into a panic.

"Lisa, what the hell happened? Where is Oriane?"

Lisa wrapped her arms around Andy, hugging him before replying to Callum's question. "I'm sorry, Callum. She has gone. I tried to get you, but none of the phones worked. I'm sorry."

Callum butted in before Lisa could go any further with her explanation. "How can she be gone? What are you talking about? What happened here?"

Lisa looked up into Andy's eyes, trying to judge what would happen next. "I have taken her to the airport in Inverness. Fred was picking her up. Guys, it's Maria. She was found dead this morning. One of her staff found her in her bed. She passed away in her sleep at Cheval Blanc le Vignoble, and Oriane has gone back there to help her mother with legal matters."

Callum sat back against the dry stone wall that surrounded the garden of the little cottage. Andy and Lisa joined him without speaking. They had all grown fond of the wise old woman, and it was hard to believe she was gone. She had only been in their lives for a very short time, but she had been a woman who left a lasting impression. None of the three of them had ever met anyone who had done more or achieved more than her. She was a legend that no one had ever heard of, and it was hard to take in that someone like this could just slip away in her sleep without anyone noticing.

After some considerable time, Lisa broke the silence. "Don't worry, Cammy. Oriane will be back. Her grandmother's wish was that she be buried in Dundee next to Jan Powlak. Oriane and her family will be here for the ceremony. For some unknown reason, she seems to like you."

Cammy pushed himself off the wall before dusting his jeans down. "If you don't mind, I am going for a walk to clear my head. You pair grab something to eat. I have kind of lost my appetite tonight."

Without saying a word, Callum strolled off in the direction of the beach, leaving Andy and Lisa still deep in thought.

"Andy, you're not going to do anything stupid, right? What I mean is, I knew you would keep your word to Maria. Her secret and my sanity were safe as long as Maria was alive.

Please don't do anything with her story until you have run it past your mother. I don't want to come and visit you in jail."

Lisa watched as he clenched his jaw. She had seen this look once before—right as he went into the meeting with her old boss. She knew then for sure that Andy would not leave the subject alone.

"Lisa, it's not right. The world needs to know who Jean Bruce was and what she achieved. She should have inspired others. Instead she was forced to hide in the shadows and let a coward be known as a hero. People looked the other way while history was distorted. I promised Jan I would not do that. I will find a way to get the story out there, but if it comes down to the wire, they can put me in jail."

Lisa had feared this was going to be Andy's decision. She pleaded with him, tears running down her face. "Don't throw yourself to the lions before speaking to your mother. She can help you, I know it."

Later, Callum returned from his walk, but the atmosphere between Andy and Lisa was decidedly frosty, and all parties headed for bed early.

Next morning, Andy awoke to find that Lisa was gone. Also missing was his Dictaphone, which contained the story of Jean Bruce as narrated by Maria Chemolie on the plane. Lisa was wise to Andy's tricks with the recording device and had guessed correctly that Andy had recorded the story. Andy read the note she had left him with a heavy heart.

> Andy, I think we need to have space to think about things. Although I love you, I do not know if I can live with your stubbornness. I will call you.
>
> Love, Matron x

Weeks went by before Andy heard from Lisa. When he did, it was a text telling him of the funeral arrangements for Maria Chemolie. The only glimmer of hope in the text message was that she wrote, "I hope to see you there." Andy couldn't make his mind up if this was good or bad, and he spent the next four hours out running, trying to clear his head. His work had suffered badly as a result of the split. He had left Callum with the lion's share of the research as he spent more and more time running or at the boxing gym.

On the morning of Maria Chemolie's funeral, Andy arrived with Callum, more nervous than he had ever been. Callum was desperate to see Oriane, but Andy was in two minds about his possible meeting with Lisa. He was in denial, and his life had taken a turn for the worse. Without Lisa, he was a moody and a sullen individual.

Andy spotted Lisa standing with the Chemolie family while the coffin was removed from the hearse. She was pale but still very beautiful. Andy wanted to go and stand by her side, but his legs refused to move. Lisa spotted him and gave him a little wave and smile before turning back to speak with the family once more.

After a few minutes, Andy could stand it no more and walked down the hill to a bench overlooking the Tay Rail Bridge. There, Andy lost track of time, and the funeral was breaking up when Lisa sat next to him, taking his cold hand in hers.

"Hello, stranger. I thought you had left for a minute until I saw you sitting down here. Are you OK?"

Andy looked round at her, trying to hide his emotion. "Busy, keeping busy. How about you? What have you been up to?"

Lisa squeezed his hand. "Oh, arranging lots of things. I'm a woman in demand. There are not enough hours in the day at the moment. You have lost a lot of weight, Andy. Are you sure you are OK?"

Andy shrugged, looking out over the bridge and then jealously at Callum and Oriane strolling along the path hand in hand before forming a reply. "I'm fine. It's good to see you. We need to catch up. What are you up to after the funeral?"

Lisa was looking into Andy's eyes as if trying to search his soul. "I am flying back to Geneva with the family, I'm afraid. Banking business to sort out there. I just popped down to say hi. Jake has got me organising a second office as we have just won a new contract to maintain military drones, so after Geneva, I am heading back to Reno. You could come out for a visit if you want."

Andy's heart leapt then slumped again as he remembered the forthcoming court case with the Royal Air Force. He dared not miss it. "Sorry, Lisa, I have this court case about the animals coming up that I really need to get on top of. Can we get together after that?"

Lisa smiled, still looking deep into his eyes. "Of course we can!" Lisa leaned across, kissing Andy on the lips and only stopping when the shout came above them. Fred was waiting with a limo to whisk them to Dundee Airport and the Falcon 900.

Andy left the graveyard more confused than when he had entered it. He arrived back at the office to find that his day was only going to get worse. He entered the office to find his mother waiting for him.

"Hello, Andrew. A little bird called Callum tells me that you have asked him to find a Spitfire pilot and get testimony from him to say that he had an aerial confrontation with a Hurricane pilot over a shot-down German aircraft. Callum has found the pilot, and he remembers well exchanging hand signals with the Hurricane pilot over who shot down the enemy plane. However, Callum has been told by me, the leading partner in this practice, to drop it. Now I am telling you right now to drop this obsession or lose your business, your friend, and the love of your life. You have a huge case coming up. I need you focused on that and nothing else. Success in that will almost guarantee your future in the world of law."

She faced her son and spoke seriously. "Andy, snap out of it. You have too much to fling it away. I have been speaking to Lisa, and I know she loves you, but she needs you to come to the party. You can't just ignore her feelings when it suits you. For god's sake, get a grip!"

Andy slumped down in his office chair, his mother's eyes boring into him. "I was at Jean Bruce's funeral today, Mum, and the funny thing was the only thing I could think about was Lisa. You are right as always. For the sake of our relationship, I will forget about Jean Bruce, and after I wrap up the court case against the RAF, I will try and patch things up with Lisa. I have been such an idiot!"

Ann Paxton sat on the edge of Andy's desk before addressing him. "Andy, no one is asking you to forget Jean Bruce. I have a hunch a story like that will get into the public domain some way. I just don't want my son going to jail for telling the truth. Now get on with finalising your case, and then marry that poor girl, you idiot!"

It took Andy much longer than expected to get a result from the RAF case. Eventually, after weeks of negotiation, the matter was finally settled, with the RAF agreeing to alter its flight plans and coming to an undisclosed out-of-court settlement that was agreeable to both parties.

Ten minutes after leaving his happy clients, Andy was on the phone to Reno, and after a lot of getting passed about, he eventually managed to get hold of Jake Shelton, who informed him Lisa was on a flight back to the UK and was in the air at that very moment. No sooner had Andy hung up than his mobile started ringing. Andy answered. Since it was his mother on the line, Andy expected to be asked about the result of the case, but he was mistaken.

"Andy, Lisa called me. She has been trying to get hold of you. I explained you were in a very important meeting. She will be landing shortly, and she wants to meet you at Jean Bruce's grave in two hours. Well done with the case—not many people win against the government. Supper is on me, and I hope you will have your girl with you when you get back. Good luck, son."

Andy fought his way through Edinburgh traffic, stopping only to pick up an important item before fighting his way across the Forth Bridge and heading north for his rendezvous in Dundee.

Andy was first to arrive at the deserted cemetery. There was not a person in sight, and Andy made his way up the winding road until he arrived at the crossroads high in the cemetery. At first, he was so busy looking around for signs of Lisa arriving that he didn't realise what stood before him. Then it dawned on him that atop the two graves stood two giant identical marble memorial stones. To the right was Jan Powlak's. Andy read the inscription, which stated that Jan had been an aircraftsman and friend of Jean Bruce.

That turned Andy's attention to the stone on the left.

HERE LIES MARIA CHEMOLIE
ALSO KNOWN AS JEAN BRUCE
GREAT BRITAIN'S ONE AND ONLY WOMAN BATTLE OF BRITAIN
FIGHTER ACE

Embossed into the base of the stone was an image of a leaping tiger cub taken from the engine cover of Jean's Hurricane.

Andy wiped away a tear as he continued to scrutinise the artwork: Hurricanes, Spitfires, and Mustangs adorned Jan's headstone while a single Spitfire high above a herd of Camargue horses decorated Jean's headstone. He was so engrossed in the beautiful craftsmanship, he did not hear the footsteps until they were just behind him. He turned just as Lisa dropped her handbag and leaped into his arms. They held onto one another for some minutes before Lisa broke the embrace, wiping a tear from Andy's cheek with her scarf. She stood back, admiring the stonework.

"It looks good, don't you think? Until now, I'd only seen photos from the artist I commissioned. It looks even better in real life."

Andy fumbled about in his pocket, and just as Lisa turned her attention to him, he crossed his fingers and went for gold.

"Lisa, I was an idiot. I have missed you so much. I don't think I can live without you in my life. I know a graveyard is a strange place to propose, but please, Lisa, will you marry me?"

Lisa looked like she had just been hit over the head with a baseball bat. The tables had been turned on her. She had planned to surprise Andy, but instead, it was she who was speechless. There was no place to sit down, so she leaned against Jan's monument. For a second, Andy thought she was about to faint and rushed to her side.

The word was a whisper when it passed Lisa's lips, and at first, it was almost lost in the wind, but Lisa recovered and repeated the word in a louder voice. "Yes."

After a few minutes of contemplation, Andy and Lisa sat on the grass in front of the headstones, looking at the ring that Andy had picked up in his mad rush from Edinburgh. It sparkled in the evening sunlight. Then Andy came to his senses.

"My mother wants to take us out for supper if that's OK."

Lisa nodded but reached across, pulling her handbag towards her. Andy watched as she rummaged about before bringing out a wrapped-up parcel.

"Here, this is for you. It is the real reason I arranged to meet you here. It was supposed to be me surprising you with a peace offering, but maybe now it's my engagement gift to you, whichever way you want to look at it."

Andy wasn't sure what to expect. He unwrapped the gift and then sat staring at it with a shocked expression on his face. He turned it over, still in shock.

"How the hell did you get this? I mean, I can't believe it! I don't know what to say."

Lisa wrapped her arms around Andy. "It was your mother's idea. Luckily, Callum knows a local author who agreed to write the book. I supplied your Dictaphone with Maria's story on it, and then I told our story of the hunt for Jean Bruce. It's perfect because you didn't write it, and it has a disclaimer that will keep the lawyers off our backs. Andy, don't you see? If people read the book, it will lead them here to the cemetery where they can check out the truth and the headstones for themselves. We have done it, Andy. You have kept your word to Jan. The truth is here. People will start to ask questions. It may not happen tomorrow or the next day, but one day, Jean will be recognised for her actions. Jan can rest in peace, and we can live our lives knowing we have honoured a great lady."

Lisa cuddled into Andy as he read the title out aloud. "What a brilliant title. *Baby Tiger*!"

THE END

ADDENDUM

> The gratitude of every home in our Island, in our Empire, and indeed throughout the world, except in the abodes of the guilty, goes out to the British airmen who, undaunted by odds, unwearied in their constant challenge and mortal danger, are turning the tide of the world war by their prowess and by their devotion. Never in the field of human conflict was so much owed by so many to so few. All hearts go out to the fighter pilots, whose brilliant actions we see with our own eyes day after day.
>
> Winston Churchill, 20 August 1940

Five hundred and forty-four Allied fighter pilots lost their lives in the Battle of Britain. Not all were British. Listed below are the numbers and nationalities of the fighter pilots from other countries who died defending Great Britain that summer.

Thirty Polish pilots
Twenty-three Canadian pilots

Twenty New Zealand pilots
Eighteen Belgian pilots
Fourteen Australian pilots
Nine Czechoslovakian pilots
Nine South African pilots
Two Rhodesian pilots
One Newfoundland pilot
One American pilot

Winston Churchill was absolutely correct. "Never in the field of human conflict was so much owed by so many to so few."

Printed in Great Britain
by Amazon

58469627R00200